THE SHINING ONES

MW01222800

THE SHINING ONES

THE UMUAHIA SCHOOL DAYS OF OBINNA OKOYE

Chike Momah

Library of Congress Control Number:		2010903505
ISBN:	Hardcover	978-1-4500-6213-8
	Softcover	978-1-4500-6212-1
	Ebook	978-1-4500-6214-5

This book was printed in the United States of America.

To order additional copies of this book, contact:
Xlibris Corporation
1-888-795-4274
www.Xlibris.com
Orders@Xlibris.com
73755

DEDICATION

In loving memory of my elder brother GODWIN (who preceded me to the Government College Umuahia, and now mercifully rests from his labors).

This is dedicated to all the OLD BOYS of my alma mater, in particular Chinua Achebe, Vin Ike, Kwamina Onuche, F.C. Jazz Egbuonu, Sam Onyewuenyi, Namseh Eno, Nicholas Azinge, and the brothers Anthony and Patrick Anwunah, contemporaries all, who touched my life in many different ways.

It is also especially dedicated, with all my love, to my children, to their mother, OLD GIRL Ethy, and to our grandchildren.

PROLOGUE

The words of the old nonsense verse sprang to my lips as I sat facing my friend Innocent Dike. I was a visitor in his home, in his village, Nnobi. In the faint glow of an old kerosene lamp, I could just barely make out his features as we sat in meditative silence. We had been talking, rather poignantly, about our alma mater, the Government College Umuahia. I was surprised I could still recall the poem. Some of it, at any rate! During a prolonged lull in our conversation, I suddenly found myself mouthing the words of the poem:

> The Owl and the Pussy-Cat went to sea
> In a beautiful pea-green boat:
> They took some honey, and plenty of money
> Wrapped up in a five-pound note.

I was quite unaware that I was mouthing the words audibly until it dawned on me that Innocent had joined me in the recitation of the poem. I looked sharply at him, surprised that he, too, remembered the words. Our eyes locked into each other's admiringly as the words tripped off our tongues in near-perfect synchrony, our voices rising and falling in a marvelous cadence:

> The Owl looked up to the stars above,
> And sang to a small guitar,
> "O lovely Pussy, O Pussy, my love,
> What a beautiful pussy you are,
> You are,
> You are!
> What a beautiful Pussy you are.

Innocent was suddenly convulsed with laughter. "You mean to tell me, Obinna, that your class also learned that poem?"

"Of course," I said. "But I can't recall in what class we learned it nor the poet's name."

"Neither can I, but can you imagine? This is a poem written for children in England. Or is it America? And we first read it in secondary—"

"Who cares? Come on! Let's continue and see how far we can go before we dry up."

So we continued:

> Pussy said to the owl,
> "You elegant fowl,
> How charmingly sweet you sing!
> Oh! let us be married; too long we have tarried:
> But what shall we do for a ring?"

At this point Innocent threw up his arms. "I don't remember any more. I mean, the exact words. But I believe the owl and the pussy cat traveled to somewhere for—let me see—something like a year or so—"

He did not remember, but I plunged on:

> They sailed away, for a year and a day,
> To the land where the bong-tree grows;
> And there in a wood a Piggy-wig stood,
> With a ring at the end of his nose,
> His nose,
> His nose,
> With a ring at the end of his nose.

I could have gone on for another four or five lines if Innocent had not called a halt to the recitation.

"A lot of gibberish," he said. "But it brings back wonderful memories. How long ago did we learn this poem?"

"Who cares?" I said. "What matters is that I was a class ahead of you and must have learned it a year before you did. That's at least fifty years ago, even if I read it in my last year in Umuahia."

"Phew!" said Innocent. "That's one heck of a long time."

For several moments, we fell silent. Then my friend said, reverently, "Umuahia was a great college."

"The best in the country at the time," I said.

"Unfortunately, it has fallen on hard times now," said Innocent, his eyes—even in the low glow of the kerosene lamp—looking wistful.

"The entire country," I said, "has fallen on hard times. When I last visited the school, about ten years ago, I nearly shed tears at what I saw. In our time, Government College Umuahia was just about the most beautiful place on God's earth. Now it has gone to the dogs."

"It's a crying shame," said Innocent. "But didn't you once tell me you made some rather uncomplimentary remarks about the school on your last day there?"

"To the principal, no less," I said. "And the big man almost bit off my head."

"What was that all about?"

"Oh! I don't know," I said, shaking my head sadly, as my mind rolled the years back to the day I sat with my classmates in our classroom, awaiting the arrival of our revered principal, Mr. Walter Graves. The year was 1949.

* * *

How does one explain a moment of madness? In one electrifying minute, I had condensed my life in the school into a startlingly negative statement. Six of the happiest years I had known in my young life had flashed through my mind's eye even as I stood up to make my statement.

There might have been some hesitation, but it was only momentary. The truth was that I had known, for at least twenty-four hours, that I was going to do, or say, something that would assuredly shock the principal. Nothing my friends said to me had dissuaded me from the course I had set for myself.

It was the penultimate day of my six years in the college. Mr. Walter Graves, a hulk of a man, stood before my class in what he had intended as a last happy farewell meeting with the senior class. And as he looked from one young glowing face to the next, he seemed as proud as any father could be, his fierce features softened, as they always were, by his wide affable smile.

He said he wanted to hear from us what we thought we had gained from the college. That simple request was the opportunity I sought, and over which I had agonized all night long. Several boys spoke ahead of me and, with not one exception, showered encomiums on the school. That was what I had expected, for there could be little argument that, in the honest opinion of every one of us, Government College Umuahia was the best secondary school in the country. There were those who thought it might well have been the best *anywhere*, period! As tribute followed tribute, Mr. Walter Graves pulled happily and thoughtfully at his luxuriant moustache.

Sitting in the middle of the class of twenty-five boys, I had plenty of time to reflect on the situation before it came to my turn to speak. Time to reflect on my personal achievements, both academic and sports, over which I felt a justifiable sense of pride! In a fiercely competitive class, I could honestly claim I had more than held my own academically, year in and year out. And though not naturally gifted athletically, I had, nevertheless, battled my way, by grit and determination, to school colors in cricket.

There was time, too, to reflect on the disappointments. First, I had not shown the same application when it came to field hockey, which I had practically abandoned just when a little more effort might have helped me turn the corner. Second, I had tried my hand at a little farming, organized by the school, and had come a cropper on two successive planting seasons—except that my second failure was infinitely worse than my first.

I had time to reflect on the friends I had made, some of whom I was now going to leave behind in the school, others of whom I would probably never again meet thereafter. I had almost no worries in my life and knew, deep down in my belly, that I was fiercely proud of my school. And talking of my belly, I had tremendously enjoyed the school cuisine, which only family pride or loyalty prevents me, even as I write this, from acknowledging as superior to the fare at home.

"And now, Obinna Okoye!" boomed the principal's voice.

With a start, I came out of my reverie. I had been so wrapped up in my own thoughts, I had truly only half-listened to the boys who spoke before me. I stood up, took a deep breath and, in as calm a voice as I could manage, spoke the words that my spark of genius—or whatever else it was—had, at that moment, put into my mouth. Unreflective and unrehearsed!

The boy with whom I shared a double desk tugged at my shorts in a desperate, but unavailing, effort to make me shut up and sit down. At that moment, had a pin dropped to the cemented floor, it would have sounded louder than the clatter of an empty kerosene tin.

In the stunned silence, the smile faded from the principal's lips as his face turned red. He stared at me in some perplexity, no doubt wondering if he should take my statement seriously or not.

"Wh-wh-what did you say?"

I looked around me, bemused and sheepish. Regret at the words I had just spoken stabbed at my heart. Though I had, sort of, prepared myself for this moment, I had not really known exactly what I was going to do nor had I rehearsed the words I would say. Even as I stood up to say my piece, I had not clearly formed the words that came out. It was as if an external force, over which I had no control, had, at that precise moment, taken over my faculties;

and the voice that spoke the words belonged to that disembodied force and had little or nothing to do with me.

But there was now no place to hide my face, no hole in which I could bury my head. I could not take back the words my mouth had spoken. That would have been just as difficult as plunging on.

Then a strange thing happened. It seemed suddenly as if the unknown force that had formed the uncompromising words now supplied a spark of vitality to my crippled mind. And I knew that, temporarily at least, I had no fear of the big man. I kept my eyes on Mr. Graves's face as I braced myself for the worst.

"I'm waiting," said the principal. "We're all waiting. Those were courageous words, Okoye, unusually courageous, I must say. And quite out of character for—"

I jumped at the opening he had unwittingly given me. "That's exactly it," I said. "That's just what I had in mind. This is a good school, sir, perhaps the best insofar as academic work is concerned. But the trouble is, sir, that none of us seems to have a mind of his own. There's nothing wrong with our being modest and humble, that sort of thing. But if—"

"That's enough!" thundered the principal, beside himself with anger, his face so suffused with blood it had turned purplish red. "That's more than a mouthful coming from you, Okoye. If what you say is true, you must be the lone exception. You certainly have a mind of your own."

He turned to the rest of the class. "Next! Okoroafor!"

"But I haven't finished yet, sir," I said.

"Oh yes! You have!"

I felt totally dejected as I sat down, my state of mind now in that gray zone between regret for my words and a blustering I-don't-carism. I was in a total daze, to all intents and purposes shut off from the rest of the class and the world, as my mind went back to the very beginning of my own Umuahia story.

CHAPTER I

In the beginning, there was Holy Pastor Brown. That was what we all called him. An Ijaw man from one of the well-known families of Abonema in the Niger Delta, he was—insofar as we understood the concept—as saintly as it was possible for a mere mortal to be. I know that he prayed morning, noon, and night every day of the week. I sometimes sneaked into the church just to watch him as he knelt on one side of the altar, devoutly mouthing his prayers.

Of course, we—my friends and I, that is—always watched him from the shadows. We did so, notwithstanding that he seldom took umbrage when he caught us in the act. Perhaps we were also keenly aware that when the pastor was praying, God was closeted with him, within his holy temple. What was it that Christ had said? "When two or three are gathered in my name, there will I be in the midst of them." We needed no other proof to believe strongly that the Holy Pastor was, all by himself, the equal of two or three persons.

His piety was not manifested only in the frequency of his prayers, but in his kindness and compassion to every person with whom he came into contact. To those miscreants who sought to do him harm, he seemed willing, literally, to turn the other cheek. Though some stories about him were doubtless apocryphal, he was reputed to have once called back a burglar he had surprised in the vicarage. And then, incredibly, he offered to share the plunder the thief had abandoned in his eagerness to get away.

The Reverend Martin Brown was the pastor of St. James Church, Aba, a Church Missionary Society church, of the Anglican persuasion. He was, by that fact, also the superintendent of the St. James Primary School. Tall, wiry, and wizen-faced, he looked anything from sixty-five to seventy years old.

The holy man had been my inspiration for as long as I could remember. As a member of the church choir, I enjoyed an advantageous position, close to the altar area, from which I watched, awed and enthralled, as he went through the rituals of the Sunday services, morning and evening. And watching him, I dreamed of the day I, too, would stand within the holy altar of God and in similarly privileged proximity to the Almighty. That attraction for the ministry, though I sometimes had my doubts, was a powerful driving force in my life.

My father, Joshua Okoye, recognized and heartily approved of my budding aspiration for the priesthood and brought it to the attention of Holy Pastor Brown. From that moment on, the delighted pastor sought in several different ways to encourage me and showed an especial interest in my schoolwork. In fact, I became a privileged and frequent visitor to the vicarage, where Mrs. Brown promptly took me under her wing.

Then in late October 1943, I went for a routine interview for admission to the government college, in Umuahia, a town some thirty miles to the north of Aba.

Words alone seem grossly inadequate to describe the tremendous impact the school compound made on my young mind. I have sometimes wondered, although distinctly uneager for the experience, what the view might be like when one first arrives at the pearly gates. The two might not be totally dissimilar.

The scene took my breath away as I stood in the center of an unbelievably smooth green quadrangle. Coming from my decidedly humble circumstances, I gazed in wonderment at the beauty of it all. And silently, I offered a prayer of thanks to God that I was where I was. For, modesty aside, the entrance examination to Government College Umuahia was commonly acknowledged to be the most competitive in Eastern Nigeria and one of the two or three stiffest to any high school in the entire country.

To one side of the quadrangle stood the longest nonecclesiastical building I had ever seen. This was the Administration Block, a curious but imposing cement-and-wood structure, sitting on solid cement stilts. Opposite it was the library building. The quadrangle was bounded on its two other sides by the dining hall and an L-shaped classroom block. I was strongly tempted to go down on my hands and knees and run my hands lovingly over the smooth grass. But I think my innate sense of decorum and dignity prevented me.

All the buildings had red roofs, and all, except the dark gray Administration Block, had entirely white walls. I had perhaps never before given much thought to such things, but now, for some reason, that combination of white walls and red roofs seemed to be in perfect harmony with my sense of colors. The dormitories, six in all, consisted of two rows of buildings: four to the front, which were close to the L-shaped classroom block, and two to the rear.

In that instant, as I stood in the center of the exquisite quadrangle, I resolved that there was not going to be any other secondary school for me, but Umuahia. It was quite a momentous decision for a kid like me to make. It was not as if I had discussed the possibilities with my father. And more importantly, I was convinced—even as I took the decision that was sure to propel my life forever thereafter—that my spiritual mentor, Pastor Brown, would be terribly disappointed with me. How could he not be, when my decision almost certainly meant I was abandoning my pursuit of the ministry? Umuahia, as a government—therefore a secular—institution was clearly not the most appropriate avenue towards the fulfillment of my priestly ambition. To that end, the normal expectation was that I would seek admission to one of the two missionary secondary schools: the Dennis Memorial Grammar School, in Onitsha, or its sister school in Okrika, both of which were Church Missionary Society schools. And I had done so. But now, the result of that examination, still expected, suddenly became irrelevant to me. Someone should have stopped me from sitting the Government College entrance examination. Now, I thought happily, it was too late.

I spun around slowly and was again struck by the sheer, unadulterated beauty of the compound. I was thrilled to the bones at the prospect of being a student of the school. But how in the world was I ever going to explain my decision to Pastor Brown? That was the rub. I had no doubt it would cause the holy man pain.

I watched admiringly as the students went about their concerns with a kind of controlled briskness that seemed entirely in tune with the air of orderliness and a lack of ostentation that were evident everywhere. I looked up and saw that even the birds, twittering musically overhead, flew in ordered formations.

A worrying thought obtruded itself into my consciousness. What if my father could not afford the school fees? I thought briefly about it and then dismissed it from my mind. Whatever gods determined the course my life would take, I told myself, could not possibly bring me face-to-face with this wonderful new world only to leave me in the lurch.

I sailed effortlessly—and painlessly—through my interview, which turned out to be an odd and quite-pleasant affair. I walked into the principal's office in considerable trepidation, my hands humbly clasped behind my back, and stood uncertainly just within the door. Seated at his mahogany desk was a fierce-looking bearded hunk of a man, with sideburns and a luxuriant moustache. Mr. Walter Graves took his time, looking me up and down with eyes that seemed to slice easily through my defenses. But then he smiled, and the smile magically melted away the fierceness of his visage.

He stood up and, clearly favoring his right leg, came and took me by the hand and led me back to his chair. In a flash, so sudden it took my breath away, I found myself lifted as if I was a bag of feathers and deposited on the principal's lap. From that rather privileged position, I found the interview something of a breeze. The only difficult question I had to answer concerned my birth date.

Perhaps fortunately for me, the principal chose not to make an issue of the affidavit executed by my father, giving my age as twelve. I might have looked twelve to him, or perhaps not. If I did, why did he have to tell me, almost conspiratorially, that he had no faith in Nigerian age declarations? And if I did not, why did he smile so graciously at me and give me a friendly pat on the back of my head?

He asked a few other questions, rather perfunctorily I thought, and thumbed through a sheaf of papers on his desk.

"You're a fine boy," he told me as he lifted me off his lap and set me down on the carpeted floor. "I think I'll see you here in January, because I believe you understand how lucky you are to be admitted to this college. All we ask of you is that you be prepared to work hard, very hard indeed."

He took a peek at his papers. "Have a good trip to—er—Aba and tell your parents that I wish them well."

I was at the door of the office when he called out to me. "You have a brother here, Samuel Okoye. I'm sure he has told you about us, no?"

"He's my cousin," I said.

"Oh, I see. You share the same last name and, as I see here in these papers, the same Aba address. Well, it doesn't matter. See you in January, young man. Good luck."

Good luck? With what? I wondered. Was the man prescient and knew I would have some difficulty explaining all this to Pastor Brown? I looked keenly at him, but his smiling face gave nothing away. I waved timidly to him and walked out of his office.

My cousin Samuel, who was really more like an elder brother, was a class 2 student. Ahead of Mr. Walter Graves, he had already told me how lucky I was. It might have been a case of familiarity breeding contempt. Or, more than likely, he was just a person of little faith. But he had given me the impression, in several little ways, that he did not believe I had what it would take to write a successful entrance examination to what he called "my college." Happily, it would soon be mine too.

With the interview successfully behind me, I spoke with Samuel before I left, with my two friends, to return to Aba. I found him at the practice nets for a game that was totally strange to me: cricket. I must confess he looked quite adept at hitting the ball thrown at him by other players from a distance of some twenty or so yards. I watched patiently until he was done. Then he sought permission from the teacher in charge of the practice and came to me.

"You're still here?" he asked, elder-brother-like. "Your interview finished hours ago. If you don't hurry, you'll be late for your train."

"I came with my two classmates, Chidi and Friday, remember?" I said. "I had to wait for their interviews. But don't worry. We have already made arrangements for the cycles that will take us to the railway station. I just wanted to say good-bye. They're waiting for me right now."

"Okay, so good-bye," he said summarily.

"Not before I tell you something."

"What is it?"

"You were right," I told him. "This is the most wonderful place I've ever seen. You told me so, but I didn't believe you."

"And what did Kofi tell you after he came for his own interview? That was about two weeks ago, wasn't it?"

"He said the same thing."

"And you still didn't believe. Why?"

"Oh, I don't know," I said. "I suppose because his interview was for a scholarship, some of us thought his head became too big for him, and that he was exaggerating—as usual."

"I'm on scholarship too," said Samuel, smiling. "Is that also why you didn't believe me?"

"Yours is different," I said. "I couldn't believe that after you saw King's College, in Lagos, you would praise Umuahia the way you did. Lagos is supposed to be the most beautiful city in Nigeria, isn't it?"

"Who told you that?"

"You did."

"I did?" he asked as if he was talking to himself. "Anyway, you're taking too long saying good-bye. So off with you. I'll see you in Aba in another month and half."

"Good-bye," I said, turning away.

"Hey! Wait a second."

"What?" I asked, turning back.

"Just some advice," he said solemnly. "You notice I'm talking to you in English, and you keep replying in Ibo. When we come back here in January, you and me, you will have to try to overcome your habit of always speaking in the vernacular. It's against the rules here."

"Vernacular?"

"Yes, you know, our Ibo language," he said.

Did he think I did not know what the word meant? I looked briefly at him and then burst out laughing. But he did not laugh with me. He was not even smiling. So I stopped laughing, shaking my head in disbelief, and turned and walked away.

* * *

On the train ride back to Aba, I had plenty of time to think about my good fortune and especially to worry about how Pastor Brown would react to my decision. The distance between Aba and Umuahia is about thirty miles, but the steam engine trains took two good hours to cover it. My greatest regret was that my best friend, Ben Nwobosi, was not with me. I had failed to even persuade him to sit the entrance examination. "Waste of time," was how he put it. "What chance do I have?" He was too modest by half.

I was nervously chewing on my fingernails when an elbow was dug into my ribs. I turned to my right and looked into the smiling eyes of one of my classmates, Chidi Ebele.

"What's the matter?" he asked solicitously.

"Nothing. Just thinking."

"About what? Your girlfriend Adamma?" There was mischief in his eyes as he said this, again digging his elbow playfully into my side.

My jaw dropped open in genuine astonishment. "Who is . . . ?" I started to ask, then checked myself from completing a pointless question.

Adamma was my best friend, Ben's younger sister, a winsome girl. She was not my girlfriend, or perhaps I had just never thought of her in quite those terms. But there was not another girl in St. James School whose company gave me as much pleasure as Adamma's.

"You think we are blind, or what?" asked Friday Stoneface, my second companion and classmate. He sat opposite Chidi and me, happily sandwiched between two young girls, and making the most of his opportunity to maximize his bodily contact with them. More precocious than most boys our age, Friday was already, at thirteen, an artful chaser of girls.

"I'm in trouble, big trouble," I said.

Chidi asked, "With whom?"

"The pastor," I said.

"Holy Brown?" asked Friday. "That's impossible." Then he added, with a knowing wink, "Especially for you."

I decided to sidestep the levity in his voice. "It's not really trouble," I said and proceeded to tell them what I thought might be the problem with Pastor Brown. They listened attentively, but with mounting incredulity.

"So," I concluded, "even if I pass the DMGS entrance exam, I'm going to Umuahia."

"So what?" asked Friday.

"You still don't understand?" I fairly screamed at him. "So I cannot go on to become a pastor."

"And you think Holy Brown—"

"Will you stop calling him like that?" I said.

Friday was taken aback by the vehemence of my objection. "Isn't that what everybody calls him?" he asked. "What's the matter with you?"

I glared angrily at him. "When other people call him holy, they mean it seriously. With you, one never knows. You always seem to be laughing when you say it."

Friday spread his arms wide in a gesture of hurt innocence. "You see my trouble?" he asked the two girls between whom he was delightfully sandwiched.

They seemed totally uninterested in his troubles, so he looked questioningly at Chidi. Chidi grunted disapprovingly and turned to me. "If you fear the holy pastor, let your father go and tell him. We know how lucky we are to be among the boys who passed this exam. Unless you are mad or something, you cannot think of going to any other college after seeing the compound. It's a fine, fine place. Didn't Kofi tell us so? And we all thought he was just blowing hot air."

Kofi Njoku Bentsil was born in Owerri, Eastern Nigeria. His parents hailed from the Gold Coast but had lived so long in Nigeria they had become, in our eyes, Nigerians. Kofi's middle name, Njoku, was a concession to the Igbo people among whom the family lived. In the Umuahia entrance examination, he had won a merit scholarship—one of ten boys, out of thirty, to do so. The scholarship interviews had taken place two weeks earlier than ours.

Kofi had returned from his interviews with glowing reports about the school. Now that we had seen the place with our own eyes, Chidi, Friday, and I declared ourselves in love with it. I know I could hardly wait for January 1944. The school cuisine, which we had sampled over the two days of the interview, was something special. I liked the prospect and promise of camaraderie with many of the students I had met. I was not even concerned about fagging for one of the senior boys. From the way my cousin Samuel had described the system, I was sure that fagging could be nothing more serious than an unequal friendship—but a friendship all the same—between a senior boy and a fresher.

I took my time but had no difficulty persuading my father, Joshua Okoye, to talk to Pastor Brown. Like me, he understood that the import of my decision was the virtual end of my priestly dreams. But faced with a choice between a secular education for his son in reputedly the best school in Eastern Nigeria and the fulfillment of other dreams via a lesser school, he unhesitatingly chose the former. He therefore agreed to talk to Pastor Brown but insisted that I, my mother, and Samuel—who was then on his end-of-year vacation—must be present. He said he hoped the holy man would understand the reasons for the choice we had made.

The Pastor received us himself and led us through his parlor to an inner, more private room. I was familiar with the room, having enjoyed the freedom of the vicarage for quite some time. This was where he always held serious consultations with his parishioners and where he received the more important personages from the headquarters of the Anglican Diocese in Onitsha.

Mrs. Brown brought kolanuts in a small wooden bowl, which he handed over to her husband. Because he was fluent in the Igbo language, though he was not a native speaker, he said a short prayer in Igbo. But he did not invoke the spirit of our ancestors, as was customary in the breaking of the kolanut. Perhaps he saw some conflict between that practice and his Christian religion. My parents each took a piece of the kolanut, but when it was offered to Samuel, he declined. I too declined, following his example, even as I heartily cursed him silently. I always enjoyed eating the nut whenever I had the opportunity and especially if my parents were not present, watching me. I knew that Samuel did too.

"So what seems to be the problem?" the pastor asked my father in Igbo. "I know from the little you told me yesterday that it concerns your son Obinna."

"It does," said my father, intertwining his fingers nervously and in ceaseless motion. "Obinna will be going to Government College Umuahia, in two or three weeks from now, to join this . . . his brother—you know Samuel here, don't you? He's my brother's son—"

Pastor Brown interrupted him with a gentle smile. "Oh yes, of course. I know Samuel well."

"Stand up when he's talking to you," said my father, gesticulating forcefully to Samuel. "Have you boys no manners? And you too, Obinna!"

The pastor's smile widened. He reached forward and placed a hand on Samuel's head. "I know you are in Umudike," he said, using the name of the village, four miles outside the township of Umuahia, where the government college was actually located. "You are surprised? I remembered there were two of you who passed the entrance exam that year from St. James, you and Samson Stoneface. Samson had a nickname, something to do with bread."

Samuel and I so far forgot ourselves as to laugh out loud. Samuel said, when he regained sufficient control of himself, "Bread Undone, sir."

"Ah yes," said the Pastor. "That's it. Bread Undone. You see, my boys, I may be an old man, but I still have a good memory." He shook his head, smiling. "But why 'Bread Undone'? Samson was fat, I know. But what has that to do with undone bread? Well, it doesn't really matter."

He seemed to thoroughly enjoy the awed expression on our faces, as neither of us could imagine how in the world the pastor knew Samson's nickname.

My father cleared his throat. "I have watched my son agonizing over this decision during the past several weeks, not knowing how to approach you in this matter. Finally, he had the good sense to come to me and ask me to speak to you on his behalf. Our people say that when an adult is at home, the goat is not left to suffer the agonies of bringing forth its young, tethered to a stake. That's why I am here now to talk to you."

He looked sideways at me. "Obinna is sometimes a child who doesn't know his right hand from his left. But he has a good head on his shoulders. He knows that if he goes to Umuahia, he will never become a pastor, and this is one dream he has had for the longest time. He does not want you to be disappointed—"

Pastor Brown raised an arm, and my father fell silent. The holy man looked from him to me, to Samuel, and to my mother.

"I see no problem here," he declared firmly. "No problem at all. God has a purpose for all of us, his children. Our best effort should be directed at discovering what that purpose is. If it is his will that Obinna will be one of his servants, Umudike will not stop the fulfillment of that destiny."

He beckoned to me, and I came and stood meekly before him. Quickly obeying an inner impulse, I then went down on my knees. Whereupon the pastor placed both hands, palms down, on my head.

"Have no fears, my son," he said. "Go to Umudike and go with the confidence that God will guide your steps every inch of the way. And you too, Samuel," he added, in turn placing a hand on Samuel's head.

My mother who, through it all, had not said a word now suddenly broke into an enthusiastic recital of Psalm 23, to the surprise of my father and much to my consternation.

"The Lord is my shepherd," she declaimed, ignoring my agonized look. "I shall not want . . ."

None of us thought to stop her, especially when we saw that the good pastor seemed content to let her go on, as with a benevolent smile and hands folded in his lap, he waited patiently.

"And I shall dwell in the house of the Lord forever."

CHAPTER II

FIRST YEAR

We watched, with some trepidation, as Mr. Walter Graves approached on the gravelly road. There were seven of us, all first-year students, some standing, others sitting, on the steps of House 1. About two months earlier, in October 1943, the big white man had interviewed every one of us. I remembered his lumbering gait as he walked, favoring his right leg. I recalled his fierce moustache and bushy sideburns. And I experienced, once again, the extremity of fear that the formidable presence of an authoritarian white man so often induced in the hearts of subject black Africans. My heart sank when, all of a sudden, he stopped, seemed to hesitate for the briefest moment and then made a right turn and walked directly toward us. "Oh my god!" said one boy under his breath, which was just about the way I too felt.

When he reached the bottom of the steps, Mr. Graves stopped again, hands on hips, and peered at us. Then a strange thing happened. He smiled at us, and at once his fearsome countenance was transformed wonderfully in a way that I recalled from my interview. I relaxed somewhat, even as I respectfully stood up.

"What's your name?" The voice was deep and resonant, matching his big frame.

"Me?" asked several boys uneasily. I was not one of them.

Mr. Graves pointed to one boy, "You!"

"Gree-goh-ree," replied the boy, nervously fidgeting with his shirt collar.

"What kind of a name is that?" asked the principal.

Another boy leaned forward and pronounced the name more correctly.

"Oh, I see, Gregory," said Mr. Graves. "Gregory what?"

"Okoroafor, sir."

"And where do you come from, Gregory Okoroafor?"

"Over there, sir," said the boy simply, pointing directly over the principal's shoulders.

Mr. Graves instinctively looked back over his shoulder in the direction indicated by Gregory Okoroafor. When he turned back, he wore a puzzled expression.

"Where is 'over there'?"

Okoroafor automatically began to point again, then checked himself. "Mbawsi," he said, looking thoroughly embarrassed.

"Mbawsi," said the principal reflectively. "I know a little about the geography of this area. Mbawsi must be about twenty miles away, isn't it?"

As none of us offered to confirm his estimate, he pointed to the boy who had helped with the pronunciation of the name "Gregory."

"And you, young man, where're you from?"

The boy stepped forward confidently. "Lagos, sir." Then he added, though Mr. Graves had not asked the question, "My name is John Agu."

The principal fixed John Agu with those piercing eyes of his, which would normally have caused most boys to go weak in the knees. But if the glare affected Agu, he did not show it. Strangely, the boy's relative aplomb seemed to surprise the big man.

I looked sideways at the boy. At the same time, he too turned, and our eyes met. I smiled at him in admiration of his courage—or whatever else it was that made him unafraid of the principal. He was a good-looking boy, very dark in complexion, and with a musculature quite remarkable for a boy of his age, which was more or less my age: anything between twelve to fourteen years. Agu sported a stylish but low haircut, with an exaggerated central parting that must have been cut by the barber himself as a semipermanent adornment.

For a moment or two, the principal's eyes continued to appraise Agu, no doubt taking note of the boy's fancy sailor-style blue-and-white jumper and his soft leather *bata* sandals. Bata sandals were arguably the best that money could buy.

"I don't think I care for your hairstyle," he said at length. "But I'm not concerned about that now. You're not Yoruba, are you?"

I knew he asked that question because Agu had said he came from Lagos. The question also seemed to suggest that the principal could not tell with confidence the ethnic affiliations of his students purely by their family names.

"No, sir," said John Agu. "I'm Ibo, but my family lives in Lagos. I was born there. But actually we come from Onitsha."

From where I stood, at the back of the pack, I desperately hoped that the principal would not notice me. I actually averted my eyes whenever he looked in my direction.

"You there!"

I kept my eyes glued to the ground, hoping that the principal was not addressing me. Someone nudged me, and I was forced to look up.

"Yes, you!" said Mr. Graves, looking at me directly for the first time. Something akin to recognition slowly dawned in his eyes. After a slight hesitation, he moved a little closer to me, looking intently at me, and then slapped his thigh triumphantly. "I remember you, quite well in fact. Let me see. Don't you have a brother here, in class 3? Okoye?"

"Cousin," I said laconically, stealing a quick glance at the other boys, embarrassed that the man seemed to recognize me much more easily than he did them.

A chubby smiling boy—the same boy who had nudged me earlier—gazed back at me challengingly. Somehow I managed to smile back. For a fleeting moment or two, our eyes held, and then I became aware that I was no longer the object of the principal's special attention. Mr. Graves was now talking to all of us as a group. "You're all welcome, my boys. This is a great college, and I'm sure you'll find your lives here richly rewarding. There are rules, of course, on which we set a high premium. The aim is to achieve good social behavior and to promote a well-disciplined *esprit de corps*."

"*Akwukwo!*" someone, probably John Agu, said under his breath, but audibly enough to make the principal look sharply in his direction. I did not know what "esprit de corps" meant. I doubted any of my companions knew. But it sounded bookish, which was what the boy—whoever he was—had in mind.

"That's another thing," said the principal, eyes still on John Agu. "One of our most important rules concerns the speaking of vernacular tongues. This is not allowed, whether Ibo, Ijaw, Efik, or any other Nigerian tongue. Also no broken English. I know some of you come from Port Harcourt and Aba. I've been around in the east as an education officer, and I know how popular pidgin English is, even among schoolchildren, in those two towns. So let me repeat: no vernacular and no pidgin."

"Oh?" said several boys in unison.

"I know," I said, causing some of the other boys to look at me. "My cousin told me about it."

"Okoye?"

"Yes, sir."

"Good for you," said the principal. "Perhaps I need to explain to your friends that we have boys here from different tribes. It would not be fair to them—"

"Is it all right if we're from the same tribe, like now?" the chubby boy asked, eliciting guttural support from several voices. "We are all Ibos. So can we talk among ourselves in Ibo?"

"No!" snapped the principal. "It is not a habit we want to encourage. You must speak in one language, English, all the time. I know I cannot stop you thinking in your vernacular, but the words you speak must be in English."

I had never before given a thought to the language in which I did my thinking. But before I could ask the chubby boy if he had, Mr. Graves abruptly changed course.

"The housemaster has a notice up on the board in the school lobby. Has anyone here seen it?" He paused, then continued, "Well, I suggest you all go and read it."With that, he spun round with surprising briskness and strode purposefully away. Seven pairs of eyes were riveted on his retreating back and that reluctant shuffling right leg. Then singly, or in pairs, we drifted away. I found myself walking side by side with the chubby boy.

"My name is Obinna Okoye," I introduced myself. "What's yours?"

"Anthony Achara," said the boy, in a whisper, looking around him nervously. "You had better be careful. Aren't we supposed to speak only in English? You heard what the principal said. And even you yourself said your brother—"

"So why are you speaking Ibo?" I asked him, laughing. "Or did you misunderstand what he said? He did not say that if you lower your voice, it is okay to speak in Ibo."

"To tell you the truth," said he, "I don't like the rule."

"Neither do I," I said heartily. "That's why I told my cousin Samuel that no one can force me to speak only in English. When I feel like it, I will speak pidgin or Ibo, depending on who I'm talking to. Samuel is in the senior class—you know, class 3. One day you'll meet him. Do you know, as soon as we arrived here today, and I spoke to him in Ibo, he told me he did not understand a word I said. I had to say it in English before he replied. Have you ever heard anything so silly?"

Suddenly I remembered something. I stopped and turned to my companion. "What did you say your name is?"

"Anthony—"

"Anthony Achara?"

"Yes, why?" he asked.

"You are the Anthony Achara my headmaster was always talking about?"

He understood my question to be rhetorical and said nothing. For my part, I stood stock-still, and studied him. We were about the same height, though he was the more heavily built. Despite a pair of wide flaring nostrils, he had a quietly appealing face and a perfect set of teeth. His eyes, deep set and adorned by bushy eyebrows, sparkled in the bright midafternoon sunshine.

"This is wonderful," I said.

"Your headmaster talked about me?"

"I don't want to make your head swell, but yes, he did. Do you remember Headmaster Akweke?"

"Akweke was your headmaster? Do I remember him? How can I ever forget him? If it were not for him, I doubt I would be here today. He was my headmaster in Onitsha, oh, three or so years ago and gave me a lot of encouragement. Then suddenly he was transferred. To Aba, I believe."

Achara looked keenly at me for several seconds. "You have quite a large head," he said matter-of-factly. "And you must be from Aba, no?"

I nodded.

"That's not a good combination," he said deadpan. "I suppose you know why he was sent to your school?"

"He never let us forget the reason," I said, smiling ruefully. "He never tired of telling us he was sent to Aba to tame us. He said he was told Aba boys were the most unruly in Eastern Nigeria."

Achara arched his eyebrows. "Sorry, but Aba boys are still the wildest in these parts. I hear that in spite of Akweke, nothing has changed."

I raised a fist playfully. "If you're not careful what you say, I'll knock your head off."

Achara said as he retreated a few paces, "That's exactly what I mean." We both laughed.

"Akweke always said you were the most brilliant pupil he ever taught," I said. "He actually predicted you'd win a scholarship to Umuahia in the entrance exam. Did you?"

Achara seemed to be struggling with himself. Momentarily, he looked down at his feet, and when he raised his head, he looked everywhere else but at me. Empathizing with him, I put a friendly arm around his shoulders.

"It doesn't really matter if you did not," I said, smiling warmly. "You passed the entrance exam, didn't you? Scholarship or no scholarship, what matters is we are all here."

"I won a scholarship," he said very softly.

"You did?" I asked, my friendly arm slowly sliding off his shoulders. "You did what Akweke said you'd do? Isn't that simply amazing?"

By this time, we had reached the school lobby, which was located in the angle of the L-shaped classroom building. And we had spoken in Igbo throughout our conversation. We were obviously lucky that no authority figure came within earshot as we walked and talked. In any case, we had kept our voices low. For my part, I was well aware that this was probably my last chance, before things got serious, to thumb my nose at a rule that even my young mind found intolerably constricting, and against which all my instincts rebelled. But if I must be truthful, I would have to admit that I was not really—and never had been—a great speaker of my own mother tongue. Broken English, being the preferred mode of communication among Aba youths, was more my thing. I suppose I was just naturally prone to rebelliousness.

We found many of our classmates in the lobby and had to jostle our way through the crowd to reach the notice board. On the board were several notices, but the one that held the attention of us freshers, as well as a sprinkling of more senior boys, was an alphabetical list of the names of the class 1 boys. Against each name was that of a class 3 student. The notice stated that the class 3 student was to be the "guide" of the class 1 boy for the school year.

Against my name was that of one Patrick Onyewuchi. Samuel had already briefed me on the fagging system. Under the system, as he related it to me, a senior student took a fresher under his wing to help and guide him through the first year. But Samuel had said nothing about the system being officially sponsored. The list was signed by the housemaster, Mr. Robert Pepple.

"Who's your guide?" I asked Anthony.

Instead of answering my question, the fellow stared at me for a moment and then said, "At least lower your voice if you're going to continue to speak in Ibo publicly."

"Okay, I'm sorry. But who's your guide?"

"Can't you see his name there?"

"Oh yes. Now I see it."

"Thomas Eleadi," Anthony Achara said. "I wonder what he's like. Why do they think we need older students to guide us?"

"Samuel said it's the normal thing in every secondary school. When his class was in King's College, Lagos—that's where his class started two years ago—"

"That's what I hear," said Achara. "Seems very strange that the first two Umuahia classes started in King's College."

"Did no one tell you why it happened like that?" I asked, surprised he did not seem to know the story.

"I'm sure you'll tell me," he said, smiling impishly.

I did not have a chance to tell him. Suddenly, from behind me, a pair of hands clasped my shoulders and spun me round. The expression on Samuel's face was not very cousinly, and his voice, when he spoke, was distinctly acerbic.

"I don't know how many times I have to tell you not to speak that language here. You don't seem to understand, but one of these days you will. Wait till a leader or a master punishes you for breaking the rule. Then maybe you'll understand. And you," he asked my companion, "what's your name?"

"Anthony Achara."

"Well, Achara, you had better look out. I don't know if you two are friends, but please don't let Obinna mislead you in this matter. You follow?"

Anthony nodded. Whereupon Samuel said to me, "I brought someone to meet you."

He indicated another student standing quietly by his side. "This is Patrick Onyewuchi," he said.

"My guide!" I said rather loudly.

We stared at each other appraisingly. I remember that my mouth fell open as if in a hypnotic trance. Then I became aware that my guide was extending his right hand to me, and I nervously reached for it. His handshake was firm without being punishingly so.

"So you're Okoye Junior."

Although unfamiliar with that form of address, I nodded and said, "Yes."

"Yes *please*," Onyewuchi said, with appropriate emphasis. "Not just 'yes.' Let that be your first lesson—or rather your second, as you seem to be already aware of the vernacular rule. You must learn to add 'please' to your answers, especially to the senior boys. 'Yes, please.' 'No, please.' But don't worry too much about all these rules. You'll get used to them as time goes on. Okoye Senior is quite right, however. You could be punished for breaking the rule."

"I can get punished for not saying 'please'?" Achara asked disbelievingly.

"No, no!" replied Onyewuchi. "I'm talking about the vernacular thing."

He held out his hand to Achara. "You're welcome too, Achara." They shook hands.

Onyewuchi had a graceful, nicely proportioned body, with strong arms and legs. In his green khaki shorts and white canvas shoes, he looked supremely athletic, an impression that was accentuated by his height. At about five feet eight inches, he was one of the tallest boys in the school and clearly one of the strongest. He was quite attractive, with his pleasant face and disarming smile, and skin the color of polished mahogany. His eyes engaged your attention, but did not challenge or provoke you.

"I'll see you later," he said, with a fleeting smile, and then turned and walked away.

"Impressed?" Samuel asked Achara and me. "Wait till you know him better. Obinna, you'll like him. I guarantee you that. You are one of the luckiest boys in your class to have him as your guide. He's probably our best hockey player, if you even know what hockey is, and quite good at football. You'll see."

"Who's your fag?" I asked Samuel. "Or does the housemaster think you're the only class 3 boy who doesn't know how to guide a fresher?"

"Is that how he talks to you?" Achara asked Samuel.

"Don't mind him," Samuel said dismissively as he moved closer to the notice board to look at the list of names, probably to refresh his memory. He had, of course, seen the list earlier.

"Gregory Okoroafor," he read out to me. "Have you met him?"

"You mean Gree-goh-ree?" I said.

"From Mbawsi, over there," said Anthony Achara.

We were both convulsed with laughter at the memory of Gregory Okoroafor pointing over the principal's shoulders less than twenty minutes earlier as we had stood on the steps of house 1.

"D'you know Thomas Eleadi?" I asked Samuel. "He's Anthony's guide."

"You mean Achara's guide," corrected Samuel. "That's his last name, isn't it? Here you call other boys by their last names always."

"Is that rule 3?" asked Achara.

"Rule or no rule," I said seriously, "I'll not call you Okoye Senior."

"Don't be silly, Obinna," Samuel said, smiling. "You know quite well that's different."

"Thank God! And, Samuel, don't worry about Gregory—I mean, Okoroafor. He was here with us not so long ago. When I see him, I'll tell him about you."

"You will?" asked Samuel, looking rather uncomfortable, perhaps at the thought of what I might say about him to his fag. After a slight hesitation, he invited Achara and me to come on a stroll with him. "We have just enough time to walk around and see a bit of the compound before the bell for supper."

"You didn't answer the question about Thomas Eleadi," I reminded him.

"Oh," said Samuel. "He's okay. Perhaps a little crazy sometimes. We call him Baba Eko. Come on, let's go, or we'll not see much before supper. This is a beautiful compound. You'll see."

"Do you need to tell us?" I asked.

CHAPTER III

I t was day 3, my first Friday, I remember. I was ravenous by the time the bell rang at six o'clock for supper. My natural inclination was to rush to the dining hall, but Kofi Bentsil held me back.

"Don't make a fool of yourself," he said, stiff with dignity. "D'you want people to say you've not seen food before? D'you even know what food it will be?"

"Do you?" I asked, slowing down to a leisurely walk, though my eagerness must have been plain to any careful observer.

"Rice and *doh-doh*," said Bentsil, smiling. "I know you like doh-doh."

"Don't you?"

"Only if the plantain is very ripe, and it is fried well, well. With you, any way it's fried, it's okay."

I too liked my plantain fried, as Bentsil put it, "well, well." But he was right. He had seen me, numerous times, buy fried ripe and unripe plantain from Yoruba women who hawked cooked food in the marketplace and on street corners in Aba.

The sweet smell of the doh-doh reached me even before I entered the dining hall. And as I gazed at the generous portion, topped by a hefty piece of meat and a rich appetizing stew, served on my white enameled plate, I knew that the dining hall was going to be one of my favorite spots in the school.

"See you later," I said, waving to Bentsil as he walked away unhurriedly to his table.

The dining hall was a large open building, with low walls, corridors along its two long sides, and four entrances without doors. The hall was located at the far end of the beautiful central quadrangle, opposite the classroom building. Seating was by dormitory, with four long tables allotted to each dormitory.

The school leader said a short prayer, and with a clatter, everyone fell to. Lacking the art of polite conversation with relative strangers, I concentrated on my food. "Hey there! You fag! Hold your knife properly."

The rebuke, accompanied by a high-pitched laughter, came from a boy two seats to my right. Instinctively, I looked up, although I was sure I was not the object of the verbal attack. My cousin Samuel had already taught me how to handle my cutlery in the correct—that is, British—manner: the fork with my left hand and the knife or the spoon with my right.

I immediately recognized the verbal assailant, and my heart sank. Three months earlier, when I came to Umuahia for my admission interview, I had seen Chima Nwanna furiously chased around a dormitory by a bigger and very irate classmate and subsequently worsted in a one-sided fight. Someone told me then that Nwanna was given to making disparaging remarks about other boys in his class. In his nastiest mood, he loved to call some of them "cockroaches"—an unflattering form of address reserved exclusively for impudent freshers, otherwise known as fags. And he was himself, at the time, also a fresher. It seemed evident to me now, as I watched him lay into his clumsy victim, that the humiliation he had suffered at the hands of his enraged antagonist, months earlier, had not curbed the causticity of his tongue.

"You're holding the knife like a dagger," Nwanna shouted at the poor boy. "How can you cut your meat like that? Bushman!"

I felt an instant dislike for Nwanna and prayed that our paths would never cross. But how, I asked myself miserably, would our paths not cross, seeing we were in the same dormitory? I was full of foreboding. Nothing about him appealed to me. Not his squat nose, disfigured by who knew how many punches thrown by exasperated adversaries. Nor his head, which was disproportionately larger than the rest of his body. That I was aware that the same description could very well be applied to my head did nothing to mellow my feelings toward him. Nwanna seemed—though that might have been an illusion—to be shorter than when I first set eyes on him. He was one of the shortest boys in the school; by a good six inches or so, he was the shortest of the class 2 boys. He stood barely four feet tall but was obviously endowed with boundless energy and a cutting tongue that promised to make life difficult for those members of my class who could not avoid contact with him.

Suddenly someone said in a hushed tone, "Black Cat appears!"

All eyes turned to the northern entrance as the housemaster, Mr. Robert Pepple, strode into the dining hall. Tall, paunchy, and with a hard, furrowed face, a perpetual scowl, and a well-trimmed moustache, Mr. Pepple had a dominating and rather forbidding personality, an impression heightened by his square and determined set of jaws. For a moment or two, he stood and surveyed the boys, nodding to himself with satisfaction. He had the air of a magistrate inspecting his court.

I leaned over to the boy sitting next to me and asked, "Do you know why he's called 'Black Cat'?"

Chima Nwanna must have been well aware that the question was not addressed to him. But I suppose he could not stop himself from butting in with his loud mouth. I was quickly discovering that he was the type of bully who hated to miss an opportunity to hurt and humiliate other boys. Actually, he first laughed out loud to gain attention. Then, assuming a pompous air, he spoke in a voice loud enough to be heard some tables away.

"Because he is black, like some of you ugly toads, and he wears rubber-soled shoes."

Pausing for effect, he continued, "You fags don't understand, of course. But you will, sooner or later. You'll see. Sometimes you don't see him coming. You don't even hear his footsteps. He just sneaks up on you suddenly, mysteriously, black as the night, like a messenger from the devil—"

Warming to his overblown and long-winded rhetoric, he seemed to lose all sense of his surroundings—that is, until he saw something in the attitude of his listeners. He stopped, looked over his shoulder, and half-jumped out his seat. For, standing right behind him, with an odd kind of a smile on his hard lips, was Mr. Pepple. Nwanna drew in his breath with a sharp rasping sound. At the same instant, Mr. Pepple planted a firm hand on his shoulder and pushed him back into his seat. I waited, hardly breathing, to see what would follow.

"Report to the staff room tomorrow morning, at eight o'clock," Mr. Pepple said, the smile that was really a scowl still on his lips.

"Yes, sir," said Nwanna. "But what have I done?"

The challenge stopped Mr. Pepple dead in his tracks as he half-turned to walk away. To say that I was taken aback by the defiant tone of Nwanna's question would be to put it mildly. I knew, if I were in his shoes, I would not have dared. I was not in the habit of so heedlessly challenging authority, as Nwanna evidently was. I have to admit I felt a grudging admiration for him at that moment.

If looks could kill, Mr. Pepple's stare would have instantly felled Nwanna. After a slight hesitation, Mr. Pepple said, "I have warned you to be more careful of the drivel that comes out of your mouth."

I did not know what "drivel" meant. Perhaps Nwanna did because he was still defiant.

"But I didn't—" he started to say, only to be cut off short.

"Shut up!" ordered Mr. Pepple. "I heard every word you said. But that's something strictly between you and me. What I'll not tolerate, and that's the reason I want to see you tomorrow—what I'll not tolerate is for you to make life intolerable for the freshers. I've received complaints—"

"From them?" asked Nwanna, who did not seem to know when to stop. "I challenge any fag here to say I've made life difficult for him."

Mr. Pepple inhaled and exhaled, staring dolorously at his interlocutor. He shook his head with the air of a man who was thoroughly exasperated. For perhaps the first time, I noticed his nervous habit of tapping the sides of his thighs with his fingers when he was angry or emotionally upset.

Then he spoke calmly, "They're probably too scared to report you directly at this stage. But one or two of the older boys have told me you've been quite uncontrollable. So eight o'clock tomorrow in the staff room."

As Mr. Pepple walked determinedly away, I stole a look at Nwanna. He was smiling smugly and had an odd kind of look on his face. I knew what that smile and the look signified but, against my better instincts, could not bring myself to abhor his behavior just because he had dared to do what I knew I could not have done.

Mr. Pepple walked up to the senior school leader's table at one end of the hall and engaged him in a brief conversation. Then he picked up a table knife and struck it loudly on the table three or four times, until he gained the attention of all the boys. He cleared his throat noisily.

"My name is Mr. Pepple, your housemaster," he announced, although there could not have been any boy present who did not already know this. "Now pay attention to the following announcements. First, for the new boys principally, always watch the notice board in the school lobby. Right now, there are a few notices you should read carefully and digest. For the moment, I want to draw your attention to two important items. Tomorrow, school uniforms will be distributed. Each boy will receive two white shirts and two pairs of white shorts for classes and one yellow shirt and a pair of green khaki shorts for games and housework in the afternoons."

His voice was a clipped, emphatic bass, vibrant, assured, and not at all unpleasant to the ears; and his delivery was as articulate and as fluent as I thought I had ever heard.

"The other thing is that under no circumstances should any boy leave the school compound at any time without an *exeat* from me. The exception is on Saturdays after the school parade, when you are free to come and go, without any special permission, until four o'clock in the afternoon. There will be no parade tomorrow, however.

"Now I'll introduce the three school leaders. Those boys in classes 2 and 3 who were in King's College, Lagos and those admitted in July last year from other colleges know that they are called prefects everywhere else. Here in Umuahia, the principal and I have decided that at this stage, and with only three classes in the college, it is a little premature to use that word. This could change next year, even though we would still be less than a full six-class college.

"As I call out their names, they will stand up, so every boy will have a chance to recognize them from here on."

He was suddenly seized with a mild cough and signaled to a boy to go get him a cup of water from the kitchen. As we all waited, my mind went back to the housemaster's announcement that we would be issued three shirts and three pairs of shorts. And I found myself wondering if this was not highly unusual. I had never heard that this was done in any other secondary school, of whatever denomination. And I was personally acquainted with several boys from my primary school and other schools in Aba who were already in those other colleges.

I already knew, from the older boys and my cousin Samuel in particular, that we would be issued all the textbooks we would need for our classes and studies. All free of any charges. And again, totally unheard-of and unprecedented in any other secondary school that I knew of, in Eastern Nigeria. And the college fees—five pounds, six shillings, and eight pence per term for tuition, board, and equipment—was the absolute lowest in the region, if not in the entire country.

The cup of water revived Mr. Pepple. "First, Clement Ugwu, the senior school leader and head of house 3."

Clement Ugwu stood up and took a bow. Short and stocky, with a close haircut, he exuded considerable bodily strength. Earlier that day, Samuel had introduced me to the senior leader. He had described Ugwu as a very patient human being, slow to anger, but so strong that those who had made the mistake of picking a quarrel with him soon regretted their rashness. Ugwu hated to fight, Samuel had said, but when provoked, he was like a lion. From the way his clothes sat on his sturdy frame, Ugwu gave the impression that they were meant merely to cover his nakedness and not as an adornment for his body. He had a habit of constantly tugging at his shorts. Perhaps he thought they would otherwise drop to his feet.

Mr. Pepple walked ponderously to the other end of the dining hall—my end—and stood by a table just across the aisle from where I sat.

"Godfrey Clarke," he said loudly, "is the second school leader and in charge of house 1."

Tall, lissome, and with thick curly hair (which he groomed meticulously), Godfrey Clarke was everything that Clement Ugwu was not. They were a study in contrasts. For, quite apart from their very apparent physical dissimilarities, Clarke was gruff, short-tempered, and cantankerous and, to boot, one of the most vainglorious persons I had ever met.

House 1 was my dormitory. My bed was the closest to Clarke's room, which was located at one end of the dormitory. It was an uncomfortable proximity, for which my cousin Samuel had already commiserated with me. Samuel had given me one piece of advice: avoid Clarke like the devil, which was easy for him to say. However, he had omitted to suggest how, in the circumstances, I could keep my distance from my house leader.

Mr. Pepple finally moved on to a third table, in the middle of the hall, the area allotted to house 3.

"Last but not least, Gilbert Enuma."

Mr. Pepple, noticing Enuma's hesitation, reached down and took him by the hand and made him stand up. Enuma was of medium height and had the type of plain, undistinguished face that is easily lost in a crowd. He seemed curiously apologetic and ill at ease about something. Perhaps he had not been attentive enough and had not heard the housemaster's instruction that each leader stand up when called. The smile on his face was brief and rather sheepish. He stood awkwardly for several seconds and then groped for his bench and sat down. His every movement was clumsy and nervous. Indeed, had the forbidding presence of the housemaster not discouraged it, Enuma's antics would have provoked loud and derisive laughter.

Mr. Pepple cleared his throat noisily. "Let me make one thing absolutely clear," he said, his voice even more peremptory than before. "And class 1 boys had better take note. The leaders have the responsibility to maintain order and discipline at all times. I will not, repeat *not*, tolerate acts of insubordination to any of them by any boy. They have my authority to punish flagrant disobedience, no matter from what quarter."

From everything I had heard, it seemed to me that these were exactly the same powers exercised by *prefects* in other schools. And I found myself wondering what the hell difference it would have made if the leaders had been called prefects. There were other disturbing questions, about which I made a mental note to ask Samuel later. Did the power of the leaders to punish other boys extend to their own classmates? The housemaster's words seemed to leave no doubt on the matter: no one was exempt. And if one felt a leader's action was unjust, was there any way one could seek redress? I looked across at Godfrey Clarke, my mind full of foreboding.

I leaned across to my neighbor. "What does 'flagrant' mean?"

"You like to ask questions, I see," he said deprecatingly. "Like your question about black cat, I don't know. I'm new too, like you. Maybe he likes to use big words. You had better shut up and listen to him."

"If you have any complaints about anything," continued Mr. Pepple, "go to your dorm leader or come to me. My door is always open. But be warned, if you choose to come knocking on my door, you'd better make sure your complaint is genuine and serious.

"Another thing. I hope you'll like the food here. It is well balanced. However, we have no objection if on your Saturday trips into Umuahia town, you buy small quantities of fruits, groundnuts, biscuits—things like that. But I repeat, small quantities! I also happen to know some boys like to buy palm oil to mix with their *okpodudu*. It seems to make the beans taste richer or something. If you buy palm oil, you must store it in the big cupboard at the northern end of the dining hall—of course, clearly labelled. No palm oil in the dormitories!

"What I'll not tolerate is for anyone to go and bother the cook. You've simply got no business with the cook. I hope that is clear.

"One thing and I am done—for now. You've no doubt all heard about the ubiquitous hyena. For those unfamiliar with the word, 'ubiquitous' means the hyena has been sighted at a hundred different places at the same time. Whether or not you believe the story that the animal is actually a disgruntled Hausa man who turns himself into a hyena and preys on living human beings is not important. I personally do not believe it. But what matters is that there is probably a hyena—or some other carnivore—out there. So we have to take precautions. I suggest that you do not wander far away from the dormitories alone, especially at night."

The mere mention of the famous hyena sent shivers down my spine. Weren't hyenas supposed to roam the more open savannas of Northern Nigeria? And to feed on carrion left by the larger carnivorous animals, like the leopards or the lions? What was this hyena doing in our thickly forested regions of Southern Nigeria? I had no answers to these questions. All I knew was what I had heard: that this particular hyena was a most unusual one and so atypical of the species that it actually attacked human beings. I had no clue how the misanthropic Hausa man was able to change, at will, from man to animal and back again to man. But though I did not understand, I think I was too scared to disavow the powers of witchcraft or other mystical forces.

No one seemed to know for sure what caused the Hausa man's bitterness against his fellow men. There were several stories. But the most often repeated was the one about an avaricious Igbo trader in Northern Nigeria. The Igbo trader reportedly dispossessed the Hausa man of land and houses in settlement of a bad debt. This at least would explain why the hyena concentrated its havoc in the Igbo country. It was popularly believed that, at the point of death, the hyena would transmute irreversibly back to human form, thus finally revealing the identity of the Hausa man. The entire country anxiously awaited the denouement to this frightening affair.

I finished my meal in a somber mood, thoughts of the hyena uppermost in my mind. After the meal, I was drifting out of the dining hall with others when I was pulled back, none too gently, by Godfrey Clarke.

"My friend," the leader asked, with a superior air, "where d'you think you're going?" "Where do I think I'm going?"

"Good Lord!" he cried, looking up to the heavens. "Are you an echo or what? Yes, that's what I asked you. Aren't you forgetting something? Now go back and do your work."

He stomped away haughtily, leaving me dazed and confused, until another boy reminded me I was on the plate-washing team for the week. As I turned and walked back into the hall, I saw my designated guide, Patrick Onyewuchi, standing some distance away, watching me. There was a curious smile on his lips and a twinkle in his eyes.

CHAPTER IV

Godfrey Clarke filled my world. In those early days and months of my life in Umuahia, there seemed little I could do, nowhere I could turn, without running full tilt into Clarke. For me, he rapidly assumed the mantle of an unforgiving nemesis. Two or so weeks had passed, and it seemed a regular Sunday, like any other. The cool, dust-laden harmattan miniseason was already over, giving way to the high humidity and excessive heat of early February. I felt rather out of sorts, but whether from the oppressive weather or something else, I did not know.

I had sweated all night long and had consequently slept badly. I woke up with my bladder uncomfortably full and headed rapidly for the urinal. That was nothing unusual; on most mornings, my first urge was to make a dash for the urinal.

I turned the corner of the bathroom annex and bumped into someone. I was thrown backward, measuring my length on the ground. From that prostrate position, I looked up into the glowering eyes of none other than my house leader. Godfrey Clarke stood stiffly upright, arms akimbo, striking—or so it seemed to me—an exaggerated pose.

I quickly regained my feet and dusted myself down, even as my bladder pressure increased by the second. But I knew to keep my head bowed, not daring to speak until spoken to.

He took his time—loads of it—before he deigned to speak. "I did not hear your apology," he said, the hoarseness of his voice at odds with his elegant, almost-delicate physique. Briefly he took his hands off his waist, but only long enough to secure the rope of his knee-length dressing gown. He was one of a select few who had dressing gowns.

"Sorry, please," I mumbled. "Good morning."

"Speak up!" he said. "I did not hear you."

I cleared my throat and repeated myself more loudly. By this time, I could barely stand still, on account of the tremendous pressure in my bladder.

"You don't have to shout, you—"

I dashed off, leaving him in midsentence. I did so, not because of a sudden rush of courage or defiance. I just could no longer restrain myself. And I did not look back once, as I ran as fast as my unsteady legs could carry me, straight to the urinal. Minutes later, relieved and very contrite, I headed back to the dormitory and to Clarke's room, obsequious apology on my mind. He was waiting for me.

"You will pay for this insult," he shouted before I could get a word out. For a moment or two, such was Clarke's fury, I feared he might have laid a hand on me. But the moment passed. "For one week from breakfast today, you will wash double the number of plates you normally wash. And next Saturday, you will be on the *matchet* parade."

My heart sank. This would be my first matchet parade, but I had already seen the amount of punitive grass-cutting that it signified. There was grass-cutting of the almost-leisurely housework variety, which all the boys, except of course the leaders, routinely did—twenty to thirty minutes of it. But there was also grass-cutting of a very different variety. The matchet parade was no ordinary parade. And grass-cutting on a matchet parade was probably the worst form of punishment, involving one solid hour (sometimes more) of unrelenting slog. It was moreover more than merely physical; it stigmatized the frequent offender as a troublesome, unruly boy. No boy wanted to be so stigmatized. Unless you were, perhaps, Chima Nwanna. He seemed the least affected by that type of notoriety. But then, it is possible that I misjudged him.

"Excuse me, please," I said, desperate to mitigate the severity of the punishment. "I did not mean to insult you. I swear to God who made me. If I didn't—you know—run off, I don't know what I would have done to my clothes. Can't you—"

"Get out of here, this minute!" he hissed indignantly. "And talking of your clothes, I'll see you later today, during the clothes inspection. You had better be ready if you know what's good for you. Any dirty clothes, and I mean *any*, even one, and you'll be in big trouble. That's a promise, Okoye. And that's something I've never been known to break."

I stood glaring at him, notwithstanding the ferocity of his words. But I was dejected and close to tears. I went and sat on my bed, wondering if it was right that a leader should be invested with such unlimited powers over his fellow students, even if they were mere fags.

I sought out my cousin Samuel after chapel and recounted to him the events of the morning. He commiserated with me but declared he could not help me out of my predicament.

"You see," he said softly, "that's why I warned you about Clarke. He is wicked. I don't know who he thinks he is. Already this year, he has threatened to put a fellow class 3 boy on matchet parade."

"His own classmate?" I asked. "I've been meaning to ask you about it. What did your classmates say to him?"

"Never mind what we said to him. Are you ready for the clothes inspection this afternoon?"

"How can I," I protested, "when he gave me so many of his own clothes to wash for him? It took me at least four hours yesterday to do so. I am not his fag, so I don't know why he keeps making me do these things for him. D'you know that up till now, I have never washed one thing for Onyewuchi, and I'm supposed to be his fag?"

Samuel thought about that for a moment or two and then said, "You know, it's not a bad idea for you to talk to him—I mean, Onyewuchi. He might be able to help you. It will be worse for you if I talk to Clarke. He knows what I think of him, and he doesn't like me either. Yes, talk to Onyewuchi, though I doubt he'll want to be involved." He paused, a smile lighting up his face. "And by the way, I'm glad you've overcome your bad habit of always talking to me in the vernacular. That's good, although your phonetics needs some improvement. But not to worry. Time will take care of it."

I playfully swung a fist at Samuel and had at least the satisfaction of seeing him take a step or two back. "What's wrong with my—whatever you called it—phonetics? It is not included in our class timetable, and as far as I know, we've not yet done it. And I don't like how you keep talking of my vernacular. Why don't you just say 'Ibo'? You're always telling how in King's College, Lagos, Yoruba boys never stop speaking Yoruba. If so, why can't I speak Ibo in this bush Umuahia?"

"The Yorubas are different," Samuel said. "With them, their language is a disease, an incurable disease. It's terrible."

"Ibos should suffer from the same disease," I said. "I hate being forced to speak only English. It's stupid."

"Stupid or not," Samuel countered very seriously, "you had better obey the rule always. It isn't even as if you speak Ibo very well. Like all Aba boys, you speak more broken English than anything else. I know you. It's only because it's a rule that you're fighting against it."

He turned and walked away. "I'll see you later," he said, waving his hand.

I went looking for Onyewuchi, in the other half of my dormitory. He was a house leader and, therefore, an assistant to Clarke in the dormitory. A wall divided the dormitory into two equal halves, each half housing fourteen boys, with each leader occupying the end room in his half. The beds were arranged in two rows of seven beds each. Access was by two doors at the front and back of the building, positioned on either side of the dividing wall.

I found him in his room, but he refused to intercede with Clarke on my behalf. He listened, very patiently, as I told him my story. He then shook his head sadly and reached for my hand and held it as he gently spoke to me.

"How will it help you if I go and speak to Clarke? Will you come running to me every time a leader punishes you?"

"But it isn't fair," I protested. "I didn't do anything to him."

"Fair?" Onyewuchi asked, a half smile curling his lips. "What is fair? My friend, the sooner you understand you're now in college, the easier things will be for you. D'you think everybody is going to treat you fairly? I can't protect you every time something goes wrong."

"You mean I must learn to fight my own battles?"

His smile widened as he nodded approvingly. "Aha! I see you're familiar with one of the principal's favorite sayings. Well, yes, that sums it up nicely. And by the way, the principal does not mean we should actually fight whenever another boy says or does something we don't like. You understand? I've watched you, and I've seen how your eyes flash wildly when you're angry. Watch it! And cheer up. Things are not as bad as you think."

I did not feel in the least humiliated, though Onyewuchi had refused to intercede on my behalf. It was his special gift that he could admonish a junior boy without, in any way, denting the boy's self-respect.

Later that afternoon, Clarke conducted the regular Sunday clothes inspection. I stood nervously by my bed and waited. When he eventually came to my corner, my anxiety increased to fever pitch as, inch by painstaking inch, he examined my bed, my locker, even under my bed. Everything he touched was clean and in its proper place: my clothes, the white bedsheets, the pillowcases, and the red blanket. He looked terribly disappointed as he straightened himself. He was turning away in disgust when an idea seemed to strike him. There was now a wicked glint in his eyes and a malevolent smile on his lips.

"Where are all your clothes?" he asked me.

"There," I said, pointing to my locker.

"All of them?" Clarke opened my locker one more time and unceremoniously took out my shirts, shorts, singlets, and various odds and ends and flung them on my bed. "Is that all? You think I'm blind or what? I know you have other shirts, especially colored ones. And what about—"

My heart sank as his attention focused on the head of my bed. "That looks suspicious," he said gleefully. "What's under that pillow?"

He took hold of the pillow and tossed it aside, revealing a pile of carefully folded but unwashed clothes lying on the bare bed planks. Grinning fiendishly, he picked up the offending clothes one by one, counting in a loud voice as he did so. When he had done, he turned to me, his triumph writ large on his brow.

"That's two shirts, two pairs of shorts, one towel, one pillowcase. Well, well. My dear fellow, what's your explanation?"

I had none. Or rather, I had, but I knew better than to give expression to my thoughts. And if I must be truthful, the fact that I had spent several hours washing his clothes suddenly seemed a lame excuse for not doing what I knew I should have done. I did not dare accuse him of exploiting my services. I was also well aware of my station in the scheme of things, especially for persons like Clarke.

So I kept my counsel and awaited the outcome with relative composure, if not serenity. My punishment was announced publicly during supper. For the next five days, I was condemned to go to bed thirty minutes early. This was a relatively light punishment for which I could think of only one explanation: it was the third punishment he had pronounced against me in the space of twelve miserable hours.

CHAPTER V

Mr. Thomas Hunter breezed into our classroom one day, in the early part of the term, his two hands buried deep in the capacious pockets of his oversized khaki shorts. He was, by reputation, an enigmatic character, with a marked penchant for the histrionics. I immediately recognized him as one of the teachers, though I had no clue what subject he taught.

Thanks to information I had gleaned from my cousin Samuel, I knew that Mr. Hunter, an Oxonian, had taught in King's College, Lagos, before coming to Umuahia. But Samuel had said that Mr. Hunter never taught him in any class. Just about the only sure thing I knew about the man was that he had been in the tropics for many years; he had a deeply suntanned skin to prove it. He was indeed so darkly tanned, he could have passed for a mulatto if his hair, that is, was not so straight.

He had a beautiful and powerful singing voice. Whenever the singing faltered, whether at the morning assembly before classes or at the Sunday chapel service, his strong, melodious voice could be heard, giving some substance to the singing and urging it on by example. He seemed capable, at will, to raise his voice to those high-pitched notes that were beyond the range of all but the most powerful voices.

Freckle faced, plump cheeked, and double chinned, Mr. Hunter stood a mere three or four inches over five feet. If he had a neck, there was precious little evidence of it. His head, plump cheeks and all, looked grotesquely small on his obese body. A shock of prematurely graying hair, above his forehead and temples, quite effectively camouflaged his balding dome. He looked close to fifty but had turned forty only a month earlier. We knew his age because the principal had announced it at a morning assembly.

Mr. Hunter stood for several moments in the middle of the room, in complete silence. Twenty-nine pairs of fascinated eyes were riveted on him as he rolled his eyes without looking at any one in particular.

At length, he took his right hand out of his pocket and pointed to the ceiling. "Smoooooooth," he said slowly, mellifluously.

Still looking up at the ceiling, he waved his right hand, palm up, seemingly at an invisible person up there, and intoned the same word three times. And all the while, he did not deign to look at us. I was beginning to wonder if the eccentric teacher was aware of our presence when he finally lowered his gaze and smiled at us. His smile widened, perhaps because he saw the puzzlement on our faces. It seemed a knowing smile, signifying that our puzzlement was exactly what he had expected.

He repeated the word one more time, "Smoooooooth." And as he said it, he gesticulated like one who was feeling the texture of a piece of cloth. Then we understood.

Apparently satisfied with his success, he next wrote three sets of words on the blackboard: HEART/HAT, BIRD/BED, FIRM/FARM. He pronounced each word several times slowly, his almost-nonexistent Adam's apple bobbing, his lips in constant motion as he shaped his mouth to the particular word.

It was a class like no other in my experience up to that point. Not once in the entire period did Mr. Hunter invite the class to repeat the words after him. He occasionally looked at us and seemed satisfied if we smiled to show we understood. For the rest, he was locked into his own world and seemed not to care what we made of his teaching methods.

The class schedule had indicated English as the subject for the session but had unusually omitted the name of the teacher. By the end of the period, however, we knew we had just had our first-ever class on the *phonetics* of the English language, taught by a natural speaker of the language. Most of us actually thought Mr. Hunter's antics amusing and looked forward to his next class. In our minds, the seed was sown that phonetics could be a diverting and entertaining subject. Indeed, for the next several days, we poked fun at one another as we tried to emulate Mr. Hunter's pronunciation and the ways he shaped his mouth.

Mr. Hunter taught a few more phonetics classes and then was inexplicably gone. His departure in the middle of the term was so sudden and so cloaked in mystery that speculation ran wild as to why he had been whisked away. It was patently clear to the boys that he had been unceremoniously removed from the college; no attempt was made by the principal to disguise that fact. Nor did the principal make any serious effort to dispel some quite fanciful rumors that the information vacuum inevitably spawned about Mr. Hunter.

As far as I was concerned, there was only one boy—in the entire college—who could throw some light on the tangled web of lies, innuendoes, and half-truths. That person was my old schoolmate, Samson Stoneface. I found him in the library and asked him my question without prevarication.

"Is it true—you know—that the government is punishing Mr. Hunter because he likes black people?"

Stoneface, interrupted in the course of writing a class essay, put down his pen, closed his exercise book, and straightened himself in his chair. He looked at the wall clock and then at me, his expression mildly irritated.

"How d'you expect me to know?"

I chose to disregard his irritation because my mission was important to me. "If you don't know," I asked, "who else can I ask?"

He looked keenly at me, and then his face broke in a smile. I knew, at that moment, that he knew why I had come to him. He was, for me, the chief information officer among the students. Had I not caught him red-handed, the week before, posting a news bulletin on the assembly hall notice board?

*   *   *

It had been an odd encounter. When I first saw the handwritten bulletin a few days earlier, I had no clue who the editor was. The bulletin was not signed. And though we had been primary schoolmates at St. James School in Aba, Stoneface was two classes my senior, and I was not familiar with his handwriting.

Then on a Friday afternoon, in the idle hour between lunch and the compulsory rest period, I saw Stoneface in the act of posting one bulletin on the board placed on the dais at one end of the assembly hall. Other than two boys chatting at the other end, the hall was empty. I looked nervously at the two boys, but they did not seem the least bit interested in Stoneface's activities. I approached the dais carefully, as if afraid to hear the sound of my own footsteps. Stoneface was pushing in the last of the drawing pins and seemed totally unconcerned about who might be watching him.

"What are you doing?" I asked.

Stoneface turned and looked at me for a moment before responding. "Why are you whispering? Is something wrong?"

"Suppose somebody sees you?" I asked, glancing quickly over my shoulder at the two boys.

"Sees me doing what? I'm not stealing anything, am I?"

I pointed at the news bulletin. "You're not afraid?"

"Afraid of what? I've been doing this for more than two weeks now. Tell me, is this the first time you've seen my bulletins?"

"Of course not," I said. "I'm only surprised it is you."

And then he said, laughing out loud, "Is it the only thing about me that surprises you?"

It was not. In truth, almost everything about him was a surprise to me. When I last saw him, at St. James, he had been so chubby he was nicknamed Bread Undone. Probably because of his rotundity he had looked decidedly short then. He had also been, with my cousin Samuel, the most brilliant boy in their class, and it had been no surprise when they both passed the entrance examination to Umuahia in 1941. The Stoneface who now stood before me was tall and quite slim. At five feet eight inches when last measured (at the beginning of the term), he was one of the tallest boys in the school. He had shed so many unwanted pounds that only the quintessential character of his face remained unchanged.

But the transformation was clearly not only physical. He had been, in primary school, timid and retiring. Now, on the evidence of what I had just seen him doing, he also seemed to be ready to challenge the authority of the principal. I was left wondering from whence this confidence, this newfound self-assurance, came.

I put the question to him minutes later as we walked away together from the assembly hall. Even his leaden footedness, inevitable for a person with his avoirdupois, and for which he was well known in Aba, had totally disappeared. Now he walked with such long strides and amazing briskness that I found myself almost trotting to keep pace with him.

"We're not allowed to read our national papers," I said. "And here you are fearlessly preparing news bulletins for students. Don't you care about what Mr. Graves will say?"

"You're referring to the *West African Pilot* and the *Daily Service*, no? This is different. D'you even know why the school banned the *Pilot* and the *Service*?"

"Everybody knows why," I replied. "Isn't it because they're always attacking England?"

"Correct. The principal wants us to remain good and loyal boys of the British Empire. That's why we can only read the *Daily Times*, which—I think it is correct to say—is the only Lagos newspaper that does not attack the British Colonial Office all the time. D'you know the *Daily Times* is published by the same company that publishes the London *Daily Mirror*? That's what I've heard anyway."

"How d'you know so much?" I asked very deferentially. "And tell me, if we're not allowed to read our national papers, why are you not afraid to put up your news bulletins that contain so much national news?"

"It's hard to explain why, but the big man himself gave his approval. You know the battered old radio set in the assembly hall? It actually belongs to Mr.

Graves. He put it there for anyone who wants to listen. So I started to go there and listen and to make notes for myself. That's how it started. Then one day another boy asked why I didn't write my notes out clearly and put them up for others to read. So I did.

"One day the principal called me to his office. He had found out it was me that was responsible. I don't know what I expected, but he surprised me. He said he was impressed by my bulletins and wanted me to include more news about the world war. I agreed."

"You didn't really have a choice, did you?"

"None whatsoever," Stoneface said, smiling. "This war against Hitler means so much to our British masters, they'll do anything to win it, including making our people believe it is also our war."

Stoneface had gone on and on about the war and how it was turning decisively in favor of what he called the "free world." It was there and then that I christened him—at least in my own mind—the chief information officer of the student body. There seemed little he did not know.

*   *   *

Stoneface had to know about Mr. Hunter and why he had so abruptly left the college. But instead of answering my question, he continued to look quizzically at me. So I started to repeat my question.

"Is it true that the government—"

"I'm not deaf, Okoye Junior," he said gently. "I heard you the first time. I just don't know how to answer your question. I think Mr. Hunter likes black people, perhaps because he seems to be a good person at heart. You know, there *are* some colonial officers like that."

I decided to take the bull by the horns. I went closer to Stoneface and whispered in his ears. What I told him made him burst out laughing. Boys at the nearby tables looked up, their concentration on their work shattered.

"Who told you that?" he asked when his laughter subsided.

"You know, people talk," I said softly, not wishing to draw any more unwelcome attention. "How many young white girls can he find here? So you know—"

"Know what?" Stoneface interrupted, like me lowering his voice. "If he likes black women, he is not the first white person in the country to do so."

I was not convinced that he was being totally frank with me on this matter. Although I had myself seen nothing, I had heard lots of talk—even in Aba—about unmarried white colonial officers having affairs with local girls of questionable virtue, all over the country. What else could they do but seek outlets for their natural urges with whatever female company was available and accessible? No virtuous native girl would dare consort with a white foreigner. And the reason was very simple: such a girl would immediately be branded a harlot, a devastating stigma.

"Look, Samson—"

"*Stoneface*! I've told you once before that here in this college, every student is called by his last name. Try and remember that and forget St. James, Aba."

"Even my classmates from St. James?" I asked. "What d'you expect me to call Kofi? Bentsil? Or Friday? You want me to call him Stoneface? I can't. And what about Samuel—"

"Don't be silly. You know Samuel is a different case. And I don't know about Friday and Kofi. I only know that last names are the rule. You understand?"

"Yes, please."

"So what were you saying?"

"Just that you know more than you're telling me—about Mr. Hunter. If the man likes black women, why doesn't he find one to marry, even if she's—you know . . . ?"

Stoneface snorted, looking at me as if I had taken leave of my senses. "A British colonial officer cannot marry an African girl—and that's all there is to it. The colonial office would not tolerate it. The officer would be removed as quick as lightning."

How he knew this for a fact, I did not know. And I did not ask him. If he said it was so, that was good enough for me.

"So then, that's why Mr. Hunter has gone. That's what you're really saying, isn't it?"

Stoneface looked carefully around him and lowered his voice further. "Maybe. But I'm honestly not sure. There's probably more to it than just his love affairs with our women. There are—or rather, were—two white teachers here whose attitude to our people is, in general, quite friendly. Too friendly, perhaps, for the British Colonial Office. Mr. Hunter was one, and now he's gone. The other—"

"I know the teacher," I interrupted, eager to show off my knowledge of our political environment. "It's Mr. Eagleton, not so? So why is he still here?"

Stoneface burst out laughing. "Don't be so impatient to see him go. Give the Colonial Office a little more time, and we'll see what they'll do."

"I don't want Mr. Eagleton to go," I said. "That's not what I meant to say."

"Of course, I know. I was only joking. But seriously, I believe they watch people like Hunter and Eagleton all the time. Take Mr. Hunter now. We were in King's College, Lagos, when he was a master there, and his attitude—"

"He seems to be following your class around."

"Stop interrupting me. As I was saying, Mr. Hunter's attitude toward our leading politicians, people like Zik, H. O. D., and the grand old man Herbert

Macaulay was a puzzle to many boys and must have worried the government. He spoke about them as if he admired what they were doing to win freedom for Nigeria. And when he talked, he did not seem to care who was listening. Many of us here who knew him in Lagos have often wondered if he was transferred to Umuahia to get him away from the political hotbed of Lagos."

*   *   *

Several days after this conversation, Stoneface took me aside after supper."Would you like to come with me," he asked, "to see Ojeozi?"

"Ojeozi? Why?"

"Why? Because I think you might be interested in his story. It's something to do with Mr. Hunter. I hope he doesn't object to your coming with me."

"Oh!" was all I could say. I was instantly interested. Ojeozi was very popular among the students. His real name was Sebastian Akueze, but this was known only to very few students. Everyone called him Ojeozi, which was actually an exact description of his job and functions in the school: a factotum, a general messenger, whose range of services included helping out in the kitchen, in the dining hall, and in fetching firewood.

"What's he going to tell you?" I asked knowing, the moment I spoke the words, that it was a stupid question.

"How would I know? Or aren't you interested?"

"How can you ask that? Of course I am. But why did he pick on you?" Stoneface looked long and hard at me, his face a picture of puzzlement and exasperation.

"What's the matter with you?" he asked and turned to walk away. "Meet me here in about ten, fifteen minutes, or so. If I don't see you, that's it. And don't you come back to me to ask me any more questions."

We met Ojeozi some thirty minutes later in the deserted dining hall. As he walked in, he was pouring some snuff out of his snuff container into the palm of his left hand. Then taking a pinch, he carried it to his nostrils, one nostril at a time, inhaled deeply, and waited a moment or two for the inevitable sneeze. Smiling with satisfaction, he dusted off his nose with the back of his hand and then gave us his undivided attention. He might have been about forty, but looked considerably younger. Short, with arms and legs bulging with muscles, he exuded tremendous power. It was said that, in wrestling, he could throw men much younger than himself. His physical strength was no surprise to anyone, since his functions included hewing wood, an activity that obviously did incalculable good for his biceps.

"So, Ojeozi, here I am," said Stoneface, speaking in Igbo. "What did you want to tell me? You said it was about Mr. Hunter."

Ojeozi looked at me questioningly. For just a moment, I thought he was going to object to my presence. Stoneface also noticed his hesitation.

"By the way," he said, putting an arm round my shoulders, "I hope you don't mind my bringing Okoye Junior with me. He likes you very much and always says kind things about you."

That was a barefaced lie, as I could not recall ever talking to Stoneface about Ojeozi. But I was not about to jeopardize this golden opportunity to hear whatever it was the man was about to tell us about Mr. Hunter. I was certain Ojeozi's story had to be an uncommon one, or we would not have gone about it with such clandestinity.

Ojeozi smiled. "I like him too. He always speaks to me with respect and kindness, even though I am a simple, uneducated person. Not all the boys do."

I was deeply touched by his opinion of me and wondered if there really were any boys who had anything bad to say about him.

"You know something, Ojeozi?" Stoneface asked. "Okoye wanted to know why you chose to talk to me about Mr. Hunter."

"Who else could I talk to?"

"You know, one of the masters?"

"A master?" asked Ojeozi. "You think I'm mad? I may be uneducated, but I'm not stupid. If I should try to talk to any of them, the words will refuse to come out of my mouth. Or like the frog, I don't know what I might say, and water will fill my mouth. And then, in what language will I talk to them? I can talk to you in Igbo because I know you will understand what I'm saying to you. I know you're the person who writes the news in the assembly hall. Everybody is talking about it—"

"You read them?" I blurted before I could stop myself.

"You're funny too," Ojeozi said. "But that's all right." He turned again to Stoneface. "What was I saying? Oh yes. I cannot talk to any of the teachers. I think you will be able to tell me what I should do. I'm coming; please wait a moment."

He went to the corridor of the dining hall, leaned beyond the edge of the building, and blew his nose two or three times. Then he came back to us and, this time, sat on a bench, again wiping his nose with the back of his hand.

"Let me tell you something," he said. "Mr. Hunter is not a good person. Because he is a white man, he thinks we cannot do anything to him."

"What's the matter?" Stoneface asked. "What did he do to you?"

"To me?" asked Ojeozi, with a surprised look on his face. "What can he do to me? No, no. It is my relative's daughter that I am talking about. She says—she's the one saying so, not me, but I believe her—she says Mr. Hunter impregnated her."

"What?" I exclaimed.

"You're not serious," said Stoneface.

"Did I say you should not tell anybody?" asked Ojeozi. "Of course, I'm serious. That's what Cecilia told me—that's her name. Mark you, her belly is not big—yet. But don't ask me how I can be sure. She only mentioned the matter to me because we were talking the other day about the college, and somehow the conversation got around to Mr. Hunter. I told her he had left the college, and she screamed and shouted that her *chi* had killed her. That was when I knew something was wrong. At first, she would not tell me anything. But I pressed her, and finally she did."

He paused and laughed mirthlessly. "It appears she and your Mr. Hunter were weaving a little basket, and it turned into a holdall."

"Wait a minute," said Stoneface. "Did you know that this . . . your relative's daughter—what's her name, Cecilia—was seeing Mr. Hunter?"

"I didn't. Although she lives with me, I had no idea at all anything was going on. I do my work and then go home. If she's not at home, I don't think anything of it. She's a big girl, a teacher in a primary school not too far from our place. Why should I worry when I return from work, and she's not there?"

"How old is she?" Stoneface asked.

"How old is Cecilia? I don't know. I know she has reached the age when you can do something with her. What will I tell her father? He entrusted Cecilia to my care because he thought it was the right thing to do for his daughter. He wanted her to leave the village and see a bit of the world. And this is the result. When she gives birth to this white child, what will we do with it? A white child! People will say that Cecilia had no proper home training."

"What'd you want me to do?" Stoneface asked the unhappy man. "Mr. Hunter has left Nigeria and, I imagine, will not be coming back."

Ojeozi looked from Stoneface to me and back again to Stoneface. There was acute misery in his eyes.

The corners of his mouth twitched with suppressed anger. "Speak to the principal," he said. "If I were to see him myself, I would not know what to say. I know you can do it. I've seen you talking to him, and I know no other student talks to him the way you do."

I could see that Stoneface was lapping up the compliment. A slow smile suffused his face as he seemed to be pondering the matter for a moment or two.

"I'll talk to the principal," he said finally. "But I can only repeat the story you told me. I don't know what you think he can do about Cecilia. It's not as if they'll bring Mr. Hunter back so he can marry your niece. You understand that, don't you?"

"Why shouldn't he marry Cecilia? Is she not somebody's child? Isn't it the same god that created all of us?"

Ojeozi suddenly shot up from his seat and walked away from us—but only as far as the corridor and close to the nearest entrance to the biding hall. We watched him as he poured some more snuff into his left palm and then brought some of it to his nostrils and inhaled noisily. He stood there, in solemn contemplation, for a long moment. Then he whirled around and came and offered the snuff container to Stoneface, who gratefully declined the offer.

"It's very good snuff, I can tell you," said Ojeozi "But, well, I suppose you're too young for it. What was I saying? Of course, I know Mr. Hunter will not marry her, even if he was here now. The day I see a white man marry somebody like Cecilia, that day I'll know the world is coming to an end. However, I still want to know what the principal will say about this and whether he will be able to help."

"I'll do my best," Stoneface promised.

"Cecilia is a good girl," Ojeozi said as Stoneface and I were walking out of the dining hall. "I just don't know what came over her. Talk to the principal. Perhaps he can help somehow."

*   *   *

A week later, Stoneface took me with him to see Ojeozi to deliver Mr. Walter Graves's answer. He refused to divulge that answer in advance to me, saying it would not be fair to Ojeozi.

"It's only reasonable," he said, "that the person who asked the question should be the first to know the answer."

"But he won't be the first," I said gleefully. "I'll hear it at the same time as himself."

"You can be tiresome, sometimes," Stoneface said, and he was not smiling.

Ojeozi was waiting anxiously for us on the steps of the Administration Block, overlooking the central quadrangle. It was dusk on a particularly steamy Saturday in mid-February. Our first meeting with the man had been rather secretive. This time, neither Ojeozi nor Stoneface seemed to care that there were a handful of students relaxing on the lawn and well within earshot of us. But we kept our voices low. Stoneface went straight to the point. "I spoke to the principal yesterday," he told Ojeozi. "He seemed to be really affected by your story, but he said that nothing could be done until the baby is born."

"And then?"

"Then he will review the situation. He did not tell me what he intends to do when that time comes. I tried to press him, but it was no use. I'm sorry."

"Is that all?"

"Yes, or rather, no. Mr. Graves said to tell you that if you like, you could see him—as soon as possible."

"Who will go with me when I talk to the principal?" Ojeozi asked, crestfallen. "Did he say you could come along?"

"As a matter of fact," said Stoneface, "I asked him the same question. He said no. He wants to talk to you alone if you want to see him."

"But he won't understand what I'm telling him. He always looks as if he does not understand me when we talk, which is not often, mark you."

An idea suddenly struck me. "Why not talk to him in broken English? He understands pidgin. I know because I've heard him try to speak it with one or two laborers. He sounds terrible of course, but you two will manage."

"Just try and remember one thing," Stoneface added. "When you tell him your story, don't put all the blame on Mr. Hunter. Try and avoid saying anything about Mr. Hunter being a wicked man who took what he wanted and then abandoned your niece. Don't forget that, at this point, you cannot even prove that it was Mr. Hunter who did it, unless Cecilia is bold enough to come out and swear that no other man has—er—touched her, if you know what I mean."

"I hear what you're telling me," said Ojeozi. "And I thank you very much."

We shook hands with him. And as he pumped Stoneface's hand, he looked at him admiringly. "You are wise for your age. Again I thank you. Don't worry about me and the principal. You have given me the courage I was looking for. Now I think I can face him without fear."

*   *   *

In the short term, nothing came of Ojeozi's talk with Mr. Graves. There were still many months to go before the baby was due—if there was really going to be a baby. "That's what the big man said," said Ojeozi bitterly. "It seems he did not believe my story. But that's all right. I am learning to be patient."

CHAPTER VI

In the classroom permanently allocated to our class, seating was in alphabetical order, by family name. Thus I found myself sharing a twin desk with the light-complexioned boy from Mbawsi, the one who could not even pronounce his own given name correctly: Gregory Okoroafor. He was so naturally nervous and fidgety, one of our white masters—it might indeed have been Mr. Walter Graves himself—casually suggested he probably had a biochemical imbalance in his brain.

For a boy with his condition, he had a beautiful penmanship, with a clean, evenly spaced, and easy-flowing calligraphy. Sometimes I would just sit back and watch him, until he rebuked me and told me to get on with my own work. His favorite subject was mathematics. His least-favored activity was athletics or any other form of sport. This, in hindsight, might have had something to do with a lack of eye, arm, and leg coordination, so essential in many forms of athletic endeavor.

He shared this disinclination for sport with Anthony Achara. Achara's distaste for games was so bad that in soccer, he seemed to have little or no idea on which of the two sides his loyalty lay. He kicked the ball presumably because he knew he could not just stand idly in a field in which twenty-one other boys were frenetically active. But he kicked it in whatever direction he happened to be facing. I had no doubt he participated in sports because it was required of all the boys. Oddly, he liked table tennis and in little time became, for him, tolerably good at it.

My own early attempt to get to grips with hockey and cricket, two games with which I was totally unfamiliar, were no great shakes. But like Achara with table tennis, I liked the challenge of cricket and stuck with it. And like Okoroafor and Achara, I had a weakness for food and thoroughly detested the almost-daily chore of grass-cutting.

We three had a number of other things in common. Such as a strong aversion to walking the four miles from the school to the town of Umuahia. We were free to do so on Saturday afternoons. Those boys who could afford it hired bicycles from petty traders who sold their wares and offered the service on the outskirts of the school compound, on the highway to the town. There were classmates who did not seem to mind the long walk. Some probably relished it, like Kofi Bentsil and Chidi Ebele though with Kofi, especially, you could never be sure if he was just putting on a show.

I could not afford the sixpence to hire a bicycle. Neither could Achara and Okoroafor. Achara indeed gave the impression that had he not won a scholarship, he might not have taken up his place in the class. Okoroafor, like me a fee-paying student, was otherwise as poor as the proverbial church rat. If he had any pocket allowance, it could not have been significantly more than mine, which was exactly four shillings for the whole term of about three months. It could have been much worse for me. My father actually gave me two shillings and wished me good luck. My tuition and boarding fees—a total of five pounds, six shillings, and eight pence, he told me with a straight face—had so depleted the family coffers, he was already at a loss how he could afford my next term's fees. It was just as well that my cousin Samuel was on a full scholarship, though that fact did him little good. His pocket allowance was only marginally more than mine, though he was two classes ahead of me. Family friends augmented our allowances with gifts, which Samuel and I somehow forgot to report to my father.

We became friends—Achara, Okoroafor and I—and did things together as often as the circumstances of our boarding life permitted us. In those classrooms where desks were not assigned in alphabetical order (the geography classroom and the science laboratories), we always sought to sit next to one another. We shared the munchables (groundnuts, biscuits, bananas, and such like), which we bought on our Saturday outings, without regard to whose pennies and half pennies had paid for them. We studied in the library together, both during the compulsory afternoon hour of study and especially during the less-regimented evening hours, before the lights-out bell.

It did not take long for me to understand why my primary school headmaster, Mr. Akweke, so often went into raptures when he talked to me about Achara. Achara was just about the most brilliant student in the class and showed no discernible weakness in any subject.

He also loved to sing but had one of the worst singing voices in the college and was quickly designated a "croaker." This was a demeaning label which, once applied to a boy, fairly or unfairly, tended to stick. To be classified a croaker was to be permanently banned from joining meaningfully in any group singing. It meant exposure to frequent and cruel taunts by other boys, even when the croaker was quietly singing to himself. "A rundown motor engine struggling back to life"—or words to that effect—was how our mutual friend Okoroafor once described Achara's singing voice. Mr. Eagleton, who taught ancient history, and conducted the school singing practices was so startled he asked Achara if he had pebbles in his mouth when he sang. And then strangely, he compared Achara's voice to Louis "Satchmo" Armstrong's, the greatest of all jazz musicians, whose name was then only just beginning to mean something to us. But I did not think Mr. Eagleton meant the comparison as a compliment to Achara. I was myself not above joining occasionally in the good-natured ribbing.

Achara was totally unaffected by the label and likened the uncomplimentary remarks on his singing voice to pouring water over a duck's back. He regarded it as his elemental right to sing, publicly or privately, when the mood was on him, which was much too often, as far as Chima Nwana—the arch-tormentor and therefore bête noir of our class—was concerned.

Those students who did not know Achara well probably only saw a quiet, self-effacing boy who knew his place in the college community and scrupulously respected the senior boys in classes 2 and 3. It took me awhile to understand that his quietly religious nature and his peaceful demeanor could not be equated with physical weakness. And to recognize that he had a steely determination that often manifested itself against gross injustice or any attempt, subtle or overt, to trample on his rights.

It was plain to see that Chima Nwanna, the bully boy, did not know Achara at all. He evidently thought he did not need to, and seized every opportunity to rag Achara about his plumpness and his atrocious singing.

Things came to a head on a wet Saturday afternoon, in late March 1944. For much of the morning, it had been thunder and lightning, presaging an unusually early beginning of the rainy season. The rain came down in buckets for a long time until its force was spent. Then it settled down to a gentle but steady drizzle. In the veranda of my dormitory, I was frenziedly ironing my shirts and shorts, eager to avoid any confrontation with my leader, Godfrey Clarke. The weekly clothes inspection was due the following day. And he still had it in for me.

Achara stood close by, leaning against a pillar of the veranda. He watched me with the superior gaze of someone who had done his own ironing in good time and not left things till crunch time. He was also humming softly to himself. If he had been content just to hum, all might have been well. But it was a favorite Eastern hymn, and Easter was due in another week or so. The season and his enthusiasm obviously soon got the better of him, and he broke into singing.

The first either of us knew that anything was amiss was when a hard punch thudded into the small of Achara's back. Because we both had our backs to the dormitory door, we had not seen Nwanna emerge from the dormitory. Momentarily winded, Achara turned toward his attacker as a second blow glanced off his right shoulder. I thought he could easily have avoided the third punch, aimed roughly at his midriff. But his lack of athletic suppleness had clearly dulled his reflexes, and the punch doubled him up, as a sharp pain seemed to wrack his whole frame.

"Stinking cockroach!" Nwanna screamed at him, his anger still apparently unassuaged even by the fury of his attack. His favorite name for any class 1 boy who did not know his place was "cockroach."

I stopped my ironing and went and stood by my friend but without a clear notion of what I would do if the situation deteriorated. I could see fire in Nwanna's eyes and feared the worst.

"What did I do?" Achara asked, straightening himself with some difficulty. "Didn't you know I was studying? Do you have to croak like that? Don't you know you fags are to be seen—"

"But not heard, I know," Achara said, looking Nwanna up and down with scornful eyes. Then he added, "Doesn't that include you July fags?"

July fags were boys who had been admitted to the college in July of the previous year (1943) to make up the serious shortfall in the number of students, mostly in class 1, but also a few in class 2. Known from then on as July fags, the name stuck and was carried over into the new year, much to the chagrin of those affected. No boy in my class, however, dared openly call a class 2 or 3 boy a July fag.

The insult momentarily froze Nwanna. "What did you say?" he asked.

Achara, though still gingerly rubbing his belly where Nwanna's last punch had inflicted pain, impudently laughed out loud. By this time, the noisy argument had attracted a few boys, who took up advantageous positions by the dormitory windows and watched, agog with expectations of fisticuffs.

"I said 'July fags,'" responded Achara defiantly. And then he added for good measure, "You're an ugly toad too."

"Achara!" I called out to my friend desperately. "Are you crazy or what?"

But I was too late. Enraged beyond control and bending himself into half his already-short stature, Nwanna lunged headfirst at Achara, catching him in the pit of the stomach. In the same motion, he brought up an arm and encircled Achara around the neck, pulling him down. They fell in a heap against the ironing table, knocking it over, and the hot pressing iron with it. Luckily, the iron fell harmlessly several feet away from the combatants.

I had seen enough. Quickly sizing up the situation, I grabbed Nwanna's menacingly raised right arm and held on to it with every fiber of my strength.

For his small stature, Nwanna certainly had astonishing power in his arms. I was struggling unavailingly to maintain my hold when, happily for me if not for him, a few boys decided to lend a hand. The fighters were forcibly separated and kept apart, though both boys seemed eager to get on with it.

Unfortunately for Achara and Nwanna, Gilbert Enuma, the timid, self-effacing school leader, happened to be in the vicinity of the fight and was inevitably drawn to the scene of the commotion. He did not ask who was at fault or what had provoked the fight. By nature uncomfortable in the face of any serious problem, he seemed particularly not to relish a confrontation with the vitriolic Nwanna. His body language, the way he kept darting his eyes surreptitiously at Nwanna, led me to believe he had already formed an opinion as to the aggressor.

"I'll be seeing the housemaster later," he announced to the combatants, looking as if he wished he were someplace else. "I believe you both know what'll happen, don't you? You especially," he said to Achara. "What's your name?"

"Achara, please."

"Have you ever fought with gloves on?"

"No, please."

"But you know what the housemaster will do?"

Dumbly Achara nodded. We all knew the housemaster's policy on fights. Mr. Pepple had repeatedly spoken to us about this. Nwanna versus Achara would be the second gloved boxing match since the beginning of the term.

"I'll let you know later what the housemaster says," Enuma said as he seemed to look the two boys over appraisingly. "I think you're well matched."

After Leader Enuma left, Nwanna smiled malevolently. He went and stood eyeball-to-eyeball with Achara. "When I finish with you," he boasted gleefully, "you'll regret coming to this college. Just wait till we put our gloves on. I already feel sorry for you."

I held Achara by the hand as, together, we watched Nwanna walk springily away. I was scared for my friend, but there was nothing I could do about anything now. When Nwanna was far enough away, I turned to Achara.

"Were you mad or what?" I asked solicitously. "Don't you know who this fellow is?"

"I was doing all right until you came and separated us," Achara countered.

I looked at him intently for a moment or two, silently wondering if he had taken leave of his senses. "D'you know how to box—I mean with gloves on?"

"No, but what's the difference?"

"What's the difference?" I cried. "You mean you don't know the—but what's the use trying to explain it to you? If you had grown up in a township—as I did—you would know. Let me tell you something. You'll feel very clumsy with those things on."

There was fire in his eyes that bespoke his fierce determination to take on the challenge posed by his mercurial tormentor, Chima Nwanna, no matter the odds against him.

"I don't look forward to this fight, but not out of fear of Nwanna. I hate fighting and perhaps shouldn't have called him a July fag. But it's too late now to take back the words. We'll see what happens."

*   *   *

The single most important component of the college policy on fights between boys was that the two boys had to be reasonably well matched in size. Age was not a serious factor if only because it was, in many cases, impossible to establish with any degree of accuracy. As Leader Enuma had remarked, Nwanna and Achara passed this test.

The fight ground was the open space between Mr. Pepple's house and the college dispensary to its left. The housemaster's house was located about three or four hundred yards to the north of the dormitories, very close to the highway leading to Umuahia Township. A pair of bougainvillea trees provided welcome shade from the scorching sun.

The fire was still in Achara's eyes even though two days had passed. Some thirty boys assembled before the housemaster's house. Gilbert Enuma was in charge of the preliminaries. He first ensured that the gloves were properly put on and securely tied. Then he reported to Mr. Pepple, who promptly stepped out of his house.

At his order, the crowd formed a rough circle, into the middle of which he summoned Achara and Nwanna. I did not particularly want to be so positioned that any time Achara looked up, he would see me. So I stood at the back of the pack, but not in such a manner as not to see the main outlines of the fight. I had watched gloved fights in Aba, and I knew how I reacted to each punch thrown, whether it landed on target or not. But especially if it landed.

"This should be a clear lesson for all," Mr. Pepple told the gathering. "Any boys who engage in a fight on college premises will be made to put on gloves. That way, they'll be given a chance, in a properly controlled fight, to work out their fury. That's a promise. Now let's get on with it. Are you both ready?"

"Yes, sir!" Nwanna shouted, raring to go.

From where I stood, I watched my friend nod quietly. I looked into his eyes, wondering if the fire was still there or perhaps had been somewhat doused by the harsh reality of his situation. The fire was gone, I thought. But it had been replaced by something even more frightening—or so it seemed to me. He was staring fixedly at Nwanna, and that stare spelled "hatred."

Mr. Pepple called for a chair from his house and sat and made himself comfortable on it. Then he gestured to Enuma to give the signal for the fight to start.

It was a hopelessly unequal boxing match. No sooner had the antagonists touched gloves than Nwanna planted a hard left fist in Achara's solar plexus, swiftly followed by a stinging right to the jaw. I winced but managed somehow to keep my eyes open and trained on my friend. All the odds favored Nwanna as he banged away with relish at all allowable points of Achara's body. Some of the punches landed, I suspected, because Achara kept darting his eyes here and there. Most of it seemed to be directed at the housemaster, as if in protest about something. He might also have been searching for me. But what could I do for him?

Suddenly he changed tactics. Nwanna swung for the umpteenth time at Achara's head. Achara managed to duck the blow this time, glory be! And then he dove for Nwanna's legs. In a flash, Nwanna found himself pinned to the ground, with Achara's not-inconsiderable weight on top of him. Before Nwanna could free himself from this humiliating position, Achara struck him in the face a couple of times.

As soon as he got up, Nwanna protested, saying between gasps, "This is supposed to be a boxing match, not wrestling." He was looking at the housemaster as he said this, which was a gross error of judgment. Achara dove one more time, and once again Nwanna was pinned to the ground, the gravelly nature of which must have stung his skin and added to his discomfiture.

At the one-minute interval, Nwanna continued his objections to Achara's tactics. "He can't do that. That's not boxing."

"This policy is not fair," countered Achara, "if I cannot fight back the only way I know how."

By this time, I had somehow worked my way, with a push here and a shove there, to the front of the crowd. I suppose I did so because it was evident that the momentum of the fight had swung, if not entirely in my friend's favor, at least to a state of equilibrium. All eyes turned to Mr. Pepple, mine very anxiously. He pondered the matter for a moment or two and then pronounced his judgment.

"You're right, my boy," he said, meaning Achara. "I'll make an exception for this fight." He looked at his watch. "Your minute is up."

Nwanna, who knew better than to challenge the housemaster's pronouncement, scowled. Achara beamed. I was surprised he could show that much elation, considering the hammering he had been subjected to by his antagonist. But then I thought he had to feel good about his chances now to give as good as he got. And indeed he did.

The remaining two rounds were a more equal affair, at the end of which the housemaster made the two boys shake hands. To no one's surprise, Chima Nwanna did so with an exceedingly ill grace, leaving no doubt in my mind that nothing had changed as far as he was concerned. I rushed to Achara's side, and so did a mob of our enthusiastically cheering classmates. There were also several boys from Nwanna's own class, and I espied one or two from class 3, who doubtless had their reasons for disliking him.

"Well, well," I said to Achara, "you were great."

He looked sideways at me as we walked back to his dormitory and made a confession. "I thought he was going to kill me there," he said.

"Perhaps he might have," I said, "had it not been for your clever—"

"There was nothing clever there," Achara said modestly. "It was desperation. What if the housemaster had said no?"

That was a good question, to which I had no answer. Or truthfully, I had. But I did not care to give expression to my thoughts on the matter. How does one tell a friend that he would have been beaten senseless, perhaps even turned into a bloody pulp? I did not want him to know that I cringed with every blow thrown by his adversary. I hoped he had not seen me, in the earlier part of the fight, lurking behind the shadows thrown by the other boys, like a coward.

"You surprised me," I said.

We had arrived at his dormitory, where he threw himself—sweat, dirt, and all—on his bed. He ached all over.

"I did?" he asked, smiling wearily. "Well, perhaps I did."

"I didn't think you were capable of dealing with the mad fellow the way you did."

"Well," he said, "you know what they say. The harmless-looking cooking pot, if ignored, will spill over and quench the fire."

CHAPTER VII

B y the end of my first term in Umuahia, I had come to terms with the strange game of cricket. Not, perhaps, to the point of playing it with an easy facility. I knew intuitively that this was not a game I would ever play with carefree abandon, no matter how proficient I eventually became.

I think this knowledge came to me—quite forcibly—the day I watched my first cricket match, played between Umuahia and a visiting team from the Methodist College, Uzuakoli, a town just under fifteen miles from Umuahia.

Augustine Onuorah, a lithe and supple class 3 boy, was the cricket captain. In practice games and in the nets, he had seemed invincible. He wielded the bat to such effect that no one could get him out easily. He kept the menacing balls adroitly of his stumps and hit the innocuous ones with consummate skill. When he bowled, he was fast and furious and ran up like a gazelle, smooth and effortless. His fast bowling obliged the batsman to be literally on his toes, very alert, and ready to react instantly to any quirkiness in the trajectory of the ball.

This last was the consequence of Onuorah's mastery of the "swinging" ball. At almost the last moment, just before reaching the batsman, the ball marginally changes its trajectory while still airborne. It is easy to see that a ball, combining speed through the air with a late change of direction, can create all manner of problems for a batsman.

Onuorah was quite simply the best and most respected cricketer in the school. He was expected to do well against Uzuakoli: garner a fair number of runs off his bat as well as prevent the opposition, with his thunderous bowling, from making too many runs in their turn at bat.

I was in for a shock as Onuorah disappointed on both counts. I watched with mounting astonishment, even bewilderment, as the cricketers from Uzuakoli hit his balls, with some aplomb, to all corners of the field. And when it came to his turn to bat, he was first struck a sickening thud on the big toe of his forward (or left) foot and then comprehensibly bowled two balls later. He must have been still smarting from the damaged toe and carelessly hung his bat outside the off stump, clearly misreading the sharp inward turn of the ball after pitching. It was, all in all, a dismal precession for our team.

It was not so much the defeat, decisive as it was, that made an indelible impression on my mind. Our defeat was—more or less—expected. The Uzuakoli team was selected from a full-strength secondary school; Umuahia's, from only three classes. It was rather the humiliating sight of such an accomplished player as Onuorah being reduced to the status of a veritable novice in the game. Subsequent matches merely served to underline the total unpredictability of the game of cricket. In no other sport known to me—football, sprinting, jumping, or other athletic specialty—did this happen quite so emphatically or so repeatedly.

Cricket was clearly a great leveler, a game in which the mighty and the talented could quite easily bite the dust, and the humble performer occasionally attain dizzying heights of unexpected grandeur. If pressed, I would say that it was perhaps this very unpredictability of the game that quietly appealed to the Quixote in me. I could dream—and did—of sometimes putting the opposition bowling to the sword. And as I warmed to the new game, I found that with hard work and a steady application to its basic principles, I gradually raised the level of my play to the point where it caught the attention of Mr. Kalaga, then the master responsible for cricket.

Mr. Kalaga, an Umuahia alumnus himself, hailed from the Niger Delta, and received his postsecondary education in the famous (some would say, infamous) Yaba Higher College, in Lagos. In the 1930s and much of the '40s, Yaba Higher College was the only Nigerian institution for postsecondary education. It was consequently an extremely difficult institution to get into. It took the best students Nigeria could offer—the *crème de la crème*, so to say—and put them through the academic mill. Conventional wisdom in the country—to the extent that we understood such matters then—was that by deliberate policy, the British Colonial Office sought to stifle the budding intellectual aspirations of its Nigerian subjects and, thereby, prevent the growth of a potentially recalcitrant intelligentsia. Expulsions were the order of the day. Many students, after sweating out several rigorous examinations, were expelled for failing to attain impossibly high standards, sometimes as late as one miserable year from completing their courses. And at the end, those lucky to survive the academic buffets obtained, not college degrees, but mere diplomas. The Yaba diploma qualified its holders for civil service appointments as *assistant* medical officers, *assistant* engineers, or *nongraduate* secondary schoolteachers. Yaba Higher College was indeed a veritable graveyard of the budding Nigerian intellectual and professional. Those whose families could afford it—and there were only a handful of these—went overseas, to Britain especially, for their university education. Britain was, of course, the mother country.

Mr. Kalaga survived Yaba. Reputedly the most brilliant student of his day, in Umuahia and in Yaba, he came through the cruel hardships of the latter, with flying colors, in physics and chemistry. He also played cricket but was only a moderate performer in the game. However, he could teach. Perhaps recognizing his own limitations, he kept a sharp eye out for the diligent and hard workers. He gave extra attention to the coaching of such boys. I was one of them. He once remarked that he was always delighted if a boy tended to linger awhile longer in the field or the practice nets, even after the school bell had signaled the end of the games period.

Other than the Methodist College, Uzuakoli, and the Hope Waddell Training Institute, Calabar, no other secondary school in Eastern Nigeria played cricket. Rumors that a game, closely akin to cricket, was played in the Dennis Memorial Grammar School, Onitsha, remained forever unsubstantiated. The fact was that the maintenance of a cricket pitch and field and the purchase of the game's equipment (bats, balls, gloves, mats, protective boxes, etc.) were simply beyond the means of most secondary schools in the area.

The college cricket team had perforce to play matches against a motley array of teams, ranging from the Masters' XIs to various combinations of the latter and the British or Commonwealth civil servants living in the township of Umuahia and its environs. District officers, as far away as Aba and Port Harcourt (some sixty or more miles away), were pressed into service to raise teams to play against the college boys.

The matches we enjoyed the most were those against the Masters' XIs, principally because they were the least serious. And sometimes, a few personal scores were settled. Even the captain, Onuorah, was not above raising the level of his game a notch or two, just to get even with a teacher that might have done him wrong. His joy was plain to see whenever he wrecked the stumps of one or two of the masters. He took especial delight in bringing about the downfall of our principal.

Mr. Walter Graves was usually the captain of the Masters' team. He was fond of boasting that in his time in Cambridge University, he missed his cricket blue by a whisker. Few among us understood, at the time, what this meant. Mr. William Quincy, an inspector of education at the Eastern Nigerian regional headquarters in Enugu, was an old friend and contemporary of Mr. Graves at Cambridge. Mr. Quincy was known to make light of his friend's claims, but he did confirm that Mr. Graves played regularly for his college there. What we saw with our eyes was that our principal was, in the words of no less a judge than Mr. Kalaga, "one hell of a cricketer." He swung his bat with tremendous power but was no longer as quick on his feet as he might have been as an undergraduate.

There were boys who did not like cricket; boys who considered it a game for snobs. They knew only soccer, rounders, and athletics and seemed to close their minds to anything else. They loved the rough and tumble of soccer and the speed and dash of track and field. They could not—or would not—understand a sport in which the players were dazzlingly accoutered in white shirts, white shorts (some teachers played in white trousers), and white sneakers (for the few who had the money for such seeming extravagance). And as if those were not ridiculous enough, there were white pads for the protection of the shins, white rubber-spiked gloves, and a clumsy white shield (called a box) for the protection of one's groin and crutch against a cruelly hard ball, hurled at the batsman seemingly with the sole aim of causing grievous bodily injury. And with the game's hunchbacked wooden bat, sometimes a trifle heavy for the smaller boys, cricket seemed designed expressly for slow, ponderous movement. Perhaps it was this characteristic—its slow deliberate pace, added to its unpredictability—that first appealed to me. I loved its accouterments, though in my first term I could not afford the cost of a pair of tennis shoes and accordingly took a painful blow or two on my exposed toes and insteps. The game was entirely new for all the boys. Everyone therefore started from point zero. No one seemed to have an advantage—initially at least—no matter how good they were in the more popular sports.

A long sloping dust road (some called it the Appian Way) led from the Administration Block to the cricket oval, about four hundred yards away. As one walked down this road, one passed the physics and the biology/chemistry laboratories on the left and the hockey and soccer fields a little distance away on the right, with conifers evident everywhere, their needlelike leaves whistling softly in the breeze. Not much more than a week's growth of grass, be it of the bountiful Bahama type or the unwelcome coarse elephant variety, was ever allowed to offend against the natural loveliness of the landscape. Hired laborers cut and trimmed the grass and lawns. But the students did their part also, either as part of our regular housework or as punishment during the dreaded weekly matchet parade on Saturdays.

"The first law in heaven is *order*," my primary school headmaster, Mr. Akweke, used to say. When or where this was revealed to him, none of us knew. He might have plucked it out of a biblical passage or surmised it from an interpretation of the scriptures, as far as I knew. I know for sure that he was never a student of the Government College Umuahia. But if he never was, he might perhaps have had a relative who was and who must have told him about the regimentation of life there.

Life in Umuahia was ordered and regulated to a degree I never dreamed was possible, from the wake-up bell to the lights-out bell. Order was imposed, with varying degrees of strictness, by a hierarchy that had the principal at the top, the school and house leaders at the base, and the masters in between. The housemaster, Mr. Pepple, somewhere just below the principal, oversaw everything pertaining to our student life with inflexibility and side-slapping determination.

A fresher, given the role and (unofficially) the title of bell fag, rang the school wake-up bell at six o'clock. Waking at six was no problem for me. In my primary school years, I woke up earlier than that to help do the household chores that had to be done before we went to school. In Umuahia, the chores were different. For the next hour, we did one of several assignments: gardening, trimming the lawns in the immediate vicinity of the dormitories, or sweeping whatever needed to be swept. If you were privileged to be a school or a house leader, you ordered everybody else around.

Then came the morning ablutions. The water supply was usually reliable. But we sometimes filled our buckets, before going to bed, just to be sure. By morning, of course, the temperature of the water would have dropped several degrees, which was something I did not much care for. Happily, my leader, Godfrey Clarke, had a habit of sending me to the kitchen, quite often, to fetch hot water for his morning bath. Perhaps he had an understanding with the cook, but the latter always obliged. No questions asked. I profited from this as often as I thought I could get away with it, Clarke being Clarke, and discreetly kept some of the hot water for my own use. My mother who seemingly loved nothing better than to take her morning bath with bitingly cold water obviously did not pass on that gene to me.

The high point of the morning for me arrived with the bell for breakfast at about seven o'clock. Breakfast was the springboard for everything that followed, at least until lunch. It set and governed my mood for the next several hours. Boiled yam and okpodudu (black beans) was my favorite breakfast. I loved to mix into the okpodudu a little raw palm oil, a thick orange-colored butterlike fat, derived from the fruit of the oil palm. This gave the meal a special and most agreeable tang. The boys were allowed to buy bottles of the stuff, which we stored in a cupboard provided for such purposes, and placed at one end of the dining hall. A bad or unpalatable breakfast often left me irritable, ill at ease, or just plain restless during classes.

Fried ripe plantains were also regular meals, not just occasional delicacies or snacks bought from roving Yoruba women in the market or street corners in Aba. Rice became staple rather than a Sunday or a festive meal. Meat came regularly with most meals, other than breakfast, and in quantities that I had never known before. The yam might be overboiled to an unappetizing softness, the soup occasionally more watery than was acceptable. The rice might be undercooked and therefore more difficult to digest and the pounded yam brittle or lumpy by turn. These were, however, relatively minor blemishes that we could—and did—take in our stride.

The nondenominational morning assembly and worship was at half past eight o'clock. This ritual of songs and prayers lasted from fifteen to twenty minutes and took place in the assembly hall, which occupied about a third of the long Administration Block. The boys sat class by class, with class 1 boys to the fore, closest to the raised podium on which the principal and the masters sat. Announcements were made by the principal or the housemaster. After the assembly, the boys trooped out, pew by pew, and down the aisle, to exit by a door close to the rear end of the hall, where the senior class sat.

I loved the singing at the morning assembly. As a choirboy, indeed a treble leader, in St. James Church, Aba, I was familiar with most of the songs and their tunes. The singing was full and lusty, participation by the boys almost 100 percent. Most times, even croakers, unmindful that their sounds jarred on the nerves of the rest of us, joined in the signing. Mr. Eagleton, who taught ancient history and conducted the singing practices, taught me to hold the songbook farther away from my mouth than I was wont to do. He taught me to open my mouth more and to cut down on that shrillness of voice that I had hitherto thought to be a virtue in singing. There was no choir, no special group to lead the singing. There was a piano but, in my first year, no skilled pianist. A few boys tried their hands at it, but without much success. It said a lot for the teaching skills of Mr. Eagleton, who was himself blessed with a good and deep voice that, in spite of the lack of good instrumental accompaniment, the collective signing of the school was of a high quality.

There were two songs that, for me, will always evoke memories of my years in Umuahia. The first of these, "All Creatures of Our God and King," I heard for the first time at my very first morning assembly in January 1944. It was sung to a catchy, pulsating tune, easy thereafter to master. We sang it with the controlled gusto and zest that came from wholehearted enjoyment, regular practice, and collective discipline. It was, for me, the school anthem.

The other song was "Eternal Father Strong to Save." This has been overwhelmingly my favorite. No other song, not even "All Creatures," comes close. There are situations in which this song brings me close to tears. There is a kind of majesty about the words and the tune that seems to accentuate the enveloping omnipotence of God. To listen to Mr. Eagleton—or until he so mysteriously disappeared from our midst, Mr. Hunter—sing it, is to feel the power of God's protection and his immaterial presence.

We went from the morning assembly directly to our classrooms. Because these were permanently assigned to the different classes, our teachers came to us in our classrooms for all subjects except geography and the three sciences: physics, chemistry, and biology. The geography room was the longest of the seven classrooms in the L-shaped classroom block, which had a lobby, with two ping-pong tables, situated at the angle of the L. Table tennis was arguably the most popular game in the college. Even those boys, like Okoroafor and Achara, who had a decided apathy for sports, took their turn enthusiastically at the ping-pong table. Physics had its own separate laboratory building; chemistry and biology shared one building.

Those were the colonial years. We probably did not know any better, but in comparing our school to the other secondary schools in the country, we invariably measured our transcendence by the number of white or expatriate teachers we had. Without exception, the white teachers were university graduates, and there were never fewer than four or five of them at any given period. Whiteness did not, of course, guarantee excellence of teaching. It did not always bring with it that sensitivity to the feelings of a subject people that, in spite of our relative immaturity, we occasionally exhibited. Quite the contrary, more often than not. There was a degree of paternalism that we were not always able to put our fingers on but that we often suspected was there.

Some of our best teachers were in fact our nongraduate Nigerian masters—in particular, those among them who had survived the rigors of the Yaba Higher College. That was how it seemed to me and to most boys in my class. We talked often about it. I do not think our judgment on this issue was much affected by our collective sense of patriotism. There was, in my early Umuahia years, no teacher to compare with Mr. Kalaga. And even Mr. Pepple, for all his frowning and his forbidding exterior, was very effective as a math teacher. And he was not even a product of Yaba.

The bell fag rang the bell at two o'clock. The bell heralded lunch, the great restorer, and marked the end of classes for the day. After lunch, a one-hour compulsory rest period followed. Everything came to a virtual standstill during this hour, unless you were a school or a house leader. They could walk around but only to ensure that no one else did.

Prep was a strictly regulated hour of study, in the library, following immediately after the rest period. This was the hour for swotting up the books or to do one's written assignment or, if one was so inclined, to take down one of the hundreds of books, fiction and nonfiction, housed in the library. A master usually supervised prep; occasionally a school leader substituted.

The solemnity, even stuffiness, of the prep hour was sometimes a little hard to take. Sometimes I just sat and daydreamed, gazing in wonder at the impressive rows of books on the shelves, more books than I had ever before seen assembled in one building. I dreamed that one day I could truly boast that I had read every one of them. I liked sometimes to idle the time away thumbing through the numerous colorful magazines, mostly British, which were displayed on the magazine racks. I confess I admired, with secret lust, the pictures of white women clad immodestly only in bathing suits, their thighs and legs and their upper torsos leaving nothing—and yet a lot—to the not-so-fertile imagination of an unsophisticated thirteen-year-old Nigerian boy. We were not used to pictures such as these.

The bell fag, an important figure in our daily lives, rang the bell at four o'clock for games. We were encouraged—if that is not too soft a word—to participate in one game or the other. Those boys not scheduled for the afternoon's games were required to do housework instead. No boys were free, in this period, to stroll or laze around the compound or to divert themselves in a manner of their own choosing. For our afternoon activities, whether games or housework, we were supplied with a set of clothes at the beginning of the term: a colored shirt and a pair of baggy khaki shorts. No other form of clothing was tolerated during this period.

The most leisurely time of the day was the period after games and housework. We had our second and last shower of the day and were then free to adorn our bodies with less austere, more colorful clothes for the evening. But even in this, the school had a strict policy that discouraged ostentation. Gaudy clothing, expensive sandals, hard-heeled shoes were disallowed. Simplicity was the rule. The principal, Mr. Walter Graves, told us he expected the more affluent boys to have some consideration for the feelings of the poorer students. I did not mind the strictures on ostentation. I had no expensive or flashy clothes. I could not afford any. The simplicity rule was made to order for boys like me. In my first term, even the commonest canvas shoes were, for me, objects of envy. My feet were usually shod in a pair of slippers cut out of used or discarded vehicle tires.

Supper, at seven o'clock, was followed by a period of voluntary study or total leisure before bedtime. Lights-out was at nine thirty for classes 1 and 2, and ten o'clock for the class 3 boys.

Electricity was a new and thrilling experience for me. In the college, I lived my life in an environment in which the hours of darkness (at least until the lights-out bell) were illuminated not by the dim and struggling light of a kerosene lamp but by the incandescence of electric bulbs. Aba, the town in which I grew up, had no electricity; neither did Umuahia, the town closest to the school and which gave it its name. The college had perforce to buy an electric generator. One of the senior boys had responsibility for the functioning of this generator, starting it at half past six in the evening and switching it off at ten o'clock.

If you were not on the dreaded matchet parade, Saturday was the best day of the week because it was the freest. The matchet parade—punishment for serious infringements of college rules—was in itself ushered in by a grand parade, which started at nine o'clock in the morning. All the boys lined up, house by house, on the lawn to the south of the Administration Block. Then followed a semimilitary parade, inspected by the principal or the housemaster. This may have been the high point of the week for Mr. Pepple, who was always in his element on these occasions. Strutting stiff-backed up and down the lines, he called on us to march with military or mathematical precision. We knew better than to laugh at his exaggerated posturings and, at his command, came smartly to attention or halted as if our lives depended on it.

We turned out for this elegant parade in our school uniform: white shirt and white shorts and, if you had them, white canvas shoes. The school uniform was, of course, supplied to the boys at the beginning of each term. In this way, uniformity of clothing was assured, and none of us, however poor, lacked for essential clothing.

The Saturday parade heralded and showcased the humiliation of the bad boys of the week, whose names were called out, loud and clear, for the matchet parade. For the next hour, sometimes more (if a boy's name was listed more than once during the week), the offenders did hard labor, usually grass-cutting, on any part of the school compound requiring attention.

Those boys who were not involved in the matchet parade were free to do as they liked for the rest of the morning and afternoon, until four o'clock. This was the time to "go to town." The town was, of course, Umuahia. We walked or bicycled to town for a variety of reasons. It might be as a diversion from the rigors, real or imagined, of our strictly regimented life in the course of the week. Or we might need a haircut or to stock up on our favorite snacks. Town was where we could get our clothes mended, our sandals repaired, our worn slippers replaced. Some had relatives living in Umuahia town, where they could enjoy real home-cooked food, always a welcome change from our balanced diet in school.

Every boy went to church on Sundays. I had thought that this would not be a required activity, the college being a secular institution. Sunday services had not been one of my favorite talking points, about Umuahia, with my cousin Samuel. So I was unprepared for the strictness of the rule that, like it or not, church attendance was compulsory. Which is not to say that I did not like it.

Protestant students worshipped in the college chapel, situated next to the principal's office at one end of the Administration Block. There was no distinction between one Protestant denomination and another. Anglicans, Methodists, Baptists, and others worshipped together. Usually, there were no sermons unless an ordained priest was present. This happened about once a month. And when that happened, there was also Holy Communion. The principal conducted the services, with the masters and the senior boys taking turns to read from the holy scriptures.

I never really understood why no provision was made for the boys of the Roman Catholic persuasion to also celebrate mass in the same chapel—before or after the Protestant worship. They had to walk to a Catholic church, about a mile beyond the college gates, on the road to the town. They were seldom heard to grumble about this arrangement. Indeed, they seemed to accept, without demur, that the official denomination of the country, as a colony and protectorate of His Britannic Majesty, was the Anglicanism of the mother country. Roman Catholicism had perforce to take a backseat.

There were no Muslims. And, come to think of it as I write this, there were no animists or what were loosely called heathens. In that epoch, in Eastern Nigeria, there were still families not yet converted to the Christian faith. Proselytization was still a vigorous activity among missionaries. But if there were any boys among us who, notwithstanding their years of Western-style education, remained infidel to Christianity, they did not come out of the closet.

*   *   *

The three months of the first term went by like a flash. And I welcomed the four-week break. The rhythm of my life in the college had been brisker than anything I had known before and was, therefore, a little exhausting. And the break meant a return to Aba, even if only temporarily. Aba was my town: the place where I grew up. I liked—or was at least familiar with—its noise and bustle. I did not always like its smell, but I could take that in my stride. It was reassuringly predictable. I knew where to go and where to refrain from going. My parents and siblings lived there, and I needed to touch base with them to, as it were, recharge my batteries.

It was also the town in which Adamma Nwobosi lived. I think I was a little surprised about the strength of my developing feelings for her. It had gradually dawned on me that my heart was aching for her. Aching for her simple good looks and the radiance of her smile. Aching for the touch of her fingers and the way she sometimes looked at me, as if she at once longed for a closeness with me but was too discreet or too prudish to rush things.

Not least, the four-week vacation meant I would be away, however briefly, from the coldhearted viciousness of my nemesis, Godfrey Clarke.

CHAPTER VIII

The majestic Asa Road winds its way more or less diagonally across the old town. With that sole exception, Aba Township consisted of straight roads set at right angles with straight streets. The houses that lined the streets and roads were mostly roofed with corrugated iron sheets; others were covered by thatch. In 1944, there was no electricity in the town. Public water pumps, sited at irregular intervals throughout the town, supplied potable water. The pumps were sometimes shut off. But we had learned, through long experience, to predict the pattern of opening and shutting. People lined up to fetch water from the pumps. Sometimes, when these lines were maddeningly long and tempers were short, fights broke out. And whenever a fight broke out, fragile water receptacles such as gourds and clay pots became endangered species. There was always wailing and ululation, mostly by little girls who feared punishment at home for the double sin of losing their pots and returning without water. I suppose we little boys, projecting our machismo, seldom gave way to such displays of our emotion.

This was my first vacation as a college boy. Though barely three months had passed since I went to high school, I came back to Aba, and to my old haunts and old friends, feeling like a little big man. I could hardly wait to relate stories of my first term in the Government College Umuahia to my family, friends, or anybody willing to listen. I think I walked with an extra spring in my step and a little more consciousness in my bearing than before. In the last days before the end of term, I had thought often and long about my family and my friends in Aba.

I had missed my parents and my siblings. My sister Grace, the first child of my parents, was two years older than I. Quiet, hardworking, and as large hearted a girl as God ever made, Grace was still struggling to finish her primary school. Men saw, in her, qualities much sought after in a wife. Accordingly, though

---

72

only fifteen, she had received marriage proposals from several Aba traders. But she was determined to complete her elementary education and obtain her First School Leaving Certificate and had turned everyone of them down. I know that my mother thought Grace was a fool to let so many opportunities pass her by. But my big sister found a surprising ally in our dad. And in our cousin Samuel, though no one, to my knowledge, had asked him.

Then there was Nneka, my sprightly and irrepressible sister, two years my junior. If I was absolutely pressed on the point, I would, I suppose, admit that Nneka was my favorite sibling. She was potentially the brainiest child of the family, very precocious, and unrivalled in any of her classes to date. But she had also learned, at her tender age, to be something of a coquette, especially when she sought a favor or an advantage. Ndubisi, the last born of the family, was five years younger than I and, I must confess, sometimes an insufferable copycat. He followed me everywhere I went, whenever he could. He liked to mimic me, in action and my mannerisms. In the years before I went to Umuahia, he would watch as our food was apportioned and then sometimes protest loudly if he thought he did not get his fair share. By which, of course, he meant that my portion was larger than his. And as soon as I became a college boy, he started talking about *when* he also would be an Umuahia boy. And he had only just turned eight! But I loved him and actually began to look forward to the day, five long years into the future, when he would join me in Umuahia. Of course, I would be in my final class then.

Outside of my family, the two persons uppermost in my thoughts as the term wound down were my best primary school friend, Ben Nwobosi, and of course his sister, Adamma. Ben's last letter to me, written from his secondary school, Aggrey Memorial Grammar School, in Arochukwu, reached me just days to the end of my first term. I knew from this letter that he would return to Aba three or so days later than I. "Are you still afraid to talk to girls?" Ben had asked in the same letter.

He did not expressly say so, but I knew the reference was to *pretty* girls. Now as I picked my way carefully through the traffic on the ten-minute walk from my house to his, I wondered if Ben knew that when I thought about pretty girls, his sister stood out as the paragon. I saw a vision of her now, in all her loveliness, unrefined and unpolished, with her tightly plaited hair, the strands of which she loved to gather and tie together at her nape. The last time I saw her, just before I left Aba for Umuahia in January, she had stood framed against the doorway of the veranda of her house, where Ben and I, as we so often did, were sharing a meal. In my mind's eye, I could still see her large glittering eyes looking intently at me as if—or so I thought at the time—she could not bear the thought that soon I would be gone from her.

"Will you write to me when you get to Umuahia?"

Her question, asked in her mellifluous Igbo, had taken me by surprise. It surprised me because I had never really been quite sure that I meant anything special to her. And I had replied, stealing a diffident look at Ben, "If you want me to, yes." Ben had prudently looked the other way.

Growing up in Aba, I was not so innocent that I did not know about boys and girls, about friendship between the two sexes, and where that friendship could lead. Some of my friends and classmates, in particular Friday Stoneface and Kofi Bentsil, often boasted about their feminine conquests. When they did that, I usually remained tongue-tied. I knew that was the reason Ben had asked me, in his letter, if I was still scared of girls. Did he think I could change that drastically, in one short term (of three months), just because we were now in high school?

I recalled what my standard 5 teacher in St. James School had once done to me. He had sat me, as *punishment* for a whole week, between two of the bigger girls in the class. That punishment had left Friday seething with envy. And there were several other boys who would have given anything to have sat next to Suzannah Elechi, whose physical endowments, front and back, often elicited gasps of desire.

Traffic was unusually heavy on Asa Road. But what peril there was on the road came not from cars (there were very few then) as from mammy wagons and especially from bicycles. Aba was a town of traders and small-time businessmen and women. For them, the bicycle was the standard form of transportation. It was also the symbol of success. People knew that a trader was doing well when he purchased a brand-new bicycle and especially if the bicycle was fitted with accessories such as light and/or a gear mechanism. The favored brands were the Raleigh and the Hercules bicycles.

I kept scrupulously to the outer edge of the road, always on the right-hand side. I did not want traffic to approach me, on my side of the road, from behind me. It used to be—before I went to Umuahia—that if I was involved in a collision with a bicyclist and got hurt in the process, my father, adding insult to injury, would cane me for my carelessness. "If you had looked where you were going," he would say, "no bicycle would have chased after you to knock you down." I did not believe my father would cane me now if anything like that happened. But I felt no urgent need to put the matter to a test.

As I neared Adamma's house, I saw ahead of me and coming toward me a line of about ten convicts. I could tell who they were by their familiar prison outfits: loose-fitting, truncated white tunics and shorts. Each balanced on his head an outsize bucket of human excrement. A wary but quite chatty prison guard, smartly outfitted in a typical warden's green khaki shirt and shorts, starchily ironed, kept a watchful eye on the procession. He talked and laughed with his charges as if they were all friends.

I would, out of curiosity, have wished that I could get really close to them. I had always wanted to know what prisoners and their jailers talked and laughed about. But the stench, increasing exponentially as they drew nearer, drove me to the opposite side of the road. I clamped my fingers on my nose, taking care to turn away from the poor fellows so they would not see my action and get mad with me. That was something we kids were always careful about. We never wanted them to get mad at us when they were on their night soil shift. We were familiar with what they could do, when provoked by catcalls or other inconsiderate behavior, with a free swing of their working brooms loaded with filth. The use of convicts for this odious public service in broad daylight was something I could never understand. There were, after all, night soil men employed by the township government specifically to perform such services.

At my knock, Adamma herself opened the front door. I saw her face immediately light up with such radiant and undisguised happiness that my heart skipped a beat. I stood awkwardly—she too—as we stared at each other for several moments. Then she silently reached forward and gently took my hand in hers. I quickly overcame my timidity and let my fingers close gratefully over hers as she pulled me into the house and then shut the door.

"Welcome," she said softly, squeezing my hand. "When did you come back?"

"The day before yesterday," I answered.

"The day before yesterday?" There was a hint of accusation in her voice.

I desperately searched for an answer. Anything to make her understand that two days was not a long time and that I came to see her as quickly as I could. But a voice came from within the house to cut into my thoughts.

"Who is it?"

"That's my mother!" Adamma whispered to me.

"Oh God!" I cried, quickly disengaging my hand from hers.

"I said, who is it?"

"It's me," I announced lamely.

"Don't you have a name?" asked Adamma's mother, coming into view. "Oh, it's you. So you have come back from your college. Let me look at you." She took her time looking me up and down and then said, "You've grown taller."

"That's what my papa and mama said too. It must be the food."

She looked at me quizzically. "What food? Or are you telling me their food is better than your mother's?" Happily she did not wait for my answer and went on, "I suppose you have come for Ben. We're expecting him today, but he has not yet arrived."

"Not today, Mama," said Adamma harshly, "but tomorrow. You keep forgetting."

"Shut up, child! Have you forgotten whom you're talking to? What is wrong with you children these days? We didn't use to talk to our parents like that."

Eager to pour oil on troubled waters, I jumped in. "Actually I know Ben's not coming back today," I said.

"Oh, you know? Then why did you—" she stopped and looked at me, then at Adamma, and she understood. She said nothing more, but the accusation in her eyes and demeanor was unmistakable.

The magic of the moment was gone, and I found myself fumbling for the right words with which to make a dignified exit. I found none. So with one last forlorn look at Adamma, I turned and walked out of the house. I had come and gone in the twinkling of an eye.

My friend Ben returned to Aba, from his college in Arochukwu, the following day, as Adamma had said. He came to visit me the same day. Whatever I had expected, Ben had not changed—or hardly—except that he was even more taciturn than he had been in primary school.

"How many inches did you add during the term?" I asked. "I added one and half inches myself. Your mother was surprised how tall I had grown."

"How many inches?" Ben asked. "I don't know. And how d'you know exactly how many inches you added?"

"Because we were measured and weighed on the first and the last Saturdays of the term. Weren't you?"

"All of you?" he asked, instead of answering my question.

"Of course. Samuel tells me this is done every term. C'mon let's see who's taller."

We stood back-to-back, and I called to Samuel to come and be the judge. It was no contest. I had previously been only slightly the taller of us two. But now I had added at least half an inch more than Ben had.

We spent the next several days comparing notes on our colleges: the food, our teachers, the games we played, what kinds of clothes we were allowed to wear to and after classes. Ben said they were allowed almost total freedom in matters of clothing after classes—so long as they were neatly turned out. His school, Aggrey Memorial Grammar School, had no regulations on the speaking of the vernacular. Which explained why, in our conversations, Ben stuck mostly to our Igbo language, and I, by force of habit recently acquired, struggled to strike a happy medium between my language and English.

"We don't have to worry about school uniforms," I told my friend, "or even the textbooks we use. The college supplies both."

"That's not fair," said Ben. "And you people pay only five pounds or so. D'you know we have to buy our own beds? We get nothing free."

In the days before we both went to high school, we used to hunt birds with our slingshots or catapults. But those days were definitely over. Instead, we roamed the streets of Aba, making the most of our four-week vacation, enjoying each other's company more intensely than we did before. As the days went by and I had more time to observe Ben, I found that he was essentially still the same simple, hardworking, down-to-earth boy I had known. He worked just as hard at home as he had ever done, helping his father in the carpentry shed at the side of their house and his mother and sisters in their daily chores.

A few days into our vacation, as we were returning to my house from an outing, Ben and I heard the strains of a popular swing tune, "In the Mood," being played on my father's organ. No one else in my family but my father knew how to play the organ. And my old man played only church music and had little use for any other type.

I hurried into our parlor and there, seated at the organ, was Titus Nwangwu. Standing just behind him, softly singing the tune, was a girl. For a moment or two, Ben and I stood transfixed within the door, staring at our friend as if he was an apparition. It was some time before it dawned on me that the girl's face was totally unfamiliar.

"What are you doing here?" I eventually asked.

"They expelled you from King's College?" Ben asked, his mouth agape in astonishment. I believe mine was too.

Neither question was meant in a hostile sense. And Titus, who understood that to be the case, seemed to be enjoying the effect he had on us. He knew what we meant. He should have been some five hundred miles away from Aba, in King's College, Lagos. King's College, by conventional wisdom, was the most prestigious high school in the country, a position that not even an Umuahian, like me, could have seriously challenged. It was not for nothing that it was located in Lagos, the capital city, whose status as a *colony* of Britain was a cut above the rest of the country, which was a mere *Protectorate.*

Titus and I had been friends for as long as I could remember. In St. James School, we were not classmates. But he had surprised the entire school by sitting the entrance examination to King's College as a standard 5 boy on the same day I sat the equivalent examination to Government College Umuahia. Astonishingly he had won a merit scholarship, thus further boosting the reputation of our primary school and adding another feather to Headmaster Akweke's cap.

Because the journey was long and tedious, Eastern Nigerians who went to school in Lagos were normally expected back only once a year, in July, for the twelve-week vacation. Titus had been in King's College, Lagos, for barely three months, since January 1944.

"And where's my father?" I remembered to ask.

Titus paused long enough from playing the organ to say, "Out." Then he continued playing.

I knew that my mother would not be at home at that time of the day, in midafternoon. She was always at her shed in the Ekeoha market, selling her wares. But I was surprised my father was not. This was usually the time for his afternoon siesta, with which he let nothing interfere. Not even if it meant he might lose a valued customer in the market. Like my mother, he had a shed in Ekeoha. But unlike her, he could not bring himself to take trading seriously and merely dabbled at it. He was quintessentially a salary-earning worker. But he had, three years earlier, lost his job as a clerk in a French trading company, when the company went under, following the defeat of France by Nazi Germany, in the world war. Had my father been home, I reflected, Titus would not have dared to play the organ. There were limits to the freedom that even he enjoyed in our home, and he enjoyed plenty of it.

"You haven't answered my question," I told him. "What happened? Why are you here?"

Titus stopped playing, pushing himself and his seat a little distance from the organ. "I have answered that question a thousand times since I came back to Aba yesterday. Everybody's surprised to see me, even my parents. You see, I didn't have time to write to them before leaving Lagos."

"What happened?" I let him see that I was on the point of strangling him if he kept us waiting much longer.

Titus shrugged. "There was a strike, you see," he said. "So the government closed our college—"

He stopped, I suppose, because he saw my eyes fixed on the girl. I asked my question with my eyes, without words. Titus read the slight inclination of my head, understood it was pointed at his companion, and smiled, pursing his lips. Our eyes met.

"This is Carole Emecheta," he said.

I could have guessed! I knew her parents as, I think, everybody in Aba did, but I had never met Carole before. She was the daughter of an Igbo lawyer and a white woman. Persons like her, being mulattos, were considered natural beauties. And indeed I thought Carole looked quite pretty in spite, or perhaps because, of her slight plumpness. She had a very charming smile and hair that was a cross between the straight Caucasian and the curly Negroid. Resplendent in a light blue blazer, with yellow trimmings, she bore herself with the self-conscious dignity not uncommon among young persons of privileged parentage. She looked so well groomed and sophisticated, I wondered how on earth Titus ever got close to her.

"Who went on strike?" Ben asked. "The teachers?"

"Which teachers?" Titus laughed derisively. "You don't know King's College boys."

Samuel just then walked into the parlor. "Who's this?" he asked, doing a double take. "Titus! What are you doing here? Shouldn't you be—"

"I know. I know. I should be in Lagos. But, as I was just telling Obinna and Ben, we went on strike, so the college was closed down for some months. They say it'll be at least two months."

"Strike?" queried Samuel. "The students, you say? But what's there to strike about? You King's College fellows have everything. I know because I was there."

"Things changed, Samuel,'" said Titus. "You remember the temporary boarding place at Bonanza? I hear that's where they put you Umuahia boys. Well, after you left, serious grumbling started about the conditions there. Even the food—"

"The food too?" shouted Ben. "I don't believe this. I thought Samuel used to say that in King's, you people eat European diet, with bread and tea and things like that?"

"And you know what?" continued Titus. "Three of the ringleaders of the strike were arrested and conscripted into the army."

"What?" we screamed.

"Yes, the army," said Titus, enjoying center stage. "We don't know if they'll be sent to Burma—you know that's where the government sends our soldiers—to fight against the Japanese."

"How d'you know that?" asked Ben.

"You mean how do I know our soldiers are sent to Burma and not to Europe? I know because I live in Lagos, and that's where everything happens."

"It must be easy fighting the Japanese," said Ben. "Isn't it the same Japanese who made all those cheap articles we used to buy before the war started?"

My friend's logic seemed rather obscure, but he had a point. I had a cousin, Daniel Ogugua, fighting in the jungles of Burma against these same Japanese. I knew, from talking to him before their troop left for the Far East, that he would have much preferred to have gone to fight in Europe, principally because that was where he understood England to be. He had been deeply affected by the Aba district officer's propaganda. Mr. Richard Littleton had organized township gatherings in the town hall and had also gone round to all the schools eulogizing the British Empire. And the centerpiece of his propaganda was that the red-white-and-blue Union Jack, Britain's flag, somehow represented the union of the white and black races of the empire. Few understood what he was talking about. None of us was able to reconcile our blackness with any of the colors of the flag.

Daniel, who was only half literate, enlisted enthusiastically, as he told the family, because of the lure of travelling to Europe and other foreign places. He only half understood the concept of striking a blow of freedom, but he had nothing against that scenario. In the event, he ended up in the Far East, instead of Europe. He was acutely disappointed but found consolation from an unexpected quarter. Some of the pictures enclosed in his letters from India and Burma showed him in various titillating postures with plump, nubile, Oriental wenches whose lush curves caused my pupils to dilate with wonder. I also wondered how much fighting he did.

"I hope," said Samuel, very concerned, "that none of the three King's College boys gets sent to fight in the war. By the way, who are they? I'm sure I must know them. I expect they are the senior boys, in class 6."

"Let me see. There was Oparaocha," said Titus.

"Opara-Trig-Ocha!" exclaimed Samuel. He turned to Ben and me. "Opara-Trig-Ocha was a genius in trigonometry. Titus, do they still call him Opara-Trig-Ocha?"

Titus nodded. "He's from Owerri, my hometown."

"And the other two?" asked Samuel breathlessly.

"Sonny Ighodaro. D'you know him? Quite fearless. He's from somewhere around Benin. Could be an Urhobo boy or Itsekiri. I don't know."

"I'm not surprised about him," said Samuel reflectively. "He was a political hothead. Always talking about Zik and Herbert Macaulay and didn't seem to care if any of the white masters heard what he was saying. And the third?"

"We never got to know for sure who that was. He was the last to be arrested, only a day or so before we left Lagos. One name mentioned is Awokoya. Tunde Awokoya. But I'm not sure."

"Awokoya?" asked Samuel. "Would that be the fat fellow with the three tribal marks? Cats Whiskers, we used to call him behind his back. Black as charcoal. I know one thing. He'll never be sent to Burma. Before they can get him into shape, the war will hopefully be over."

He paused and then added, "But that's a terrible way to punish secondary school boys for leading a strike."

"And there's nothing anyone can do about it?" I asked.

Titus and Samuel turned their gaze on me pityingly. "You don't understand, of course," Samuel said. "Our politicians can say what they want, but the Colonial Office will pay no attention."

I could hardly take my eyes off Titus. And I kept thinking what a difference three or four months made. When I was able to take my eyes off him, I focused them on Carole, in wonder at his temerity in bringing her to my father's house. This was no longer the Titus I knew. When he left Aba for his first trip to Lagos, just four months earlier, he had been a somewhat bumbling, nervous boy. Now, on the evidence of what I was seeing, his clumsiness had disappeared, replaced by a relaxed fluency of bearing and motion that I—kind of—liked. He seemed remarkably self-assured.

There was just one more thing to do as I remembered the last time all of us (minus Carole) had assembled in this same parlor. I went and pulled Titus off the piano stool and made him stand back-to-back with me.

"Now, Samuel," I said, "tell us who's the tallest."

As soon as I said the words, I knew how he would react, and he did not disappoint me.

"You mean taller," he pointed out. "There are only two of you."

I waved aside his pedantry. "We already know who the shortest is," I said, looking pointedly at Ben. "You only need to judge between me and Titus, and then we'll know who the tallest is."

Samuel smiled tolerantly. He nearly always did, unless I spoke to him in Igbo in our college in Umuahia. I loved him, I suppose, as one loved a big brother, which means I could never resist the temptation to tease or even taunt him when the opportunity presented itself.

Now he moved a little away from Titus and me for a better perspective. Then he shook his head.

"It's difficult to judge," he said. "I think you're the same height."

I felt deflated. "That's not possible, Samuel. C'mon, man, you mean to tell me that in just four months, Titus has caught up with me?"

Someone giggled, and I turned to the sound. Ben had his mouth half covered as he struggled to suppress his laughter.

"Must be King's College food," the uncovered half of his mouth said.

CHAPTER IX

My mother's voice was still ringing in my ears as I boarded the train at Aba for the journey back to Umuahia for the second term, 1944. I could still feel the sting where, twenty-four hours earlier, she had pinched my earlobes in her frenzied determination to ensure that her words sank deep into my consciousness.

My mother, Margaret, was a very demanding woman. She was generous and kind but usually asked for something in return. Pressured relentlessly by me, she had finally agreed to supplement our pocket allowance, by matching what my dad gave us. Dad promised Samuel and me four shillings each, doubling what he had given us for the previous term. My mother added four shillings but extracted three promises from us. Conditions that, she said, were nonnegotiable.

"I know that sometimes when I tell you something," she complained, her voice shrill with passionate concern, "it enters one ear and goes out by the other, especially you, Obinna. Samuel is not so bad, but you, you are almost as bad as your sister Nneka, who does not even listen."

She had gripped me then by my two ears and pulled me close, screaming her words at me.

"I listen to you and Samuel and your friends, the way you boys talk. I don't know what happened to the one called Titus. Lagos did something to him, which I don't like. Otherwise, how do you explain what happened that day he was here with that white girl—"

"She's not white, Mama," Samuel said, a corner of his mouth curling up in a soft smile. "She's mulatto."

She looked at him with eyes that might have seemed hostile had it not been for a gentle light dancing in them. I knew she loved it whenever Samuel addressed her as mama. Just as he was like a brother to me, my mother loved him like a son.

"What's the difference?" she asked. "Isn't her mother white? Anyway, what was I saying?

Oh yes. You boys did not know, did you, that I would return to the house as early as I did. And there you were, with Titus and that girl holding hands. What is the world coming to?"

"Mama," I protested. "What's so terrible—"

"Shut up, child. This is exactly what I'm talking about. They hold hands in public, and you say it's all right? Do you hear anyone protest when you and Ben hold hands? That's because you're both boys, and everyone knows it means nothing. But when your friend holds hands with what's-her-name, it makes me wonder about the future."

"The future, Mama? Just because a boy and a girl hold hands? Mama, please you're hurting my ears." I put up a hand to restrain her from almost tearing off the organs.

"And I'll tear them off if you don't watch your tongue. I want a promise from you and Samuel that you will not behave like Titus."

"How?" Samuel dared to ask.

"Don't pretend you don't know what I mean. Girls are trouble. You start by holding hands and, very soon, the handshake has gone beyond the elbow, as we say. Listen, you two. I am a small person, and I know it. You see this my room in which we are? Apart from the bed and that armchair, do you see anything else in it? That's because we are poor people. But we manage. We don't want trouble that is bigger than us. I tell you, I have seen a lot of things in my life. I have seen how you can bring trouble down on your head sometimes by the company you keep. But what is the use going into these details. It is not everything that the wine tapper sees from the top of the palm tree that he talks about. You understand what I am telling you?' She had then let go of my ears and gone and sat in her armchair. It was custom-made by a grateful relative, a carpenter who owed my father for past favors. I fingered my ears gingerly, checking them out. Ear-tweaking was my mother's favorite punishment whenever we children strayed from the straight and narrow.

"Are you listening to me? I don't want you bringing girls here. If you think, because you are college boys, that you've outgrown my control, you don't know me, which brings me to something else. You must promise me another thing. I want you to read your Bible regularly. And say your prayers every night before you go to bed." She paused, looking at me in that special way she had with her eyes that always seemed to make me feel uncomfortable. "Obinna, I don't know what's happening to you. Not so long ago, you were always talking about becoming a pastor. I don't see you now reading the Bible as you used to do, and—"

"Mama, I told you I lost my Bible last term."

"I know what you said," said my mother, "but that's no excuse. There are at least two Bibles in this house that you could have used—mine and your father's. Anyway, if you look behind you, on that window, there's another Bible for you. I got it for you yesterday. Take it and treasure it."

"Mama, thank you," I said. "I promise you—"

"I don't want empty promises. Our people say that the spoken word is the heart that one sees. But you children of nowadays play around so much with words it is difficult to be sure what you are really thinking. Just one more thing. Strangers may come to see you in your college and say we gave them this or that to give you. You'd better be careful what you take from anyone you don't know well, especially anything to put into the mouth. There are people who may be envious of you being in Government College Umuahia.

"I see you smiling. Even you, Samuel. I'm always talking about this, not so? You're tired of hearing me telling you not to take things from strangers and put into your mouth. But what does the Bible say? A word is enough for the wise."

It occurred to me that she got that wrong. If she believed what the Bible said, why did she feel the need to go on and on about the same subject? Perhaps she did not think Samuel and I were wise boys?

Her words kept reverberating in my ears even after we arrived back in the college compound. She had kept her promise regarding our pocket money. This was something for which I thought I deserved all the credit. My dad had turned a deaf ear to my pleas for additional pocket money and told me why. Samuel, he said, had used his allowance so wisely in the previous term (my first, Samuel's seventh) that he had spent only sixpence. And I thought I had done quite well myself spending just a little over three shillings. I did not like being judged on the basis of Samuel's excessive frugality and told my mother so. Happily for me—and Samuel too—she had allowed herself to be persuaded by my argument. She had even gone beyond the promise of more pocket money and bought me my first pair of white canvas shoes and his second pair for Samuel. I wore mine proudly on the train ride, showing them off whenever possible.

It was on this train ride that I first encountered "the man with the broken jaw," as he was popularly called. He was truly a hideous, terrifying spectacle, with a grossly disfigured mouth. Just looking at him was, for me, rather embarrassing. His upper and lower jaws had been cruelly and permanently yanked open, with the scarcely recognizable lower lip glued to the upper reaches of his chest. Whatever did this to him—some said it was a fire, others that it was some dread disease—also seemed to have destroyed the muscles that controlled the opening and shutting of his eyelids. His eyes consequently remained fixedly open. How he slept, no one could fathom. Flies hovered around his face with relative impunity. He dribbled horridly, eating or talking. His words, when he spoke, were at best muffled and difficult to follow. But he always seemed to have a lot to say.

His story, when I finally managed to piece it together, was astounding. He was, he said, the victim of the wickedness of a jealous classmate. He had been the brightest boy in his class and very popular. Strangely, his confidence in his popularity had been his undoing. The medicine man he and his family consulted had revealed the name of the student and the precise incident that had caused the disfigurement. It was not apparently anything he had eaten, which would have been a simple case of poisoning. He had, he said, stepped over an innocent-looking heap, comprising the entrails of a chicken and some ashes, in the middle of a road in the town Uzuakoli, where his college was located. At least that was what the medicine man said had happened. I had my doubts about the man's story. My mama and papa had told us, over and over again, that they did not believe in the occult, like the good Christians they were. But how could one be sure? I knew what I had to do: follow scrupulously my mama's advice to be careful about what "entered my mouth." That was the easy part. But how to protect oneself against the mystical powers of evil spirits? No one offered to explain how stepping over the entrails of a chicken could cause such unspeakable havoc to a man's anatomy. The man with the broken jaw had himself felt no need to explain cause and effect to his listeners.

"Which means, quite simply," said Kofi Bentsil, "that he assumed everybody understood."

"What d'you mean?" asked Friday Stoneface.

"Don't tell me you believe a word—," said Achara.

"You have to protect yourself," Bentsil declared firmly.

We were lounging at the end of the Library building close to the dining hall, counting the minutes to the bell for supper. We swapped stories about our vacation experiences and talked in hushed tones about the evil that men could do to their fellow men.

"Protect yourself?" Achara asked. "You mean even here in our college? Do you have something in your dorm for your protection?"

Kofi Bentsil tried to backtrack. "I didn't say I have. But it depends, doesn't it, on what you believe?"

"Are you sure," asked Stoneface, "that you don't have some Hausa ju-ju hidden under your pillow, even now as we talk? We all know the Hausas make the best talismans and charms in the country."

"I'm not concerned about what you think," said Bentsil. "I'm used to people saying things about me."

Stoneface and I exchanged knowing glances. We knew what Bentsil was alluding to: an incident that took place when we were in our penultimate year in St. James School, Aba. On the morning of the first day of our end-of-year exams, Kofi Bentsil had not only been late to school but had also come in reeking strongly of an unfamiliar and peculiar perfume. Perhaps illogically, this gave rise to ugly rumors about examination charms and jujus.

Kofi lived the rumors down, which was quite easy for him. The fellow had such an "I don't care" attitude that nothing ever seemed to bother him. Plus, those of us who knew him well did not think he needed any ju-jus for the class exams. He was generally considered the best in the class or, perhaps I should say, modesty apart, one of the best two or three. I also knew that the only opinions that counted for him were principally Friday's, Chidi's, and mine. And it was, not coincidentally, the same foursome, in a class of some fifty-five boys, who passed the entrance examination to Umuahia.

CHAPTER X

Chidi Ebele and I were walking to a hockey game when we saw the principal. He was leaning over the balustrade of his office, watching us. Then he called out loudly, "Ebele!"

"Sir!"

"Come to my office. And you too, Okoye."

We immediately went on our guard. Mr. Walter Graves did not summon a boy to his office unless there was an extraordinarily good piece of news or the boy had done something deserving of serious reprimand or punishment. I had a feeling it was really Ebele that the principal wanted to see and that I was merely an appendage.

"What did we do?" Chidi asked me under his breath.

"I know I've done nothing," I said.

I was right. About my being an appendage, that is. The telegram that Mr. Graves handed over to Chidi merely told him that his father was gravely ill and that his mother wanted him to come back to Aba immediately.

"My father is dead," Chidi said simply.

The principal looked at me and nodded very faintly. The glint in his eye told me he understood and that it was the reason he had asked that I come along too. To be some kind of a support for my friend and classmate.

Initially, Chidi's tone was almost unemotional. He ran his eyes over the telegram a second time, staring hard at it as if willing it to reveal some deep dark secret. When he looked up a second time, his emotion began to show, as tears welled up his eyes.

"The telegram doesn't say what kind of illness," he said, "but I know he's dead."

"You're perhaps jumping to conclusions, don't you think?" asked the principal, placing a hand on Chidi's shoulder.

"Sir, you don't know our people. If Mama wants me back, then Papa is dead."

"I'm sorry, Chidi," I mumbled, choking on the words.

"How many days can I take?"

The principal looked at me and said, though without much conviction, "You could be wrong, my boy. But you can go. How many days?"

He pondered the question briefly and then said, "How about three or four days? Yes, four days. You don't really need more than that. There's nothing much a boy as young as you can do that your relatives cannot take care of. Right?"

"Yes, sir. Thank you, sir!"

"Go with God's blessing, my boy. I hope your mama is a strong woman. Be kind to her and do your best to cheer her up. Are you the oldest child?"

"I'm the first son, sir. I have two older sisters."

"Well then, if you're right in thinking the worst, you are now the man of the family. See to it you do not disappoint me. Have a good trip."

"Thank you, sir," said Chidi, blinking back tears.

The principal motioned us out of his office. At the door, I turned to look at him, and what I saw astonished me. He was staring ahead of him, with eyes that did not blink. But the expression on his face was so soft and kindly I thought I saw some moisture in the big man's eyes. He saw my action and waved me away even more peremptorily than before.

In exactly four days, Chidi Ebele returned from Aba. They were four days that affected him so much, he seemed transformed from a mere boy to a very mature adolescent, if not a young man. In those four days, he told me, he had had the time to ponder the principal's injunction that he take care of his mother and siblings and that he be the person the family looked up to. He soon discovered, he said, that he needed those challenging words from the one man in the entire universe capable of delivering them to maximum effect.

"As soon as my mother saw me," he related, "she started to cry very loud. And she went on crying until I started to cry too. I held her as we cried together. I tell you, I didn't know I could cry so much. But that was not the only surprise."

He said he quickly became aware that his oldest surviving uncle (two or so years younger than his father) had designs on his grieving mother.

"At first I couldn't believe it when my mother told me that my uncle Josiah wanted to marry her."

"Marry her?" I asked. "Are you sure you understood what she told you? How can your uncle marry her?"

"The same question I asked," said Chidi, half smiling.

The truth shocked him, and me too when he explained it to me. He soon learned that it was not an uncommon practice. Tradition apparently allowed his uncle Josiah to "offer a knife" to the widow. If Chidi's mother had accepted the knife, the arrangement would have been sealed, and she would have been added to the number of Uncle Josiah's wives.

Chidi was aghast at the notion that his uncle could be transformed, by this process, into being his stepfather (father really, there being no words in the Igbo language for that category of fatherhood). So he sought the advice of some other relatives, arguing that Uncle Josiah already had two wives of his own and eight children.

"And you know what every single one of my relatives told me?" Chidi asked rhetorically. "That the custom is really for the benefit of the widow and her children."

"Meaning you?" I asked as if I did not know what the answer would be.

"Guess," he challenged me. "Of course! My uncle, I was told, would take care of us and our mother. I told them my mother does not need anyone to take care of her or her children."

Chidi and I talked briefly about the custom and were of one mind on the matter: it was an abhorrent and a loathsome custom, period. It needed Achara who knew much more than either of us about our people's customs and traditions to give us a perspective that we had completely overlooked.

"The practice," he explained, "is not really as bad as you think. It may be difficult for you township boys to understand, but think of a poor widow in the village who is left without the means to take care of herself and her children. Many are, you know."

Achara pointed out something else. The giving of the knife was actually a privilege accorded only to those widows who enjoyed a good relationship with the dead man's brothers. It was a mark of total acceptance of the widow by the family of her deceased husband.

"Well," said Chidi, "that may be so, but I persuaded my mother to refuse the offer and to do everything in her power to prevent anyone touching anything belonging to us."

I could not fault him on either count. Especially with regard to his family's assets. I knew, as most of our friends did, that thanks to the industry of his father, those assets were not inconsiderable.

It did not take me long to recognize the transformation in Chidi. He had been a rather introverted, timid boy. Now he became more and more outgoing and convivial. In almost everything he did, he seemed much more relaxed, more confident than before. He even began to talk about girls and dancing. And though the second term was then still young, he began to plan his activities for the next vacation.

I do not know for sure if this had anything to do with the way he played his sports. I suspect it did. Clearly one of the school's outstanding talents in football, he now seemed to play with added zest, dazzling teammates and opponents alike by the wizardry of his dribbling and the deceptive speed of his footwork. His football skills indeed were sadly wasted on Government College Umuahia, which did not set a high premium on the game.

Chidi took to field hockey as naturally as fish takes to water. This was a game that neither of us had ever seen before we went to Umuahia. In those early days, we did not even use standard hockey equipment. Our hockey sticks were crudely fashioned out of bamboo roots. With this passable implement, Chidi so mastered the art of the game that he went one step further and invented a masterpiece that no hockey coaching manual ever mentioned. By a sleight of hand and stick, so fast the naked eye could barely follow it, he would flick a stationary ball into the air and dribble it while it was still airborne. It was beautiful to watch, but very dangerous. The hockey master was at first enthralled by the sheer dexterity of it all. Soon, however, he firmly discouraged the airborne dribble, because frustrated opponents were apt to lose their temper and swing wildly with their sticks.

I recognized, from quite early on, that I did not have Chidi's natural aptitude for hockey. It seemed my manifest destiny that I had to work harder than most at those games I played with any degree of seriousness. As it was with cricket, so it was with hockey.

It was indeed at Chidi's persistent urging that I gave hockey an extended trial and eventually decided I liked it enough to take it seriously. Patrick Onyewuchi, my guide and mentor, was—before Chidi's genius took center stage—arguably the best hockey player in the school. He had his doubts initially about my potential in the game but soon took me in hand, seeing how determined I was. Talk about flattering to deceive! There was another hockey player sadly also taken in by my seeming determination to come to grips with the game. Joseph Nwobi, a class 2 boy from the town of Awka, was a player of only modest ability. Tall and gangly, he ran with arms flailing and a lumbering, jerky motion, his head and torso seemingly at odds with his limbs. He strove mightily to generate speed, but the net result was like much ado about nothing. Mr. Knight, biology and hockey master, played Nwobi at center half, a midfield position where his flailing, windmill style often gave pause to frightened opponents. In little or no time, he made the position his own in the first team.

Nwobi and I became friends in the course of the second term, and the story of that friendship was a rather strange one. A week or two into the term, I found a letter on my locker in the dormitory. The handwriting was unfamiliar. The envelope carried no postage stamp, nor was there a postmark on it. In any case, letters received through the regular mail were normally distributed to the boys in the dining hall during lunch. With only a slight hesitation, I slowly opened the letter and pulled out a single sheet of light blue paper.

A light blue writing sheet had its special significance. And, not to put too fine a point on it, it had amorous undertones. Love letters between schoolboys and girls were usually written on lightly colored paper, blue being one of the preferred colors. I looked at the bottom of the paper and saw that it came from Joseph Nwobi. A little flustered, I began to read. And as I read, I wondered why he had chosen this method of communication. The handwriting was upright and regular, the letters small and compact. It was, without doubt, penned with great deliberateness. Love letters usually were.

In a short letter, Nwobi came straight to the point. "I like you," he declared in the very first line, "and I want you to be my friend."

I lowered the letter and looked around me to see if I was being observed. There were happily very few boys in the dormitory, and I breathed a sigh of relief.

"I have been watching you and thinking how to approach you. The other day I saw you talking to that fellow (who, I think, should remain nameless). Just be careful with him. I know him well. He will promise you many things, but don't trust him. As for me, I don't make any foolish promises. But if we are friends, I can help you in many ways."

That was the burden of his letter. He did not elaborate on the ways he could help me. But I was so disconcerted by the tone of the letter I did not worry too much about such details. I was not at all sure to whom he made reference. I suspected it was Mike Ukwunta, with whom I had sat and talked in the dining hall a few days earlier, long after the hall had been practically deserted. Deserted, except for a handful of boys. And now, as I read Nwobi's letter, I seemed to remember he had been one of that handful. But he did not appear to have paid us much attention. I could not even remember the topic of my conversation with Ukwunta or any other boy. The more I pondered this, the more I was embarrassed. And then strangely, my mind began to focus on Joseph Nwobi.

He was nicknamed *Slacker*. But he was not lazy, only occasionally slow. In retrospect, I really do not think the sobriquet was fairly bestowed on him. It was just one of those things that happened. He was a class senior to me, so I was not around at the genesis of it all. But a classmate of his told me that Nwobi had been late to an afternoon prep and, on another occasion, to a practice hockey game. And that was all it took. The nickname was given and, in the final analysis, it was really an endearing term. His classmates, as well as the class 3 boys, flung the nickname at him to his face laughingly. We, in class 1, used the name only in whispers and undertones and when we talked about him behind his back.

I did not know how to react to a proposition I found acutely disconcerting. I promptly rejected the idea of a written reply nor did I think it a good idea to go out of my way to deliver an answer in person. Thoroughly bemused, I decided my best course of action was to do nothing. I would play it by ear. I lay on my bed and stared straight up at the ceiling.

How long I lay there, I do not know. But suddenly, I sat bolt upright, startled by the rather unusual sound of the dormitory door shutting and doing so with a loud bang. Leaning against the door was none other than the Slacker. He wore a diffident smile, perhaps reflecting his inner nervousness. Or his embarrassment. Luckily for him, there was no one else in the dorm.

He came and sat on the bed next to mine and pointed at the letter, which I still had in my hand.

"You've read it?" he asked. I nodded.

"So?" he asked, a little impatiently.

"What?"

"Don't be silly," he said. "You know what I mean."

It was an awkward moment. I had no answer to his question and remained silent. Neither of us could look the other straight in the eye for more than a fleeting moment. It was that time of day when most boys congregated near the dining hall, awaiting the bell for lunch. Nwobi who, in spite of his nickname, was not known for tardiness at mealtimes did not seem to be in much of a hurry. I suppose he saw this as his golden opportunity. For not only were there no stragglers in the dorm, but Nwobi did not also have to worry about my leader and nemesis, Godfrey Clarke. It was public knowledge that they disliked each other intensely.

"I think I know what's bothering you." Nwobi said, essaying a smile. "You think I just want you to be my fag, not so?"

I found my voice.

"Why did you write—I mean, instead of just talking to me?"

"Would that have made any difference? I would have asked exactly the same question."

"I mean," I said, hastening to amend my question, "you didn't need to write or even ask me the question. We could have just become friends, you know."

He took my statement as a positive response and immediately apologized for the letter. "I didn't know how else to approach you. I'm really sorry. And I'm not looking for a fag to wash my clothes or anything like that. I just want us to be friends."

I think my problem was that I could not conceive of a friendship between two boys that was based on a specific proposal to that effect. And as I pondered where all this was headed, the bell for lunch mercifully rang.

I ate in a daze, my mind preoccupied by Nwobi's proposal of friendship. And for the next several days, I went to great lengths to avoid him. When our paths crossed, as they often did on the hockey field, my overwhelming feeling was one of awkwardness.

*   *   *

Word got out about Nwobi's letter, and I was teased endlessly about it by some of my classmates. Especially Kofi Bentsil, Friday Stoneface, and sometimes even Chidi Ebele.

"Did you notice the color of the sheet of paper on which he wrote the letter?" Stoneface once asked as we sat in our classroom.

"And the envelope too," said Ebele. "Light blue. The color of love."

"If he wants so much to be your friend," asked Bentsil, "has he ever invited you to go to the Uppers with him?"

"Do you know, you're really a scatterbrain," said Chidi Ebele. "What has the Uppers do with what we're talking about?"

"It's his favorite spot in the compound," said Bentsil evenly.

"That's not fair," I protested. "Have you ever seen him going there?"

"Aha! Now you're defending him. If you want to know, yes. I've not only seen him going there, but I've also seen him there."

"I don't believe you," said Stoneface. "That means you've been there yourself, and I know you wouldn't dare."

Bentsil stiffened. "Wouldn't dare" was like a red rag to him. All three of us knew, from our many years of interacting with him, that a challenge like that nearly always brought out the worst in him, which was why I was sure poor Stoneface had spoken before he had had time to reflect. He looked sorry immediately after the dare left his mouth.

"I'm making for the Uppers," Bentsil announced calmly. "Come along, if *you* dare."

CHAPTER XI

I was astonished, and so were Ebele and Stoneface. We looked at one another and then at Bentsil. He seemed to be enjoying himself. His eyes sparkled with irrepressible humor. His tone was challenging; his attitude nonchalant.

"I'm making for the Uppers," he said for the second time. "If you want to follow me, come along. If not, don't come."

"You are mad," Ebele told him.

"And if we're caught?" I asked.

Bentsil was always the most daring of us four. When the mood was on him, he seemed to have no fears at all. In primary school, he had certainly had no fear of the cane-wielding Headmaster Akweke. He thought nothing of approaching the most unapproachable girls. But, I said to myself, that was in the primary school. We were now in a secondary school, an altogether different world. A world in which we, as fags, were at the lowest point on the school totem pole. And we knew it.

"Who will catch us?" Bentsil asked. "Another orchard thief? We could ask the person what he is doing there."

None of us could immediately challenge the power of his logic. But neither were we eager to join him in this adventure and for a very good reason. The housemaster had repeatedly warned that any boy caught in the school orchard would be "summarily dealt with." We knew what that meant: two matchet parades on consecutive Saturdays. Even the principal was sometimes known to take a hand in dealing with the misdemeanor. He gave the miscreant what he fondly called "six of the best." And those boys who had been subjected to the treatment averred that when Mr. Graves brought the cane down on their behinds, he generated tremendous power. And they ached for several days.

I did not give myself much time for reflection. Looking back now, I am sure Kofi Bentsil counted exactly on that. He knew I was a sucker for a challenge thrown by him. But I should have remembered what that proclivity had cost me in our primary school days. We were rivals, Kofi and I. A rivalry that was not confined to our academic work. Once, in Aba, I had joined him in brazenly setting foot where no native boys were allowed, unless we were part of the household of a European master. As servants, of course. And as if that was not bad enough, we had shot our catapults carelessly. We were trying to kill a bird but accidentally shot a stone through the glass window of a white man's residence. We were arrested and reported to our school. Headmaster Akweke, in front of the entire school, first admonished and then severely caned us. I don't believe the punishment made the least impression on Kofi.

I clearly recalled the catapult incident. Recalled too—and very painfully—the disgrace and the caning. And just as clearly, I had not learned my lesson. I just simply could not say *no* emphatically to Kofi.

"When d'you want us to go?" I asked.

"Now," said Kofi. "This is the best time. No one—at least no one in his right mind—will even think of going there at this time of day."

"Oh," said Stoneface, "so you agree you must be out of your mind."

Bentsil made a disparaging face and beckoned to me. "Let's go."

It was a hot, humid Saturday afternoon in mid-May, with scarcely enough breeze to ruffle the leaves on the trees. It was the type of heat that discouraged outdoor activity, unless unavoidable.

A tree-lined lane led from the Administration Block, past the hockey field on the left and two senior (that is, white) staff residences, to the orchard. The orchard was popularly called the Uppers. I did not know why. I never asked. The plantation was quite a distance from the dormitories. The approach to it, for the most part, was up a gentle incline. Perhaps this last was why it was so called.

The orchard was, in my eyes, a marvel of modern agriculture, with its rows on rows of dwarf banana and orange trees. One could pick the fruits without the aid of a pole or the need to climb thorny orange trees. I was fascinated by the small-sized pineapples, which turned a green and violet hue on ripening. I was more familiar with the bigger variety, yellow when ripe and sweetly delicious to the palate.

Bentsil and I picked our way through the oranges and then the bananas, with anxiety gnawing at the pit of my stomach. From time to time I looked at my companion and marveled at his sangfroid. By the time I had eaten five or six oranges and probably as many bananas, I had little or no appetite left for the pineapple, my favorite fruit. I had thought to save it for the last. I was ready, even anxious, to go back to my dormitory. But Kofi was not yet done and would not hear of it.

"Relax, my friend," he said, his mouth full and nearly choking on the words. "Do you see anybody here?"

As always, I did not wish to appear the more fearful or chickenhearted of the two. My instincts shouted that it was time to leave. The coast was clear. We had had our fill of the fruits. And satisfied our derring-do. But my sense of pride stilled that inner voice. So I shrugged in resignation and stayed close to Kofi as if I was his shadow.

"Who the hell—?" demanded an unfriendly voice right behind us.

I whirled around, my heart jumping into my mouth, and recognized the bearded, burly white man who now stood before us. Mr. Barnabas Knight, a graduate of London University, was the senior biology teacher. He was also the hockey master. We were not acquainted with him, except on the hockey field, since he taught biology only to classes 2 and 3.

"What are you doing here? Not that I need to ask. I can see for myself." I remembered what Kofi had said he would ask whoever caught us in the orchard. And in the split second it took me to think about it, I tried to imagine even Kofi asking the biology master, a white man to boot, what *he* was doing in the orchard. I stole a glance at my friend, thinking to see his ego and confidence blown sky-high. Instead what I saw—and heard—shocked me. He had not only not lost an iota of his calm demeanor, worse, he also struck as relaxed a pose as the circumstances allowed. And then he told the most barefaced and astounding lie I thought I had ever heard.

"We're doing our homework, sir."

"Your homework?" queried Mr. Knight, his voice and body language saying he had now heard it all. "With your mouth full of—whatever it is you're eating?"

"We're sorry, sir," said Bentsil. "We shouldn't have eaten the fruits, but—well—we couldn't help ourselves."

"That's funny," said Mr. Knight, but his laugh was distinctly unfunny. "You *were* helping yourselves as I can clearly see. But what's this about homework? Whose homework?"

"Mr. Kalaga, sir."

I was stunned by the fluency and aplomb of his lying and stole another quick look at him. Mr. Kalaga was the physics and chemistry teacher but had been prevailed upon by the principal to also teach class 1 botany temporarily.

"Mr. Kalaga?"

"He was teaching us about the structure of trees and branches."

"And of course he asked the class to come to the orchard to sample the oranges and bananas," said Mr. Knight. "Naturally."

"No, sir, not exactly—" Kofi stopped, seemingly stumped for words for the first time since the encounter began.

Mr. Knight smiled, revealing a gap in his teeth that detracted somewhat from an otherwise handsome face.

"Your friend," he said, looking keenly at me for a moment or two, "doesn't seem to know what you're talking about. *He* looks as guilty as hell. What are your names?" We told him whereupon he produced a small notebook and a pencil from the hip pocket of his capacious shorts.

"How'd you spell the names? Slowly now. I'm not yet familiar with your native names."

Touching the tip of the pencil to his tongue, he scrawled the names on the notebook, then carefully put it and the pencil back in his pockct. He rubbed his palms together vigorously. Perhaps he was enjoying our discomfiture. Mine at any rate.

"Mr. Kalaga said you should come to the orchard to do your homework?" The inflection in his voice sounded like an accusation against Mr. Kalaga.

"I didn't say that, sir. It was just that when he said—"

Mr. Knight raised his hand imperiously to silence Kofi. "I shall be talking to Mr. Kalaga about this, and you'll be hearing from me later. Meantime, I suggest you get out of here. At the double!"

I did not need a second urging. I did not even stop to see if Kofi was behind me. I walked briskly away and did not pause until I had put a good distance between me and the gate of the orchard. I was by then out of breath. I sat against the trunk of a whistling pine tree and waited for Kofi.

He came along at a more leisurely pace, his eyes and bearing still somehow defiant. He held his head high. I looked him up and down as he approached and shrugged in total resignation.

"I don't think I'll ever understand you," I said.

Astonishingly Kofi took that as a compliment. "Don't worry," he said. "I'm telling you nothing will happen."

"How can you say that? Haven't you heard of this man? Supposing he actually goes and asks Mr. Kalaga about what you said?"

"Supposing? Of course, he'll ask Mr. Kalaga." He came and sat by me. "Didn't we study trees this week in botany?"

"But the teacher never told us to go anywhere near the orchard. You just stood there and told one great big lie."

"You'll see," was all Kofi could say.

I did not share in his optimism. But there was now precious little I could do about anything. Mr. Knight had a reputation as a hard man, with a marked propensity for putting the boys on matchet parade for the slightest infringement of the rules. But he was also known to be scrupulously fair-minded.

As we sat, leaning against the trunk of the whistling pine, I asked Kofi why, of all the masters, he had picked on Mr. Kalaga to be involved in this sordid affair.

"You know Mr. Knight doesn't like him," I complained.

"That's just rumors," he said dismissively.

The story was that Mr. Knight, as the senior biology master, had not been particularly enthusiastic about Mr. Kalaga teaching class 1 botany. We knew this was for a mere two or three weeks, necessitated by the convalescence of the junior biology master, Mr. Asinobi. Like Mr. Kalaga, Mr. Asinobi was an alumnus of the Yaba Higher College, Lagos, where he got his diploma in the subject.

Mr. Knight apparently wanted to take over class 1 botany himself, but as the story went, he had been "persuaded" by Mr. Walter Graves to let Mr. Kalaga do so. Whatever the truth of the story, my classmates and I were thrilled to the core at the prospect of having Mr. Kalaga as our botany teacher. He had in fact taught the subject the previous year, for just three months, before the arrival of Mr. Knight. And he had apparently done an excellent job. It was always so with him. Whatever he set out to do, he did well. Or he would not have touched it in the first place.

Mr. Kalaga was popular among the boys. He spoke excellent English, was clear and precise in his diction, and went to great pains to ensure that the class understood what he was saying. We suspected that the principal took all that into consideration. Mr. Graves might also have known that, as class 1 boys, we would relate more easily to a fellow Nigerian than to a somewhat forbidding white master. Mr. Knight, though none of us could argue his knowledge of his own mother tongue, was not the easiest speaker of the language to understand. There was a hoarse quality to his voice that muffled or distorted his articulation.

For two or three weeks, I was on tenterhooks, but the wrath I feared did not come. Mr. Knight did not summon me nor, as far as I knew, did he summon Kofi. Kofi's unconcern, if that was possible in the circumstances, actually seemed to increase. Whenever I brought up the subject, he waved it aside. "I told you not to worry."

Then one day, Mr. Kalaga sent for me. I immediately suspected the worst and ran to dormitory 2, Kofi's dormitory. But he was not there. Full of foreboding, I then crept at a sluggish and unwilling pace to the master's house.

Mr. Kalaga's house was a two-bedroom structure, with a medium-sized living room, a wide veranda at the front, and a smaller one at the rear. The kitchen was an annex that one entered from the back veranda. The lavatory and the shower room were some fifteen or so yards behind the main building, close to the rear hedge of the compound. It was situated next to the housemaster, Mr. Pepple's house. The main road to Umuahia town ran right behind both houses.

Mrs. Kalaga opened the door. Very dark skinned and in her late thirties or early forties, she had a homely oval-shaped face, large heaving breasts, and, when she smiled, a rather sad smile. She peered long and hard at me through her horn-rimmed spectacles before letting me in.

Kofi Bentsil was standing by the dining table, set close to the end wall of the living room farthest from the entrance door. Seated at the dining table was Mr. Kalaga himself, a benevolent middle-aged man, whose genial disposition and near portliness masked a fierce determination and an iron will. Like his wife, he was bespectacled. Unlike her, he barely looked at me as he waved me to the side of the dining table opposite to where Kofi stood.

Looking at him as he sat there, it was difficult to imagine that, in his younger years, he was a pretty good half-miler. Nor that he was a glutton for work. For in addition to his temporary stint as the class 1 botany master, he of course taught his specialist subjects of chemistry and physics. Mathematics came naturally to him. He was the cricket master in my first year and even helped a reluctant Mr. Knight to teach us the hockey game. He coached athletics.

Mr. Kalaga smiled expansively and took off his spectacles. Then leaning far back in his chair, he intertwined his fingers at the back of his head. The intense sunlight that permeated the room, coming in through the windows, made him blink from time to time as he now focused on Kofi and me.

Then he addressed me. "Mr. Knight spoke to me—oh!—I forget how many days ago, about the day he caught you two in the orchard."

He paused, I think, to let the words sink in. As was his wont, he spoke slowly, in measured tones. It was as if he loathed to let each word out before the previous one had been properly understood and digested. That is the best way I can describe his manner of speaking. That way, he seldom needed to repeat himself. I loved to listen to him and often wished I could talk like him, each word clearly enunciated, the voice sonorous and vibrant.

But not today. I was ill at ease and, for perhaps the first time, wished that Mr. Kalaga would rush his words to shorten my agony. I raised my head to look at Kofi. His face was expressionless. His eyes were fixed, staring straight ahead.

"But I already knew what he was going to tell me, thanks to young Bentsil here." This time Kofi looked directly at me and smiled with satisfaction.

"You'd better wipe that silly grin off your face," Mr. Kalaga spoke sharply to Kofi and then continued. "Do you know why I chose to confirm your impudent lie to Mr. Knight?"

I remember saying to myself that it was not my lie, impudent or otherwise. I had told no lie. In fact, I had hardly said a word to Mr. Knight. But though the thought flashed through my head, I knew better than to try to excuse myself and my misbehavior.

"Simple," continued Mr. Kalaga. "Once, I too was a thoughtless boy, like both of you. Like you, I liked nothing better than to meet the challenge of rules and regulations head on. Luckily for the school, there was no orchard here when I was in my junior classes, or I wonder what I would have done to it. Seems like a century ago. I was pretty high-spirited in those days. Don't misunderstand me. I do not condone what you did. I do not condone the breaking of school rules. I warn both of you to never ever do such a stupid thing in the future. I've watched you in my classes, and I know you are better than this. I like some spirit in my boys, just as long as neither of you intends to make this type of behavior a regular occurrence."

He stopped and peered at Kofi and me in turns. He was silent for so long that I surmised he was deliberating on our punishment. Or how best, at least, to reprimand us. I was right.

"You may go back to your dormitories," he finally said. "But! Consider yourselves on probation. You know what the word means, don't you?" As neither of us volunteered an answer, he added, "Well, if you don't, go to the library and look it up in a dictionary."

It was on the tip of my tongue to thank him, but he would have none of it. Firmly, but with a smile, he waved us out of his living room. Kofi and I walked in silence until I was sure we were out of earshot of the master's house. Then I stopped Kofi and made him turn to face me.

"Can you tell me something?" I asked him.

"I'll tell you even before you ask because I know what you want to ask me. Mr. Kalaga told me sometime last term that I could come to him with any problem."

"He did?"

"You don't believe me? Okay. Please yourself."

I was still incredulous. "When did he? I mean, I've never seen you talking to him, except in class."

Kofi put on his most haughty air. "And at cricket practices and athletics."

So that was it! Kofi was an excellent high jumper and was already showing quite a flair for cricket. It would therefore seem natural enough that Mr. Kalaga might take more than a passing interest in him.

The sudden relief from the weeks of pent-up tension was more than my stomach could take. A tightening in the pit of the stomach presaged a rush to answer nature's call. I left Kofi where he stood and made straight for the students' lavatory, which was close by.

I grabbed the toilet roll, placed for our convenience on a stool just within the entrance to the lavatory. I counted out the *three* sheets allowed by the rules. I added another three on a whim and then topped it all off by counting out two more. I tore the eight sheets off and was walking to one of the semiopen enclosure when a voice behind me made me jump. I recognized the voice even before I turned to confront my nemesis.

"What d'you think you're doing?" asked Godfrey Clarke.

"Nothing," said I, knowing what was coming.

"How many sheets is that?"

"How many? I—er—don't know?"

"You shouldn't have counted them aloud," said he. "I heard you clearly. How many are you allowed to use?"

"Three."

"And you tore off seven. Why?"

I could have given him a million reasons why. Like, how stupid the three-toilet-sheets rule really was. Like, if all the boys obeyed the rule strictly, many would walk into their classrooms and the library and the dining hall still reeking of odors from an uncompleted job. Like, how I've seen some of the senior boys tear off as many as ten or even more. Had it been any other of the school leaders, I might have attempted to explain my conduct. And I might have suffered nothing worse than perhaps a serious warning. But Clarke was Clarke, whose outstanding quality was never to have mercy, who never saw an infringement that he did not visit with the maximum penalty. Especially if the culprit was named Okoye.

So I kept my counsel and counted and tore off four of my eight sheets, folded them neatly, and placed them on top of the roll of toilet paper. I might still be cheating by one sheet, but I saw nothing wrong with taking a little advantage of Clarke's hearing lapse.

"See me in the Leaders' room later," said Clarke, "and I'll tell you what your punishment will be."

CHAPTER XII

Patrick Onyewuchi was my official guide, which meant, in popular parlance, that I was his fag, and he was my master. But I never knew him to be authoritarian in our relationship—except when he needed to be, for my own good. He did not like to impose himself on anyone, whether a classmate or a junior boy. He seemed to like to let me come to him with my problems or to discuss situations that were unfamiliar to me. He would listen attentively and then try to set me on the right path.

I do not recall that he ever once asked me to do anything worthwhile for him. Even his laundry. This was something that many of my classmates routinely did for their guides. I would have loved to do Onyewuchi's laundry and to fetch hot water for him from the kitchen on cold mornings for his bath.

I did these things for Godfrey Clarke: washed his clothes, fetched him hot water, ran stupid errands for him. And I heartily cursed him with every ounce of energy I expended on his behalf and every minute it took me to do so. I tried to offer my services to Onyewuchi, but he would have none of it.

"Why?" I asked.

"Because you are not my servant," he replied.

"So I am Clarke's servant?"

"Well," he said, "what can I say? Clarke is different."

"Can I ask you something?"

"What?"

"Were you anybody's fag when you were in class 1?"

"We were then in King's College, Lagos."

"I know. Were you?"

"Yes, why?"

"Because," I said, "I want to know if you never washed clothes for your master." Onyewuchi smiled. "It was different in Lagos," he said softly. "The school didn't appoint official guides for class 1 boys. The senior boys just picked the boys they wanted to befriend, and that was that. In fact, it was a class 5 boy, not class 6, that asked me to be his fag. We became friends, that's all. He did not ask me to wash his clothes."

"I see," I said. "Okay then, can you do one small thing for me?"

"If possible, yes. What is it?"

I hesitated for a moment. I remembered that several times in the past, when I had gone running to him for help or advice, he had chided me for not standing on my own two feet. "Fight your own battles," he would say, echoing the principal's dictum. The problem was that no one, not even Onyewuchi, could explain to me satisfactorily how a mere class 1 boy could take on the likes of Godfrey Clarke.

"Can you talk to Clarke," I asked, "and see if he'll let you bring me over to your half of our dormitory? With my bed next to his room, anytime he pokes his head out of his room, it's me he always calls to do one thing or the other for him."

"You want to come over to my side of the dormitory just to get away from Clarke? You think that'll solve your problems?"

"Yes, please."

"And which boy do you want to replace you, with *his* bed next to Clarke's room?"

That was all it took to deflate me. I heaved a long sigh of resignation to my accursed fate. But I was not yet through with my guide.

"All right," I said. "How about this? Next time he asks me to wash his clothes, can I tell him that you gave me lots of your clothes to wash, to say nothing of mine also? Maybe then he'll leave me alone."

Onyewuchi laughed shortly and then was silent for a moment or two. "Well, if you think it will help you," he finally said, "you may do so."

"Yes, please, it will help me. I'm sure of that. He knows how I hate doing anything for him, and that's why he makes me do them. He's wicked."

"He's just vain," said Onyewuchi, trying to defend the indefensible, "not wicked. He likes to look his best, that's all."

"Is that why he's always looking for a chance to punish me? I know what you're going to say, that I'm not the only boy."

"You're not, and I'm glad you know it. There is nothing any of us, not even the senior school leader Clement Ugwu, can do about him, unless of course he does something really stupid and in the presence of a master or somebody like that."

This conversation took place, as best as I can recall, in the middle of the second term and about a week after Kofi and I had been reprimanded by Mr. Kalaga for our orchard misadventure. It had not ended quite satisfactorily for me. But at least it gave me the courage to take one last stand against Clarke. I resolved that never again would I wash any of his dirty clothes. I was not at all sure what he would do if matters came to a head between him and Onyewuchi, on this or any other matter concerning me. I kind of feared for my guide in the event of such a confrontation, but I hoped he was "big" enough to handle Clarke and other boys like him.

There was a confrontation between them, some two weeks later, but it had nothing to do with my running errands for Clarke or doing his laundry. It was rather mostly about Okoroafor.

Gregory Okoroafor hated games but did not mind housework. By contrast, I disliked housework but was developing a penchant for games, particularly cricket and, to a degree, hockey. Playing games was fun. Cutting grass or cleaning the lavatory building was an unwelcome chore. But despite our dissimilarities, Okoroafor and I became friends. Our friendship had in fact begun on the first day of class, in our first term. By the accident of the alphabetical arrangement of seating, by family names, we found ourselves sharing a double desk in the classroom permanently assigned to class 1.

It was the prep hour, in the library. Okoroafor felt a dull, throbbing pain in the thumb of his left hand and told me about it. We then became so engrossed in discussing the pain and what to do about it that we failed to hear the bell for the end of prep. We therefore did not hurry to our respective dormitories to prepare for the games period. Then when the bell was rung for games to start, we realized our error and made a dash for our dormitories. Too late!

Godfrey Clarke was the leader supervising volleyball on that day. Oddly, for such a vainglorious character, Clarke was quite good at the game. The fact that he was tall might have had something to do with it. Whatever it was, Clarke could, and often did, hurl himself at the ball, even when doing so left him inelegantly eating earth and dust, at full stretch, on the sandy floor of the court.

Okoroafor and I arrived at the court fully ten minutes late, which caused Clarke to smile fiendishly. He called a temporary halt to the game in progress and turned to us.

"Late again, I see," he said.

I could not tell if his remark was directed at me, at both of us, or only at Okoroafor. I knew I was hardly ever late to any game, or if I was, it was never to a session supervised by Clarke. So I said nothing. And neither did my friend.

"Any reason for your lateness?" Clarke asked as if he really wanted to know.

Okoroafor started to explain, holding up his left hand. But Clarke, raising his own left hand imperiously, interrupted him.

"Hold it! See me in the leader's room immediately after supper. Both of you."

As chance would have it, Onyewuchi was also in the leaders' room, located at the end of the library building close to the dormitories, when Okoroafor and I reported to Clarke.

Clarke was not interested in the reasons we adduced for our lateness to the volleyball game. He was—or seemed—totally indifferent to my friend's painful thumb. "If the thumb is so painful," he asked, "how did you manage to play with it? I was watching you."

He had to watch *all* of us, or he would not have been carrying out his duties of supervision. But it occurred to me that there were several and different levels of watching. There was the intelligent, dispassionate, perhaps even compassionate watching. The type that understands or tries to understand, and shows some humanity and flexibility as the circumstances require. But there was also the wickedly tendentious watching, the type motivated by a keen desire to ensnare and then, of course, to inflict punishment. If Clarke had watched Okoroafor intelligently, I have no doubt he would have observed that a painful thumb could scarcely have made any difference to the level of play of a boy who was patently one of the worst volleyball players in the school. Okoroafor did not once use his left hand during the entire course of the game. But as far as Clarke was concerned, however, Okoroafor had played his usual lousy game. Therefore there could not have been anything particularly wrong with his thumb.

Clarke pronounced our sentence. "Matchet parade for both of you."

I cast my eyes around for someone who would dare to tell Clarke what he could do with a judgment arrived at without due consideration of the facts. Someone who could stand eyeball-to-eyeball with him and warn him that a sentence so lightly and carelessly pronounced on his fellow school boys, however lowly, would inevitably lead to a lack of respect for the judge himself. And even for the law he stood for.

My eyes fell on Gilbert Enuma, a school leader like Clarke and therefore his equal in authority and power. And on Onyewuchi, my guide and friend, a house leader who was not at all the equal of Enuma and Clarke—except in the inner and spiritual power that comes only to those to whom that grace is given by reason of their humanity and humaneness.

Onyewuchi had obviously been chatting with Enuma before Okoroafor and I walked into the leaders' room. They had fallen silent as the brief interchange between us and Clarke unfolded. They heard Clarke's sentence and must have been stuck by the total absence of any real opportunity for us to state our case.

Enuma did nothing. Onyewuchi, after a moment's hesitation, called to Okoroafor. "Let me see your thumb."

Okoroafor and I, unmindful of Clarke's eyes on our backs, moved deeper into the room, and Okoroafor held up his left hand to Onyewuchi. But it was Enuma, not Onyewuchi, who first examined the painful thumb. He peered closely at it, applying a gentle pressure, evidently to see how Okoroafor would react. Okoroafor winced immediately and drew back his hand, then held it out again to Onyewuchi.

"It looks swollen," Onyewuchi said after a pause. "It must be very painful. What happened?"

"I don't even know," replied my friend. "I don't remember anything hitting it. It just started to ache."

"Could be whitlow," said Onyewuchi. "You'd better go to the dispensary tomorrow if it still aches."

"He's probably telling a lie," suggested Clarke.

"I don't think so," said Onyewuchi.

I watched my guide intently, wondering what he would do. He, for his part, was looking at Enuma, almost certainly out of deference for Enuma's higher rank. Enuma, typically for him, chose to say nothing.

"Get out of here!" Godfrey Clarke barked at us.

Disappointed, we stepped out of the room, but on a sudden impulse that came to both of us simultaneously, we stopped just beyond the door and waited. I was not disappointed.

"I don't think your decision is fair to them, at least to Okoroafor," I heard Onyewuchi say to Clarke.

"I beg your pardon?" said Clarke.

"You didn't give them a chance to explain anything. That's not fair."

"Why don't you mind your own business?" Clarke retorted. "I know Okoye is your fag—"

"That has nothing to do with anything," said Onyewuchi. "As a matter of fact, I'm more concerned about the other boy, Okoroafor. You can see—if you take the trouble to look—that his thumb is really bad. Why don't you have a look for yourself?"

Enuma finally woke from his stupor, because it was his voice that said, "You know, this boy Okoroafor, he's a good boy."

"And he's your fag, no doubt?" asked Clarke.

"Oh no! Nothing of the sort."

"So what's your business in this matter?"

Clarke's contempt for the diffident, bumbling Enuma was well-known in the school. He was known to have once expressed the opinion that Enuma had not merited his appointment as a school leader. The story may well have been apocryphal, but when I asked Onyewuchi about it, he had chosen to neither confirm nor debunk it.

Onyewuchi made one last attempt to change the course of events. "I'm appealing to you," he said to Clarke, "to change your decision. Or at least to hear what the two boys have to say. Okoroafor's thumb—"

"I'm afraid I cannot change the punishment."

"Listen, my friend," Onyewuchi said soothingly. "You know I don't like to interfere in this sort of situation. The only reason I'm doing so is—"

"Because of your fag, Okoye."

"I don't know," said Onyewuchi patiently, "what Okoye did or did not do in this affair and what excuse he had for being late to the game. At least listen to them, and you might be able to find out exactly what happened."

"I'm sorry, but my decision is final."

Okoroafor and I should have eavesdropped more carefully, because the next thing we knew, Onyewuchi walked out of the room, obviously bristling. He caught us in the act as we stood behind the door and illogically—or so it seemed to me at the time—turned his anger on us.

"How long have you been standing there?" he asked.

"We heard everything," said Okoroafor glowingly.

"And we thank you—" I began.

He cut us short. "For what? If I wasn't so angry with the fellow, I'd be very, very angry with you two. You're in big trouble already, and you don't want any more from me, I'm sure. If you know what's good for you, you'll disappear from here immediately. Before Clarke sees you."

"He can do his worst," I said defiantly.

"Don't be stupid," said my friend. "Let's go! Come on!"

As we walked away, I looked back at Onyewuchi. He stood where we had left him. He was staring at us. And I swear there was deep compassion in that stare.

CHAPTER XIII

"When the Egyptian pharaohs were building their fabulous cities and the monumental pyramids, most of Europe was inhabited by half-naked savages, eating wild berries in the forests of Europe."

As near as I can remember what he said, those were Mr. Eagleton's exact words. I am not at all surprised I remember the words so clearly. I do not know about my other classmates, but those were words I was not likely ever to forget. It is as if they are permanently engraved, in stone, in my memory.

The subject was ancient history; the teacher, Mr. Eagleton. Ancient history was my favorite subject. Mr. Eagleton was one of my favorite teachers. I loved to listen to him as he recounted the wonderful stories of the pharaohs of Egypt, of the wars between Sparta and Athens, and of Alexander the Great who, at the young age of thirty-three, ran out of places to conquer and, incredibly, shed tears on account of that fact. I learned from Mr. Eagleton that the code of Hammurabi of Babylon was several centuries older than the laws of Moses, whose Ten Commandments, I had thought, were the earliest form of their genre. I thrilled to the knowledge that the birth of civilization took place, not only in the valleys of the Euphrates River in the Middle East, but also in the Nile Valley and Delta of ancient Egypt, an *African* kingdom. And coming nearer home, Mr. Eagleton told us about the achievements of the ancient and illustrious West African kingdoms of Ghana, Mali, and Songhai, which flourished at about the time Europe was emerging from the Dark to the Middle ages.

In recounting these stories, Mr. Eagleton, himself a European, did not exhibit any trace of condescension in his voice or his manner.

Ancient history fascinated me. But the more recent period of history, or rather that part of the subject dealing with the colonial expansion of Britain in Africa, was dull and drab by comparison. Even at our tender ages and though much too cowed to express our feelings openly, there were several among my classmates who had what I can best describe as a sense of racial degradation as the colonial story and the unspeakable horrors of the slave trade unfolded. However, journeys of exploration and discovery per se were stirring. Mungo Park's "discovery" of the Niger and David Livingstone's journeys to Southern and Central Africa were the foremost among those stories.

I think, on the whole, that I worked harder at my books in the second term of my first year, 1944, than I had in the first. Indeed the first term had floated by so quickly it had ended before I had properly adjusted to the different academic requirements of a secondary school. Coming from a primary school in which I had been clearly one of the best (or I would not have been in Umuahia), it had only slowly dawned on me that, without a single exception, every one of my classmates could make a similar claim with respect to his primary school. And with that awareness came the realization that competition among us would be extremely stiff and that no boy was going to be a pushover.

That realization came slowly. The excessively intense "mark grubbing" (the sometimes mindless, always obsessive, striving for the best scores in all tests and written works), which was to become the chief characteristic of the academic competition among us, manifested itself in all its disturbing ramifications a little later. But already I sensed that to excel, I had to work twice as hard as I ever did in primary school. Or I would be left "carrying the *canda*," a popular phrase for "finishing at the bottom of the class." I did not want that. Neither did any of my classmates.

I liked botany and zoology. They were "drawing" subjects. I was not a great artist, at least not in comparison with my cousin Samuel, whose exceptional gift in art revealed itself from when he was a very young boy. But evidently some of his talent had rubbed off on me. I was one of the two best artists in the class, excelling in the drawing of insects, birds, plants, and the like. Though I struggled with others when it came to textual matter, my ability to draw clearly gave me some advantage in these two subjects.

The entrance examination to the school had tested our abilities principally in arithmetic and English. I suppose every one of us in the class had a notion that he wrote good English or at least wrote it well enough to have achieved success in that highly competitive examination. I was never really comfortable with English, if only because, as a subject, it was very elusive. Attaining proficiency in it seemed—and still seems—to me to be an eternal struggle. Arithmetic was different. I knew for sure I was good in it. Unfortunately for me, mathematics in Umuahia did not comprise only arithmetic. I found out that I also had to contend with its other two—and for me—unfamiliar branches: algebra and geometry. I did not find either easy, and my performances in them were at best spotty and erratic. My confidence suffered as a result. In the first-term examination, I did something I am not proud of. I was so frustrated by the complexity of one of the geometry questions that I leaned over to Okoroafor, when the master was not looking, to seek some help. If any other boy saw this exchange, no one, to this day, has confronted me with it. None lodged a complaint to the master.

The only science subject I had done in primary school was nature study, which was really nothing more than an elementary form of biology. Umuahia brought me into a collision with physics and chemistry. Both subjects gave me endless trouble, though the teacher was the incomparable Mr. Kalaga. I just seemed unable to get a proper handle on the two sciences. Physics was, I think, my worst subject. Matter and energy, sound and motion, heat and light were all natural phenomena, part of my everyday life experience. But there was nothing natural about them, as concepts with which I had to grapple mathematically, in the classroom. I approached every physics class with some trepidation and was wont to be occasionally absentminded. Sometimes, when I could contrive it, I distracted myself in ways that I knew the teacher would disapprove of, if he caught me.

I enjoyed reading works of fiction. This was both a matter of voluntary distraction as well as almost an academic requirement. This was the first time I was truly exposed to reading for the sake or the love of reading. My primary school had no collection of books I was aware of. Aba, the town in which I grew up, had no public library worthy of the name. The British Council, that most worthy cultural arm of British colonialism, had not as yet begun its civilizing mission to the darker corners of the Nigerian Colony and Protectorate. That was to come later.

I got into trouble on a number of occasions for reading a novel when I should not have. Like the day Mr. Kalaga caught me. He was teaching us about the atom. This was in the middle of the second term. I recall, to this day, the words with which he introduced the subject.

"An atom," he told the class, "is the smallest indivisible part of an element that can take part in a chemical reaction."

Somewhere along the way, he lost me, which was the signal for me to take out a volume of Rider Haggard's *King Solomon's Mines*. I placed the volume discreetly on my lap, below the desk line, where I was sure Mr. Kalaga would not espy it.

"By the way, Okoye, what d'you think you are doing?"

I had not seen him approach my desk. In my confusion, I got up, a little too abruptly, dropping the book to the floor.

"Sorry, sir," I mumbled.

Mr. Kalaga's smile, as he regarded me solemnly, seemed only skin deep. "Have you been listening to anything I've been saying?"

"Yes, sir. I have."

"You couldn't have," he said, "unless you think you can read and listen to me at the same time."

He bent over and picked up the novel, scanned the title page, and then returned it to me.

"I've read this story," he told me, still smiling. He paused for a moment or two and then said, "Your punishment is to write me a summary of the story, in about two hundred words. Bring the summary to the next physics class."

"But, sir," I dared to protest, "I'm only halfway through, and I'm a slow reader."

"Then do a summary up to the point you've read."

He turned, took two or three steps, and spun on his heels to face me once again. "You seem to be running into trouble with me too frequently for your own good. You'd better look out!"

I did not turn in the summary at the stipulated time, because it turned out to be much more difficult to compose than I had thought. In fact, a little over two weeks and several physics classes passed before Mr. Kalaga asked me about the summary. It was doubtless stupid of me, but that passage of time had led me to hope he had forgotten about me and the volume of Rider Haggard.

In the upshot, Mr. Kalaga put me on a matchet parade for my troubles. And I still had to produce the summary.

Religion was the first class every Monday. This was purely and simply a forty-minute discussion session. We looked forward to it because it was a diversion from the strict rigors of the other subjects. Every conceivable religious topic was broached, either by the teacher or the boys, and discussed without inhibition. Did the miracles actually happen? Was Christian baptism the inflexible requirement for eternal salvation, as the words of Jesus Christ implied? If so, what about the millions of Jews who had lived and died before Christ? What about Muslims and Buddhists and the adherents of other religions? And more importantly to me, what about the "heathens" of Africa who never had a chance until the late nineteenth century and the early part of the twentieth to receive the gospel of Jesus Christ? The teachers, untrained as they were in biblical exegesis or in religious instruction, could not supply definitive answers. They knew it, and we knew it. Yet, despite the relative lightheartedness of the discussions, very few words that were sacrilegious or profane were spoken.

The second term examinations came and went, and I thought I did quite well. However, since the results of the first term's exams had not been published, I was not sure how I could measure whatever progress I might have made. No one told us if the results this time would be published. I really did not care. The four-week vacation was a week away, and that was all that mattered.

———

Then the principal dropped two bombshells. One was the departure of Mr. Eagleton, the history master. The other, and perhaps the more momentous, was the promotion of six of my classmates to class 2, to take effect at the beginning of the third term.

Mr. Eagleton was my favorite white teacher, a good man, and widely admired by the boys. In everything he did, he showed good taste and class. He carried himself with dignity but generally spoke to us as a friend, with little or no trace of condescension. He had seen action in the world war, which was still raging, specifically in the North African theater of the European conflict. He was seriously wounded in the initial phases of General Rommel's blitzkrieg across the scorching sands of the Sahara. At the time a second lieutenant, he was honorably discharged and was able to resume his teaching career.

I remember him not only for the wonderful stories he told us, as our history teacher, but also for one play he produced toward the end of the term: *The Apple Pie.* I have forgotten almost every detail of the play except that it was a signal success and thoroughly enjoyed by the school. It was the first time I ever saw an apple pie or even heard of it. It looked so appetizing, the picture of it is indelibly engraved on my mind. I envied the actors in the play. They each got a piece of the real thing after the play was done.

There was general puzzlement as to the reasons for Mr. Eagleton's departure and an almost-tangible sense of loss among the boys. There were no rumors about him and women, white or black. There was only a feeling that a good man was being let go by an unfriendly and reactionary authority: the British Colonial Office. I remembered vividly my conversations with Samson Stoneface on the occasion of the equally sudden departure of Mr. Hunter, the phonetics teacher, in the early weeks of the first term. The scandal surrounding Mr. Hunter and Cecilia, niece to Ojeozi, had virtually ended the day Cecilia miscarried. The principal had declared the matter at an end, as far as he was concerned. Ojeozi was very bitter about that decision, but even he knew there was nothing anybody could do about the outcome to the ugly incident.

Mr. Eagleton had a clean bill of health as far as scandals were concerned. Samson Stoneface said so, and that was all I needed to know. Perhaps Mr. Eagleton had been a little too sympathetic to the national struggle for political self-determination and independence. Had he not almost given his life for "freedom"? He had, in extolling the achievements of ancient empires native to West Africa, given us some sense of our self-worth. I know that when he left, it was almost as if he took a part of me. Perhaps I exaggerate some of this. It is entirely possible that time has somewhat hallowed my memory of him.

The unexpected promotion of six boys from class 1 to class 2 shook the entire class. No warning had been given before we wrote the exams, about this eventuality. It is a moot point if such a warning would have made any difference to the outcome. No results were released. The promotions had been as much a surprise to the beneficiaries of the principal's decision as they were to the rest of us. There was, however, a reasonable consensus among us that at least four of the six merited their promotion.

Anthony Achara was one of the six. And emphatically one of the four. There was no question in my mind that had the results been released, Achara would have been either in the first or, at the worst, second place in the order of merit. That's how good I already knew he was. I thought Bentsil might have been among the six. When I shared my thoughts with him, he admitted to being terribly disappointed. But then he said something that surprised me.

"It's just as well," he said, "that we don't know the positions."

"Why?" I asked. "I would have liked to know where I placed."

"Can you imagine how it would feel if you were seventh?"

"Me, seventh?" I asked, laughing. "Impossible."

"Speak for yourself," said Kofi. "I know if I was seventh, God! I think I would have gone crazy."

"Yah. I think I know what you mean."

Anthony Achara was elated. I reminded him about what my headmaster in primary school (and his, three years earlier) had said about him.

"Is this," I asked him, "the rain Mr. Akwete prophesied you would make to drench us?"

His look told me not to be silly; his mouth said something else. "We will get to spend only one term in class 2 before going up to class 3 next January. How do they expect us to cope?"

"Don't be silly," I told him straight. "Your trouble is that you're too modest."

CHAPTER XIV

The mood of the boys was somber as we reassembled in our classroom at the beginning of the third and last term of our first year. We had been twenty-nine at the beginning of the year. We were now down to twenty-three. Somewhat chastened by the unexpected promotions from the class, we took what comfort we could from one another. Some of us had lost our best friends to class 2. A few thought they should have been among the six. Most of us assumed that the promotions had been based on an order of merit, though unpublished. But there were some who were suspicious.

My father was philosophical about it when, during the vacation, he called Samuel and me to his bedroom.

"What happened," he told me, "is in the past. Look to the future and make sure you are never caught unawareness again. It is said that a buttock stung by an ant becomes wiser. Samuel, I charge you to make sure he does what he's supposed to do. If you have to tear off his ears, do so, if that will make him listen to you. I know how stubborn he can be."

Samuel and I exchanged glances, and then he spoke up for me. "Papa," he said, "Obinna doesn't need me pulling his ear. I know he will do the best he can."

I did not think he knew me that well, at least not as far as my application to my studies in Umuahia was concerned. But I smiled gratefully at him and promised to do my best henceforth.

And I did. I studied hard, determined to make my old man proud of me. I knew it was unlikely that there would be more midyear promotions from my class, but it had become for me a matter of personal pride and honor. I was going to be the best I could be. If no tangible rewards followed, I would at least have the satisfaction of being counted among the best and brightest of the class.

It was in fact the Slacker, Joseph Nwobi, not cousin Samuel, who most helped me academically at this stage.

Our friendship had blossomed to the point where I was entirely at ease in his company. While not neglecting his own studies, he seemed ever ready to encourage my efforts. He did things for me but seldom asked that I do anything for him. I no longer had to walk the four miles into town. I had often done so to save as much of my pocket allowance as I could, since I was desperate to impress my parents with my frugality. Now, unless Nwobi was sick or was on the dreaded matchet parade, which was a rare occurrence, I rode to town with him on a bicycle hired by him. I liked going into Umuahia, even when I had no compelling reason to do so. The bicycle ride was a thrill. So were the pounded yam and bitter-leaf soup we were regularly served at Nwobi's uncle's home in the heart of the town.

There was, however, one catch in our relationship. His generosity was sometimes overwhelming, therefore, embarrassing. Taken singly, they were mostly little things. Like him insisting on paying for my haircut. Or buying such items as bread and coconut, on which we snacked as we rode back to the college, if we were not already full. And sometimes even when we were. Like jumping in front of me to pay for a merchandise for which I was in the act of proffering the money. Like buying me my first fountain pen.

I often protested. Sometimes vehemently. But to no avail. He seemed indeed to take my protests as some kind of a rejection of his friendship. That was never my intention. He was just so keen to help me that he completely overlooked the little matter of my sense of personal dignity and self-esteem.

He could afford his generosity. I was well aware of that fact, though it scarcely diminished my discomfort. His father, an Awka trader in Onitsha, had two adjoining sheds in the famous OTU market, the largest open market in Nigeria, perhaps in the entire world.

Uncharacteristically for a trader of the times, the senior Nwobi gave his son a very generous pocket allowance. My pocket money was officially six shillings—for a term of about three months! I say officially because in reality I had ten shillings. There were cash gifts from family friends that Samuel and I once again failed to report to my father. However, six shillings or ten, Nwobi's allowance was several times that amount. Three pounds, or sixty shillings, was an amount only few other boys could boast of. He himself revealed this to me in a rare moment of unguarded conversation.

I came to rely on Nwobi increasingly for help in my studies. After supper, we would often study together in the library. He made me work hard at my algebra, my weakest point in mathematics. He found ways to make me study even when I was disinclined to do so. More often than Samuel, he did the

115

big-brother thing, pushing or coaxing and sometimes deliberately needling me into reading my books.

He warned me about my attitude to the new English teacher. Mr. James Theodore, belying the Greek meaning of his name, did not seem like a gift from the gods. He came to Umuahia following the departure of Mr. Eagleton. He may have been sent to us as a replacement, but he did not teach history nor did he show any interest in producing plays. Mr. Eagleton sang beautifully. Mr. Theodore, had he been a student, would have been branded a croaker. His voice was gravelly, but not like Louis "Satchmo" Armstrong's. When he sang, his voice was unmelodiously flat.

He taught his subject harshly, and inevitably we did not appreciate his method. But Nwobi, quite early on, put me on guard against rushing into premature judgment of the master and his strange ways. Mr. Theodore had a simple but pitiless rule of marking; for every grammatical or spelling error, he deducted one point. And he was, to boot, exceedingly stingy with his marks. I seldom did, but there were not a few boys who ended up with scores below zero. When that happened, he would deduct the negative score from the score for the next essay or test paper.

Nwobi's point and, I must say, Samuel's too, was that in the long run, Mr. Theodore's methods could be highly beneficial to our mastery of the language. I did not know if time would prove his point, but I had no use for Mr. Theodore's two favorite ways of showing his displeasure. He had what he called a "love tap" and a "hatred tap." The love tap, the milder of his two forms of punishment, was a crack with a sturdy twelve-inch ruler across the fingers of the offender, palm up. The hatred tap was a more painful crack on the knucklebones, palm facing down. And as he administered the tap, he nearly always smiled, seemingly enjoying the victim's agony. Some likened his smile to that of Lucifer. If Mr. Eagleton had a benevolent attitude to our struggle for national self-determination, Mr. Theodore could barely suffer our collective shortcomings.

"I'm sick and tired of this *African* stupidity!"

If he did not say this to us once, he must have said it a thousand times. And as he spoke the words, he always seemed at the point of tearing out his hair in exasperation. There was another phrase he loved to throw at us. "Oh! *Renascent* Africa!"

His tone of voice, far from being laudatory, left us in no doubt whatsoever that he did not think Africa was renascent or would probably ever be. And to rub salt into our wound, he borrowed the phrase from the title of a book by Nnamdi Azikiwe, the foremost politician on the Nigerian national scene and the bête noir of British colonialism. *Renascent Africa* was Azikiwe's most celebrated work.

There was no doubt about it: the man had a decidedly short fuse. But he seemed confident that none of us would dare raise a voice in protest. None did. Umuahia was not Lagos. And the government college of my time was not King's College. Mr. Theodore had taught in King's College, Lagos, for a few years before he was transferred, in late 1944, to Umuahia. There were stories, which we perhaps lapped up a little too eagerly, that Mr. Theodore was once, and quite possibly twice, beaten up by the boys in King's College. If the stories were true, there could be little doubt as to the cause. But evidently he had not learned his lesson. He probably believed that after the political hotbed that was Lagos, the more sedate political climate of Umuahia would be a safer place to vent his feelings about Africa and Africans.

I was not alone in wondering why teachers like him even wanted to come to Africa. And more importantly, why they did not cut short their tour of duty as soon as they determined that young Africans were not, so to say, their cup of tea.

I thought about all this, but I also took to heart the cautionary words of cousin Samuel and my friend Nwobi. So I gave Mr. Theodore the benefit of the doubt and concentrated on doing the best work I could do in my English language papers. Though I was never really sure about this, I came to believe, in the course of the term, that I actually found favor in his sight. Other than this, there were times I wondered if he had normal human feelings. It turned out he was married. But that did not significantly lessen my wonderment. As it is said, a corpse might fill a coffin, but that does not mean that it is the body of a worthy person.

Stories soon began to circulate that Mr. Theodore was one of the markers of the English language paper in the Cambridge School Certificate examination, a high school diploma test. This was a not-inconsiderable cause for alarm, as none of us cared for our English paper to be marked by him. Then we got over our concern and instead began to feel sorry for the other schools. We were confident that an obvious conflict of interest would eliminate him from marking the papers of his own students in an examination, which we believed was taken in every country where the British Union Jack flew. The senior class, cousin Samuel's, had the most to fear on this score. But even they were only in class 3, still two years away from sitting the Cambridge examination.

*   *   *

It is difficult to describe the thoughts that went through our minds as we—my classmates and I—watched the successful candidates in the year's entrance examination as they arrived for their admission interviews. Twelve months earlier we had gone through the same process. I myself had arrived at the college wide-eyed in wonderment at the sheer beauty of the compound. It was easy to see that several of the interviewees were just as awestruck as I was.

That first sight of the new class of fags-to-be was a thrill. It would be their turn, as it had been ours, to be told that "fags were to be seen but not heard." To be taunted endlessly as cockroaches if they ever dared to be fresh with us senior boys. To be scorned mercilessly if their table manners or their handling of the dining cutlery was less than impeccable. To be taught to say "yes, please" or "no, please," which we had been told was the respectful way to respond to our seniors. To be exposed to the likes of Chima Nwanna who, through my first year, had scarcely shown any signs of letting up on us. Which of these boys would Godfrey Clarke pick on?

I felt some sympathy for, not to say empathy with, them. I did not know how I would relate to them. But I did not think I had it in me to call them the names I had been called. Or to make them do chores for me as I had done and was doing for a few of the senior boys.

Michael Anyanwu was another matter. This was one boy that I knew I would not spare the slings and arrows that I myself had endured. As a friend, of course. I knew him very well in Aba where he was a pupil in St. Luke's School, a Roman Catholic primary school. He was a close friend and schoolmate of a cousin of mine, Simon Chidube. Three of us, sometimes with my friend Ben Nwobosi, often went bird hunting together, with our catapults, or roamed the streets aimlessly during our evening leisure hours. Michael and Simon were Roman Catholics and had this insufferable superiority complex about their Catholicism. This was where they drew a rigid unbending line. I sometimes crossed that line and went with them to their Roman Catholic Church services. But they never once returned the compliment. For them it would have been a cardinal sin to step into an Anglican church. That was what their reverend fathers had taught them, and it was binding.

I loved to tease them mercilessly about their stuffy religiosity. When Michael came for his interview, I was eager to seize the opportunity to torment him some more and to gloat over the appearance—if not the reality—that Protestants were favored over the Catholics in the college. Our Sunday morning services were held in the college chapel. Catholics had to trudge close to a mile, to a village, for theirs. But I decided I would bide my time till the conclusion of the interviews. The chance never came.

It was the second week of November. The rainy season had ended though occasionally the clouds looked menacingly dark, and thunder and lightning now and again troubled the fainthearted. I took Michael on a long leisurely walk down to the cricket field. There I showed off some of my cricket strokes, using a discarded bat that had seen better days, which I picked up from the veranda of the cricket pavilion. Michael was suitably impressed and struggled to understand the complexities of the game. A sudden downpour immobilized us there for the better part of an hour, and we sat and talked.

Michael wanted to know everything about the college and the students: what the teachers were like, how good the food was, how the students interacted among themselves, what rules governed the students' lives, and how strictly those rules were applied.

I took my time describing what life was like in the college as we took a circuitous route back to the dormitories. I showed him the soccer and the hockey fields and, taking a detour, stopped at the entrance to the orchard. We were careful not to venture within the gates. But my bemused friend saw the impressive rows of stunted fruit trees, with their fruits temptingly within easy reach.

Michael burst into my dormitory in the early afternoon of the following day. And I knew straightaway that something was terribly amiss. He huffed and puffed and for a long moment was too winded to talk coherently.

"What happened?" I asked.

"You won't see me here next January," he announced dramatically, making himself comfortable on my bed.

"You and me can't sit on the same bed," I told him as I tried to wave him to my neighbor's empty bed.

"Why?"

"That's what our white teachers say. I think they're afraid of something, you know."

He looked at me in silence for a moment or two. Then the expression on his face changed, and I knew he had experienced an epiphany, an inspirational flash of understanding. And he laughed. But still he did not budge.

"Dem dey craze," he said, lapsing into broken English momentarily.

"No pidgin, please," I told him.

"I know. Someone told me already. You're all crazy here or something."

I was getting impatient. "How did your interview go?"

"Bad! Very bad. They took my scholarship away. Something I won with my pen and my brains! They said I don't need it."

"I don't understand," I said.

"Me too!" Michael said, standing up. "Look at my clothes. My shirt, trousers, canvas shoes. The principal said my parents must be rich to be able to buy me these clothes. So I asked him what's so wonderful about them."

"You did? And—"

"He didn't answer me."

I looked him over slowly and saw nothing extraordinary about his clothes. He wore a light blue jumper, coming down halfway between waist and knees.

Spotlessly clean white trousers. And a pair of white canvas shoes. In my eyes, they did not suggest wealth. But what did I know of such matters?

"So because of your clothes you cannot come in, in January?"

"I can come, but as a fee payer. That's what they told me. I'm the one saying I won't come. I'll go instead to CKC, even if I pay fees there."

CKC, Christ the King College, in Onitsha, was the preeminent Roman Catholic high school in Eastern Nigeria, a good school but, in the judgment of every Umuahia boy, not the equal of our Government College.

"Wait a minute," I said. "I'm getting confused. Are you saying you'll go to CKC rather than come to the best college in the country if you have to pay fees?"

"Yes!"

"What will your father say about this? By the way, you know the fees here are the lowest in the east, don't you?"

"So?"

"Don't be stupid, man. I don't think your father will agree with you."

Michael suddenly remembered something else and laughed. "This is funny. There was another boy. Tall. Much taller than us. He said the principal told him he must be older than fourteen. So he failed in his interview. Is this how white people think?"

"I don't know," I said, casting my mind back twelve months. "There was a boy last year who lost his scholarship because the principal said his parents can pay his fees."

"What happened?" asked Michael. "Was it his clothes?"

"No, it was not like that. He came for his interview in a car. That's what I heard."

"His father's car?"

"I don't know, and I never asked."

"Is he here?"

"Of course, he's here. He's not stupid."

"Are you saying I'm stupid?"

"You are if you really mean what you're saying."

"You can say what you like. No one is going to take my scholarship away and think that it's okay."

I knew Michael to be a strong-headed, obstinate boy. He was very difficult to shake once he made up his mind. When he left the next day to return to Aba, his resolve not to accept admission to Umuahia as a fee payer had not diminished an iota. I was angry with him for his pig-headedness and because he and I had often talked about how wonderful it would be if we were together here. I was angry with my principal because of the total unfairness of his decision regarding Michael's scholarship. I considered it so arbitrary it almost made me cry. I was angry with myself on account of my powerlessness to undo a crying injustice. The entire episode left a bitter taste in my mouth.

*   *   *

I put Michael and his stubbornness firmly behind me when I needed to, when it came to crunch time for the end of year exams. I worked hard because I wanted to keep to my resolve to be among the best in the truncated class. In the upshot, I was not at all disappointed. And I knew then that I had it in me, with steady application to my studies, to be a force to be reckoned with, the rest of the way. The manner in which my guide and mentor Patrick Onyewuchi wrapped his arms around me in a bear hug and the softer embrace of my friend Nwobi made the third term's effort worthwhile. Cousin Samuel smiled expansively, wagged an enthusiastic finger at me, and said, "I always knew you could do it."

I could hardly wait to tell my parents in Aba about my result.

CHAPTER XV

SECOND YEAR

Very early in my second year, one of the new boys sought me out and introduced himself.

"I'm Dike," he said. "Innocent Chukwuka Dike. From Arochukwu. You are Obinna Okoye?"

I nodded. "Yes. From—"

"Oh, I know where you're from," said the lad. "But don't you have an English name?"

"You mean when I was baptized? Everybody calls me Obinna, at least in Aba. Here we're called our last names."

"But—"

"If you really want to know, it is Christopher. But you're not going to start calling me that, are you?"

"Don't worry," said Dike. "You're a class 2 boy, and I'm only a fag."

I looked him over. Dike was lanky and slightly taller than average for class 1. His skin looked like it could have used a generous dose of Vaseline. Or the more popular *ude-aku*, a lotion extracted from the palm kernel.

"I was in the Central School in your hometown, Orifite," he said, grinning toothily. "And the school owes me thanks for the great honor and distinction I brought to it."

"Meaning what exactly?"

Drawing himself to his full height and puffing out his chest, he said, "In the entire history of Government College Umuahia, I am the first pupil of your Central School to pass in the entrance exam."

"You are?"

"Yes. And in so doing, I raised the status of the Central School, and now everybody in the area knows the school."

I did not know whether to laugh or to reprimand the fresher for his audacity. But something about him warmed my heart. He carried himself straight as a rod and had large luminous eyes and a dimple on his right cheek that deepened when he smiled, which he did often enough. I briefly thought about his exaggerated claims and decided to let him enjoy his little triumph for what it was worth to him. For the moment, at any rate.

"I thank you on behalf of my town, Orifite," I told him. "How many years were you there?"

"Three. My uncle is a teacher in the school."

"Good. Welcome to Umuahia."

We shook hands as I looked steadily into his eyes. What I saw in those orbs convinced me I had not heard the last of Dike's innocuous braggadocio.

"I'm sure you will like it here," I added. "Looking at you, I can see one thing right away. You will benefit from the excellent food."

"In which house are you?" he asked.

"School House."

"So am I," he said. "That's good."

"We'll be seeing then," I said, giving the new boy my version of the "colonial" smile—the fleeting, condescending smile with which a white district officer so often received the homage of his good natives. It was my way of trying to put the fresher in his place, which was how it was supposed to be.

Chima Nwanna and a few of his classmates had done exactly that to us as class 1 boys. They were still doing so, though we were now in class 2. Nwanna stood out of course. His treatment of us had been so pernicious, he had seemed bent on destroying any meaningful relationship with any boy in my class. It was so bad, some of the boys began to talk about banding themselves together to deal with his menace. Having miraculously escaped a few ambushes, his luck finally ran out the day he walked innocently into our classroom. The class had just been severely berated by Mr. Theodore as a bunch of lazy, good-for-nothing Africans. Or words to that effect.

Particularly because we had expected more respect, now that we were in class 2, we had been more upset than we had ever been. When Nwanna chose that moment to walk into our class, several of us zeroed in on him. None bothered to ask him what he wanted. We ordered him to leave immediately but somehow omitted to leave him any avenue of escape. Nwanna stupidly compounded his problem—and he clearly saw that our attitude was belligerent—by reminding us of our lowly status in the college. And that we still stank "like cockroaches," always his preferred term of endearment.

I do not believe Nwanna knew a whole lot about what happened to him that afternoon. Only that, in the melee, he was struck upward of a hundred punches on all parts of his body, including several shin-shattering kicks. Actually no bones were broken, but that was not of much concern to us. Only after some calm was restored did we listen to Nwanna's protest that he had come to deliver a message to one of us from a housemaster. Mr. Pepple, no less!

Mr. Pepple, we mostly all knew, did not much care for Nwanna's generally defiant attitude and his lack of restraint in his conduct to the junior boys. But he took very strong exception to what we did to his messenger. He complained, as we were later officially informed, that we had "mobbed Nwanna while on official duty." And the principal had agreed with him.

For our riotous behavior, the entire class two was put on the Saturday matchet parade. But we did not mind the penalty we paid. For most of us, the satisfaction of beating up on our common foe far outstripped the severity of the punishment.

*   *   *

As I reflected on Innocent Dike and his class of thirty new boys, I felt neither the urge nor the motivation to talk meanly to them. Besides, there were one or two among them who looked strong enough to break me across their knees.

These did not include Dike. Standing about the same height as myself, there was nothing formidable about him. He looked too frail to arouse fear in even the most fainthearted among the class 2 boys. I knew if I had to, or if he ever stepped over the line with me, I could take my chances with him.

I shared the same dormitory with him: School House. School House was one of the three houses into which the school was now divided. The other two were Nile House and Niger House. Each house consisted of two dormitories. Each had its own house master. It was common knowledge that was not how Mr. Pepple would have ordered things. But no matter: that was how the principal, Mr. Graves, wanted it. And Mr. Graves was a man who, once decided on a course of action, remained unyielding to any opposing viewpoint. That was the persona he projected, and that was all we saw. Mr. Pepple, who obviously would have preferred to have remained the lord of all he surveyed, had no other option but to acquiesce.

In place of the school leaders of my first year, the principal appointed a school captain and two school prefects. Their authority, as it was when they were school leaders, cut across the houses. Below them were house prefects and subprefects, with their authority limited to their Houses. Clement Ugwu, senior school leader the previous year, was made school captain. From my perspective, he richly deserved his position. Godfrey Clarke was appointed a school prefect. Not a few of the boys thought he was luckier than he deserved. I took consolation in the fact that at least he did not supplant Ugwu as the head student. Gilbert Enuma, the third school leader, was demoted to the position of a house prefect. He had been, by consensus, the weakest of the school leaders. But he was such a good-hearted person that I almost regretted his demotion. He took his misfortune as he took most things: with little or no display of emotion.

To universal acclaim, Patrick Onyewuchi was elevated to the position of a school prefect. The heartbreaker for me was that he moved to Niger House as the head of that house. He was no longer my official guide. But I had bonded with him in a way that rendered our strictly official connection irrelevant and of no consequence.

"This is not fair," I wailed to him. "Why couldn't they leave you in School House where you were?"

"Because Godfrey Clarke is already there, I suppose."

"They should have moved him to Niger House. Didn't they hear all the complaints the boys have been making against him?"

We were in Onyewuchi's room in his new dormitory. It was a long, narrow room. His bed was set deep into the room, close to the end wall. The bedsheet was immaculately white, the blanket the usual bloodred color of the college. A four-drawer locker, a wooden chair, and a small table were the only other furniture in the room.

Onyewuchi sat on the chair by the table. I sprawled on the bed but kept my feet off the blanket and the bedsheet. I did so because my feet were covered with dust, from the fickle harmattan, which was still raging though it was late in January. The harmattan is a dry-season cold spell, with dust-laden winds blowing south into Nigeria from the Sahara. It covers everything in a film of dust. If I had a sweater, I would have brought it out. I had none, so I had to live a lie and pretend that the coolness in the air did not get to me.

"Move Clarke to Niger House?" queried Onyewuchi in a mildly irritated voice. "Okoye, you are now in class 2. You should by now be able to go on with your life without worrying too much about people like Clarke. You're no longer in the same half of the dormitory as himself. So why does it matter so much to you what he does?"

The rebuke in his voice was unmistakable. So I changed the subject.

"Who's your new fag?" I asked.

"A Calabar boy, Okon Ebong."

"He's lucky. By the way, can I still come and see you from time to time?"

"Of course," said Onyewuchi. "That's if you can spare the time."

I laughed at the idea. "Spare the time? It's you that will not have time to see me, now that you're a school prefect."

"Don't worry about that."

"Can I meet this fellow, Ebong?"

A boy walked into the room. "Did you call me?" he asked. "I thought I heard my name."

"My god!" said Onyewuchi. "You have sharp ears. I must be careful how I talk about you. Ebong, this is Okoye Junior. I was his guide last year." Then, turning to me, he added, "I don't need to introduce him, do I?"

Ebong and I shook hands, appraising each other. He had a big head. That was a feature we had in common. But in spite of that slight disproportion of head to body, he looked surprisingly athletic. His musculature gave him an appearance of power and strength. That and his compact frame. When he walked into the room, I was struck by the springiness of his step and his balance. Overall he seemed marvelously coordinated physically.

Although it was well past the games period, a time of day when the boys donned their more colorful clothes, Ebong was clad in the simple white shirt and khaki shorts supplied by the college. No canvas shoes or sandals nor even the simplest slippers adorned his feet.

"Where're you from?" I asked.

"Uyo," he replied. "But I lived with my uncle in Calabar."

"Uyo is not far from Aba, where I came from, only forty miles or so. Isn't that the place with the famous hospital, with doctors who're actually reverend fathers? I hear it is the best hospital in Eastern Nigeria. Is it true the reverend fathers do miracles there, and that no matter how sick you are, once you go there, you'll be cured?"

"Who told you that?" asked Onyewuchi. "It's just stories. But I know they have an eye specialist, and he does eye operations."

"Can you imagine that?" I asked in wonderment.

Ebong and I walked out of the room together, united in our shared bond with Onyewuchi. When I thought we were out of earshot of the room, I said to Ebong, "He's the best guide in the whole college. You'll see. I like him very much." To which Ebong replied with a nod and a pursing of his lips.

In the weeks that followed, I got to know the new boy quite well. One thing was soon apparent: he was just about the poorest student in the place. But I could not understand why. We scarcely talked about his father, whom he might have lost while still a toddler. "I don't really remember him." That was how he put it. But he also told me his uncle Bassey, his father's younger brother, was a well-to-do businessman in Calabar. Ebong talked endlessly about him. About how grateful he was to Uncle Bassey for supporting him through primary school, even though he had his own children. Ten of them or thereabouts. Which was probably why Ebong came to Umuahia virtually empty-handed and, as far as I was able to determine, with barely a change of clothing. Uncle Bassey paid Ebong's school fees: five pounds, six shillings, and eight pence. He also paid for Ebong's transportation to Umuahia. Then, presumably satisfied he had done as much as could reasonably be expected of him, bade his nephew good-bye and wished him well.

In his first term, Ebong's bedside locker was the barest I ever saw in any dormitory. He could not indulge in so simple a luxury as buying a half-penny's worth of groundnuts. Or a small bottle of palm oil to mix with his beans for that special flavor, which I knew he loved as I, too, did. He wore his hair longer and thicker than most boys did because he could not afford the cost of a haircut. And naturally, combing his hair became something of a strain. Because he was shy and retiring, he seldom made demands on his friends. It seemed he had learned, through the long experience of his penury, to do without most things other boys had. I never saw him waste money or his food. I sometimes watched him at mealtimes. And always, he ate his food with a slow and deliberate thoroughness, his orange seemingly without ever spilling one drop of its precious juice, and his banana with scant regard to its total wholesomeness.

Ebong was good with his hands. I cannot aver that he loved carpentry. I never saw him whistling or singing to himself as he worked the tools and the wood. Grim-faced and unsmiling, he evidently saw carpentry as a means to an end. He mastered the art to such good effect that in his first term, he made his own clothes box—the first he ever owned, he told me—and even produced a few extras that other boys bought from him. He constructed little boxes, with sliding lids to hold such items as pencils, pens, erasers. The boxes had sides held firmly together not by nails, but by beveling. Beveling was an art I never mastered myself. The truth was I was not much enamored of carpentry.

From almost the first moments I watched Ebong handle a cricket bat, a hockey stick, or a paddle tennis racquet, I was struck by his exceptional ability to catch on to the techniques of any game with consummate ease. The paddle tennis (popularly called *padda*) was the closest thing to lawn tennis available to us in our early years. It was played on a smaller court and with a lower net than in regular tennis. The racquet was flat, oval shaped, short handled, and wooden. The padda court was located just by the library, close to the prefects' room.

Ebong and my classmate Chidi Ebele were kindred spirits. Many were the hours they spent playing against each other on the padda court or at the ping-pong table in the lobby of the classroom block. I watched them with a mixture of admiration and not a little envy, mindful that no game, none whatsoever, came as easily to me as to my two friends.

127

But it was in cricket especially that Ebong's star quality shone at its brightest and best. Augustine Onuorah, cricket captain for the second year, Mr. Kalaga, and even the big man himself, Mr. Graves, quickly recognized Ebong's uncanny ability. Ebong never admitted to having ever played the game, only that he had seen white men play it in the Calabar area, maybe half a dozen times or so. But he had done so as one would watch an unfamiliar but eye-catching sport. And from a very respectful distance.

I had learned, myself, to appreciate the finer points of the game, though I was not as yet completely adept at playing it. And I could tell right away, as I watched Ebong's flowering, that the fundamentals of good cricket—the straight bat, judgment of the line and length of the ball, the forward and backward defensive strokes—came almost instinctively to him. He seemed, as much in attack as in defense, to have what Mr. Graves described as the ability to "read" the ball early. That is, early enough to fashion the appropriate stroke with time to spare. He therefore seldom needed to hurry his strokes.

Even in that first term of his life in Umuahia, his talent attracted bowlers. Every boy who thought he was a passable bowler wanted to bowl to Ebong in the practice nets. Few made any significant impression on him.

The story soon began to circulate that the college had finally unearthed a genius at cricket. And the full flowering of that genius was eagerly anticipated by all.

CHAPTER XVI

Mr. Kenneth Nwoke seemed ill at ease when halfway through the term, in mid-February, Mr. Graves brought him to our class and introduced him as our new history teacher. By the end of the introduction, I thought I understood from where his nervousness came. So did several of my classmates.

Simply put, Mr. Nwoke was much too fresh out of high school himself to be a teacher of any subject. Certainly not in Government College Umuahia. Or for that matter, in any of a handful of other prestigious high schools in the country, including his own secondary school, the College of Immaculate Conception, a well-regarded Roman Catholic institution in Enugu.

Mr. Nwoke had sat the Cambridge School Certificate examination only a few months earlier. At the time of his induction into the faculty of Umuahia, the results of that examination were still awaited. And to cap it all, he was not a trained, certified teacher, even of the higher elementary certificate variety.

He did not bring himself to Umuahia. We understood that. It was our revered Mr. Graves who did. Or if the appointment was made at the headquarters of the Department of Education in Enugu, the big man must have been a party to it. Else, Mr. Nwoke would not have come to Umuahia.

What our principal's motives were in bringing a relatively unformed, very young man to Umuahia as our teacher was beyond our ken. It might have been his good looks. But even as that thought obtruded itself, I rejected it. Most of the other boys also did. None of us ever knew Mr. Graves to be swayed, in his important decisions, by such a superficial consideration. Mr. Nwoke spoke good English if he was not unduly nervous or rattled. Perhaps that was the overriding factor in his favor.

He was an upstanding young man and was always attired in scrupulously clean clothes: usually a white shirt, brown khaki or gray flannel shorts that reached down just below his knees, long socks, and a pair of highly polished brown or black shoes. For him, it seemed to be an unbending article of faith to be always immaculately turned out. Even when he was the master in charge of games for the evening.

As we got to know him better, we warmed to him. We knew he strove his hardest to justify the principal's faith in him. But there was little any of us could do to help him overcome his sense of humiliation when it became known he had achieved a poor pass in the Cambridge examination. A grade 3 pass was so disappointing, he reportedly offered his resignation to Mr. Graves. But whether he actually did or not, he remained on the teaching staff. And continued to teach history to class 2.

Mr. Nwoke reached the nadir of his Umuahia experience on the day of Mr. Quincy's visit. Mr. Quincy was your typically gruff, overbearing British nemesis of the *bad* Nigerian teacher. Cambridge University-educated, like our Mr. Graves, he was also, like the latter, hunky and awe inspiring. He had a reputation for not suffering fools gladly. Unfortunately for the teachers he "inspected," none knew for sure what his definition of a "fool" was.

The moment Mr. Quincy, with our principal in tow, walked into our history class, Mr. Nwoke appeared to suffer a sudden seizure. Moments earlier, he had concluded a lesson on the Prophet Mohammed and the rise of Islam in Arabia and was at least ten minutes into the story of the Buddha.

Momentarily paralyzed by the unexpected appearance of the formidable education inspector, he soon came out of his stupor. And then he did the strangest thing. Instead of continuing with his lesson on the Buddha, Mr. Nwoke reverted to the Prophet Mohammed. In his agitated state, he stumbled frequently over his words, seemed occasionally to mumble incoherently, and repeated himself again and again. Even his semantics deserted him; he seemed to forget that Arabs were simply Arabs and not "the people of the Arabs" as he repeatedly called them.

Through it all, Mr. Quincy looked on with the aloof and condescending bearing of a man who had seen it all. From time to time, he exchanged glances with Mr. Graves. What our principal thought of Mr. Nwoke's performance, I could not tell from his vacant expression. And what Mr. Quincy would have had done had the principal not been there to, as it were, provide a protective shield for his panic-stricken protégé was a moot point. Mr. Quincy had a reputation for getting physical with any teacher of whose performance he strongly disapproved. Thankfully, he restrained himself, perhaps because he thought that, for the moment at any rate, Mr. Nwoke's discomfiture was punishment enough.

Almost to a man, the class shared the teacher's humiliation. Perhaps, if that was possible in the circumstances, more poignantly than he did himself. I saw a few boys who discretely covered their faces with their hands. As if by burying their ostrich heads in the sand, the ugly scene would simply evanesce. I looked on woodenly, afraid of moving any muscle on my face lest I gave my agony away. But there was a boy who, in the course of this unedifying spectacle, got up, cool as a pitcher of water, and impudently attempted to bring the teacher back to the subject of the Buddha. The boy with whom he shared a double desk promptly pulled him down. And thereafter, mercifully, he kept his mouth shut.

Days later, at his next history lesson, Mr. Nwoke surprised the class by tendering an unreserved apology to us.

"I knew he was visiting," he explained. "But I did not expect he would walk into my class just like that."

Even I could have told him, from my experience as a pupil in St. James School, Aba, that Mr. Quincy loved to surprise teachers. A school might know he was coming, but no teacher knew for sure if the inspector would come into his or her class. Mr. Nwoke continued, "When he walked in, I had to think very quickly. And I thought it would be easier for me to just go back to a topic with which I was familiar through having just taught it than to continue with the one I had just started. I'm glad I did. At least I felt more comfortable with the story of Islam—"

Someone in the back of the class sniggered. It was the same boy who, days earlier, had tried to embarrass the teacher by his ill-timed intervention. Sylvester Uwakwe was really a clumsy buffoon who thought he was funny. But all he achieved was often to offend the sensitivities of his classmates. Now, once again finding himself the object of collective resentment by the entire class, he quickly looked down, covering his mouth with one hand. But nothing could mitigate his insensitive and irrational conduct.

"I was not born yesterday," said Mr. Nwoke, staring long and hard at Uwakwe. "I'm new to this job, and I know you all know that. But I am learning every day, and I don't think I will ever forget what happened here last week."

"What will Mr. Quincy do to you?" a boy asked.

"I don't know. I hope the principal will put in a good word for me."

I am convinced that the encounter with Mr. Quincy significantly raised the level of empathy that the class felt for Mr. Nwoke. We saw him thenceforth less as an unqualified teacher than as a very young man who, through no conceivable fault of his own, was thrown in at the deep end. And oddly, he came through this period of his seeming humiliation reincarnated. Previously diffident, even stodgy in demeanor, and somewhat lacking in humor, he now became a lively participant in the life of the college. To the point where he was unafraid to propose that a netball match be arranged between the school and the Women's Teacher Training College, in Old Umuahia town. That was quite a novel suggestion. And it had many boys salivating at the mere thought of coming into physical contact with some scantily clad bodies of the opposite sex.

Mr. Nwoke not only proposed the idea, but he also went ahead and arranged it. I say he proposed it, but as we later learned, the idea had not originally been his. He had an aunt, one Mrs. Dorothy Ezeoke, who was a teacher in the women's college, where she doubled as the netball coach. On one of his visits to her home, she threw down the gauntlet. The story had it that he initially scoffed at the challenge but promised to talk to one of the senior masters in his college. He then spoke to Mr. Pepple who astonishingly accepted the challenge and encouraged Mr. Nwoke to clinch the arrangement.

Mr. Nwoke had only two weeks to get a hastily selected team into shape and to pass on some tips on the finer points of the game, which he gleaned from his aunt. The women were generally older than the boys, but this was of little or no consequence to the latter, who were simply raring to get close to their opponents.

On the afternoon of the match, a record crowd gathered on the makeshift grass court, close to the soccer field. A handful of the local residents, who lived on the perimeters of the college, had heard about the game and sneaked into the compound, agog with expectations.

I had surprised myself by volunteering for the team. But I was passed over as not quite tall enough. As if a mere difference of three or so inches had anything to do with a lighthearted match. Or with accuracy in shooting the ball through the nets in a girls' game that none of the boys had ever played.

The women won the match handily enough and then were entertained to an excellent meal in the dining hall and sent on their way. An hour later, Mr. Pepple summoned the entire government college team to his house. Nwobi, who was a member of the team, asked me to come along, and I did.

Mr. Pepple was furious and roundly scolded the team.

"Can anyone here explain to me," he asked, "why the women somehow managed to get the ball whenever there was a scramble for it?"

For a moment or two, no one spoke. Then, from where he and I were standing, at the back of the pack, Nwobi offered an explanation. Very injudiciously as it turned out.

"We did not want to hurt them," he said softly.

"Who said that?" demanded Mr. Pepple. "Step up so we can all see you."

Nwobi shuffled forward hesitantly, to derisive cries of "Slacker!"

"Now, repeat what you said."

"We didn't want to play too hard," said Nwobi.

Mr. Pepple regarded him for a while, pursing his lips. "I suppose you didn't. But don't tell me you didn't want to hurt them. I watched all of you, and you, Nwobi, you were one of the worst offenders."

"What did I do?" Nwobi asked, courageously but unwisely.

"What did you do? I'll tell you what you did. All of you! What you did was leave the ball and play breasts instead."

That was, I have to say, typically and flagrantly hyperbolic. If it was the same game I had watched, I saw none of the boys playing breasts.

"We did our best," suggested Nwobi but now without much conviction.

"You most certainly did not. What you did was give our college a bad name." "But, sir, I thought everybody had a good time," said Nwobi. "The crowd enjoyed the game and laughed a lot."

Nwobi should have known, but obviously did not, that he was not cut out for the role of team leadership or spokesman. He should have known, but on this occasion did not, when enough was enough. Mr. Pepple seemed indeed to be taken aback at Nwobi's unaccustomed boldness.

"The crowd laughed a lot," said the master. "But they were laughing at your collective frivolity. They were laughing at you because your antics amused them. They could see you had some difficulty distinguishing one round object from the other."

Nwobi burst out laughing, only to realize a moment or two later that he was the only one who found the situation funny. He stopped laughing, but the harm had been done. Mr. Pepple was so furious he was stumped for words for what seemed a full minute. Then he dismissed us.

"You stay back, Nwobi. I'm not through with you yet."

I waited for my friend some three hundred yards from the master's house. After about ten minutes, I saw him emerge from the house. I could not read his face, though he seemed to be smiling as he approached me. But it was not *his* type of smile. It seemed vacuous and totally unfamiliar.

"What happened?" I asked.

He shrugged in the manner of one who did not care and said, "Nothing much. He put me on the Umuahia Run."

"Umuahia Run?" I shouted. "For what?"

"As if you don't know," was all he said and walked on. I followed, a step behind, on the narrow winding dirt path.

"But that's—"

"Excessive for my offence? Tell you the truth, I really don't care."

He did not care, but I did. He was known as the Slacker, and he was certainly not one of the most fleet-footed athletes around. But he had the second most important attribute for the grueling one-mile run: stamina. Boys like him easily clocked six minutes and under for the distance, which was the required time. So he could afford to be nonchalant. Indeed, for the good athlete, the run was more like training than punishment.

It was not only the distance of the Umuahia Run that made it for me the worst punishment, but whoever designed the run (the principal or Mr. Pepple, or both) also clearly and expressly configured it to inflict pain and torture. The last section of the course, from the vicinity of the cricket oval to the Administration Block, was unrelentingly uphill.

The physical agony was not all. The middle passage brought the runner tantalizingly close to the orchard, at just about the point when dehydration might cause the runner to tarry long enough to steal and eat an orange. It was pure torture. If one tarried and took longer than six minutes to cover the course, one was in serious danger of repeating the run.

Godfrey Clarke was the first prefect to inflict the run on me for returning late from a Saturday outing to the town. He had that supercilious smirk on his well-oiled face that I had come to thoroughly detest as he pronounced my punishment. I had expected to do some grass-cutting. I even pleaded for a double dose of grass-cutting or a combination of grass-cutting and plate-washing. But Clarke was adamant.

"I have no hope," I told him, "of doing this thing in less than seven minutes."

"You know what that means, of course."

"That's why it's not fair for slow runners like me."

"You should have thought of that," he said, dismissing me with a wave of his hand.

"But how was I to know you were going to punish me in this way?"

"That's a stupid question," he retorted, his patience exhausted. "If you break a rule, you must be prepared for the consequences. No one knows his punishment before committing an offence."

The weather for the run was not at all clement. It thundered intermittently, and soon it began to rain, which turned sections of the course slushy and treacherous, conditions not calculated to help me achieve my best time. But the rules did not provide for postponement in the event of bad weather.

I did the run in the company of two other boys. At least we all started together, and I kept pace with them for about twenty yards. Then they were off like hares, and I did not see them until the completion of the course. I did it in eight minutes and waited for Clarke's Damoclean sword to descend on my head. But it did not. Though my two companions had apparently done better than I by more than one minute, Clarke, tempering justice with unaccustomed mercy, pronounced my effort satisfactory. He disdained to explain why. But I put it down to the stormy weather. And that was the end of the matter.

Or so it should have been. But when I thought I had forgotten the run and even Clarke's magnanimity, my friend and erstwhile guide, Patrick Onyewuchi, raked up the matter.

Supper was done, and I was in the library flipping through the pages of an issue of *Life* magazine when I should have been studying. I had not seen Onyewuchi approach from the direction of the prefects' room until he was right behind me.

"You know," he said, "you argue too much."

"Pardon?" I said, turning to face him.

"You like to argue," he repeated. "I was watching you and Clarke the other day when he told you your punishment would be the Umuahia Run."

The other day? That was at least a week earlier. I had not seen or spoken to him in all that time. We were no longer in the same house. And his elevated rank as a school prefect, with more responsibilities than when he was my official guide, had somewhat distanced him from me. I know I tried repeatedly to bridge the widening chasm, but he was not always available.

"You saw me arguing with Clarke?" I asked.

"You had no case, and yet just because you didn't like the punishment, you began to argue."

It was on the tip of my tongue to ask him if he had ever seen any boy who liked his punishment. But there was something in the way he was looking at me that discouraged any flippancy.

"I was only pleading with him," I said instead.

"Was that what you call pleading? If so, I wonder how you would sound if you were really arguing. Listen, Okoye. You know I've watched you since you came here, and it's not as if that was the first time I've seen you argue. I'm just telling you because it is something you need to be aware of. I know you can change. I think I was like that in my first year. But I've changed. And so can you."

CHAPTER XVII

The principal looked larger than life as he stood on the assembly hall dais flanked, in no particular order, by the masters. Except that Mr. Pepple always found a way to stand shoulder to shoulder with the big man and to lean sideways to whisper words of counsel into his ears. The boys mostly put it down to old habit, formed when Mr. Pepple was the lone housemaster in the school and was considered the principal's right-hand man and counselor in all things affecting our welfare and our discipline. But now, in my second year, there were three housemasters.

Mr. Graves cleared his throat noisily and got the attention of the assembly. "Tomorrow, Thursday, is the last day of the term and the school year. I know you are all eager to go home to your parents for the Christmas vacation and to all the festivities and masquerade shows associated with Christmas. I wish you all a merry Christmas, even as we look forward to the new year. I hope you will return with renewed vigor for the challenges ahead, especially the senior class, who will be in their Cambridge School Certificate year, the first class since the reopening of Umuahia to sit that important examination.

"I have two announcements, both good and not so good. First, the good news. The winner of the prize for the college badge competition is Silas Izuchukwu. His design is simple and captures most closely the essence of the college motto: *in unum luceant.*"

There was an enthusiastic round of applause for Izuchukwu as he stepped forward to receive his prize of three pounds. I joined in the applause, but only perfunctorily, as my mind struggled with the acute disappointment I felt. Not for myself, but for my cousin Samuel.

From the moment the principal announced the competition, about three weeks earlier, I was confident that Samuel's artistic genius would prevail over all. The principal had translated the words of the motto into English since Latin as a subject was not, at the time, taught in the college.

"In translation," he had told us, "*in unum luceant* means 'May they shine as one.' A noble and charming sentiment, with which I am sure you will all agree."

A loud voice from the rear of the assembly had asked, "But what does it really mean, the motto? To do a good design, one needs to fully understand it."

The principal, a little surprised at the question, had then launched into a long exposition and, disregarding the hilarity his words caused, even quoted from the scriptures.

"In one of the most compelling passages in the Bible, Jesus said to his disciples, 'Let your light so shine before men that they may see your good works and glorify your Father, who is in heaven'—or words to that effect. It is the goal of this institution, as it is of every school, to produce young people who will be a shining light in what they say and do to the less-fortunate members of the community." He had paused for a moment and then added, "And the light will of course shine brighter if you pull together as one."

I had given the competition a halfhearted try and given up, perhaps a little too hastily, when I saw Samuel's genius at work. His design showed three hands holding aloft three flaming torches, the collective glow from which brilliantly illuminated the firmament. It was judged by one and all as, artistically, the most harmonious in the blending of the colors and, aesthetically, the most pleasing to the senses.

Izuchukwu had little or no pretensions as an artist. As far as any of us knew, he had done nothing of note prior to the competition. His design had two torches—one white, one black—embedded respectively on contrasting dark and white backgrounds. None of the boys privy to his design—and I was one of them—gave his submission the least chance of being picked.

But Mr. Graves, whose mind was as impenetrable as a dense tropical forest, clearly chose the competition to drive home an important lesson: that simplicity can often be a great virtue. We learned our lesson, and Izuchukwu carried away the prize.

"Now for the bad news," said the principal as I struggled, in my mind, to come to terms with Izuchukwu's triumph. "As a result of the end-of-the year exams, a few boys will have to repeat their classes next year, 1946. As I believe you all know, there is no automatic promotion from one class to the next, here in this college. A notice will go up on the bulletin board in the lobby later today. I suggest you read it before you leave tomorrow on vacation."

That was it. The principal showed no emotion as he gave us the bad news. He offered no compelling reasons why the school felt the need to keep a few boys back from advancing to the next higher class with their classmates. We called it *demotion*, I suppose, because the flavor of that word accorded with the utter degradation the affected boys felt.

I did not cover myself in glory as I had done in the end-of-year examinations twelve months earlier in class 1. My father, scarcely believing his eyes as he read my report, was moved to observe that the boys who had placed above me in the order of merit "did not have two heads." He was right. Not only did they not have two heads, some of them had not even worked as hard as I had done. What went wrong, I did not know. I only knew I should have done better. The competitiveness in the class was beginning then to intensify. It was to get even more stifling as the years rolled by. But I think we were all well aware of this trend as a result, especially, of the unexpected promotions, in the middle of our first year, from our class.

My personal dissatisfaction with my performances, however, totally paled in comparison with the humiliation suffered by two of my classmates, who were denied promotion to class 3 with the rest of us. One of the two was none other than Chidi Ebele. He was devastated. And so were we, his companions from St. James School, Aba. Kofi and Friday sought me out, and together we went and spoke with him and did the best we could to commiserate with him and to share his grief. But there was only so much we could do for him.

"How can I explain this to my mother?" Chidi asked, staring vacantly into space. "Why are they doing this to me?"

That, indeed, was the question. This was Umuahia at its worst. Of course, we mostly all knew the double-edged reputation of the school, even before we sat its entrance examination. We had heard it was a very hard school. But it was universally acclaimed the primus inter pares, if not indeed the nonpareil among the secondary schools in the entire country, which was of course the reason every discerning parent wanted his son there. And which, precisely, was where the rub lay.

Umuahia picked the best pupils from the primary schools in our part of the country, literally the *crème de la crème*. It did not need the wisdom of Solomon to see that even in a class made up of the best, it was as inevitable that some boys would rise to the top as it was that others would sink to the bottom. No matter how diligently the boys worked at their books. And no matter how plain it was to see—and it was very plain to see—that every boy strove, with heart and soul, to outperform everyone else academically. In the judgment of the entire class—and we talked about little else for the longest time—there was not a single one of us who was not smart or intelligent enough to move with the rest of us into the next class and to cope with the academic demands of the new class.

The greater shock, if that was possible in the circumstance, came when we discovered that one of the boys who had suffered a fate similar to Chidi Ebele's in class 3 was the number one public enemy of my class: Chima Nwanna. I did not know whether to cry or to laugh. Though his vitriolic tongue and intemperate behavior toward us had noticeably moderated over the past year, several among us still bore him ill will for his unrelenting hostility to us in our first year. Now, in the new year, in class 3, we would catch up with him. I know I agonized, over the Christmas vacation, how I would interact with him as a classmate.

If my academic performance did not set my father's heart ablaze with pride, nor mine neither, Samuel's did. A natural for the sciences and mathematics, Samuel was consistently in the top three or four—well, maybe five—in his class.

I watched my father intently as he read our school reports. He read mine first. This was my sixth report, and Samuel's umpteenth, but the ritual scarcely ever changed. My father would summon both of us to his presence in the parlor of our house. He would, almost ceremoniously, open and spread out the reports on the dining table. His table, that is. We kids had none we could call our own.

He always read mine first. If he had anything to say to me, he invariably waited until he had read Samuel's. And then he would compare and contrast to his heart's content. He was always harder on me than on Samuel, perhaps because I was his son, and Samuel was only a nephew. And perhaps also because, in truth, Samuel's reports seldom gave him much cause for harsh words.

My father's face was aglow as he read Samuel's report. I watched, entranced, as his eyes moved ever so slowly from left to right as they scanned the lines, and his lips and mouth worked tremblingly as he struggled here and there to read the words. After a while, he looked up. At me, not to Samuel.

"This is good," he said to me. "Samuel is second, again. I don't know if it is the same person who is always above him, but this is good. What was your position? Let me see." He picked up my report, looked at it briefly, and said, "Eighth," and then looked intently at me, his eyes and face conveying a succinct message without the use of words.

Then as he continued to read Samuel's report, a strange thing happened. His face clouded over. He shook his head vigorously as if to clear it of any cobwebs in his brain. He must have read whatever it was two or three times before he handed the report to Samuel and pointed to the lower section of the sheet.

"I don't understand what your principal is saying there," he said, but in a manner of one who fully understood but wanted independent confirmation of what he had read.

I took the report from Samuel, though he seemed unwilling to hand it over, and read the principal's comments on him. Samuel was argumentative and stubborn, the report said. But that was not the worst of it. The principal ended with a direct threat of expulsion from Umuahia if Samuel did not significantly improve on his behavior in the new year.

My first thought was that this was a case of mistaken identity. That the principal's strictures were meant for me, not Samuel. My second thought was that if indeed Samuel was argumentative, that was a flaw he shared with me. I recalled the day Patrick Onyewuchi had told me bluntly that I was argumentative to a fault. And he was a pretty good judge of character.

When did a little stubbornness, I asked myself, constitute a flaw so grave that one of the best students of his class had to be put on notice of expulsion? I had no answer to my question. I doubted that anyone, except perhaps Mr. Graves himself, could have supplied the answer. Or could he, really? I understood immorality, depravity, wickedness, mendacity, or other forms of turpitude as behavior sufficiently reprehensible as to merit even the cruelest and the most unusual forms of punishment. But argumentative? What else did that word mean other than a little show of spirit or some fire in the belly?

My father was flabbergasted. He took back Samuel's report from me and read it one more time. Then he folded it carefully and put it back in its envelope.

"I have often wondered," he said sadly, shaking his head in disbelief, "if some white men put their food in their anus and not in their mouths. What your principal says here does not make sense to me. I mean, does he know Samuel? I don't like praising anyone in his presence, especially you two. Because whenever I do, your heads swell. And then if your mama asks you to pick up a broom, you think you are too big to bend over.

"But I'll tell you one thing. The man does not know this my Samuel. Perhaps our hot sun has affected his head."

He stopped for a moment and looked at me with such fixity that I became a little uncomfortable. "Are you sure," he asked, "that this was not meant for you?"

"Papa!" I shouted. "What did I do now? You are not with us in Umuahia, so how can you—"

"Listen to him!" growled my father. "I don't need to be with you in your college to know what you can or cannot do. I know that once an idea enters your head, you don't let go, no matter what anybody else says. I'm surprised I have not heard reports of anyone beating you up for arguing too much."

Samuel spoke up for me. "Why should anybody want to touch him? He's not a troublemaker. In fact, there's only one boy, a prefect, with whom he used to be constantly in trouble."

"Aha!" exclaimed my father.

I gave Samuel a dirty look. "Who asked you? Papa, this fellow is wicked. He doesn't like me and thinks just because he is a prefect, he can do what he likes."

"What's a prefect?" my father asked.

"They're senior boys appointed by the principal to take charge of the students' activities outside of the classes," said Samuel. "They can punish boys who do not behave well."

"You're a senior boy, Samuel. Are you a prefect?"

Before Samuel could respond, I laughed and said, "Him? A prefect? He's too quiet. He doesn't bother anyone, and no one bothers him. He hardly talks of anybody."

"That's why I don't understand your principal," said my father, waving Samuel's report for emphasis. "Samuel, you listen to me. Don't let this report discourage you. You're a good boy. I've passed the stage of dancing so people will give me money. What I tell you is what I know to be true. You respect people, even those who are not in authority over you. If you behave differently in your college, I don't know, perhaps because, as Obinna said, I'm not with you there. Be careful, especially of that madman, your principal. You know what they say, that a madman and his sense go together. Avoid him if you can.

"As for you Obinna, I have little to say about your report other than that it is not so bad or particularly good. Your result tells me you did not work hard enough."

"But, Papa!"

"Shut up, Obinna. Let me finish what I'm saying. You tell me Chidi and some other boys will not be promoted. I feel sure that none of them thought anything like that could happen to him. Especially Chidi. I know he used to fly, like you. What happened to him? Could it be because of his father's death? I wonder.

"What I'm saying is that you should both be alert and make sure nothing like that ever happens to you. A stubborn person doesn't need to be told when fighting has broken out. When he sees other fleeing, he will do likewise. Always be on your guard. Work hard. If you know what upsets the principal and your teachers, try to avoid doing those things. That's all I want to say."

As we turned to go away, he stopped us.

"I just remembered something. But I need your mama to be here when I talk about it. Obinna, go and call her. And even if she hasn't finished her supper, tell her it's very important."

I found my mother enjoying her after-supper tea. She liked her tea boiling hot but always took it with her spoon, blowing hard on it, before carrying the spoon to her mouth. Ndubisi and Nneka, my two younger siblings, hovered around her as they often did when she was supping. I used to do the same in hopes of handouts from whatever she was eating. But I was a college boy now and well past such childish things.

"He says I should call you," I told her.

She knew who "he" was. So she put down her teacup and spoon on a stool by her chair and went with me.

"Anything wrong?" she asked my father.

"No, nothing is wrong," he said. "You haven't seen these reports, have you?"

"No."

"There, take them and read later. But that's not why I called you. No, there's something else."

He paused, clearly for dramatic effect. He knew we were all hanging on his words.

"Have you noticed," he asked my mother, "that Samuel and Obinna have been behaving oddly for quite some time when in church?"

"When in church?" I asked, wondering what was coming.

"What have they been doing?" asked my mother. "They go to church regularly, which is good. You know how some college boys are. Just because they are in college, they think they can come and go as they like. But not these two."

"You mean you haven't noticed that they sometimes leave the church just before the sermon?"

Samuel and I rapidly looked at each other. And I knew he was thinking the same thoughts as I did. We had wondered when my parents would get around to this matter. But I kept a tight face. So did Samuel, as we waited.

"Now that you say it," said my mother, "I think yes, I knew there was something. In fact, only yesterday—"

But my father interrupted her. "I wanted to ask them, in your presence, why. So, my boys, start talking. As your mama was about to say, you did exactly the same thing at church yesterday. And that was the first Sunday of your holidays. I'm listening, but make it short because I have one or two things to say about it."

I jumped in before Samuel—always a slow starter in such situations—could get a word out. I think I did so because I wanted my father's hammer to fall on *my* head, not on Samuel's. A little chivalry on my part perhaps, but it was mostly pure reflex.

"In our chapel services in college," I explained, "there are no sermons. So we kind of got used to services without sermons, which we believe are not really necessary—"

"Hold it!" barked my father, looking sternly at Samuel. "Who's 'we'? You mean you and Samuel? And what makes you think it is for you to say what's necessary and what's not? Let Samuel talk. He's a senior boy in the college. Let him explain this thing you are both doing."

"It's like this, Papa." He had lived so long with us, he called them Papa and Mama as naturally as I did. "The principal conducts services on Sundays, and he never preaches. So our services are short."

"I see," said my dad. "You think the sermons here make the services too long for people like you?"

"Actually, whenever a pastor is invited to conduct the service, he preaches," said Samuel. "And we even have Holy Communion for those who are confirmed."

"And do you walk out from the service before he starts his sermon?" asked my mother.

I jumped in again. "That's different! He's a pastor."

"I don't understand," she said. "If you listen to his sermon, why don't you do the same here?"

"We always stay," I replied, "when the pastor preaches. But as you know, many sermons here are preached by lay readers."

"I want to make sure I understand what you're saying," said my dad. "You do not believe, I take it, that these lay readers know what they're talking about. Is that it?"

The way he was staring at us discouraged any thought, at least on my part, of responding to that last loaded question. I looked sideways at Samuel. But he would not return my look.

My father got up from his chair and came and stood close to Samuel, eyeball-to-eyeball. He was then still an inch or so taller than Samuel, who at five feet eleven inches was one of the tallest boys in the college.

"Now you listen to what I have to say. And I don't want my words to enter in one ear and exit from the other. You may be college boys, but that doesn't mean you know everything. Your principal does not preach on Sundays, and you think therefore that sermons by persons who are not pastors are useless? Is it not the same principal who wrote what he wrote about Samuel? Or are we talking about somebody else? What does he know?

"Are you two listening to me? Or am I not loud enough? You will henceforth do as I say. I didn't bring either of you up to look down on people who did not go to college or who are not pastors. If holy Pastor Brown picks the person to preach, you will stay and listen to that person—even if he is a trader. I myself have preached twice in the church. You have to understand that when a person like me climbs the pulpit, he puts himself in God's hands completely. And he speaks from the fountain of his lifelong experience and the wisdom that comes from his exposure to many things and many situations. If you listen with your heart and your head, you will get something of value from such a sermon. D'you understand what I'm telling you?"

"Yes, sir."

"Good," he said, placing his hands on both our shoulders. "I'll be watching you—"

"And so will I," my mama cut in, the expression in her eyes almost hostile in their determination.

"When you return to your college," said my dad, "you will of course do as you like. But here in Aba, it is going to be a different story. By the way, how many weeks is your holiday?"

"Five weeks," Samuel said.

"Enjoy it," said my dad, smiling expansively.

* * *

It was a joyless and barren Christmas vacation. We watched the masquerade dances and ate ourselves silly on Christmas Day. That was nothing unusual. What was, was that my friend Ben Nwobosi and his entire family traveled to their home village of Obosi and stayed put there for almost the duration of my vacation. So I did not get to see much of Adamma. And whenever I managed to see her, her mother hovered around us. Quite possibly, she was beginning to see me as some kind of a threat to her daughter's virtuousness. There were moments, indeed, when I felt flattered by that kind of attention.

And then there was Chidi Ebele, for whom the vacation was one prolonged period of agony and misery. I felt what he felt, perhaps not as poignantly, but very deeply. We talked endlessly about his situation and what he should or should not do about it.

"I can find another college," Chidi said repeatedly.

I did not want to hear anything like that. But how could I tell my friend and classmate to return to a school where we would no longer be in the same class? "What does your mother say about that?"

"My mother? Well, she doesn't quite agree with me."

"Why?" I asked, though I knew the answer.

"She thinks I'm better off in Umuahia than anywhere else. But what does she know?"

I knew the answer to my question because I had, unknown to my friend, talked with his mother. I felt no guilt about this. It was a chance encounter that gave me the opportunity that I probably would not have deliberately sought. Mrs. Ebele was walking past my father's house, carrying what looked like a heavy bag of stuff she had bought from the Ekeoha market, which was close by.

I was chatting with a friend when I saw her. I ran to her and offered to relieve her of her burden. She smiled gratefully as I took the bag from her.

"Thank you, my son," she said, patting me on the head.

I asked her the question that had been burning in my heart for several days, and I did so without prevarication. It was too convenient an opportunity to miss.

"Ma," I said, "Chidi has been saying he will not return to our college. Has he talked with you about it?"

"He has," she said. "And he's very angry."

"So am I. And so are all our friends."

"But you don't think he should look for another college?"

"No," I said without hesitation.

"That's what I've been telling him. And all he says is that I don't understand. But what do I not understand? When his father was encouraging him to do the entrance exam to Umuahia, I understood the reason. Chidi kept talking about King's College and sometimes DMGS."

"He did?" I asked, scarcely believing my ears. "I did not know this. We were in the same class, in the same school, and I never once heard him mention those schools. Did he tell you why?"

"He did not need to. His father and I knew the reason. He did not want to go to a school that is in the bush, far away from the town. Township life has spoilt him."

That might have been a consideration for me too. But I had cousin Samuel, who was some kind of a role model for me. I always looked up to him. He was an Umuahia student, and that was all I knew or wanted to know. I had felt a need to be where he was. Perhaps, also, I needed to show that what he could do I could do. He blazed the trail. I followed.

In truth, however, the Dennis Memorial Grammar School, in the big town Onitsha, had been a strong attraction for me, but for a very unusual reason. It had something to do with my burning desire, in that period of my life, for the priesthood, for which I needed—or so I had thought—a missionary school like DMGS. But that was before I went to the Government College Umuahia for an admission interview, and fell hopelessly under her spell.

"So what will Chidi do now?" I asked.

"He will return to Umuahia," she said quietly, but with such steely conviction that I knew the battle was won. "Even if he repeats one class, Umuahia is still the best. What's the hurry?"

So as our Christmas vacation drew to a close and I talked one more time with my friend, I knew he really had no other option than to return with me to Umuahia.

CHAPTER XVIII

THIRD YEAR

The atmosphere in the class at the beginning of my third year was uneasy and awkward. Chima Nwanna, our bête noire, especially in our first year, was now our classmate. When we first knew his fate, at the end of the previous year, several of my classmates had sworn that they would exact their pound of flesh from him in the new year.

But human nature is of course totally unpredictable. If I did not already know this, it was a lesson I was to learn soon enough. When my class finally had Nwanna at a terrible disadvantage as he sat in our midst, a strange thing happened. Very few of us understood what it was. Nor why we did not raise a collective fist to buffet our helpless, hapless enemy. We had no qualms, months earlier in our second year, to pounce on him and beat him almost to a pulp. And all he had done was walk uninvited into our classroom. And of course being Nwanna, he had the temerity to call us names, even as we surrounded him with malice aforethought. We paid the penalty for that day's ugly work. But we had no regrets.

The change came about gradually. For a week or so, there was silence. Clumsy, boorish, sometimes embarrassing silence. During this period, we spoke to him virtually only when he spoke to us. Some, like me, simply did not know how to react to him. The more charitable among us smiled at him politely or acknowledged his presence with a nod or some other gesture. Quite illogically, I thought he would remain the same aggressive, acerbic person I had known previously. I really had not reckoned with the possibility that his humiliation might have doused some of his fire.

Something began to stir in me. I had this strange desire—in truth, a quite irresistible urge—to talk to him. To be a little more friendly toward him. I think I began to have this urge when I noticed that my unease was his unease and that my awkwardness mirrored his awkwardness. I watched him closely and soon detected several fumbling attempts on his part to come closer to us. I knew I was no expert in such matters, but how else explain his eagerness to offer help or advice whenever he saw an opportunity? Or his oft-repeated efforts to join in the ebb and flow of ordinary conversations? When he tried this, it seemed, as often as not, to have a chilling effect on others. For my part, this was not simply due to a lingering hostility toward him. I just felt some discomfort caused by my new and daily proximity to him.

Then one day, I happened on Nwanna and Anthony Achara in quiet conversation, which, in itself, was a minor miracle to me. The last time I saw the two of them exchanging words, their fists were also flying. That was almost two years earlier, when Achara was my classmate in our first year and Nwanna, the bully, had taken serious exception to Achara's cacophonous singing.

I was soon to learn that in the interviewing period, a lot had happened to mellow their relationship. They had been classmates for a year and a term. Time enough for them, as Achara told me later, to learn to talk civilly to each other. To live and let live—or, as Achara put it, for the hawk and the dove to learn to perch on the same branch. Achara learned to turn a blind eye when Nwanna was in his most volatile mood. Nwanna, for his part, knew how to play deaf when Achara hummed or sang.

They shared one favorite subject: English. Achara was the best writer of English in their class; Nwanna was not far behind. So almost naturally, they began to develop a mutual respect for each other.

The tragedy for Nwanna, and which was the reason for his nonpromotion, was that in a stiflingly competitive environment, he was unable to maintain the same level of performance and efficiency in several of the other subjects. Not even in those subjects, especially history and literature, in which his proficiency in the language should have given him some advantage.

I saw them in the school lobby, chatting and watching two games of table tennis that were in progress. Table tennis was one of Nwanna's passions, although he achieved only a moderate success at it. He spent a lot of his leisure hours, when perhaps he should have been studying, playing ping-pong. Achara also had more than just a passing interest in the game. It was one of only two games, *padda* was the other, in which he actually knew his right from his left. He had a habit of surprising those opponents who, contemptuous of his general lack of sporting ability, underestimated him.

I walked up to them and, on an impulse, challenged Nwanna to a game. "If you win," I told him, "you can have my chicken tomorrow at lunch."

Nwanna's eyes dilated in surprise and wonder as he recognized the challenge for what it was: a big one. Chicken was every boy's favorite dish. More so, as it was served to us only once a week, on Sundays. If I did not feel confident I could beat Nwanna, I would perhaps not have risked my chicken. In reality, however, I had another motivation—in pursuit of which the potential loss of my chicken was the least of my concerns.

Those were the first kind words I think I ever spoke to Nwanna. I did what I did impulsively, taking the bull by the horns. For a brief moment, Nwanna was speechless. But I think I knew he would jump at the opportunity for a friendly interaction with an erstwhile antagonist.

"Do you mind?" he asked Achara.

"Who cares if he does?" I said before Achara could get a word out. "He'll be no competition for you."

"See who's talking," said Achara. "Have you forgotten how many times I've wiped the floor with you?"

"Wiped the floor with me? Where did you learn that expression? Anyway, you've beaten me only when I let you do so. We're friends."

Achara turned to Nwanna. "You asked me if I would mind. I don't, but on condition he'll stay and play against me after you two are done. And then we'll see who's the better player."

"That's not fair," I protested. "I might be too tired then. Why don't we leave it for another time?"

"That's the worst excuse I've ever heard," said Achara. "Boys play four or five games in a row and never get tired. If you're scared I'll beat you—"

"Me! Afraid of what? That's it. I accept."

I could see, as Achara and I engaged in this friendly banter, that Nwanna was gazing at us and doing so with a sad smile on his face. And I thought I knew what must have been going through his mind. It was easy to see that he seldom smiled these days. Every minute of every hour seemed to hang heavily on him. He had few friends. On the contrary, the story of his life in Umuahia had been virtually an unending catalog of boys he had antagonized by his thoughtless remarks and behavior. It had not seemed to bother him much who liked or hated him. Until now! I know if I were in his shoes, I would probably feel as if I was at the bottom of an abyss, one thousand feet deep, looking up at everybody and everything. He had changed. Now he was desperately looking for friends. Or if not friends, at least boys with whom he could enjoy a regular cordial relationship. He was groping, quite simply, for the warmth of a human hand.

My challenge must have touched a hidden, tender chord in him. He hesitated for a moment, then reached out, took my hand, and pumped it two or three times. "Let's play," he said. "One table is free."

And we played ping-pong as we never played before. I did not care if I won or lost. Neither, I think, did he. My chicken at lunch the next day might have been at risk if Nwanna won overall and chose to enforce the wager. But the game he and I played symbolized for me much more than a piece of meat. I was reaching out to a lonely classmate who needed a friend. Nwanna played like one who had at last found a helping hand.

It was a rambunctious merry-go-round of table tennis, and by the time we were done, I was thoroughly exhausted. The contest for supremacy between Achara and me was largely unresolved. I won as many games as I lost. Whereupon he claimed victory.

"At least," he said, "I think I've wiped the grin off your face."

I did not remember grinning—in a superior manner, that is—at him. But I was content to let the matter rest there for the time being.

"Tomorrow," I said, "is another day."

The next day, though not at *his* insistence, my chicken went to Nwanna.

*   *   *

This was the year of the introduction of what became known as the Textbook Act. Mr. Walter Graves made the announcement at the end of a morning assembly in the assembly hall. He looked, as he always did when he made his most important pronouncements, to be in a somber mood.

"Effective today," he announced, "there will be no reading of textbooks at the following times: during the games period, even if you are not down to play any game; during the afternoon rest period, which means between lunch and prep; and of course, after the lights-out bell.

"Your teachers and I are highly gratified," he told us, "by your obvious determination to do well in your studies. We know how hard many of you work at your books. We have become aware that even after lights-out, several boys find ways to continue studying. But we are concerned that boys who study all day long might be overreaching themselves.

"You may not know this. But excessive devotion to bookwork is a real danger. That is why I and your teachers are very serious about this new rule. Be warned. Any infringement will be severely dealt with."

The principal did not elaborate on the dangers to which he alluded. And no student bothered to ask the question. We did not need to. I thought I knew exactly what he had in mind. Most of the boys did too. Although there was as yet no instance of it in Umuahia, stories abounded about other colleges where some students had apparently read themselves into a state of mental paralysis. The new vocabulary, much bandied around, included "brain fag," "mental breakdown," and similar expressions. All of them dark forebodings of the dire consequences of excessive swotting.

But few cared. Because academic competition in every class remained intense, nothing the principal said or did, no punishment or fear of it, no level of vigilance by the masters or the prefects—nothing—seemed capable of diverting any of us from our primary goal: to excel in every written paper, test, or examination. The prefects themselves were mostly not above a little skullduggery in this matter. They had something other boys did not have: small private rooms they could call their own in the dormitories, where they could—and often did—study after hours, when no prying eyes could see them. Or so they thought.

I do not know how it sounds to say it myself. Perhaps a trifle immodest. But no matter. I was among the best students of my class. Having, in the last term of my first year, sworn to God, my father, and myself that I was going to be the best student I was capable of being, I worked as hard as I needed to, to achieve that aim. And after I somewhat disappointed myself—and evidently my dad too—in my second year, I was resolved never again to let a lack of effort stand in my way.

I was not among the best in every subject. With the odd exceptions here and there, that was pretty nigh impossible. Anthony Achara was one of those exceptions. Given the very high caliber of the students, it was a wonder that there could be such boys.

Mathematics bothered me. So did physics. Neither subject was what I could call my cup of tea. But I worked hard at them and eventually achieved some success in both. To the point, at least, that neither subject very adversely affected my overall placing in the terminal, or the end-of-year, order of merit.

Both subjects came quite easily to Gordon Agwuna. He was easily one of the best and brightest in the class. He was readily acknowledged by most as the best in mathematics. But he was an insufferable egotist. When six of our classmates were promoted in the middle of our first year, he was one of a small number who thought the promotions were handled with less than absolute fairness. He used innuendoes and half statements to imply that had the process been totally fair, he might have been one of the six.

Agwuna in all he did exuded arrogance. That might have been only self-confidence, but it came over as cockiness. When he helped a classmate with a mathematical problem, he always seemed to do so with condescension. There never was, or so it seemed to me, a problem in the subject that he considered beyond his ability to tackle and to solve. Always provided the problem did not have a level of difficulty clearly beyond the reach of the class.

Like an algebra test we took at the end of the second term. One of the questions proved intractable. At the end of the test, Agwuna went up to the master, Mr. U. U. Ofong.

"Sir," he said, "I think there must be something wrong with question number—"

"I beg your pardon, young man," said Mr. Ofong. "Something wrong, did you say?"

He looked Agwuna up and down briefly with what seemed like hostile eyes. But we knew better than he probably thought. We knew Agwuna was one of his favorite students, something he had demonstrated to the class time and time again. Often in not-so-subtle ways. Mr. Ofong was one of those teachers who showed fondness for those boys who excelled in their subjects. And Agwuna was the best in mathematics.

"Yes, sir," said Agwuna, standing his ground, knowing in what high regard the master held him.

"You are either more courageous than you should be, or you are a fool, young man. What question?"

"Number 5, sir."

"And what seems to be wrong with it, Agwuna?"

For just a brief moment, Agwuna faltered. But he soon recovered his poise. "Sir," he said, "I think there might be an error in the question or—"

"Or what?"

"I don't know, sir. Perhaps it is just too difficult for this class."

Something in the assured manner of the boy who stood fearlessly before him might have convinced Mr. Ofong to take a look at question 5. Then he went to the blackboard, chalk in hand, and set about putting Agwuna in his place. He worked at it for about fifteen minutes and then took a second, and more prolonged, look at the question. Frowning a little, he took out the master copy and studied it for a moment. When he looked up again, the expression on his face told us Agwuna had been on to something.

When the master recovered from his surprise, he did something I never thought I would see. He extended his right hand to our classmate, who looked at it hesitatingly for a second or two, and then grabbed it.

"You are quite right, my boy," the teacher said. "I made a slight error in copying out the question on the board."

A slight error? But it was a significant-enough error to render the question impossible of solution. Need I add that it was the highlight of the year for young Gordon Agwuna? And it won him the last lingering acknowledgment from all of us as the class mathematics supremo.

Agwuna was not an easy person to come close to. I know I tried. I tried because, despite his cockiness, there was something about him that stirred a chord in me. I could not put my finger on what it was. Perhaps that very air of cockiness, which he wore around him like a cloak, only really served to mask his vulnerability. He seemed especially not to want to be too pally with those boys whom he considered his most serious academic rivals. Kofi Bentsil and Gregory Okoroafor were prominent in that group. So was I.

Agwuna found a kindred spirit in Chima Nwanna. Opposites attract, don't they? Agwuna was tall and slender. Nwanna was short and robust. Agwuna was one of the two or three brightest in the class. Nwanna was not promoted to class 4 because he was very, very far from being one of the smartest of his class. They, however, did have one quality in common: a certain haughtiness of bearing and demeanor and a disdain for lesser human beings, which was so evident in Nwanna's attitude to my class in our first and second years. Nwanna's arrogance still showed in flashes, though he was now more mellow in his interactions with his new classmates. He could still turn up his nose at those prefects who crossed him and at those of his classmates who found it difficult to overcome their hostility to him.

Agwuna and Nwanna became fast friends. In an environment in which the boys called one another by their last names unless they were brothers or cousins and such like, the two friends called each other *dianyi* ("mate," in loose translation). They bonded so closely that an attack on one was virtually an attack on the other. When either got into trouble with a prefect, which Nwanna was more prone to, the other often became embroiled in the ensuing altercation. There were times when I was tempted to tell Agwuna that he was carrying the notion of "my brother's keeper" too far for his own good. But I always held back, minding my own business.

Since our table tennis challenge games, Nwanna and I had gotten much closer to the point where we might have been regarded as friends. But unlike Agwuna, I think I had a clearer idea of where to draw the line between the legitimate demands of friendship and a sense that each of us had to accept responsibility for his own foibles and transgressions. Only when Godfrey Clarke got into the picture did I tend occasionally to lose my objectivity.

Nwanna could have been the link between Agwuna and me. I cannot recall how hard he tried, but my relationship to Agwuna seldom went beyond the merely polite and respectful. We remained, as it were, mentally ossified on either side of our mutual friend, locked in academic rivalry, straining to get the better of each other and others every day of every week of every month. Nothing else seemed to matter to either of us. With Nwanna making only a feeble effort to help us connect, neither Agwuna nor I knew how to reach out to each other.

*   *   *

We had three adjoining farm plots and, together, worked hard to plant the seed yams given to us by the school. Nwanna's enthusiasm for this quite-serious diversion was an eye-opener for me. He had certainly not looked the type for farming. Agwuna, whose ostentatious lifestyle came pretty close to flouting the school regulations, initially gave the impression that a hoe and other farm implements were for uneducated "natives." But when we got down to it, they both tilled and planted with astonishing zeal.

Truthfully, I merely tagged along, not wishing to be categorized among the lazybones. I did not want to farm. But I went along with it nevertheless and worked with might and main to plant the seed yams and—initially, at least—to maintain my plot in a weedless condition.

Farming was a diversion for the boys in the sense that it was conceived, from beginning to end, as a relief from too much concentration on our textbooks. The principal said so in so many words.

"My aim," he told the assembled boys, "is to flesh out the principle embodied in what has become known as my Textbook Act. Yes! I hear what goes on. In prewar Umuahia, the students farmed. And had it not been for the three years the college was turned into an internment camp for Germans and other enemies of the Allied powers, there would by now have been a large acreage here under constant cultivation. If prewar Umuahia students could farm, so can you.

"But a second, and equally weighty, reason is—as I suspect you've all heard already—"

"To prevent us from swotting all the time!" a boy loudly proclaimed.

"I don't much care for that word," said Mr. Graves. "But yes. Besides, farming is an ennobling vocation—or avocation, if you understand the difference."

"We do!" said a chorus of voices.

"I'm sure you do. So there it is. Seed yams will be weighed and distributed tomorrow afternoon. Farm plots will be allocated later on the same day. And good luck to one and all. The college expects every boy to do more than just his best.

"In due course, the harvested yams will be weighed, and the college will pay each boy for anything above the weight of the seed yams supplied to him."

I was unfamiliar with the word "avocation," which sounded to me like the antithesis of "vocation." But no matter. I did more than my best, as the big man had called for. I made my ridges, planted the seed yams, and, to some extent goaded and energized by Nwanna and Agwuna, weeded my plot faithfully.

But I soon tired of the relentless effort required to keep up with the other boys. Or perhaps I expected mother earth to weigh in with her bounty and give me a good harvest. Nwanna, after a prolonged period of pushing and prodding, gave up on me. Agwuna was—well—Agwuna. In a voice dripping with sarcasm and contempt, he called me a township boy "who did not want to get his hands dirty."

My harvest was an unmitigated disaster, of course! When my harvested yams were weighed, the principal was in shock.

"What happened?" he asked me. "Your yams look very miserable."

If the man was looking for an explanation from me, I knew better than to give expression to the thoughts that flooded my mind at that instant. What happened? I could not admit to my principal that I had been lazy, extremely remiss, indolent, or whatever other damning adjectives fitted my case. I had not wanted to farm in the first place and had realized, too late, that it had not been intended to be a compulsory activity. The principal had said, on the day he launched the program, that the college expected all the boys to do their best—or words to that effect. And I thought that meant only one thing.

"What were you thinking?" The principal's voice cut in on my reverie.

"Nothing, sir. I did my best."

"That's your best? I never heard of a farmer who harvested less than he put into the soil unless there was a natural disaster or something."

"I'm surprised too," I said.

"You realize you actually owe the college as a result of your negative harvest?"

I uttered the first words that came to my mind. "I don't mind paying, sir—"

He laughed out loud, looking at me as if I had gone crazy. "You! Pay the college? How d'you intend to do that? Write to your father for the money? In any case, even if you could, the college does not want your money. We are not in this for profit. All you have to do is try harder next time."

"Next time, sir? But I thought—"

"For you and others like you, if any, it is compulsory. I want you to try again next year. Look to it, my boy, that there'll be no more excuses."

I had no excuses. Only shame at my performance. A sense of shame made all the more acute when I watched the likes of Nwanna collecting rich rewards from their honest endeavors. Agwuna collected too; he who, by the logic of being born and bred in the city of Enugu, should have been an infinitely more indolent farmer than I was.

He and Nwanna happily backslapped each other, effusive in their mutual congratulations. I was happy for them too as we huddled at the assembly hall end of the long balcony running the entire length of the Administration Block. There was a short line of students waiting their turn to have their yams weighed, every one of them looking confident they would come out on the plus side of the ledger.

"It's not fair," I said. "I think I worked just as hard as some—"

Their laughter stopped me. Then Agwuna said, "You don't really believe what you're saying, do you? The whole thing is your fault. How many times did we ask you to go with us to work on our farms, and you found some reason not to go? How many times?"

"Dianyi," Nwanna said to Agwuna, putting an arm consolingly around my shoulders, "please don't be too hard on him. Okoye, we are congratulating ourselves not to make you feel bad, but because if we don't, do you see anybody else congratulating us? You know what the lizard said when it fell from the top of a tall tree and happily scampered off, bobbing its head?"

"I don't," I said.

"Well, it said if no one else will praise it for surviving that fall, it will praise itself."

"You didn't fall from any tree."

"You just don't understand," Nwanna said. "It's merely a saying of our people. But what does a township boy like you know about Ibo proverbs?"

"But you said it in English," I observed.

"Oh, don't be silly. Don't you know that's because we're not allowed to speak Ibo here in the college?"

Only a year earlier, he might have said the very same words with biting sarcasm and a contemptuous nod of his big head. But Nwanna was no longer the acerbic Nwanna of old. Somehow, now he spoke almost gently and in a jocular manner, taking the bite out of his words.

"Isn't that your friend Ebong, there in the line?" Agwuna suddenly asked.

I looked and indeed saw Ebong in the queue, even as I wondered how Agwuna knew that we were friends. Our eyes met, and Ebong waved to me. As always, though it was a Saturday afternoon, when boys were free—within limits, of course—to wear what they chose, Ebong was attired in the regular school uniform of an off-white shirt tucked into khaki shorts. His feet—glory be—were now shod in sandals, which he could afford only by the sweat of his brow.

Ebong's harvest was just about the most bountiful of all. As I watched him inching forward in the line, I knew he was going to collect big. And he—who, perhaps more than any other boy in the school, had the best reasons to toot his own horns on account of his industry—looked extremely bashful as he patiently awaited his turn. Evidently, he had never heard the tale of the lizard that fell from the heights and lived to tell the story—and to praise itself.

Ebong still needed all the money he could garner by his own endeavors. His rich uncle, who lived in Calabar, had not significantly raised his pocket allowance, which therefore remained, to my knowledge, the most niggardly in the school. It was no wonder that he did his farming as he did everything to which he put his hand: with a single-minded determination to be the best in the college.

*   *   *

My third year was a year of sharp contrasts. My disastrous efforts at farming saw me plumbing the lowest depths. Academically, it was my *annus mirabilis*, the year I soared to the loftiest heights it was possible to attain in the class, which was very satisfying and all that. But as with my cousin Samuel the previous year, Mr. Walter Graves injected a caveat into my school report that cast a dark cloud over everything.

"Obinna Okoye," the principal wrote in the year's final report, "is too high-spirited. He has a natural inclination to disobey and to argue. He needs to curb these tendencies."

He might have added, as he did in Samuel's class 4 report, that if I did not improve, I would risk expulsion from the college. But he really did not need to. That risk was implicit in the tone of the comment. I had no dictionary in my father's house to look up the word "curb." But I think I knew what it signified.

"You must have done something," my father said, "to make your principal give you such a bad report. Or is it that he just plain hates the two of you?"

Neither Samuel nor I could answer that question to my dad's satisfaction. However long and hard I reflected on the past year, I could not recall any major incident that seriously merited the principal's strictures. I had a few passages with some of the school and house prefects, but even Godfrey Clarke had not been as difficult as in my first or second year. Once I had snuck out of the dormitory in the dead of night, accompanied by a friend who was not a classmate and armed with two candles. We had headed for a small quite obscure room in a part of the Administration Block where, we thought, we could study without fear of discovery. But Clarke, who seemed to have an uncanny nose for such shenanigans by the boys, surprised us. Strangely, he chose not to punish us himself. Instead, he said he would report us to the housemaster. If he did, nothing came of it. And as far as I knew, the principal did not hear about it. Or he would have summoned us to his office, perhaps for his "six of the best."

That had been, by far, the most serious breach of discipline by me throughout the year. But I did not think it merited the gravity of the principal's remarks on my conduct. It could be, I finally reflected, that the cumulative effect of all my conflicts with those in authority over me, however minor when taken singly, must have been too much for Mr. Graves to overlook.

A natural inclination to disobey? Patrick Onyewuchi had accused me of being argumentative. But were the two flaws one and the same thing? Onyewuchi was a pretty good judge of character. And if so objective a friend thought I argued more than I should have, there was nothing more to be said. He never, however, said anything about disobedience.

Samuel's end-of-year report made no further allusion to his stubbornness. In any case, he had been, like others of his class, mostly occupied by the challenge of the Senior Cambridge School Certificate examination, which the class 5 boys sat toward the end of the year. The results were expected by March or April of the following year. This was the first school certificate examination of the post-World War II Umuahia.

Samuel's class was quite nervous about the examination. That was plain to see. The rest of us were nervous also. For them, as well as for us. Much was expected of them in this first test of the academic excellence of Umuahia. We looked to them to help reestablish the preeminence of our college among the high schools of Eastern Nigeria. It was not an unreasonable expectation, notwithstanding that there were several quality schools in competition with ours.

CHAPTER XIX

FOURTH YEAR

A new year, 1947. A new class. It started with a shocker, which should not really have been one. Chima Nwanna did not return for the new year. But we knew he would not. In the last days before the end of the previous year, the class had been shaken when we heard he had been expelled from the college. Probably the only boy who had received the news with anything approaching equanimity was Nwanna himself.

No, it should not have been a jolting surprise. But when we reassembled in our new class and Nwanna was—conspicuously—not among us, many of us relived the shock of his expulsion.

Nwanna had been something of a stormy petrel in his earlier years. And even after his ego had been considerably deflated by his nonpromotion from class 3 to 4, he had retained some of his defiant, refractory spirit. But he had become somewhat chastened in his last year and had taken his disgrace with as much fortitude and good grace as could reasonably be expected.

The bristling hostility some of us had felt toward him, which had been still evident when we first found him among us as a classmate, had mostly dissipated by the year's end. Now there seemed no good reason, no logic in his expulsion. We saw him only as a victim of an excessively stringent and unsympathetic authority. The overwhelming feeling was of anger and frustration. Nwanna had placed in the bottom third of the class in the order of merit. But he had placed above four or five boys. And only one boy—the last in the order—had been denied promotion to class 4. It seemed to us as if our principal was determined that the school should earn its reputation—a reputation for toughness in matters of conduct and, of course, for academic excellence. An institution that would heedlessly weed out a student for the reason of a little show of spirit.

We asked ourselves, what other school would have expelled a Chima Nwanna? And we thought we knew the answer to that question.

On the penultimate day of his last term in Umuahia, Nwanna had invited Agwuna and me for a stroll. We walked down the dust road, lined by the evergreen whistling pine trees, which led to the hockey and the soccer fields. We walked as we always did, with Nwanna in the middle, between Agwuna and me. We were his friends, but we were not friends. We simply seemed incapable of any emotional connection, either of serious antagonism or of friendliness.

"I want," Nwanna said, "to tell my story to you two because I feel closest to you in the class."

We talked as we walked. Nwanna spoke in a strong, steady voice, with little or no display of emotion. Agwuna tried to be strong. But his voice, on occasion, was tremulous. I cannot recall how I sounded. By nature, however, I think I was the most emotional of us three.

"The principal summoned me to his office yesterday. And straightaway, I knew it would not be good news."

"You knew?" I asked. "You mean you expected this?"

"Yes and no. Depends how you look at the situation. I kind of suspected the big man would seize any opportunity to expel me, and yet I kept hoping he would not. Maybe 'hoping' is the wrong word. You see, things reached a stage where I didn't care anymore. I was ready for anything. Agwuna knows what I mean."

I looked across at Agwuna. "What does he mean?" I asked, feeling like one who had been left out from our mutual friend's confidence.

Agwuna wore his maddeningly supercilious face. "You were so busy swotting," he said. "You did not see what was going on around you."

"Now that's not fair," protested Nwanna.

By this time, we had reached the hockey field and made ourselves as comfortable as we could, sitting on the edge of the embankment bordering the field.

"What's not fair?" Agwuna asked.

"You knew only because I told you. Don't talk as if you don't know you're as much a swot as he is. I think you are even worse than Okoye."

"Thank you, Nwanna," I said. "As always, you tell it as you see it." Nwanna picked up a dry twig and idly broke it into many pieces. And as he spoke, he threw the pieces, one at a time, in different directions.

"I walked into the principal's office," he said. "And he actually rose from his seat as if he meant to come forward from behind his big mahogany desk to receive me. Anyway, he didn't. But he offered me a chair. I was just beginning to wonder what I had done to merit such respect from Mr. Graves when he hit

---

me with the . . . er . . . news. He wasted no time or emotion. He said what he said in the fewest words possible in the circumstances."

"What did he say?" Agwuna asked.

"Just like that?" I asked in the same breath.

"I'll never forget what he said, I don't think. He looked me directly in the eye and then said, 'Nwanna, I'm afraid you will have to go.'"

Nwanna stopped and stared straight ahead of him. Out of the corner of my eye, I watched him. Momentarily, he appeared to struggle with himself. I could not quite read the expression in his eyes, which—notwithstanding his earlier, perhaps pretended, nonchalance—seemed a trifle worried. I remained silent, letting him take his time. Agwuna too seemed to recognize the poignancy of the moment and kept his thoughts to himself.

Nwanna picked up another long twig and began to break it into many pieces. "I asked the principal, 'Why, what did I do?' And you know what he said? He told me I would have to go because he was sure I would do better in another college. He said he knew I'd had a pretty difficult time in Umuahia. That I had never properly adjusted to the place. That he was concerned about the example to other boys. I told him I didn't know what that meant and could he please explain."

"You said what?" I asked.

"You know me, or should, by now. The man had just told me he was expelling me from the college. I felt I could talk quite freely and that nothing I said or did—nothing—would make him change his decision. He laughed when I asked him to explain. Then he said I was much too independent, too spirited for the college—or words to that effect. That I was always questioning authority, and *that* was quite simply unacceptable. I asked him if my performance in class and in the exam had anything to do with my expulsion. He told me that, well, yes, it had, even though I wasn't the worst in the class."

Nwanna paused, giving vent to a long sigh, as if of relief. Again, I watched him narrowly, but no longer out of the corner of an eye. I faced him directly because some of the things he had just told us struck home, as if they were directed at me. And the critical words that buried themselves, like shafts, deep into my consciousness were the same words the same principal had written in my report: "too spirited." It was all very disconcerting.

Of a sudden, Nwanna stood up, took hold of several pieces of the twig, and hurled them all, with one gigantic effort, as far as he could. Then he looked at Agwuna and me, in turns. And there was madness in his eyes.

"It was then that I told the man I didn't gave a hoot and that he could do his worst. And you know what? I felt good saying those words to him. Oh yes! It felt sooo goooooood!" He made a fist and then relaxed it.

I could scarcely believe my ears. I could not see myself, whatever the provocation or however desperate my circumstance, having the temerity to speak to Mr. Graves with such abandon. But Nwanna was Nwanna. He had, latterly, been looking rather like a gem to some of his classmates—that is, to those of us who liked our gems cut rough. He was no longer the enemy.

"I was—and Agwuna knows this—not totally taken unawares by all of this. People who don't know me think I'm stupid or something. For the past several months, almost the entire year in fact, I've been preparing myself quite carefully. You must have seen me studying harder than I've ever done before. If you did, you must have wondered why I didn't do significantly better in the exam.

"The reason is this. All through the year, I've concentrated on class 4 work. That's what I said. Class 4 work."

He had seen the disbelief in my eyes and shook his head slowly, with a smile. A smile of intense satisfaction. A smile that lit up his face as I had seldom seen it lit up.

"Class 4 work?" I asked. I was not sure I had heard right. I looked across at Agwuna, but he kept a strictly—and studiedly—impassive face. He had known all along, or at least for a long time, what Nwanna was up to.

"Yes, class 4 work. What did I need class 3 work for? That was what I did last year, no? My plan, which worked out quite well, was to borrow notes from one or two of my friends in class 4—including their prep work. I studied the textbooks they studied. And I did all that for one important reason. If I was to be expelled from Umuahia, I was determined to sit the school certificate exam in the same year as my former classmates. There!"

"Excuse me," I said, hoping that my increasing disbelief showed in the way I was looking at him. "You just said you plan to sit the Cambridge exam—or is that not what you're talking about?—one year before *our* class. Where d'you plan to do this? At home, in your father's house?"

"It's been done before, or haven't you heard of some Nigerians who've done it? But that's not what I have in mind. And please wipe that smile from your face. There are many other colleges one could go to. Umuahia is not the only—"

"Nobody says it is," I interrupted. "But after Umuahia, you'll surely not want to descend to any of those dreadful colleges like they have in Onitsha—you know the ones, don't you?"

"I do. I'll try the good ones, like DMGS or perhaps the Methodist College in Uzuakoli. I'm not a Catholic, so it'll probably be pointless trying CKC."

"Besides," added Agwuna, "you're not a football player."

I knew to what he alluded. CKC (Christ the King College in Onitsha) seemed to place such a high premium on its soccer reputation that it was generally believed to favor, in its admission practice, if not policy, those boys whose skills were highly rated in the game. I did not like to judge other colleges. I only knew that mine—for all my ranting and grumbling—was the best that there was. I also knew that CKC was (with its sister college in Enugu, the College of Immaculate Conception) the best soccer school in Eastern Nigeria.

"And if the good ones don't admit you?" I asked.

For a fleeting moment, Nwanna's face clouded over. It was as if he suddenly saw his predicament starkly, in all its negative ramifications.

"Why," he said slowly, uncertainly, "I'll try the not-so-good ones. I'll find a college, most likely in Onitsha, and do the best I can. But I'm absolutely determined to show Mr. Graves!"

The next day, we said our final good-byes. But not before we hugged and held each other in a long, quite emotional farewell. And as we parted, he held up an arm, pointing a finger for emphasis, and said, "Remember what I told you yesterday. I'll show Mr. Graves!"

"I'm sure you will," I muttered to myself as he clambered onto the mammy wagon that would take him to Umuahia town on the first leg of his journey to his hometown or village. Wherever that was.

That was the last time I set eyes on Chima Nwanna. Or heard from him. To this day.

*   *   *

But I heard quite a bit about him. From Agwuna, who had maintained some contact with him during the vacation. Now on the very first day of the new school year, Agwuna and I talked about him. It felt strange not having Nwanna as a buffer between us. But I got over that feeling. There were other boys huddled with us in the library: Anthony Achara, Joseph Nwobi, Gregory Okoroafor, and one or two others.

"He told me before I left Enugu," Agwuna told us, "that the New Samaritan College in Onitsha admitted him to their Cambridge class. So things are working out well for him, as he had hoped."

"I know one thing for sure," I said. "If he does well in the Cambridge exam—in fact, if he passes at all, even in grade 3—it will be, for me, the outstanding performance in this year's exam. And you know why, don't you?"

"No!" said a chorus of voices, but not Achara's.

"Because Nwanna would have proved the big man wrong?" Achara offered, looking at me, seeking agreement.

I nodded and said, "Think of it. Nwanna was expelled, not only for his behavior, but because the big man judged him weak academically. In Nwanna's mind, it must be that Mr. Graves does not expect him to pass in the exam.

And we all know Cambridge is the exam by which all things are judged. So if Nwanna actually sits the exam this year, one year before our class does, and if he passes, his case would be the most conclusive proof that no boy should be expelled from Umuahia for academic reasons. Or even detained in any class."

"Maybe the college expects all of us to pass in grade 1," suggested Agwuna.

"If that's what they expect," said Okoroafor, "then they might as well expel as many as ten boys from each class before they reach the Cambridge class."

"Which is quite out of the question, of course," said Achara.

"Then they should leave us alone!" I said, with feeling.

My friend Nwobi—who had listened, mum as an oyster, to all this—now launched into an animated discourse. "I'm one of those who believe that Nwanna is deeper than he looks and sometimes acts," he said. "I believe he can do it. For one thing, he'll do well in English, as you all know. And that's the one subject that's responsible for the high number of failures in colleges like New Samaritan and some others in Onitsha. And after the drilling he got here in math and science, he should be more than all right in those subjects. Nwanna is a very determined person. If you dare tell him he can't do something, he takes it as a challenge."

He paused, looked around us to ensure that no unwelcome ears were listening, and then lowered his voice to speak in Igbo, in flagrant disregard of a golden college regulation: "You know what our people say. *Onye kwe, chi ya ekwe.*"

"I'm afraid Okoye does not understand what you just said," said Agwuna, intentionally needling me.

He succeeded, but I bit down on my lower lip to hold my feelings in check. "I know what it means," I said. "It is one of my father's favorite sayings. Doesn't it mean that if you are positive, your chi or guardian spirit will also be positive, and you will then succeed?"

I looked around me with pride, happy to have wiped the superior grin off my rival's face. Nwobi nodded appreciatively and continued, "No, I have no fears for Nwanna. In due course, it will be interesting to compare his result with ours. It's just nine or ten months to go for my class, and I wonder if I'll ever be quite ready for the exam."

"Me too," said Achara. "I get nervous just thinking about it."

"Oh please," said Okoroafor, "don't be so modest. We all know that you can sleepwalk through the Cambridge exam and still come out with flying colors."

"Spoken like the true Silas Marner," said Agwuna, who could never resist an opportunity to tease. "You'd better not sleepwalk through this year, or you'll find yourself near the bottom of the class."

"Who're you calling Silas Marner?"

Okoroafor was angry. He did not like being called Silas Marner, though he knew there was nothing he could do to stop anyone taunting him with that name.

The nickname came about because, for one brief moment, Okoroafor dozed off (or perhaps only daydreamed) while the class was reading George Eliot's *Silas Marner*. Though he flew into a rage the first time he was called Silas Marner, the name stuck. In time, he knew it was futile to protest. Another boy was nicknamed Captain Bligh because, just once, he broke wind rather loudly while the class read the great sea novel *Mutiny on the Bounty*. The redoubtable sea captain was of course never recorded as having broken wind. Only that he "*messed* on the lower deck" or "messed regularly" with the ship's surgeon. And in the Nigerian lingo of the time—and to this day—to mess is to break wind.

"What's the matter with you, my friend?" asked Agwuna. "I didn't give you the name. If you don't like the name, then try not to fall into a trance whenever we're doing history. We know you don't like history."

"So how about it?" Okoroafor asked, still a little miffed.

"What did you just say?" asked a voice from behind me. "*How* about it?"

I recognized the strange, cultured voice and spun round. The Yorubaman stood not quite three feet from me, arms akimbo, with a quizzical expression on his face. "*How* about it?" he repeated.

"Oh, sorry, sir. I should have said, '*What* about it'?"

"That's better," said the Yorubaman, his gaze taking in the entire group. "Achara! Nwobi! I'm disappointed. You're both in class 5 and should have immediately corrected him."

"Yes, sir," said Achara as if he meant it. "I was just about to do so when you came. Actually, sir, for a boy who went to school in his village, Mbawsi, he's not so bad."

Even Okoroafor recognized the banter in Achara's voice and took no offense.

"Now now," said the Yorubaman, "you mustn't tease. But I see your remark was well taken. That's good."

CHAPTER XX

We called him the Yorubaman almost from the day he joined the staff of the college. Mr. Bisi Babatunde (BA in history from London University and BA in English from Cambridge University) arrived in Umuahia about halfway through the last term of the previous year, 1946. The principal made a great to-do about his coming to our college, announcing with pride—before the man's arrival—that we were extremely fortunate to be bringing to Umuahia one of the best educated Nigerians. He had graduated, Mr. Graves proclaimed, second class, upper division. In both subjects, I think the principal said.

We called him the Yorubaman because that was what he was. It was a singular honor, that sobriquet. And an affectionate one too. But to this day, it puzzles me why he was so singled out. We had two Efik masters, but neither was called the Efikman. None of our Ijaw teachers was known as the Ijawman or perhaps the Saltwaterman. No other master was given a fond nickname so directly linked to his ethnic group. In calling Mr. Babatunde the Yorubaman, I know there was no malice aforethought. No deliberate intent to hurt feelings. And certainly, no conscious or subconscious tribalism (that hated word!) at play.

He got to know about his sobriquet inevitably. But so far from taking offense, he seemed indeed to enjoy it and sometimes actually used the name, in the third person so to say, to draw attention to what he needed done by the class. "So says the Yorubaman," he would say after giving us his instructions. When he did that, he seemed to be giving his instructions added emphasis.

He stood out from the other staff, and not only the Nigerian staff, by what we chose to see as his superior academic credentials. As far as I knew, he was the only master with a "double-barreled" degree, one-half of which he had earned from one of the two or three most hallowed groves of academe. About five feet ten or eleven inches tall, he had the jet-black complexion so typical of the quintessential Yoruba and a nervous habit of "brushing" back a very close-cropped hair with his left hand. I sometimes wondered where he picked up that habit. Perhaps in England?

He was an excellent teacher of the English language and literature. Hardworking too. And infinitely more amiable than Mr. James Theodore, he of the love and hatred taps (the unloved cracking of a hard ruler across the palms and the bare knuckles of his victims). Mr. Babatunde came to Umuahia as a successor to Mr. Theodore. The latter had left the college soon after the principal got wind of a conspiracy among the boys to waylay and beat him up.

I was not involved in the conspiracy. Never having once received his "tap," though I suffered vicariously with those who did, my personal feelings toward Mr. Theodore were, at worst, indifferent. But I heard about the conspiracy, and I suppose I did not disapprove of it. I was not sure what exactly drove the conspirators to their dark and desperate design since they never gave it utterance. I know I had become sick of the man's constant refrain about our collective "African stupidity." A sentiment to which, I suspected, the principal's attention must have been drawn, but which Mr. Theodore continued to mouth with astonishing impunity. Perhaps, too, some of the senior boys might have had more than their fill of the master's ruler crashing down on their knuckles.

Mr. Theodore, when he taught in King's College, Lagos, had once been beaten up by the students there. Two students, to be precise. They had cornered their man, the story went, in the dark of the night, in an unlit area of the college grounds. Then with their bare hands, they had mauled him badly. And he never found out which boys had done the foul deed.

The Umuahia conspirators swore to duplicate what the Lagos boys had done. The story we pieced together afterward was that they wanted to so work him over that he would never want to see an African face again. The ringleader of the group was one Ochea Okochi, a boy known to be fiercely proud of the warlike qualities of his Ohafia people. He never tired of bragging about it. He told his group, apparently, that he would prefer to deal with Mr. Theodore single-handedly. But he was no fool. He might need two or three of the group, he said, to stay close, lurking behind trees, should their prey prove to be more resourceful in self-defense than seemed likely. Europeans, he said, were sometimes tougher than they looked and could bring to a single-handed combat knowledge of the martial arts about which we Nigerians were mostly ignorant.

A fifth columnist might have passed the word to the college authorities. The principal did not wait to see if the boys would carry out their threat. Quickly and quietly, he sent word to the regional head office of the department of education in Enugu. The next day, Mr. Theodore reported to Enugu. A few days later, he was reportedly seen in Lagos. The story we heard, and which might have been deliberately fed to us, was that our English teacher took an emergency leave of absence, from which he would probably not return. He did not return. I cannot vouch for some of the details I have recounted here. But I have a strong sense—many of us did—that Mr. Theodore was sent home to England because it was in the interest of his physical health.

It certainly proved to be in the interest of the collective mental well-being of the students. Taken solely by itself, Mr. Theodore's departure was spiritually uplifting. Mr. Babatunde's arrival made it doubly so. Not only did it seem unlikely that the Yorubaman would ever denigrate the intelligence of his fellow Africans, he had no use for harsh methods in any of the forms so routinely favored by his predecessor, the little Englishman Mr. Theodore. He cracked no student's knuckles. He did not deduct marks for every little error we committed in our English papers and tests and then charge the negative score, if there was one, against the student's next paper. He was not as sadistically stingy with his marks when he graded our written work as Mr. Theodore was. In a word, the Yorubaman was—well, normal. He was also generous. Within a month of his arrival, he was so favorably impressed by the standard and the quality of the work done by the students in English that he openly acknowledged the efficacy of Mr. Theodore's approach.

His approach, as we soon discovered, was to listen to the boys. He listened and took note of the things we said in our everyday communication among ourselves and with our teachers. And the way we phrased what we said. In English, of course. Then he began to compile a list of the more common errors of grammar and our use—or abuse—of English phrases and expressions. And he then wrote the list on a part of a blackboard that he permanently set aside for that purpose in one of the classrooms.

TABOOS: Words and Expressions to Avoid

That was his label for the list. The list grew until he thought there were no more to be added. And perhaps no more space to accommodate additional offending words and phrases. As I write this, my memory on this matter lapses. But I recall that one of the things that most got his goat, because it was much favored by the boys, was our use of the word "with." We would commonly say, for example, "I am with the book" when we should have said, "I have the book." He discouraged, but did not ban, the use of "due to." He told us that the jury of eminent grammarians was still out on that issue. But in many instances where we used the phrase, we would have been more correct to say "owing to" or "because of." He hated to hear us say, as we so often did, "so therefore" or "supposing if." He condemned their use as ugly and rather tautological.

We had fun trying to avoid the taboo words. And we mocked mercilessly those boys who constantly trod on Mr. Babatunde's grammatical minefield. But I can say, I think correctly, that the taboo list did us a world of good.

There was no trace, in our ears, of the heavy Yoruba accent in Mr. Babatunde's diction. He neither spoke, nor did he seem to attempt to speak like an Englishman, notwithstanding that he went to Cambridge. He spoke rather softly, had a ready vocabulary, and probably the clearest and best articulation of any teacher in the college, white or black. He taught English as only an excellent African teacher could teach an African class. He understood our difficulties because—in modern parlance—he'd been there, done it. And having studied the finer points of the language at the most distinguished institution, bar none, in His Majesty's realm (sorry, Oxford!), he came to us with the best possible qualifications.

He had two strings to his bow. But if I had to pass judgment on the relative strengths of those two strings, I would say that English came first, history second. Not by a wide margin though. I think he enjoyed the challenge of teaching us a foreign language, with all its imponderables. English was not, never has been, a cut-and-dried subject, possibly with the exception of its grammatical rules. But style, the manner in which we struggled to express our ideas in writing and in speech, what someone once described as "the dress of thoughts," *that* was the challenge. And he rose to it. Else, he would not have bothered with his *taboos*.

History, or at least the way we took it on, in my high school years was, by contrast, more factual than otherwise. About the only challenge there, other than the effort to master the facts, was when an examiner might make a statement relating to an event and then say, "Discuss."

During his two or so years in Umuahia, the Yorubaman taught only aspects of the history of the British Empire and, inevitably, of the West African slave trade. Williamson's *History of the British Empire* was his bible. We read the book or, perhaps I should say, he read it to us, like a set book in literature. He lamented the fact that very little had been written about what he termed "the real history of Africa," particularly as it concerned West Africa and Nigeria. Other than the ancient history of Egypt and the relatively more recent and glorious stories of the three noted Sudanese empires of Mali, Ghana, and Songhai, it almost seemed, he would say, as if our people had no history at all. He promised us he would, one day, do something to help fill that yawning and regrettable lacuna.

* * *

One day, I found Achara in the library, after supper, swotting. It was that time of day when we were fancy-free in our attire and in what we did to occupy ourselves. Quite unusually for him, Achara sported a brightly colored jumper with floral designs, over a pair of off-white trousers. I believe it was the first time I ever saw him in trousers. But he was now in his Cambridge School Certificate year. A very senior boy. And a school prefect to boot. He had to look the part, I suppose.

I took the chair next to him, dropping my pile of books on the table.

"How is it going?" I asked for openers.

He knew it was me but pretended to be so absorbed in his work that he had not noticed my approach. Now he looked up and regarded me with eyes that he tried to make hostile, but failed. Then he smiled.

"How is what going?" Which was exactly the reaction I had expected. So I played along.

"Studying for the Cambridge man," I said. That was a new expression, "the Cambridge man," which had crept into the vocabulary of the students, particularly in the class scheduled to sit the examination at the end of the year.

"It's not going at all," Achara said, frowning.

"You're very funny, you know. The exam is—let me see, this is the middle of February—at least eight, nine months away. And you're worried. If you ask me—"

"I didn't."

"If you ask me," I persisted, "I predict you'll achieve the best result in the whole of Nigeria. Mark my words. The Yorubaman says you are the best in English. I'm sure he meant the best he has taught anywhere, though he didn't say it quite that way. I also know you're the best or just about the best in your class in math, history, chemistry, and perhaps geography. So!"

"Did you come here to study or what?" Achara asked.

"Okay, I'll stop bothering you. But I don't like to see you looking worried about Cambridge. It might affect me too, your nervousness, when my turn comes next year. You know what nervousness can do to a person."

"I know what it did to me once," said Achara. "I didn't tell you about our geometry paper last December, did I? Just as we were about to enter the exam room, one boy came to me with a problem that had been bothering him. I looked at the problem and advised him to drop a median from the vertex of the triangle to the base. Then we walked into the room. Can you believe the same question appeared on the exam paper?"

"What happened?" I asked as he paused for a moment.

He shook his head sadly and for a long while just stared vacantly at me. I stared back.

"You won't believe this," he finally said. "It's something I still don't understand. What happened? Simple. I forgot whether I was supposed to drop a median or a perpendicular to the base of the triangle. I became extremely nervous."

"So what did you do?"

"I knew I had to drop something. So I calmed down and drew a line from the vertex to base but did not identify the line. I did the best calculation I could manage and put QED at the end."

"How badly did it affect your score in the paper?"

"It didn't. I scored 97 percent. And you know what? I didn't lose the three points on that particular question."

"The teacher—that's Ufong, isn't it?—must have made a mistake in totaling your score," I said.

"He made a mistake, all right," said Achara, smiling. "But it was not in totaling my score. He gave me the full points for that number. I think what must have happened—"

"I know what happened," I asserted, interrupting him. "Some teachers have their favorite boys—"

"I am not one of his favorites," Achara protested.

"But you're one of the best in his subject. That makes you a favorite. Obviously, he saw your QED and didn't bother to read your calculations carefully enough. He's not the only teacher who has favorites. I know because something like that happened to me, but I won't tell you in what subject."

"Why?"

"Because you'll know the teacher concerned."

"Hey! That's not fair. I just told you mine."

"You didn't," I corrected him. "All you did was mention the subject, and I knew right away."

"Just tell me what happened or leave me to continue my work," he said, quite artlessly. But I had seen the cunning look in his eyes and chose my words carefully.

"We did a paper," I recounted. "And this teacher made a comment on mine, that it was profuse, diffuse, and confused. And still, I had the best score in the class, 16 over 20. Since that day, the other boys have never let me forget it, and a whole year has passed. How d'you explain my score?"

"I can't," Achara said. "But clearly, it is not math or any of the science subjects. Profuse, diffuse, and confused? Can't be geography either. Must be English or history—"

"I better leave you alone to study," I said, packing up my books and beating a hasty retreat.

"That's just a tactical withdrawal!" Achara shouted after me. "You're afraid I'll make you tell me."

I did not bother to look back.

CHAPTER XXI

For the umpteenth time, the wily West Indian bowled his leg break outside the off stump, hoping to turn the ball, on pitching, away from the batsman. He had packed the off side with seven fielders, with the clear intent to stem the batsman's flow of runs. He had cause to worry about the batsman, Okon Ebong. The West Indian knew, as did his captain, Mr. Walter Graves, that his team's best chance of success lay in tying down the young boy whose cricketing genius had blossomed wonderfully.

From the other end of the pitch, I watched my friend fretting. He fretted because he seemed unable to pierce that packed offside field, no matter how hard he hit the ball. Ebong was a permanent fixture in the cricket team, though he was only in his third year. I watched, with not a little envy, as he met each ball with the full face of his bat—in dead center. And he was fretting!

What did he want *me* to do? I was on trial, in my first game in the team. My problem was not an inability to pierce a close and watchful field. My problem was infinitely more fundamental. I was seldom able to make any meaningful contact with the wily bowler's leg breaks. I was bamboozled by the wicked turn he imparted to the ball. Sometimes the balls turned prodigiously. Sometimes only just enough to beat my defensive bat. What runs I was able to garner, I did mostly from the trundler at the other end.

Ebong and I met in midpitch for a brief caucus before Mr. Lloyd—the West Indian—was due to begin a new over. It was a strategy caucus. We spoke in whispers because it would have been stupid to let the opposition, some of whom walked close by us, hear our battle plan. Ebong suggested it was time to change tactics and to attack.

I was not sure what he had in mind. So I asked him, "What d'you think I've been trying to do?"

171

He looked at me as if I had lost my mind. "We have to attack," he repeated and walked briskly back to his end of the pitch to receive the first ball of the over.

"Speak for yourself," I said, but softly and to his back.

So for the umpteenth time, Mr. Lloyd delivered his leg break. He was actually in his final delivery stride and might not have seen the movement at the other end. Ebong countered that last bowling stride and the intended leg break by two quick forward strides of his own. He met the ball on the full toss before it could touch the ground and change direction. He swung his bat mightily, made the sweetest contact I had ever seen, and lifted the ball clear over the head of the lone ranger in midfield.

Mr. Lloyd, hands on waist, watched unbelievably as the ball fled to the boundary line. He smiled knowingly as enthusiastic applause rolled like a wave around the field. He went determinedly back to his mark, charged in, and delivered what seemed like an identical ball. Ebong also did the identical thing and hit the ball, on the full toss, to the boundary.

"So that's what you meant," I said to Ebong when we met one more time in the middle of the pitch at the end of the over.

Before he could reply, Mr. Lloyd came up to us and said, smilingly, to Ebong, "Those two shots were baseball shots, not cricket."

"Baseball, sir?" Ebong asked. "What's baseball?"

"An American game," Mr. Lloyd said. "Somewhat like rounders, with which I'm sure you're familiar. I do not recall ever seeing you play such a shot before. That's pure improvisation. I'm impressed."

"Thank you, sir," Ebong replied, wiping the sweat off the sides of his head with the sleeves of his white shirt. "Sometimes this straight-bat business doesn't help."

"What you played," said Mr. Lloyd, "could also be called a cow shot. And it's not wise to overuse it. But I'm impressed. I'm enjoying your display because I see you have a good cricket head on your shoulders."

"A big head too," I added jovially. "The biggest in the college."

"See who's talking," Mr. Lloyd said, laughing. "Anyway, I'll talk to your principal about you, Ebong. I wish it was possible to pluck you right out of here and transplant you to the West Indies to develop your game."

I suppose the man needed to underline the difference between Ebong and me because he bowled me in the very next over with a ball that I had expected to turn, but which held straight. I did not hang my head in shame as I walked back to the pavilion. I think I knew I had done as well as might have been expected in my initiatory first-team match. At least I had survived a few overs of keen probing by a wily bowler who, I knew, had played good-grade cricket in Jamaica.

To this day, I do not know if the West Indian spoke to Mr. Walter Graves about Ebong. I only know that whenever I was lucky to be Ebong's batting partner, I always wished some of his ability would rub off on me. But then I would look at his wide shoulders and his muscular arms. And I knew I could never generate the power he did when he struck the ball. I knew I was close to being selected for the first team. Both the principal and Mr. Kalaga had, on occasion, complimented me on my basic straight bat. But the basics, they also told me, were not enough. As they put it, I needed—more than anything else—to instill some measure of confidence in my abilities.

Ebong told me the same thing. "You can play well," he said. "But every time you go to bat, you look worried and nervous."

"Aren't you ever nervous?"

Ebong laughed shortly. "Of course I'm nervous, but I try not to show it. And once I make good contact with the ball—you know, in the middle of my bat—my nerves settle down. And then I know it will take a really good ball to get me out."

While the opposition was desperately looking for that good ball, Ebong put their bowling to the sword and plundered runs, like a batsman to the manner born. "Plunder" might perhaps suggest that he used violent methods or that he robbed and defrauded the opposition. His style was thrust and cut, as with a saber. He cut and deflected the ball delicately and defended with the straightest of bats. Only when he drove the ball massively off his front foot or reared back to pull or hook was there the slightest hint of violence in his play. When he walked to the wicket to bat, expectations rose. If he failed to score or if the gods were not in the mood to let him prosper fully, he seemed to be merely demonstrating that he was human.

*   *   *

It was perhaps proof of the hold the game of cricket had on my young mind. But the night before the team for Benin was announced, I had a dream. It was all really too silly for words. In one part of my dream, the principal, no less, informed me of my selection for the team. He called me to his office. He first shook hands with me and then told me I was in. In the other part of my dream, I was in the middle, batting—in the best of all possible worlds—opposite the team's batting prodigy, my friend Ebong. But while he struggled, I prospered. Suddenly, the game seemed ridiculously easy as the runs flowed like a fast-moving river off my bat. I believe it was that most unlikely scenario—him, struggling; me, batting with poise and majesty—that brought my dream to an abrupt and jolting end. I sat up confused, wondering where I was. When I realized what I had just been doing, I fell back on my pillow, with a moan and a sigh. I could not go back to sleep but tossed and turned on my bed for about an hour before the wake-up bell mercifully ended my misery.

It was Patrick Onyewuchi who brought me the good news later that day. He came to my dormitory, about a half hour before the games period was due to start. He came with his friend and classmate Thomas Eleadi—a breezy, jovial, barrel-chested boy—and Anthony Achara.

"What are my neighbors doing?"

That was Eleadi's signature greeting, the only way he seemed to know to announce his presence. It was, as always, a rhetorical question.

"*Baba-Eko*," I intoned, "give us a song."

That was the standard, unchanging riposte to Eleadi's inquiry that needed no answer. But Eleadi was in the senior class. And only his classmates, his friends, and those boys who thought they could get away with the familiarity dared to address him in that manner.

Baba-Eko was a slight corruption of the nickname of Long John Silver, the unsavory, one-legged, ham-faced fictional buccaneer in R. L. Stevenson's popular novel, *Treasure Island*. "Now, Barbecue," Long John Silver's shipmates would demand, "tip us a stave." And the fearsome villain would oblige with the old sea song: "Fifteen men on the dead man's chest. Yo ho ho and a bottle of rum!"

I had no clue how or why Eleadi merited the pirate's nickname. He was not much given to singing and was indeed a croaker. His appearance did not inspire awe. Quite the contrary. Because of his conviviality and his gregarious nature, Eleadi was popular. Quite likely, his nickname originally had nothing to do with Long John Silver. "Baba" in Nigerian usage means "father." Eleadi was portly, suggesting a father figure. He had lived briefly in Lagos, otherwise also known as Eko.

I had long established my credentials with him and could therefore take the liberty without giving offense. Shared friendships brought us together quite often. Eleadi, Onyewuchi, and Samson Stoneface were classmates and friends. Onyewuchi and Stoneface, my mentors in my first year or two, were now more friends than mentors to me. Through them, I had fairly frequent contacts with Eleadi and soon developed the habit of calling him Baba-Eko.

"We've brought you good news," Eleadi announced expansively as they approached my bed.

"Good news? What is it?" I asked, my heart beating wildly. I knew it had to be about the cricket team, concerning which strong rumors had circulated all day and which had caused me to dream dreams of pure fantasy.

"You've been chosen for the trip to Benin City," said Onyewuchi, making himself comfortable on the empty bed next to mine.

I jumped off my bed, punched the air with gusto, and let out such a bellow that several of my dormitory mates sprang up in fright.

"I'm in the cricket team!" I shouted, my heart full to bursting point. Momentarily losing control of my emotions, I first lustily embraced Onyewuchi, then Eleadi, taking both by surprise. I was going to do the same to Achara, but he adroitly dodged my encircling arms and stood to one side, eyeing me. There was something in the way he was looking at me, with an odd smile on his lips, which aroused my suspicion.

"Don't tell me you knew about this?" I asked him.

"'Know' is a strong word—"

"He knew, all right," said Innocent Dike, standing by the entrance door of the dormitory. How long he had stood there, I did not know. Though we were in the same dormitory, he had his bed in the other half of the building, separated from my half by a partition wall.

Dike came and took my hand and pumped it a few times. "Congrats," he said. "But you must be the last of the team to know about it. I knew at least an hour ago."

"What? Are you in the team?" I asked, amazed.

"Meaning you don't think I'm good enough?"

"You're not," said Achara emphatically. "You think because—what is it you're always bragging about? Something to do with your bat being straight—"

"The straightest in the college," said Dike pompously.

"Your bat may be straight, but where are the runs? Without runs, no team wins a match." Achara then turned to me. "Don't mind him. Congrats. I'm glad for you."

So was Dike, notwithstanding that he sometimes put on a swaggering, slightly cocky manner. I never forgot my first meeting with him, a week or two into his first month in the college. I was in class 2 then. He had sought me out, he said, to introduce himself to me. He was, he told me with fierce pride, the first and only pupil to pass the Government College Umuahia entrance examination from the central school of my village, Orifite. And by that singular success, he had brought honor and glory to the school and—I think he added—the entire village. As if I, who had preceded him into Umuahia by one year, was not really from Orifite, just because my primary school had been in Aba.

"Why is the team going only as far as Benin City," Dike asked, "to play against Government College Ibadan? Perhaps the college cannot afford the cost of going all the way to Ibadan?"

"That's what was agreed by the two principals," said Onyewuchi. "Benin City is about halfway between Umuahia and Ibadan. The two teams will be hosted by Edo College in Benin City."

"This is the first time you and me are in the same team," I told Onyewuchi. "The only difference is you've won your colors. One day, who knows, I'll win mine too."

"We could have been teammates in another game if only you had stuck to it."

"You mean hockey, don't you?"

"Yes, Okoye, hockey. You gave up on the game just as you seemed to be beginning to play it well. It's something I'll never understand. You disappointed Mr. Kalaga and Mr. Knight too."

"I tried my best," I said. "It's just that the game sometimes seems so wild. I'm afraid of other players' sticks. I've been hit quite often even when I didn't have the ball near me. Perhaps I'm really a coward, and I'm just looking for excuses."

"If you were a coward," Baba-Eko asked, "d'you think you would have gone as far as you've done in cricket? You don't seem to fear fast bowlers. And didn't you recently enroll in the boxing club? You have more courage than you think."

What he did not know, and about which I was in no hurry to explain to my assembled friends, was that I had joined the boxing club only on a dare. A dare by two acquaintances. I should have said two friends. But what manner of friend would suggest so fearsome and violent a sport to another. When I joined the club, I did so, though every fiber of my being, and all my instincts, cried out vociferously in protest.

Austin Okeke, a class below me, was a natural-born fighter if I ever saw one. I had sometimes watched him box and found his basic approach very simple. He liked to move in close to give your jaw a good, solid whack, regardless of the punishment he himself took in the process. Paul Ogbo was smooth, tactical—indeed a stylist. He was only in his second year in the school but was, at about five feet five inches, quite tall for his class, if not his age. He was very adept at fleeting around his opponent, at hitting without being hit, and at pretending that his opponent's punches carried little or no sting.

Okeke and Ogbo were the two boys who successfully goaded me into boxing. They challenged my manhood, or was it my honor? I never really knew which. And I succumbed like a boy who did not have his own mind. I joined, thinking that boxing gloves softened the sting of a punch. Instead, I found that they greatly increased the surface that received the punches. Enough said!

"I don't know how long I'll remain in the boxing club," I told Baba-Eko, who, in praising my courage, was trying to make me feel good about what I was doing.

* * *

176

The next day, the cricket team was officially announced. It included a host of my friends: Ebong, of course, and Onyewuchi; Kofi Bentsil and Chidi Ebele, my old schoolmates from Aba. Ebele had so far overcome his initial and deep disappointment at his fate at the end of our second year, that it was getting to be difficult to remember that we had been classmates for close on a decade before then. As expected, the team captain was Augustin Onuorah. Chris Obidike was also in the team. A class 3 boy, his selection was probably the most exciting of all. Small and frail looking, Obidike nevertheless had probably the best eye-and-hand coordination of any boy in the team, which enabled him to bat in a manner that caused gasps of wonder and disbelief. His timing, that innate ability to make contact between his bat and the ball at the most auspicious moment and for the best results, was something no other boy had. Not to anything like the same degree. Not even Ebong.

Whereas Ebong's genius was grounded on a superlative orthodoxy, Obidike's brilliance showed little or no respect for the basic principles of batting enunciated in cricket manuals. As he batted, Obidike maintained a smiling, somewhat-supercilious expression on his face. It was often difficult to determine if he was enjoying himself, even as his stroke play gave enormous pleasure to his teammates and the spectators. He always managed to convey the impression that he was a cut or two above the fray. And that the struggle to excel and the ebb and flow of the game were too mundane for him.

Three days later, the team left for Edo College, Benin City. The college lorry, in which we travelled, huffed and bumped its way from Umuahia through Owerri to Onitsha, on the majestic River Niger. A ferryboat, the *Shanahan*, then ferried us across the river to Asaba for the last leg of our journey, eighty-something miles, to Benin City. For the most part, the roads were not macadamized, which meant that we ate a lot of dust. I had no idea—still do not—how many miles we traveled to Benin City. My guess would have been close to two hundred miles. I know that if we had travelled all the way to Ibadan, to meet our sister Government College team on their home ground, we might have done some four hundred miles, which would have meant twice the amount of dust that assailed our mouths and nostrils. The trip took place in late January, in the middle of the dry season, when the harmattan, a dust-laden North-East wind from the Sahara, blows toward the West African coast, turning everything in its path brittle dry and overlaid with dust. Especially vegetation and the human skin.

This was the first time I had crossed the River Niger. As the *Shanahan* rolled and wove its way past shallow, sometimes-treacherous segments of the great river, I leaned over the deck railings and watched the intimidating waters flow by. This was the river in whose depths, according to popular lore, the famous Mammy Water lived. She was a river goddess, whose exquisite and beguiling beauty could lure the unwary into an untimely and watery grave. There was a European trader, whose name was Jonas Sanders, who lived in Onitsha, close to the banks of the river. Legend has it he was the only human who could dive to the depths of the river to meet and carouse with the mystical goddess and live to tell the tale.

My mounting excitement, as the lorry sped on, had less to do with the river goddess than the prospect of seeing the ancient city. Benin City, properly so called, was the greatest of the historical cities of Southern Nigeria, if not indeed of West Africa. European historians, writing from their warped perspective, laid much emphasis on the bloodthirstiness of some of the rulers of the Benin Empire, especially the last great king, Oba Overami. But we had begun to learn, from the Yorubaman, not to put all our faith in the story of our people as recounted by those who propagated the notion that we had little or no history worth the telling. My heart swelled with pride at my first sight of the ancient city, with the quaint ruins of the old city wall bearing testimony to its historicity.

Edo College was then what was called a government middle college. It was government-owned and funded, as were the two colleges whose teams were due to meet there in a cricket match. But whereas Umuahia and Ibadan government colleges were full six-year high schools, Edo went only up to the fourth year, class 4. The college then helped those class 4 boys who wished to complete their high school education to find other schools for their final two years.

The two cricket teams arrived within a few hours of each other and were housed in two separate dormitories. I did not know what the school did with the students whose beds we took over. Perhaps they doubled up with other students on their beds, which was something I felt sure Umuahia would not have permitted. Two boys could not even sit on the same bed, never mind sleep.

We were barely settled in when who should saunter through the doors of our dormitory? It was the captain of the Ibadan team. Whether he intended it or not, it was—in my judgment—a smart psychological move. His name, he told us, was Andrew

Ighodaro, from Sapale. If he did nothing else, he came across as a very confident young man who knew his way around, was completely relaxed in the company of strangers, and could engage in small talk with the practiced ease of a man of the world, which might have been something, it seemed to me as I gazed at him, that Ibadan did for him. Ibadan was then Nigeria's largest city, larger even than Lagos, and only a stone's throw, so to say, from the gay, high-living, and freewheeling metropolis. It seemed, by contrast, as if we Umuahians were rustics, coming from a village.

Ighodaro was a good-looking mulatto boy, about six feet tall, trim and athletic, and with the slightest suggestion of a swagger in his walk. More than anything else, it was that slight swagger that bothered me. Just looking at him, I think I experienced something akin to an inferiority complex. Desperately, I hoped he did not affect my teammates the same way.

"I hope you all had a good trip," he said after chitchatting for a few minutes. "How many miles is Umuahia from Benin City?"

Someone said 180; another said 200. But no one seemed sure. None thought to ask him about the distance from Ibadan to Benin City to test *his* geography. What most struck me in our conversation with the dashing young man was that all we did was react to him. None, not even our captain Onuorah nor my mentor Onyewuchi, took the initiative in any aspect of the conversation.

"I'm looking forward to the game," said Ighodaro as he stood up to return to his team's dormitory. "I hope it will be a good game."

It was. If memory serves me right, I managed to score 10 runs. Ebong fought hard and long to good effect, scoring some 35 or so runs. Onyewuchi struck a few good blows; Chris Obidike, several. Thanks mainly to those three, the Umuahia team scored a total of about 130 runs. Ighodaro, who opened the bowling for Ibadan, bowled his medium-fast off cutters sharply into the batsman, off the pitch, and often at a disconcerting height. How I kept him off my stumps, I really have no clear memory, as I write this. But I did and proudly too. He took, I think, three wickets; but mine was not one of them. His prize wicket: Obidike's.

But he was not yet done with us. Not content with his three wickets, he stepped into the breach, with his bat, when his team faltered, chasing our score. Umuahia should have won, but Ighodaro would not let us. It was in fact not so much that he scored some 30 good runs, but that the manner and the timing of his doing so were impeccable. He wrested the initiative from us when we thought we smelled victory. Against his broad bat, there seemed nothing our bowlers could do. Not even our captain Onuorah, who had a good match, capturing several wickets. We fielded well but could not stench his runs. And when he hit the winning run, he knew—as we did—that he had snatched an improbable victory out of the jaws of defeat. Ighodaro's last act, when we left early the next morning to return to Umuahia, was typical of the man. He once again came to our dormitory to wish us a safe trip and to congratulate us on our valiant effort.

"It was one of the best matches I have played," he said, "in all my years in Government College Ibadan. Better than the six or seven I have played against King's College."

His mention of King's College, Lagos, affected us poignantly. To a man, our team hoped and prayed that one day, we would have an opportunity to

179

measure our strength against that college as we had just done against Ibadan. King's was the best known of the three big government colleges for boys. And it had, reputedly, the best cricket team.

A little chastened, but happy overall, we began our journey back to Umuahia. At Asaba, we waited at least two hours before the *Shanahan* came to ferry us across the Niger to Onitsha. Suddenly, as we waited, Chidi Ebele tugged at my shirt, and pointed across to the other side of the road from where we stood.

"Isn't that Orizontal, there by the pleasure car?"

I looked and saw him and recognized him at once. He was truly a sight for sore eyes, magnificently built, tall, broad-shouldered, impossibly handsome, and sporting an ash gray suit with the now-familiar double-breasted jacket. The jacket was so long, it reached to midthigh.

Prince Akweke Abyssinia Nwafor Orizu, scion of the royal house of Nnewi in Eastern Nigeria, was popularly called *Orizontal*, a play on his last name and the word "horizontal." He espoused what he described as horizontal education, typically American, as opposed to the vertical—or perpendicular—education, typically British.

In America, he preached and wrote, education was available to all and was broad-based. In Britain, in sharp contrast, education was the privilege of relatively small numbers and tended to be rather narrowly focused. But what most galled him was that Britain, as the colonial power, imposed her educational philosophy on a hapless Nigeria. It was this pernicious influence that he set out to correct, a task which he seemed determined to make his life's work. To that end, he had, while still in America, set up a philanthropic organization, the American Council on African Education. And in the name of that council, he had obtained hundreds of tuition scholarships from various American sources for the benefit of African students.

This was the first time I had actually seen the man so close, I could have walked across the road and touched him. I might indeed have done so had I not, at that precise moment, seen the young girl who got out of the car and stood by him. She, I also immediately recognized. She was the daughter of a well-known Igbo leader, Mr. Zephniah Obidigbo, a strong man who ruled his household with a firm but benevolent hand. He was known to be very strict with his daughters.

"Let's go and talk to them," Chidi Ebele urged me, noticing my hesitation.

"I can't," I said. "I won't."

"Why?"

"D'you know the girl standing by him?"

"I don't," said Ebele. "But what does it matter?"

"You don't know her," I said. "So it's easy for you."

"What's the matter with you? I'm going, even if you won't come."

"Why are you surprised?" asked Kofi Bentsil, just then joining us. "It's the same old Obinna. What's it they say, that the leopard cannot change its spots? Did he ever tell you what happened between him and Adamma—you remember her? She was his bloke."

"I do," said Ebele. "No, he didn't tell me. But I'm sure it's a long story, and I don't have the time now."

He crossed over to the prince and the girl, closely followed by Bentsil. I watched, from my distance, as my two friends did what I was too timorous to do. And as I watched, my mind went back to Adamma. And to the awful hash I had made of our relationship. Ebele was wrong; it was not a long story. Adamma's mother had smelled more than a rat, when there was not even a rat to be smelled. Whereupon she had put her foot down, declaring her daughter off-limits to me. I remembered how she had put it. "You Aba boys are all the same." Thus condemned, by association as it were, I stayed away but remained friends with Adamma's brother, Ben. Bentsil, when I told him the story, all but called me a coward. I think the way he put it was that I had no backbone.

"What took you two so long?" I asked my friends when they came back from across the road. "What did they say to you?"

"None of your business," Ebele told me, laughing. "You didn't want to go with us. Why d'you now want to know what we talked about?"

"Don't be stupid. Did the girl recognize me?"

Bentsil shook his head slowly, looking at me all the while. "D'you think we went over to talk to her about you? We were only interested in the prince, not the girl. However, we did manage to find out one thing, but I'm not telling you—"

I pounced on them, catching them unawares, and wrestled both of them to the ground. None of our teammates intervened, I suppose because they heard us laughing. But I was not laughing. We grappled for a minute or so, and then their combined strength overpowered me as they pinned me to the ground.

"Good God!" said Ebele, gasping. "You want to kill us because of the girl?"

"I will," I said, even as I lay prostrate, "if you don't stop showing off."

They released me as they stood up, dusting themselves off. I did the same, but my eyes were still wild.

"Okay, what was it you wanted to know?" asked Bentsil. "Ah yes, what she said about you. The answer is . . . *nothing*. We didn't ask her if she recognized you. But she's on her way to the United States."

"That's what she said?"

"She did. And so did he. They are travelling together, as a matter of fact."

"But what's she going to do in America?" I asked.

181

"She's actually one of—how many did she say?" he asked Ebele but did not wait for his answer. "Ten or so students, she said. They'll be travelling with Orizontal to America in the next week or two. On his scholarships. How lucky for them."

I looked across the road. But the prince and the girl had left the scene, with their pleasure car, on their way to Lagos and the United States. The merciless tropical sun was beating down on us as we waited for the ferryboat. For the rest of the journey, I could think of nothing else but my shameful timorousness. I had missed an opportunity. A golden opportunity to ask the girl, Catherine was her name, about her family. And especially about one of her younger sisters, Evelyn, whose existence and winsomeness had begun to intrude on my consciousness more and more.

As our lorry drove into our college compound, the team struck up the traditional song of defeat:

"Deeply wailing, deeply wailing . . ."

I joined in the singing; but I was, in truth, wailing for myself.

CHAPTER XXII

I first met Mr. James Wolf the day I went with my classmate Gregory Okoroafor to see the principal. Actually, I had no business with Mr. Graves. I went with Okoroafor only because he said he needed my moral support. He wanted, he told me, to lodge a complaint with the big man. A complaint that had to do with the dining hall classification of the boys according to whether we were heavy, moderate, or light eaters.

It was, if the truth be told, a fun classification. It gave rise to a lot of hilarity and leg-pulling as most of the boys did whatever they could to avoid classification among the light eaters.

"My concern," the principal had announced weeks earlier, "is that too much food is being wasted."

He made his announcement at a morning assembly. Mr. Graves informed us that he and the housemasters had mulled the dining hall situation for a few months before he decided to launch the novel idea.

"The reason is clear," he said. "The portions are much too much for many boys."

There was an instant murmur of protest. One voice, rising above the general din, said there were those for whom the portions were not even enough. "Are we going to suffer with those whose needs are less?"

"Who's talking about suffering?" the principal asked. "All we're trying to do is group boys rationally. The food will then be apportioned according to the groupings. This should lead to less wastage."

Chris Obidike, sitting two rows in front of me, raised his hand to gain the principal's attention. "Who will decide who the heavy eaters are?" he asked when the big man pointed to him. "Or will the grouping be by size or what?"

There was general laughter, joined in by the masters and even the principal. Small and slim in build, there was not an ounce of extra fat on any part of

Obidike's body. But we all knew he liked his food, his favorite dishes being the *okpodudu* (the black beans), yam, and rice.

"I can assure you," said Mr. Pepple, moving to stand by Mr. Graves, "that you will be grouped with the big eaters. Bodily size will play little or no role in the groupings. The prefects know who eats a lot and who doesn't. We might not get it right 100 percent initially. But we'll adjust as we go along."

As far as Okoroafor was concerned, they did not get it right. Not initially. And not even after he had lodged several complaints. Modest to the point of self-effacement, he at first allowed himself to be placed among the small eaters—that is, until he found that it was seriously affecting his mood and temper. I know he protested to one or two prefects. But to no avail. Then one day, he was punished by a school prefect for some intemperate language when he argued, one more time, that he should be reclassified.

"That's it!" he told me. "I'm going to the principal."

"To do what?" I asked as if I did not know. But I thought he needed to be pulled back from the brink of a precipitate and ill-considered action.

"Don't try to stop me now," he complained. "What you can do is follow me."

"You're crazy," I said.

"Crazy or not, I need your moral support. But you don't have to enter the man's office with me."

As if I would have dared, given what I thought about his idea.

"You tell me," he challenged me, obviously still struggling to convince himself. "You yourself are with the big group. And I can name several others who do not eat more than I do."

"So?"

"Don't you understand? We all pay the same fees—at least those of us who are not on scholarship. And that's what I'll tell the principal."

"You're joking?" I said.

But I knew he was deadly serious. I had seen the fire in his eyes, and I was familiar with its portent. I went with him to the principal's office, arguing strenuously with him all the way until we got there. Then I stayed back in the corridor of the office and waited. I sharpened my ears in an unavailing effort to catch the exchange.

After what seemed ages, the big man himself came to the door of his office and beckoned me in. I knew straightaway that Okoroafor had told him that I was lurking somewhere outside the office.

Mr. James Wolf sat in a straight-backed chair at the far end of the office. I knew it was him, though I was meeting him, in the flesh, for the first time. He sat, leaning forward, an unlit pipe dangling from a corner of his mouth. He had arrived a week earlier. The senior boys said he came from the antipodes (more specifically, New Zealand). I knew he taught English literature to class 6 and was supposed to be crazy about cricket.

In just one week, he had built up a reputation as a person who called a spade a spade. When I walked into the principal's office, he was in the process of doing just that. He took the pipe out of his mouth and stabbed the air repeatedly with it, by way of emphasis, as he spoke.

"It was a crazy idea," he said, "right from its inception. If you ask me, I think this young man has a good case. Scrap the whole thing. That's my recommendation. Scrap it."

He was a spoilsport. That was my immediate reaction to him. *What did he know*, I asked myself, *about the boys and how we ate?* I liked my classification with the big eaters, because I loved to eat. I had argued strenuously with my friend, but not because I thought that his complaint lacked merit. I was simply concerned that too many complaints—justified or not—would eventually doom the dining hall experiment. They did exactly that. The complaints and, quite likely, the intervention of such powerful masters as the antipodean, Mr. Wolf. But I did not know that at the time as I stood respectfully to one side of Mr. Grave's large office desk.

"Have you met Mr. Wolf, our new cricket master?" Mr. Graves asked me.

"No, sir," I said. I did not want to look at him after what he had just recommended to the principal.

"Okoye Jr. was a member of the team that played against the Government College Ibadan."

"I see," said Mr. Wolf. I was well aware that he was staring at me. But I remained rigidly immobile.

"Now off with both of you," said Mr. Graves. "I'll review your complaint, Okoroafor. You're not the first and will probably not be the last to complain against the new arrangement. We'll just have to wait and see."

So I had been called into the big man's office just to meet the new cricket coach. As we walked away from the Administration Block, I saw that my friend was strangely taciturn. All he would tell me was that he had said exactly what he had planned to say to Mr. Graves. But it did not seem to have helped him feel better about anything. He was however thankful that Mr. Wolf was there.

I did not share that sentiment. I was still feeling resentful when, a day or two later, Mr. Wolf appeared at our net practice. He was only in his late thirties or early forties, but he already walked with a slight stoop and seemed to lean more heavily on his walking stick than I thought appropriate for a man his age. It was a fancifully carved stick with a silver handle, which, we later learned, he said he had picked up from somewhere in the Far East on his way to Nigeria.

He came to the nets with his wife, one of the most gorgeous white women I had ever seen. I surmised that they were childless, or they would surely have brought the child with them.

Mr. Wolf stood to one side, with his wife, and watched us for a while. He made signs to Mr. Kalaga, who was supervising the practice, to go ahead and not pay him any attention. After about ten minutes, Mr. Wolf came forward and spoke briefly with Mr. Kalaga. Only then did the latter do the introductions. The first to be introduced, naturally, was the team captain, Onuorah. Then the rest of us.

"This is Mr. Wolf, from New Zealand," said Mr. Kalaga. "He will be our new coach." He then turned to Mr. Wolf. "If you need me, sir, I'll always be available to assist you."

"Thank you very much," said Mr. Wolf. "I'll certainly use all the help I can get. This is the school team, right?"

"Yes, sir," said Onuorah, stepping forward. "Would you like to have a go at it, sir?"

Mr. Wolf took his time looking from one boy to the other. Then he smiled sunnily and said, "I suppose you're all curious to see what the new coach can do with the bat."

It did not sound like a question, so none confirmed his supposition. We waited as he picked up a bat and hefted it momentarily, for weight and balance no doubt. Dropping his walking stick, he took his position in the nets. He had the strangest stance at the batting crease as he prepared to receive his first ball. Taking middle and leg, he planted his bat exactly at middle, with the blade of the bat facing his legs directly. We had been taught to show the blade either to the approaching bowler or to the mid-on.

Mr. Wolf stuck his rear end out exaggeratedly and wiggled it several times in an obvious effort to relax his entire body. Only then did he look up to signify to the bowler that he was ready for the first ball. I cannot recall exactly what we expected, but Mr. Wolf batted in quite a masterly fashion, without causing us to gasp in wonderment. His bat was as straight as it was possible to be, perhaps a little more so than seemed absolutely necessary. It was, some of us thought, his way of underlining the importance of a straight bat as a fundamental requisite in the art of batting. He was, after all, our new coach.

"There is no game in the world quite like cricket," he told us as he linked arms with his beautiful wife. "I'll leave you all now. But here's some food for thought. Next year, 1948, will be the centenary of the birth of the greatest cricketer who ever lived. Anyone here know his name?"

"W. G. Grace, of course," offered Mr. Kalaga.

"That's good," said Mr. Wolf. "But actually, I meant the question for the boys."

"Who was W. G. Grace?" Onuorah, our captain, asked.

"Who was . . . ?" asked Mr. Wolf, totally taken aback by our ignorance. Then his expression changed. "You really don't know? Or are you playing me for a sucker?"

I did not know what "sucker" meant, not to talk of playing him for one. Except, of course, that it sounded like the other word for "football." But somehow, we knew he was not talking about football. We were surprised that he was surprised, so in the end, he had to tell us who the man was.

"W. G.," he said, "was the father of modern cricket. Let me put it this way. He took batting in the last quarter of the nineteenth century from what you might call the village blacksmith's game to the exquisite form we know today. He was the first to make a regular habit of scoring more than a hundred runs off his own bat in game after game, after game. In his career, he did so exactly 126 times."

"More than a century of centuries," added Mr. Kalaga. Mr. Wolf smiled and nodded in affirmation.

He was consumed with an inordinate passion for the game. He seemed ready and eager to talk about cricket morning, noon, and night. Doubtless he dreamed about it in his sleep. We soon learned how ill-advised it was to run into him—anywhere, anytime. We developed a sixth sense about it all: to "see" him before he saw us and then to run and hide. Or if there was no place to hide, to change direction and turn through 180 degrees. Or just plain scamper off. If you did not do any of these things or if he caught up with you, you were doomed to a session in the art of batting. He used his walking stick as a bat to demonstrate all the strokes in his batting repertoire. He would lean into an imaginary ball and drive it straight or "through the covers," explaining the difference between the two. Then he might launch into a demonstration of the dead-bat forward or backward defensive stroke. If you had not, by this time, found an excuse to run away, he would show you the square cut, emphasizing the power and savagery of the stroke. Or, all delicacy and poise, an imaginary and beautiful late cut. Being, himself, essentially a back foot player, he was particularly partial to the forcing strokes off the back foot, especially the hook and the pull.

There were boys who found Mr. Wolf's obsession with the game funny—boys, who, from a safe and respectful distance, laughed at what they termed his "ludicrous antics." I was not one of them. How could I be when, in time, I found I was one of a small band whom he habitually ferreted out, even when we thought we were safe and secure in our dormitories? He said we had "some potential" in the game. Ebong and Obidike were part of the group, which, I suppose, should have been very flattering for a frankly moderate performer like me.

If he had been content to talk only cricket, I might have found the will power to endure the imposition. But the man soon added rugby and the strange American game of baseball to his bag of games. When he collared you, you could never be sure which of these games he would pull out. I had only heard mention of the American game from Mr. Lloyd, the West Indian, a month or so earlier. But he had likened the game to rounders, not to cricket. Mr. Wolf went to some pains to draw an affinity between baseball and cricket.

He boasted that his country, New Zealand, was the greatest power in the world of rugby. He said the team was called the All Blacks. Whereupon, quite innocently, I remarked that I was not aware that Maoris were black skinned. He seemed to take offense at my remark.

"The name has nothing to do with the color of anybody's skin," he said, frowning. "And what's more, the team is not made up entirely of the Maoris. In fact, there are, I think, only three or four of them in the All Blacks."

The cricket season ended at the end of the first term, in late March, when the rainy season began. And then to my absolute horror, Mr. Wolf somehow obtained the principal's permission to introduce rugby. For the introductory phase, Mr. Wolf announced that he was looking for a combination of robustness and speed in his "guinea pigs." To be fair to him, he did not employ that expression. But that was what they were to us, and that was what we called them—guinea pigs, the boys he experimented with.

On his criteria, I felt untouchable. Just about the only thing robust about me was my larger-than-life head. As to speed, if my life depended on it, I could not have done the one-hundred-yard sprint in less than fourteen or so seconds. Nothing blistering there. Of my fellow cricketers, Ebong was robust but lacked speed. Chidi Ebele combined the two attributes. Obidike had some speed but should have been too slight in build to qualify. Nothing deterred, Mr. Wolf selected all of us. Obidike asked permission to decline the invitation. He stated flatly that he was not interested and rejected all blandishments on the part of the master.

I did not have his courage and allowed myself to be coerced into participating in a game I found I detested. I dropped hints, in several little ways, of my lack of enthusiasm. But if Mr. Wolf noticed, he did not let on.

Then one day, at practice, the situation boiled over. I played so shabbily, my friends warned me I was courting trouble. They warned me because they must have seen that I was putting on a deliberate show. If I was in a scrummage, I maintained stiff legs when I should have helped my team's cause by helping to kick the ball to the rear of our pack. If I was called upon to throw the ball into a scrummage, I threw it in a manner to give advantage to our opponents. I moved wooden-leggedly when the play called for hard running. If I caught the ball at all—a rare occurrence—I threw it back with little regard to whether my teammate or an opponent caught it.

I knew Mr. Wolf was watching and taking it all in. But I was like the dog (in the Igbo proverb) that, when it becomes suicidal, loses its ability to smell excrement. There is an English equivalent: whom the gods wish to destroy, they first make mad.

At the end of the practice session, Mr. Wolf summoned me. With him was a new teacher, Mr. Rock. Mr. Rock was Irish and—almost inevitably, being Irish—was much taken with the game.

"That was just about the worst display I ever saw," said the Irishman, very red in the face. "What did you think you were doing in the field?"

"I tried my best, sir," I said. "But with the drizzle—"

"What drizzle?" he asked, getting angrier.

It was in fact still drizzling as we spoke. Not to talk of some lightning and thunder. I gestured with both my arms at the inclement conditions. But the two masters were unimpressed.

"It drizzled on the other players too," said Mr. Wolf.

"If that was your best effort," chimed in Mr. Rock, "then you're not even worthy to step into a rugby filed. What's your problem?"

Irrationally, perhaps, I decided that this was the moment of truth. I took a moment or two to form my words as I looked from one interlocutor to the other. For some reason, I particularly resented the attitude of the Irishman, who was known to have quite a temper. He taught Latin to the junior classes. Latin was a new subject, introduced at the beginning of the year, for classes 1 to 3. I had therefore never been taught by Mr. Rock and did not really know him, except by reputation.

"I don't like the game," I finally declared. "I don't want to play it, and as far as I'm concerned, it's a stupid game."

As soon as I spoke the words, I wished I could take them back. But I had lost all sense of smell, even of human excrement, the most malodorous of all. The irascible Mr. Rock stared at me with eyes that seemed on the point of popping out. Temporarily, I forgot Mr. Wolf, who was himself no slouch when it came to raising Cain. I suspect the extraordinary courage I displayed in my choice of words must have given the masters pause. Courage? Perhaps "stupidity" would be closer to the mark. When I remembered to look at Mr. Wolf, I saw that his back was turned to me. I did not see his face again until I reported, at Mr. Rock's bidding, to the principal's office the next day.

Mr. Graves was in a dark mood. And so was Mr. Wolf, who was there. No surprise, that. But Mr. Rock was not present, for which I did not know whether to be thankful. I do not recall what I expected by way of punishment. If I gave the matter any thought, my mind might have run the gamut of the usual punishments: the matchet parade, the Umuahia Run (my least favored), perhaps even the principal's "six of the best," his favorite expression for flagellation.

The punishment was original. And infinitely more humiliating than anything I could have imagined.

"For the next week, starting on Monday," pronounced the big man as his eyes bored into me, "you will sit in the front row at the morning assembly."

"Every day," added Mr. Wolf unnecessarily. Did he think I did not understand Mr. Graves's simple English?

I understood the words they spoke, but it took a moment or two for the full significance to sink in. For my mind to really grasp the enormity of the sentence.

"You mean, sir, that I will be sitting with class 1 boys?" I asked, though I knew what the answer would be.

"That's exactly it," said Mr. Wolf. He took out his pipe from the hip pocket of his brown khaki shorts. He then selected a match and lit the pipe, all the while looking steadily at me. He puffed two or three times and then added, "You will lead the procession out after each morning assembly."

I did not take too kindly to the grin that spread over his face. A wicked grin if I ever saw one. And I had begun latterly to think, on account of my cricket, that I was one of his favorite students.

"Why?" I dared to ask. "What did I do to deserve this punishment? All I said was that rugby is a—"

Mr. Wolf would not even let me finish my sentence. "Who cares what you think about the game? It was the manner in which you said it. You were very disrespectful to Mr. Rock and me."

"My boy," added the principal, "you have to learn that sometimes it is not just the words that matter, though they are important. Much more significant is how you say them and the context in which the words are spoken. D'you understand?"

I did, but I could not bring myself to give him the satisfaction of my affirmation. It occurred to me that the evil genius behind this ultimate of all humiliations might have been the absent Mr. Rock. Once upon a time, in my primary school years, my standard 5 teacher had sat me for several days between two of the biggest girls in the class as punishment for an offense I cannot now recall. There were, amazingly, boys who envied me that punishment.

I did not think any of my Umuahia classmates would envy me now. To be made to sit with class 1 boys, when it was not of my choosing, was a worse mortification than being forced to sit between two girls. I found myself wondering if there was something about my personality that inspired in my teachers this clearly aberrant form of punishment.

The following week was my worst in my Umuahia years. How I went through it is unfathomable now to me. First, there was the wide-eyed surprise on the faces of the class 1 boys as I took my seat next to them. Then the sniggering when the principal explained to the assembly why I had to sit where I sat. A consequence, he said, of my blatant disrespect for two of the masters. I must have developed eyes in the back of my head because I could swear I saw looks being exchanged among the boys. And because the procession, after the assembly, was a kind of an inside-out affair, starting from class 1 in the front rows, I was forced to run the gauntlet through the entire assembly.

In the first two days, at least, I could not raise my eyes to those who stared at me. This was especially mortifying when I filed past the rows of seats where my class 4 mates sat. I could not pretend to put a bold face on my humiliation. Nor did I dare cry. That would have made a bad situation infinitely worse. I walked like an automaton, looking neither to my right nor to my left, my body stiffened by the rage burning in my entrails.

Friends came to ask me what really had led to this punishment. To those who asked, I told the truth—*my* slant of the truth, which had nothing to do with disrespect for the two masters. Some came to commiserate with me. But in the final analysis, I was alone, utterly alone, in my world of shame and embarrassment. None could share this world with me to, as it were, reduce my agony. A boy suggested that I should "show them" by walking with a swagger when I led the procession. But I knew that any attempt on my part to thumb my nose at the principal or Mr. Wolf or the irascible Mr. Rock, would be to expose myself to ridicule and perhaps worse.

Mr. G. C. Mokelu, the geography master, called me to the staff room in the middle of my week of despair, late in the evening, when he knew we would have the room to ourselves. G. C. Moks, as he was popularly called, was one of my favorite teachers. In the Dennis Memorial Grammar School, Onitsha, where he had taught for several years before Mr. Walter Graves enticed him to Umuahia, G. C. Moks was called the best teacher of geography in the world. We might not have been as lavish in our praise of him in Umuahia, but we could not imagine how anyone could be a better teacher of the subject.

Physically, he was not the most prepossessing master in the college. Lean and angular, he had jaws so fiercely prominent and so square we nicknamed him Jaw-Bones. With the jawbone of an ass, the book of Judges recounts in the Bible, the legendary, unshorn Israelite Samson had thunderously slain a thousand Philistines. Our Jaw-Bones transformed geography from a tepid, indifferent subject into an almost-inspirational discipline. His maps—whether physical, demographic, or economic—were vibrant and eloquent accompaniments to his teaching. His notes (which he dictated to the class only after he had thoroughly explained the subject matter) were simple to read, easy to understand.

191

"I wanted to see you," he began, "because I have watched you sitting with the boys three classes your junior. And I have keenly felt what I think you have been feeling."

I stood meekly before him, my hands clasped behind my back. I stared at the wooden floor of the room, unable—because of my sense of shame—to even look him in the eye. Now he waved me into a chair and asked me to relax.

"I will talk to you frankly," he continued. "Our people say that if an adult is in the house, the she-goat is not left to suffer the pains of delivery while tethered to a stake. I have observed you over the past year or so since I joined the staff. You're one of the best students in my subject. For that, I'm happy. But I don't know if anybody has told you this. You are sometimes very impulsive in your behavior. I wish you could sometimes stop yourself, especially when you're aroused, before you say something you might later on regret. I have heard the full story of the incident at your rugby practice. Now you listen to me and listen well. You should not have spoken as you did to Mr. Wolf or Mr. Rock. You don't know these white people—"

"But I only said . . . ," I started to explain and then stopped.

"I just told you I heard the full story. I know what you said. Listen. I have had some experience in dealing with white people. They think they are the lords of the universe, and perhaps they are. As an individual, you can stand up to them, but then you better be sure you can deal with the consequences. If it is their word against yours, then, young man, you are sunk. It is best to go softly with them, even if it makes them think you are a fool or something like that. You simply don't take them on unless you think you're their equal. Take someone like Mr. Babatunde now. What can they do to him? He has studied in the best universities in England. He is better educated and knows their language better than most of them.

"A word is enough for the wise. Or as we say, the buttock when stung by an ant is the wiser for it. I am sorry, my boy, but you have to accept that your punishment is at least partially your fault. Learn from this experience. Keep your head high. And stop carrying on as if your world has come to an end."

He got up from his chair and came and stood by me. I knew what that meant: the end of our talk. I did not know if he saw—or felt—my gratitude. But as I looked up at him, a moment or two before I also got up, he gently tapped me on one cheek.

"Remember what I said. Hold your head high."

CHAPTER XXIII

My cousin Samuel's class received the results of the Cambridge School Certificate examination, which they had sat in December 1946, early in the second term of their last year, 1947. The class did Umuahia proud. As expected, all the boys passed. The great majority, just over twenty of the twenty-eight boys, achieved a grade 1 pass. The remainder were in grade 2. All but six or seven passed with "exemption from London Matriculation," a much-coveted honor. We understood the "exemption" to mean admissibility without other impediments into a university.

However, at the time, there was no university in Nigeria. Only the Yaba Higher College, then the only institution of higher education in the country. Yaba took in the best and brightest of the country's high school graduates and trained them for a variety of professions. But in the end, it awarded diplomas, not degrees. And in the two, three, or more years its students studied there, they were put through the academic mill. Several were expelled, sometimes when they were very close to getting their diplomas. Many Nigerians saw Yaba as a veritable graveyard of the country's budding intelligentsia. It set its students impossible standards—for mere diplomas and national certificates!

None of Samuel's classmates looked forward to Yaba. As Samuel put it, if they were going to be grilled mercilessly in a college, it should be in a college that awarded degrees. There would at least be some consolation in that. Degrees would mean almost automatic qualification for appointment into the senior cadres of the civil service. Yaba diplomates were appointed to the lower cadres, as *assistant* medical officers or *assistant* engineers and such like.

Samuel and his classmates dared to hope and dream about a university education only because they had heard that something like that was in the offing. Rumors abounded that the British Colonial Office was close to a decision on an improved structure of tertiary education in West Africa. But in the best traditions of that ponderous office, it dragged its feet.

The Elliot Commission on Higher Education in West Africa was set up in 1944 or thereabouts. The Colonial Office sent it to West Africa to survey the terrain and its peoples. And then, of course, to recommend on the need for a university for the hundreds of high school graduates turned out by the four British territories of Nigeria, Gold Coast, Sierra Leone, and Gambia. The four countries then held their collective breath while the Colonial Office pondered the situation and the recommendations of the commission.

Finally, two—or was it three?—years later, it reached a decision. A university college, to be tied to the apron strings of London University in a "special relationship" was set up in Ibadan and was ready to admit its first students in 1948.

Effectively, that decision killed off Yaba Higher College and its diplomas. Samuel was happy about the prospect of going to a university and had no tears for the demise of Yaba. The Colonial Office might have been extremely dilatory in the matter, but Samuel felt something akin to gratitude to it for the timing of its decision. However, he and his classmates, ready for university studies in 1947, had to cool their heels and their eagerness for just one year.

The "special relationship" with London University was of little or no concern to him. We all understood that expression to mean that London University would oversee the gradual development of the fledgling college to full maturity as a university. For how long? No one knew for sure. The popular assumption, the British being the British, was that this tutelage would spin out for as long Britain could hold on to her West African colonies.

Samuel was confident he would be among the successful candidates when it came time to sit the entrance examination to the new institution. In the meantime, he sat and passed the Posts and Telegraphs (P and T) examination, a civil service recruitment test.

"In the year before Ibadan," he told me, "I can earn some money that may come in useful in the university."

"You mean for the fees and things?" I asked.

"Of course."

"But you may not need it," I said. "I'll bet anything you will win a scholarship."

He looked at me and smiled expansively. "You sometimes know the right thing to say. Thank you. I hope I'll justify your confidence."

"Somehow," I said, changing the subject slightly, "this place is not going to be the same when I come back here next term, alone."

"You don't need me," he said seriously. "You never did. Maybe Onyewuchi, but not me. You used to run to him, especially in your first year. But you're all right now. You don't need even him. And happily for you, Godfrey Clarke is also leaving for the P and T. You need nobody now."

He was wrong. I was not happy Clarke was leaving. I was not sad either. The truth was that the fellow was no longer of much concern to me. He pretty much went his way, and I went mine. We seldom moved in the same orbit. He was a school prefect, with considerable powers to inflict pain and suffering on those boys who fell foul of the regulations or his interpretation of them. But I suppose I had learned, through my long experience of crossing him, when to take evasive action if he loomed anywhere in my sight.

He remained, to his last day in Umuahia, something of a human peacock. I could never come to terms with the meticulous care with which Clarke groomed his hair and his body, as if he was a girl. I could not stand his partiality for the *ude-aku*, a nice-smelling ointment extracted from the palm kernel, with which he shamelessly bathed his body, head to toe. His liberal use of the substance—notwithstanding the intense, unrelenting tropical heat—always made my flesh crawl. It was anathema to me. Samuel often complained that my skin looked whitish and flaky because I would not apply such ointments. That was okay. I could live with that criticism, especially coming mainly from my cousin.

Onyewuchi was in the P and T group. They were expected to report to that department in September. This meant that they required a special dispensation from the principal to skip the third term of the year—their last. Mr. Walter Graves had no objection to this and happily bade farewell to the group.

It was not so easy for me to bid farewell to my guide, mentor, and friend Patrick Onyewuchi. The elements on the last two days of the second term were gloomy in the extreme. It rained hard too. My heart was just as gloomy, but I would not let my eyes rain tears. I put on a show of stoicism, though the impending separation from my friend rent my heart.

He was munching on his favorite combination snack, groundnuts and coconut, when, in answer to his call, I went to his room. Ebong, his mouth stuffed full with biscuits, sat on a chair, a picture of melancholy. He was not a boy who ordinarily wore his heart on his sleeve. To see him now looking dejected, and twiddling a cricket bat when he clearly was not thinking cricket, affected me.

It was Onyewuchi's idea of a farewell party. On his bed was a small assortment of sweet biscuits, crackers, groundnuts, and coconut pieces in varying shapes and sizes. There was nothing to drink except water. Wordlessly, I fell to.

"I'll miss both of you very much," Onyewuchi said.

"We'll miss you too," I replied, including Ebong with a sideways look at him and a wave of my hand. "You are a wonderful person. The best friend any boy could have wished for. Look at Ebong. Doesn't he look already lost, like a sheep without a shepherd? Look at him."

The object of my commiseration said not a word. He had discarded the cricket bat, which he carefully propped up against the bed. He was now standing and just staring at Onyewuchi and me, in turn, as we spoke.

"He'll be all right," said Onyewuchi. "Won't you, Ebong?"

"Somehow, I don't think so," I said.

"Come on, Okoye! Leave him alone. Anyone who's as good as Ebong is in so many different things should be all right. He's the best cricketer in the college—"

"I beg your pardon?" I said, smiling. "I scored more runs than he did in the last match last term, remember?"

"He's one of the best two or three in hockey," Onyewuchi continued as if I had not spoken. "By your own efforts, Ebong, you are now able to raise enough pocket money to take care of your needs. There's nothing much I can do for you now. In fact, there never was much I did for you, anyway."

It might have been a collective case of a rare disease called *modesty* and which perhaps afflicted all the P and T group. My cousin Samuel had expressed pretty much the same idea when he told me I would not need him and that I never did, anyway.

"That's not true," said Ebong before I could get a word out. But then, he did not elaborate. He was a boy of very few words, except when he talked sports. Then he would unwind his tongue and wax eloquent.

"It's not true," he repeated, his eyes asking me what more needed to be said. So I too lapsed into silence, letting the expression on my face speak for me.

It did, because I saw Onyewuchi looking hard at me.

"I don't know what your problem is," he said to me. "You've only ever had one serious problem—"

"Clarke," I said. "I know."

"I'm glad you know. Now he too is leaving. You are now, in class 4, one of the senior boys in the college. Other boys now look up to you. Next year, class 5—and you know what that means?"

"Cambridge," I answered.

"You know I have confidence that you'll excel in that exam."

"Thank you," I said, looking down. "I'll do my best. In fact, I always do my best, except in the eyes of the principal."

"That's only in your conduct, of course."

"What does he want me to do?" I asked. "Why has he twice threatened me with expulsion?"

"We've been through this several times," said Onyewuchi. "What was it he said in your last year's report? 'He has natural inclination to disobey.' I'm afraid he's right. Especially where Clarke is concerned."

"Only with Clarke," I said emphatically.

"Let's not get into that. Just do the best you can, and you'll be all right."

"I hope so."

"There's just one thing I want to ask you."

"What?" I asked.

"Why are you the worst farmer in the college?"

He laughed as he whispered the question. But it was no laughing matter. Least of all, to me. I stole a quick glance at Ebong, who might have heard the question but pretended he had not.

"That's not fair," I whispered back to Onyewuchi. "I did the best I could."

But did I? I had asked myself that question a million times since the disaster of my second attempt to grow yams, in expectations of a reasonable harvest. My assertion to Onyewuchi that I had done my best now rang hollow. I knew it and, which was more mortifying, I knew he knew it.

It had been a disaster, worse than in the previous year. Something got to my seed yams, perhaps before they could sprout a new life. Must have been insects or worms or other parasites. My harvest, once again, was the laughingstock of boys who had nothing better to do than make fun of other people's misfortune. When my harvested yams were being weighed, I averted my eyes from the scales. But then, illogically, I asked the housemaster what the scale read.

"Let's just say," said Mr. Pepple, smiting the side of his thigh as he was wont to do, "that ignorance should be bliss for you."

That had been the ultimate humiliation: not knowing how much my yams weighed. And I knew I would be teased unmercifully—by friend and foe alike—for my ineptitude in this endeavor. So I steeled myself against the barbs.

"Will you do it again?" Onyewuchi asked, his tone milder, less sarcastic. "I mean, farm?"

"Should I?" I asked, looking him in the eye.

The school bell rang for supper, and we knew it would be the last supper all three of us would eat in the same dining hall in Umuahia Government College.

"Tomorrow is my last day here," Onyewuchi said. "But I'll say my good-byes now. I'm not sure if I'll see either of you in the morning before everybody heads home on vacation."

He went and shook hands with Ebong and patted him fondly on the back of his head. He then came to me, extending his hand toward me. But I deftly moved inside of the out-stretched arm and encircled him with my arms.

"There," I said as we disengaged. "I've been wanting to do that for a long time."

"Thank you both," he said as we linked hands and walked out of the dormitory and into the pouring rain.

*　*　*

I actually thought I had gotten Adamma out of my system. I could not deal with her mother's obvious hostility and lacked the courage to go visit her at her home. Her father, quiet and unobtrusive, pretended I did not exist, though he was well aware that his son Ben and I had been best friends in primary school. He saw us share Ben's meals several times. He might also have noticed with what favor I looked at his daughter. But if he did, he said nothing. Sometimes, I found his silence more disconcerting than his wife's unfriendliness.

Adamma boldly came to my father's house two days after I returned to Aba for the August 1947 vacation. She did not send word to me that she would visit. She was herself now a high school student in her second year in the Holy Rosary College. This was an all-girls school in Onitsha. Perhaps she thought that her new status freed her from absolute and total obedience to her mother's wishes. Or perhaps she was not completely forthcoming to her parents as to where she was going.

I was taken aback when I saw her. And mightily pleased too, I might add. Her smile, as she stood in the doorway of the room I shared with Samuel, was radiant. She used to have her hair braided. Now she wore it like a boy, barbered. I never saw hair, cut so low, look so beautifully in tune with the rest of a girl's body.

I could not tell if she was even aware of it, but there was something about her allure that bordered on the quietly sensual. Her artless beauty I had always found beguiling. Now I found her slightly fuller figure rather more physically appealing than I was—how do I put it?—comfortable with.

There was no doubt about it. I was mightily pleased to see her. But I was confused too. Confused by the strong urge I felt to take her in my arms, even as one-half of my brain, it being my remembrancer, recalled one of the Ten Commandments. Why my half-baked gray tissue assumed that taking Adamma in my arms would inevitably lead to sin, I could not tell. But it chilled me, freezing me in my tracks as I made a half move toward her.

She saw my hesitation and smiled knowingly. It was, it seemed to me, a coquettish smile too. A smile that proclaimed, in an odd kind of way, that she was now no longer the artless little girl I had known in days of yore. It was the smile of a pretty girl whose prettiness had grown in her own consciousness to the point where she was aware of the magnetic quality of her personality.

I do not recall who first moved. I was still struggling with my reluctant brain when, somehow, I found myself entangled with Adamma. Talk about magnetism! We were now in the middle of the room, holding each other so tightly we could only breathe with difficulty, heavily. No, we did not kiss. I had not learned to do such things. Nor had she, as far as I could judge. The fierceness of our embrace, if that is what it was, said it all. The next thing I knew, we fell in a heap, a tangled heap, on the bed I shared with Samuel.

Someone coughed in the corridor leading to the room and, in a trice, we untangled ourselves and sat up as if that was all we had been doing. Samuel came in, without knocking, which was as it was supposed to be. Neither of us ever thought it necessary to knock on the door before entering. Until now. Now he stopped as his eyes slowly took in the situation. He peered long and hard at Adamma, the room being very poorly lit by natural light coming in through the lone window giving upon the parlor.

He did not apologize for interrupting the proceedings. Instead, he smiled and said, "You remember that I'm leaving for Port Harcourt in the next hour or two, I hope?"

I had forgotten. Or to be totally truthful, Adamma's unexpected visit had wiped all else from my memory. I looked at her sadly, my twisted smile and a slight shake of my head telling her—as clearly as if I had spoken the words—that that was it. For now, at any rate.

I was still breathing heavily, which was something I could not understand. It was not as if Adamma and I had been tossing uncontrollably on the bed. Or doing something we should not have been doing. We had simply held each other closely, quietly savoring the rare moment of our physical closeness—knowing better than to take the moment, delirious and intoxicating as it might have been, even one step further.

In that all-too-brief moment of such sweet privacy as I had never before experienced, my mind, following its own twisted logic, turned to Kofi Bentsil. And to Friday Stoneface. Two friends and classmates who were, even then, rather more worldly wise than seemed appropriate for that period of our adolescence. I did not think about Chidi Ebele. But I asked myself what Kofi and Friday would have done had they been in my shoes. I was laughing inwardly at myself and at the utter pointlessness of my question, when cousin Samuel so unceremoniously barged into the room. It was pointless because I knew the answer to the question. Or if "know" is too strong a word, at least I had a pretty good idea what it was.

Adamma got up, straightening her dress as she did so. Her visit had been brief and, so to say, to the point. Barely a half-dozen words had been exchanged between us. We had, somehow, found no use for them to articulate what we felt. We just did it—at least, what we could or needed to do.

———

199

With Samuel looking from her to me, and no doubt waiting for an answer to his question, Adamma reached for my hand and held it, squeezing it once, twice, and then let go. She kept her eyes on me as she walked slowly backward till she was past Samuel. Then she turned and walked out of the room. And the sweetness that she had brought with her, and which had seemed to permeate and pervade the room, went with her.

Strange as it may seem, I felt no bitterness toward my cousin Samuel. Far from interrupting, he had probably saved us, though I might not have felt so at the time. I think I did the right thing to apologize to him.

"I'm sorry, Samuel," I said, getting off the bed. "I shouldn't have—"

"I'm the one that should be sorry," he countered. "I didn't know she was here."

"It wouldn't have mattered. This is your room also."

"It was," Samuel said. "In another hour or so, it will become yours entirely. As you know, I'll go from Port Harcourt straight to Lagos in about a week or so."

I helped him put the finishing touches to his packing, my mind in a whirl. I had never before owned a room exclusively by myself. For almost as long as I could remember, Samuel and I had shared the room. He had lived so long with us it was difficult sometimes to remember that his parents lived in Port Harcourt, a distance of some forty miles from Aba. His father was my father's elder brother, born of the same mother, though my grandfather had married, in all, three wives. I had two other surviving uncles, half uncles actually. Both were traders. They plied their wares in Northern Nigeria and only came home to our village of Orifite for the Christmas festivities. This was an annual pilgrimage by which they set great store. But they were not much in my life, and I was often hard put to it to remember their names.

Samuel did something I had not suspected he was capable of doing. Ordinarily, he was not much given to sentimentalities. He very seldom showed emotion. But on this last day of his long sojourn with us, after he and I had properly secured his two-piece luggage, he came and stood in front of me. For just long enough for me to begin to wonder what he had in mind, he stood and stared at me. And then he said the words I never thought to hear from him.

"Obinna," he said, his eyes boring into mine, "you know you are the brother I never had, a younger brother. I don't need to tell you that my parents and two sisters mean everything to me. But this house is the home I've known for—what?—at least ten years. I even have to think hard to remember when my father brought me to your father. But I remember clearly the words he spoke as he handed me over to Papa. 'Joshua,' he said, 'take my son and treat him like one or yours. You will know better what to do for him than me. I only stayed in school long enough to read the Bible and write a few words.

But whatever you do, don't ever let him forget. You understand what I mean? He must never forget, no matter how far he goes.' And I knew exactly what he meant by those words."

"And you've never forgotten," I said as we pulled each other into a warm embrace.

"How could I ever forget the parents who had me?" he asked, a strange light shining in his eyes, his question addressed to no one in particular. "I'm just so lucky to have two papas and mamas. That's a blessing no one can ever take away from me."

"Careful now," I said, smiling. "Don't make me jealous."

Family prayers were said over Samuel about an hour later, both my parents returning to the house earlier than they were wont to do. I went with Samuel to the motor park, carrying one baggage on my head. The weather cooperated somewhat, it being the August break in the middle of the rainy season—a regular climatic aberration caused by some kind of an annual shift in the pattern and direction of the trade winds, which I have never fully understood.

Samuel found the lorry he wanted, paid up, and took his place close to the tailboard of the vehicle. But not before he had once more embraced me warmly and said, "I expect great things of you in Umuahia. Keep the Okoye flag flying."

Soon, the vehicle, a mammy wagon, started up with a cough and a loud spurt and began to ease off from its allotted space. Samuel waved, and I waved back and went on doing so until the vehicle disappeared from sight round a bend.

It was a more wrenching moment in my life than I had expected it to be, this separation (of a sort) from a cousin who was really a brother. Or was he a brother who was really a cousin? It was rather confusing. I had, for almost all my life, taken Samuel for granted—a given. Someone with whom I had interrelated—sometimes thoughtlessly, often, I think, rather indifferently, hardly ever thinking that the emotional bonds between us were deeper than either of us would have cared to admit.

Now suddenly, he was gone from me. Separations have this maddening habit of coming on us suddenly, even when we know they are coming. So as I stood and stared at the departing mammy wagon, with one arm raised even after the lorry had disappeared from view, I began to wish we—Samuel and I—had had more time to do this separation with appropriate solemnity.

There was a lump in my throat that would not let me breathe freely and easily. I did not fight it, for I knew what it was doing there and whence it came.

*   *   *

The Yorubaman caused something of a stir when he announced, at a morning assembly, that he would take the entire class 5 out on a picnic. Excited applause began to reverberate around the hall. Then the master held up an arm for silence.

"Don't get ahead of me," Mr. Babatunde said, loud and clear. "Wait until I tell you when the picnic will take place, and then I hope you will still applaud."

He leaned toward the principal, who was standing next to him, and whispered a few words in the big man's ear. The principal nodded two or three times, emphatically, as if in encouragement.

"The picnic," the Yorubaman then announced, "will be on Sunday, two days hence."

The entire assembly froze, not just Achara's class. His class was the class immediately affected by the announcement. But there was, in the minds of every one of us, a sense of shock that the school would give its imprimatur to an idea that seemed like a punch below the belt.

From the back row, a loud voice was raised in protest. "But that's the day before the start of the Cambridge exam!"

Another voice, which I recognized as Nwobi's, added, "And that's our last day for swotting!"

Murmurs of support rolled like a giant wave over the assembled boys. But it was useless. The principal maintained the impassivity of his face, a clear sign—if any was needed—that all protest was in vain. The Yorubaman was not smiling either.

"It's for the good of the class," he explained. "It does no boy any good to study until the last possible moment before such an important exam. Brain fag, as our Nigerian expression has it, might set in and ruin a boy's chances of achieving the best performance of which he is capable."

That dramatic announcement, with the near uproar if engendered, was the high point of the third and last terms of my fourth year, which, otherwise, passed very uneventfully. It would be an understatement to say that it caused quite a lot of dismay, and not only in Achara's class. My own mind jumped twelve months ahead, when it would be my turn to sit the examination. If the Yorubaman was still around—and even if he was not—my class seemed sure to suffer the same fate as Achara's class.

Nothing like this had ever happened in the college. As far as any of us knew, nothing like it had ever happened anywhere else. Not even in England. To be thus deprived of what we saw as our last best chance to pick up on those tidbits of knowledge that might otherwise escape our attention, seemed a cruel blow indeed.

"How can they do this to us?" Nwobi grumbled as, later that day, we sat in the library, studying.

Achara looked up from his books. "To tell you the truth," he said, "I see nothing wrong with the idea."

"You must be the only one who doesn't," I said. "He's one of my favorite masters, but if he tries anything like that next year—"

"Yes, tell us," urged Achara as I paused. "What will you do? Refuse to go?"

"I might."

"You wouldn't dare," said Achara.

"I could pretend to be sick," I said without much conviction. "Or something like that."

After a short suppressed bout of laughter—suppressed on account of other boys concentrating on their books—Nwobi looked steadily at me for a moment or two.

"It's not a bad idea, when you think of it," he said, challenging Achara with his eyes.

"Meaning . . . ?"

"Meaning I might do so," said Nwobi. "They should have told us about this picnic a week ago instead of today. What it means now is that I have to read for *two* days tomorrow Saturday. And yes, I know. You don't have to tell me it is impossible to do so."

"I'm glad you know that."

"It's easy for you, Achara. But you obviously don't understand how hard it is for the rest of us to lose one whole day."

"Why don't you just give up, my friend? You may be surprised how well it might all turn out to be. As for Okoye, I really don't understand why he is getting panicky already one year before his turn. As they say, to be forewarned—"

"Don't give me that!" I said vehemently. "Just watch me."

Achara laughed. Nwobi too, though there seemed to be little mirth in *his* laughter. His eyes looked pensive.

"Watch you? I'm afraid I can't do that," said Achara. "I hope to goodness I won't be here to watch you."

"D'you think," asked Nwobi, going off into his own little world of unrealism and daydreaming, "that there's a chance the Yorubaman is not serious about this picnic?"

Mr. Bisi Babatunde answered that question some thirty or so hours later on Sunday morning. Shortly after the Anglican chapel service, the school lorry rolled out of the college compound, with all class 5 boys aboard. If there were any doubting Thomases before then, there were none after. We knew, all of us in class 4, that the Yorubaman was for real. That what he said was what he did, and would do. In December 1947 and, if he was still around twelve months later, in December 1948.

I had watched Nwobi as he took his seat next to Achara in the lorry. He had looked to me as if he was at peace with himself, when he finally understood that he had no other options. That gave me heart. I knew then that if he could reconcile himself to the picnic, so could I when my turn came.

CHAPTER XXIV

FIFTH YEAR

James Wolf clutched the hard white ball to his chest with his right hand and covered both with his left hand. The feeling that he seemed anxious to hide the ball from view was heightened when he stole a surreptitious look, first to his right, then to his left, and finally behind him. Suddenly, still clutching the ball to his chest, he lifted his left knee as high as it would go, pivoting slightly to his right as he did so. Next he withdrew the hand that held the ball, extended it backward, and finally let fly the ball at an imaginary opponent who, he said, would be positioned about twenty yards away from him.

A small group of us, all cricketers of sorts—each one of us handpicked by him—stood and stared at him. It was fascinating histrionics, with his earnestness and enthusiasm for his mission, plain for all to see. The midafternoon sun beat down on our heads. Fortunately, however, the harmattan was blowing; and we were comfortable with the heat. Not one among us dared object to the master's choice of a Saturday for this extracurricular activity. But because he thus violated the sacrosanctity of our freest day of the week, we felt like victims. Or, stated differently, we were the human guinea pigs for Mr. Wolf's experimentation.

He was on a mission, he told us. "In England," he said, "they play cricket, but not baseball. In America, they play baseball but think cricket is much too dull and slow for their temperament. I would like to see Nigeria go the way of Australia, where much cricket is played and some baseball."

He said nothing about his home country, New Zealand, in this regard. So we were left to surmise that there was no baseball there and to ask ourselves why he now chose Nigeria for this particular mission. Wasn't charity supposed to start at home?

"In baseball," he said, "you pitch the ball, not bowl it as in cricket. That means you can throw the ball with no concern about the straightness of the arm. You all know that in cricket, if you bend the bowling arm at the elbow or jerk the ball at the batsman with a throwing action, it is illegal. Baseball permits any delivery action, straight arm or bent."

He taught us a whole host of things about the American game. We learned that the person to whom the ball is pitched is called the batter or hitter (not the batsman, as in cricket). The batter stands only twenty yards from the pitcher (twenty-two yards in cricket). A ball hit behind the batter and a line drawn from the batter's box to the left and right corners of the field is called a foul ball. Such a ball is immediately called dead or out of play if not caught by a fielder. The batting side does not advance on such a hit, however long it is. He taught us that the ball has to be pitched in the zone between the armpit and the knees of the batter and must pass over a plate at the batter's box, or it is ruled a "ball," meaning that it is not a fair delivery.

It was all very confusing, especially to those of us who were still struggling to develop, or fine-tune, our cricketing skills. He showed us a baseball bat; and we saw straightaway that, because of its rounded form, the point of contact between it and the pitched ball was, in reality, only a thin line. Because we were used to the flat surface of the cricket bat, we looked at one another wonderingly. It was clear to us that hitting with such an implement would be a hundredfold more difficult than with an honest cricket bat.

Someone asked the master why he went through his series of antics, looking to his left, right, and behind, before pitching the ball at the imaginary batter.

"Because, my boy, there might be a teammate of the batter at first, second, or third base. You have to watch him closely, or he might take off as you deliver the ball and steal the next base."

We laughed, but Mr. Wolf did not laugh with us.

"Stealing," he said earnestly, "is a serious and very important part of the game. There are players who are quite adept at it. Runs are very hard to come by in baseball. And since a run is scored only when a batter goes from one base to the next until he reaches home plate, it should be clear that stealing bases helps a team as much as any other aspect of the game."

We nodded in understanding, but without enthusiasm. I could not empathize with Mr. Wolf in his zeal to introduce the strange game to us. I was in the first term of my fifth year, 1948, which was, above all, the year of the Cambridge School Certificate examination. I was not the worst swot in my class, but I could ill afford the time for a new game. A game that, because of its superficial affinity to cricket, could quite easily ensnare boys like me.

Quite deliberately, I made up my mind not to like the game. And close on the heels of that decision came conviction. A conviction that baseball was inferior to my game. I convinced myself that baseball was merely a modified, but more dangerous form of rounders, a game little boys, even girls, played in primary school. I convinced myself that baseball could not hold a candle to cricket for the variety or the sheer beauty of its stroke play. There could be nothing, in the American game, to compare with the imperiousness of the straight drive nor the elegance and gracefulness of the cover drive. Nothing to surpass the delicacy of the late cut or the impishness of the glance when the ball, at the moment of impact with a "dead" bat, is deflected away from the body, to the delight of the batsman and the mortification of the bowler. Was the quintessential baseball stroke not the shot that heaves a ball from the outer fringes of the batting plate and deposits it somewhere, or anywhere, to the left side of the outfield? A stroke that in cricket goes by the rather undignified label of a cow shot, easily the riskiest, crudest stroke in the game. In England, Mr. Graves was fond of telling us, the cow shot was a stroke favored by the village blacksmith, all shoulders and powerful muscles, who would abandon his forge, come the weekend, for the occasional game of cricket in the village green.

Mr. Wolf made us play baseball for the whole of that first term of 1948. He told us it was strictly voluntary, but we did not believe him. As I told Achara, quite early in the term, the game might indeed have been genuinely voluntary for him, for Okoroafor, and for other boys of their ilk. But I knew I had no choice in the matter. Nor had Ebong nor Bentsil nor Ebele. As cricketers, we represented Mr. Wolf's best hope for the new game—period. He had a habit of tracking us down if we failed to show up for one of his sessions. And for me, that was a fate worse than an hour at the matchet parade. A little bit of hyperbole perhaps, but it came pretty close to how I felt.

I stayed the course faithfully and never let an unkind word about the game pass my lips—especially when the master himself was around. I had learned my lesson, which is not to say that I made any serious effort to master the art of baseball. Generally, when it was my turn at the batter's box, I flailed away with might and main, usually with little or no contact with the ball. And I kept doing so until Mr. Wolf took notice and asked me if my eyesight was failing me. It was, actually. But I would not have blamed the poverty of my baseball stroke play on my declining vision.

Happily, the game died a natural death. There just did not seem to be any enthusiasm for it, even among the cricketers. Perhaps *especially* among the cricketers. I believe many of us saw some kind of a conflict between the two games, in most of their fundamental and basic principles of execution, with bat and ball.

It was at about this time that we noticed that Mr. Wolf was sprouting a beard. He went on growing it, and a straggling moustache to boot, until the skin of his face was barely visible. His lips too almost disappeared from view.

I was curious, but like my teammates, I refrained from asking any questions. Then one day, at a cricket practice, and unprompted, he told us why he grew his beard.

"Is there anyone here who hasn't heard of the great W. G. Grace?" he asked.

A few boys raised their hands. I did not, because I remembered that less than a year earlier, he had asked us at another cricket practice if we knew of the great man. The boys who raised their hands were either new members of the team or older hands who chose to "play the master for a sucker." His words, twelve months earlier, not mine.

Mr. Wolf looked briefly at us and shook his head. "Well well," he said. "I'm surprised. The greatest ever, and you haven't heard about him? W. G.—that's what he's commonly called. W. G. was the father of modern cricket. This year, 1948, is the centenary of his birth."

He pulled at his luxuriant beard for a moment or two, reflectively, and then said, "W. G. had the most monstrous beard, which gave him quite a fearsome visage and must have struck terror in the hearts of some poor bowlers who came up against him. It was said that the quickest bowlers sometimes aimed for his beard with their bumpers."

"What happened?" someone asked, in a voice reflecting considerable concern for W. G.

"What d'you think?" asked Mr. Wolf, his happy smile splitting his face from ear to ear. "W. G. was a great hooker of the ball. Need I say more? He was the nonpareil. I wear my beard in tribute to him. And I'll keep it on till the end of this year."

I found myself wondering how his beautiful wife could stand all that hair.

*   *   *

Mr. Walter Graves had announced, at the end of the previous year (my fourth), that there would be a change in the school year. The school year had been the same as the calendar year. Now it would be September to August. The establishment of the University College, Ibadan, we were told, had something to do with the change. It was set to admit its first set of undergraduate students in September 1948. The change also reconciled our school year with the prevailing system in the rest of the world. Meaning, of course, the Western world. Europe and America, to be precise.

We—the students, that is—were not asked if we liked the change. The principal talked about the *summer* vacation. But in Nigeria, we have no summers—only the rainy, and the dry seasons. For much of the northern hemispheric spring and summer, from late March through September, it does nothing else but rain in my part of Nigeria. And the late summer months, we were told, would be the time of the long annual vacation for the University College, Ibadan—for those of us who would be lucky to gain admission to that institution. But who wanted to have the long annual vacation when one did little else but stay indoors because of the incessant rain? That would have been the best time of the year to concentrate on one's academic work, in a classroom or a library. But no one asked us what *we* thought.

The Ibadan University College was in our future—our dream for the future. There were some among us, in my class, who had reasonable expectations of success in its entrance examination. But first, there was the Cambridge School Certificate examination to sit and to pass.

The direct and immediate consequence of the change in the school year was that my class would be in class 5 for only two terms. What would have been the third term of 1948 would, by the change, become the first term of 1948/49, my sixth class. Achara's class, like my cousin Samuel's a year earlier, had written their Cambridge examination in the last term of their fifth year. The very notion that my class would write the same examination in the first term of our sixth year rankled in our collective mind. Why couldn't they leave well alone?

Every examination I had hitherto sat paled in significance in comparison with this one. It was an examination that would open the doors to the future. It was also the end of the road academically for those who would have no further opportunities to aspire to a university or other forms of tertiary education. It was an examination that had the capacity to make or unmake a person. Because the syndicate, or board of examiners, was as remote from us as the moon was from the Earth and knew not friend or foe in our Umuahia class, its absolute objectivity in grading the boys was taken for granted. We dubbed the syndicate the *Cambridge-Man*.

A saying arose among the boys that "the Cambridge-Man will decide." It was a saying that underlined the fierce competitiveness in the class. A competitiveness in which few of the boys seemed willing to concede superiority to others, no matter how often and how regularly bested by them in tests and examinations. Those boys who, time and again, came out on top were the principal targets of this war of words. They stood to lose the most if the Cambridge-Man did not rank them in the top flight of the class, a distinction to which they had become accustomed.

I was one of *them*. And I knew therefore that I was among those who had to prove themselves, one more time, in order to win some grudging respect from the other boys. For reasons that I knew had nothing to do with the acuity or vacuity of my intellect, I began to worry about the examination. I worried that I might never be adequately prepared for the full rigors of an external examination, set by a faraway syndicate that did not know *me* from Adam. In other words, the half-serious banter about the Cambridge-Man was getting to me. What if indeed I had achieved my level of success because I was a favorite of several of our teachers? The Cambridge-Man had become, for me, a bogeyman.

*   *   *

In the midst of all this worrying, I found solace and contentment in my friendship with one of the littlest boys in the college. Alfred Onwudinjo was a fresher and stood only just over four feet tall, with a blessedly pleasant face and an infectious smile.

Our paths had crossed in the unhappiest of circumstances, for me. For the second time in the space of twelve short months, Mr. Graves had inflicted the ultimate humiliation on me by making me sit in the front row during the morning assembly with the class 1 boys. Again, for one long week. It is odd how twelve months can seem a very short span, yet one week can feel like an eternity.

I had been found guilty of speaking disrespectfully to a person in authority: one Festus Ezekwe, the school captain. A class 6 boy, just one class senior to me, Ezekwe and I had in fact been on quite friendly terms—that is, up until the incident that goaded me into using some extravagant, but unwise string of words. Indeed, in an interhouse competition about six months earlier, in the final term of my fourth year, I had met Ezekwe in probably the strangest boxing match ever staged in the college.

Because we were in the same weight group—the heavyweights—we found ourselves matched against each other. But it was not a fair match. He was older and, more to the point, stronger and more experienced in the art than I was. It would have been a very lopsided contest had I not used my head and found a willing partner in Ezekwe.

As we touched gloves, I decided that discretion was indeed the better part of valor. No words were exchanged between us. But my body language was eloquent. It was my good fortune that Ezekwe, somehow, quickly caught on to that language.

I would feint and jab, but very lightly. Ezekwe, who ordinarily packed a knockout punch in his right hand, also feinted and jabbed. But taking his cue from me, he jabbed without his customary gusto. Not wishing, as it were, to tempt the devil, I scrupulously refrained from doing what I did best: throw my favorite combinations of right and left. Ezekwe threw a few, experimentally I suppose. But soon sensing its utter pointlessness, he desisted as the match progressed. I had barely worked up a sweat when the three-round match ended.

Ezekwe got the verdict and the points for his house. I came away from the match with body and skin intact, but no points for my house. It was, some boys remarked afterward, the only boxing match they ever saw in which both contestants smiled throughout its duration. As Ezekwe and I embraced at the final bell, he patted me on the head in a friendly and conspiratorial manner. Briefly, I held him tightly and smiled innocently.

Then one day, about six months later, I failed to show up for a matchet parade, on which I had been put by a meddlesome prefect for a relatively minor infraction. On the Saturday of the matchet parade, it had rained without cease, and violently too, though the start of the rainy season was officially still about a month away. When the school captain asked me about my absence from the parade, I lied outright.

"You know," I said, "I didn't hear my name called."

He looked at me as one would a little boy who was trying to be cleverer than his teacher or father or something. And then he laughed. That laughter stung me. So when he sought to put a hand on my shoulder as we stood and talked in the prefects' room, I pushed his hand away, and none too gently.

Achara, who was also a school prefect, was in the room and watched the deteriorating interaction between me and Ezekwe with mounting concern. I knew this by the way he was looking at me, with eyes that pleaded with me for some restraint. Getting, I suppose, no satisfactory response from me, he now stepped up to me. Quietly, he grabbed me firmly by one arm and pulled me as far away from my interlocutor as he could, within the room.

"What's the matter with you?" he asked. He spoke softly, but I could see the fire in his eyes. Or if it was not fire, it might have been anger. He was angry with me. But I was past caring.

"He has no right to laugh at me like that," I said, looking over my shoulder at the object of my displeasure.

"He was only trying to be friendly," Achara pointed out. "You just told him a barefaced lie, no?"

"I did not."

"You did, my friend. Everyone—and I mean everyone—clearly heard the names of those on the matchet parade, which, if I remember correctly, were called out twice. And you think you can stand there and say you didn't hear your name? I thought it's only your eyes that are giving you trouble."

Ordinarily, I would have laughed at this piece of witticism. But I was in no mood for pleasantries.

"If I lied," I said, "let him prove it."

Quite deliberately, having now lost all sense and sensibility, I had spoken loudly. Loud enough for Ezekwe to hear me and with enough acerbity to show him I did not care.

"Excuse me," said Achara, with dignity. "Please pardon the interference."

For just a moment or two, he stared at me sadly. Then he turned and walked back to his seat. I too walked back deeper into the room and went and stood in front of Ezekwe.

"What's the matter with you?" Ezekwe asked me.

"That's the same question Achara just asked me. Why does everyone think there's something the matter with me? I told you I did not hear my name."

Ezekwe just narrowly stopped himself from laughing out loud a second time. I could see by the way he tried to cover his mouth with one hand that it was a bit of a struggle to maintain his composure. When finally he recovered full control of his emotions, he turned to Achara.

"Can you tell your friend here—"

"Leave him out of this!" I interrupted harshly.

It was then that Ezekwe made his fateful decision. He modulated his voice in a manner, I supposed, to underscore the solemnity of the occasion and his regret at doing what he was compelled to do.

"You leave me no choice in the matter, Okoye Jr.," he said. "For failing to show up for your matchet parade and then, on top of that, trying to lie your way out of it, your punishment is doubled. That means—"

"I know what it means," I interrupted. "To begin with, since Samuel left the college, no one calls me Okoye Jr. anymore. Secondly—"

"Sorry," he said quickly. "Force of habit."

"Secondly, you can't be serious about doubling my punishment."

"You asked for it. I'm sorry."

"That's not fair," I said, looking across at Achara. But Achara turned his face away from me. "I'm a class 5 boy now."

"Then act like one!"

"Go to hell!" I burst out. "What gives you the authority to do this?"

"Why don't you go and ask the principal?" said Ezekwe, gathering up his books and things. "I'll be reporting the matter to him. It will be your chance to ask him that question."

"Do your worst!" I fired at his back as he was walking away. "Blow your pipe there till you burst!"

If memory serves, those were the same words someone spoke to the legendary Pied Piper of Hamelin. And they were words the entire town of Hamelin, in medieval Germany, rued when the piper led their children into the cavernous mouth of a mountain, which then closed up and swallowed them. Nothing so dire happened to me, but I was to sorely regret my outburst.

Mr. Walter Graves, with impish delight no doubt, decided to repeat my previous year's punishment. I was mortified at this degradation.

It was some consolation to me that Ezekwe, when he heard about my punishment, actually sought me out and apologized.

"I never expected he would make you sit with class 1, again. I'm really sorry."

"Never mind," I said, though I minded very much. "Maybe you could talk to the principal?"

"I'll see what I can do," he said, sounding sincere.

If he did, it made no difference. The very next morning, at the assembly, I took my unaccustomed place in the front row with the newest boys in the school.

Alfred Onwudinjo sat next to me. I had seen him around, but there had been no connection between us. I sat stiffly, very self-consciously, my shame writ large on my face. *He* broke the ice between us.

"Good morning," he said plaintively.

"Good morning, Onwudinjo," I replied, looking straight ahead of me.

"You know my name!" he cried softly, evidently delighted that I did.

Only then did I turn to look at him. He was smiling from ear to ear. Briefly, I wondered what there was to smile about. Or did he feel honored to be sitting next to a class 5 boy? I smiled back at him. At least I think my face did.

That was the beginning of our friendship. The chemistry between us was good and instantaneous. From that moment on, Onwudinjo was like a kid brother to me. Thenceforth, too, it seemed to me, he looked up to me as a big brother, friend, and counselor. Counselor? I asked myself that question repeatedly, as time went by, and the days stretched to weeks and the weeks to months. In my more objective moments, I knew I myself needed some counseling. But I supposed that from the deep fund of my own Umuahia experience, good and not so good, I could in fact counsel young Alfred. And I did.

He was shortsighted and needed corrective spectacles. I too was shortsighted and needed corrective spectacles even more desperately, particularly because of my involvement with cricket. My batting had been languishing somewhat, and I feared I might lose my place in the team. So I suggested to Onwudinjo that we travel together to Port Harcourt during the Easter vacation to see an eye specialist.

"But I don't know anyone in PH," he said.

"No problem," I said. "We'll stay with my uncle there."

"How can?" Onwudinjo asked dismissively. "They don't know me, and I don't know them."

"So come with me, and you'll get to know them. In fact, I'll write to my uncle today, just to warn them we're coming."

"But there isn't enough time for him to reply before the end of the term. Suppose they don't like the idea?"

"Stop worrying," I said. "I don't need a reply from my uncle before I can take you there. He's my father's senior brother. You didn't meet my cousin Samuel here. He left last year. We're like brothers actually. His parents live in PH with their other children. There's no problem."

"Oh, I don't know," said Onwudinjo uncertainly. "But if you say so, then I suppose it's okay. Do they have a big house?"

I laughed. "A big house? Does he need a big house just to accommodate the two of us? No, I'm afraid he doesn't even have a house. They have only two rented rooms, but that's okay. We'll manage. I've been there several times, with Samuel—that's the cousin I told you about—and my elder sister, and there was no problem. You lie down where you see a space. I know my uncle. He'll like you. You'll see."

"I hope so," said my little friend, still full of doubt.

"Just make sure you write to your parents and let them know you'll be going to PH for your glasses, straight from the college."

"I'll do so immediately," said Onwudinjo. "I already wrote to them about the glasses, and I'm expecting some money from them. I had told them I will likely go to Enugu for the glasses."

"Enugu? D'you know anybody there? Or d'you have relatives?"

"Well, my father knows some people—"

"Forget them! You should go to a place where you know somebody—me."

His money came, in the nick of time. Mine too, a few days earlier. The trip to Port Harcourt was a very pleasant one for us. We were most cordially received by my uncle and aunt, Matthew and Esther Okoye. Uncle Matthew, about two years older than my father, was the less educated of the two. He seemed too, for most of his life, to be engaged in an unending struggle to make ends meet. But he never complained—to my hearing. He preferred, he always said, to thank God for his three children, of whom, as he put it, Samuel was now a young man who talked fearlessly with white men but never failed in his duties to the parents who bore him. I know he was sincere when he thanked God for his brother Joshua. "In taking Samuel at a very tender age into his family," my uncle said to God, "Joshua ensured that Samuel had the best education available. He is the proof that a person who has the support of good people is more blessed than he who has wealth but few friends."

I had no idea how tedious Onwudinjo might have found some of this, but I knew most Igbo families took their daily prayers seriously. But there was never any doubt about the warmhearted welcome we both received. And when, four days later, Onwudinjo left Port Harcourt to return to Onitsha, where his parents lived, I could tell he was suitably touched when my uncle pressed him to accept a gift of one shilling. It was an amount that I knew the family could only just about afford to give away.

"Take it," said my uncle to my little friend. "And buy some bread for your brothers and sisters."

My uncle, I knew, had no idea if my friend had any siblings or not.

CHAPTER XXV

I never got to know who thought up the idea. It was one thing to play soccer matches against schools like the DMGS, Onitsha, or the Methodist College, Uzuakoli. Perhaps even against the Hope Waddell Training Institute, Calabar, whose acronym HWTI was ungraciously rendered as Here We Train Idiots. (For the record, let me say here and now that none of us in Government College Umuahia thought they trained idiots in HWTI. It was just one of those things for which there really is no explanation. I doubt anyone remembers anymore how it all started.)

The Dennis Memorial Grammar School, in the unpolled but consensual opinion of Umuahia boys the next best high school in the entire Eastern Nigeria, had a soccer team that held no terrors for us. In my time, we lost fairly regularly to them, beat them once in a while, and generally gave them a good run for their money.

The Uzuakoli Methodist College was more on a par in soccer with us. If we lost occasionally to them in that sport, we more than compensated by beating them quite regularly at cricket. So regularly, in fact, that before I was through with Umuahia, we had given up playing cricket matches against them altogether. The contests had become so very lopsidedly in our favor they were no longer much fun.

Hope Waddell played just one soccer match against us and beat us handily enough by the score—if memory serves—of 3-1. They were good, very good.

But play soccer against the likes of the two preeminent Roman Catholic secondary schools in the region? The Christ the King College, Onitsha, and the College of Immaculate Conception, Enugu, had soccer players equal to the best players in the country. Some of their players were good enough to merit serious consideration for selection into the national teams of the time. I do not want to speak ill of my principal or my teachers. But whoever thought up the idea of pitting our soccer skills against these two schools might have lost his mind.

Early in the second, and last, term of 1948, my fifth year, we hosted the soccer team from the CIC, Enugu. One of our masters, the Yorubaman I think, said something about soccer being only a game. If it was only a game, why did we put an all-consuming effort into our preparations? Our team practiced and practiced. And then practiced some more. I was never absolutely sure of this, but I heard that the team was clandestinely served eggs and some other special dishes that the rest of us never saw on our dining tables. The cricket team was never served eggs. Perhaps we did not need extra nourishment to beat the teams wc met.

We had not learned our lesson after the drubbing we received at the hands (feet, actually) of the other Catholic school, the Christ the King College. In a match, on their home ground in Onitsha, they scored ten goals to our one. "One for every Umuahia player, except the goalie," said Chidi Ebele, a member of the team himself. Why he excepted the goalkeeper, I could not tell. The poor goalie, when he could be persuaded to talk, confessed he was so dazzled by the blinding speed of the opponents' footwork that he could never tell at what moments they took their shots. The defeat had been so comprehensive and the manner of it so humiliating that the team forgot to sing the lyrics to our traditional song of lamentation: "*Deeply wailing, deeply wailing . . .*" That at least would have forewarned us, as we crowded around the school lorry to welcome back the team, that they had lost the match. They had lost their voices too, it seemed.

The school did everything to revitalize our soccer team in preparation for the CIC match. But there was not one of us who did not think the outcome would be just as bad for us, though we were to play on our home ground. There was, in all this, only one slim ray of hope for us. Not hope that we would win, but that the defeat might be less humiliating than that against the Onitsha college. The CIC team was actually on their way to play a much more important match against the redoubtable Port Harcourt team, one of the strongest city teams in the country. The stop to play against our Government College team was therefore little more than a warm-up practice game for their team.

A more-than-usually-heavy downpour washed out the game on the appointed afternoon of the match. So it was rescheduled for the next morning, a Saturday. That rescheduling, unexpectedly, gave us our second slim ray of hope. The CIC team was expected in Port Harcourt, some eighty or so miles from Umuahia, that same Saturday. We dared therefore to hope that they would treat the match against us even more cavalierly than they would have done, so as not to risk injuries to their players. We hoped and prayed.

Meanwhile, to kill time during the washout, the CIC players diverted themselves at the ping-pong table, watched by several starstruck Umuahia boys. Friday Onoh, the CIC center-forward, popularly known as "untouchable" because of the brilliance of his dribbling, played against Chuka Onwudike, reputedly the best defensive schoolboy soccer player in the country. In the course of the game, Friday mishit the ping-pong ball so that it flew over Onwudike's head. Nonchalantly, Onwudike spun on his heels and deftly flicked at the ball with his left foot before it bounced. Mouth agape, we watched as the ball hit the wall behind him and, rebounding neatly, flew back and landed in the dead center of Onoh's half of the table. I knew, as did several of the Umuahia boys, that this was no fluke and that Onwudike had intended that the trajectory of the ball, after he flicked at it, would be exactly as it turned out to be. The oohs and ahs and, I suppose, the awed expression on faces like mine impressed even the two CIC players. Chuka Onwudike smiled appreciatively and took a bow.

The next morning, Umuahia beat the CIC team by four goals to three. We were elated, naturally. But we did not kid ourselves into thinking that we had, overnight, developed into a great team. We rejoiced at our victory, though it was plain to see that our opponents had merely toyed with us. Our first goal had in fact been the result of a careless piece of showmanship by the CIC goalie. Even as he seemed to be waving to someone in the crowd of onlookers, he attempted to collect the ball that rolled slowly toward the goal. He must have taken his eyes off the ball because, to our utmost astonishment, it passed just under his fingers into the empty net.

It did not escape our attention that, for a team that set great store by their reputation as just about the best (or second-best) team around, the CIC boys took their defeat, not just in stride, but laughingly. Our egos were not bruised for the simple reason that we had none—in soccer. All we knew or cared about was that everyone had a good time. The CIC team left within an hour of the end of the game for their much more important encounter with Port Harcourt. And with that victory securely in our collective pocket, Umuahia never afterwards sought a rematch against the CIC team. At any rate, not in my remaining time in the college.

*　　*　　*

Government College Umuahia might have lost many more soccer matches than we won. But other than cricket and perhaps field hockey, there was one activity in which we could proudly claim supremacy over all others. Or almost all others. That activity was books and academics. No school in the whole of Eastern Nigeria, with the possible exception of DMGS, Onitsha, could touch us in that regard. That was our boast, even if we could never really prove it to the satisfaction of students from those others schools. Especially the boys from Dennis Memorial.

The Cambridge examination results for Achara's class were issued early in the second term of 1948. As the whole world expected, that class covered itself in glory, every bit as much as the previous class, my cousin Samuel's, had done. Achara led the class, also as expected. The major surprise—certainly to the entire school, quite possibly to himself too—was that Achara scored only a C (credit) in the English language paper. He should have achieved an A (distinction). We knew he was the best around. Our teachers all said so. His classmates acknowledged it. His innate sense of modesty, however, would not let him accept the laurels.

No matter, I know he was a disappointed young man, though he got a distinction in every other paper. It is entirely possibly that Achara's result in the English paper was the reason for the Yorubaman's unusual exchange of correspondence with the Cambridge Board of Examiners. I cannot, of course, vouch for the absolute veracity of the story that, at the time, certainly struck us as somewhat bold and audacious for a Nigerian. As we understood the sequence of events, Mr. Bisi Babatunde wrote to the Cambridge syndicate severely criticizing the form and content of the English examination papers set for African students. We were not privy to the exact nature of the criticism. But it must have struck home. The syndicate certainly took the matter seriously enough to set a slightly modified sample paper and to send it to Mr. Babatunde, with a suggestion that he try it out on the class next in line for the examination. That was my class. Mr. Babatunde, in his turn, sent to the syndicate a suggested model of an appropriate English paper for future examinations.

For my class, the situation was extremely intriguing. Having become aware of the highly unusual exchange of correspondence, we were eager to discover in what ways the content of the paper differed significantly from the English papers set in the previous years. Not to put too fine a point upon it, we found none. The questions on the grammar and structure of the English language remained as immutable as ever. The passages used for analysis did not appear to have more African allusions than before.

I was one of two boys who scored an A in the paper, which the Yorubaman had marked, he told us, with the same level of stringency with which Cambridge examination papers were marked. My classmates were willing to accept that John C. Jibunoh, the other boy who scored an A, had always been the best in the subject. His distinction was therefore not a surprise. Mine seemed to be. And they let me know it. Over and over again. I was the favorite of the Yorubaman, they taunted. One of his favorites, anyway.

"Wait till December!" they chanted. "The Cambridge-Man will decide!"

By then, I had become quite inured to this form of teasing. And so I let the refrain wash off me like water off a duck's back. My confidence, at this point, was at an all-time high—most of the time. There were, I must confess, moments when it sank abysmally low. I did not know why, but I took it all in stride. Those moments of diffidence were, I suppose, a natural reaction to the daunting challenge of confronting the first of the two major examinations of my high school years. The second, the entrance examination to the new University College, Ibadan, was to come three or so months after Cambridge.

In an odd kind of way, I actually began to look forward to the Cambridge examination. This, doubtless, had something to do with the fact that the two previous classes, my cousin Samuel's in 1946 and then Achara's in 1947, had both done Umuahia proud. I did not see, and none of my classmates saw, any reason to think that ours would be different. It probably also had a little to do with the fact that in the final order of merit for our fifth year, 1948, no classmate placed above me. It was the apogee of my academic endeavors, up to that point, in Umuahia.

Just before the end of my final term in class 5, the results of the first-ever entrance examination to the Ibadan University College were released. And once again, Umuahia had added another rousing page to its glorious history of outstanding academic achievements. My cousin Samuel's class had waited one year for this examination. They had then sat it with Achara's class.

The University College awarded three major and about a dozen minor scholarships, based solely on merit, in the entrance examination. Achara won one of the three major scholarships. No surprise there. Samuel and four other Umuahia boys won minor scholarships. My friend Nwobi and a handful of others secured ordinary passes. The principal, Mr. Walter Graves, who tended to be niggardly in singing our praises, described all this as "without doubt, the most stirring performance by any school in the country." I believe those were his exact words. And we knew he meant every word because, as he spoke, he was pulling and stroking his moustache reflectively.

"The staff and I have decided to start an honor roll," he announced to a morning assembly a few days before the beginning of the first so-called summer vacation. "When the college reopens in September, you will see a wooden board in this assembly hall high on the wall, there."

He pointed to a section of the wall, to his left, as he faced the students, high above the central window of the hall.

"The names of the scholarship winners in this year's University College entrance exam will be inscribed on it. It should be an inspiration to the succeeding classes and will remain a testimony of excellence through the ages."

It all sounded a little high-flown, but I believe he was serious. I know that it immediately set my mind working. Or perhaps just plain daydreaming.

About the future and how hard it would be to get my name inscribed on that board.

Later that same day, I lounged with Achara, Joseph Nwobi, and Innocent Dike on the steps of the Administration Block, facing the resplendently green quadrangle. It was a humid evening, clouded over, with not a star visible in the heavens. But we gave scant thought to the threatening skies. Uppermost on our minds was our coming separation. Achara and Nwobi were excited about the new University College to which they were headed, full of hope for the future and—it seemed to me—reasonably confident in their ability to cope with whatever destiny might thrust their way.

"Your name should be on that board," said Achara to me, "in a year's time."

"It should," I replied rather immodestly, "if all goes well. I won't pretend about it. I'd like my name there with yours or, failing that, with Samuel's. But as we all know, there can be surprises—"

"Are you telling me!" said Nwobi. "Here I am, going to Ibadan in three months' time. I didn't think I had any chance in the entrance exam."

"Stop being so modest," Achara said.

"Modest about what?" asked Nwobi. "Listen, I won't mention any names. But there must be at least six or so boys, and I'm sure you know them, who should have—"

"Should have," said Achara, "but didn't. That's all part of the game."

"I don't know what game you're talking about," I said, "since you hardly play any. But I think I understand what you mean. There's always an element of surprise in every exam. I might not even pass in the entrance exam, not to talk of winning a scholarship. But—"

I stopped because my friends were staring at me. And the expression on their faces said, as clearly as if they had spoken the words and done so in unison, that I was stark raving mad.

"What?" I asked, looking at them in turns.

Wordlessly, they exchanged glances. Then Achara, smiling sweetly, shook his head slowly a few times.

"I know your game," he said. "And don't you dare say anything again about me and games, or I'll challenge you—"

"To ping-pong," I interjected. "What else? It's the only game you play."

He looked daggers at me but, I knew, without venom and then made a motion as if brushing aside my interruption. "I think you're angling for us to praise you outright, to tell you there's no way you could fail in the entrance exam."

"I kind of agree with you," said Nwobi, avoiding eye contact with me. "But don't be so hard on him."

221

Mercifully, Innocent Dike changed the subject, slightly. He had been content to look from one person to the other, saying nothing—conscious, I suppose, that he still had some way to go before he needed to worry about the Ibadan entrance exam.

"D'you think Umuahia will continue to win so many scholarships every year?" he asked our two senior friends.

"Isn't that obvious?" asked Nwobi. "That's exactly why I asked the principal when he first mentioned the honor board—"

"Was that before he announced it at the assembly this morning?" asked Dike.

"Yes. And I asked him how long he thought it would take before the board fills up."

"I see your point," said Dike. "What you're saying is that perhaps only the names of the *major* scholarship winners should be there."

"Which means," I said, "that for this year, only Achara will have his name inscribed."

"Yes. And that would be a real honor roll. Listen, my friends, one thing is certain. If there are only three major scholarships each year, Umuahia cannot be sure to win one of them every time, no matter how good we think we are."

"Agreed," said Dike. "I know one thing. If the Central School in Okoye's village had such an honor roll, you know, for those who pass in the Umuahia entrance exam, there'll be only one name on it—"

"Yours," I said. "I know. And if you want to hear it again, congrats! But I swear, if you mention this thing one more time tonight, I'll not be responsible—"

I left my sentence in eloquent suspense, knowing that sometimes words are inadequate to express strong feelings. Or as in this case, a hint or threat of violence. An unserious hint, of course. My friends burst out laughing. But so as to maintain my threatening mien, I did not join them.

Instead, I asked Nwobi, "What did the principal say?"

"To my question? He said he didn't think the university could possibly continue to award as many scholarships—you know, major and minor—as it did this first time."

"I'm not sure I understood what he said quite that way," said Achara. "I don't remember his exact words, but I believe what he was trying to say was that it was okay to give honor to whom honor is due in this first entrance exam, which is, in a way, historic."

"And let what happens in the future take care of itself, I imagine?" I asked. "I sincerely hope the University College didn't give away so many scholarships just to give itself a good name on its first—how shall I say?—outing. I pray Dr. Mellanby repeats the gesture next year. I want my name on that board."

"Stop worrying," said Achara. "You just wait and see."

That was easy for him to say. But before I could take him on, young Dike jumped in.

"What will you read in the university?" he asked.

"Mine is easy," said Nwobi promptly. "I'm really only good in the arts subjects. So I think it'll be history, geography, and English for me, though math is not too far off. No physics or chemistry—"

"And you?" I asked Achara.

"I don't envy him," Nwobi cut in. "When you're just about the best in every subject, how can you choose? If you ask me—"

"No one asked you, my friend. Let me speak for myself." Achara paused for a few moments, then went on, "I suppose I could take the engineering subjects or—"

"Didn't I tell you?" asked Nwobi jubilantly. "He doesn't know yet. I'm sure he was going to say 'or medicine,' no?"

"Yes," said Achara defiantly. "Or medicine. Why not?"

"Whatever you choose," I said, "I know one thing for sure. You'll be the best."

Our eyes held for a long moment. Then he looked away, almost sadly. It was as if his mind was burdened by what might have seemed to him the exaggerated expectations of his friends. How could I expect anything short of superexcellence from a friend who had established himself as quite simply the nonpareil in Umuahia Government College? Was he not the same boy about whom my primary school headmaster had predicted, even before we sat the entrance examination to Umuahia, that he would show us who the master was. Something about Achara making "the rain that would drench you." *You*, being Kofi Bentsil and me, and others who might be lucky to be offered places in Umuahia Government College.

"It's funny," I said, looking steadily at my friend. "D'you remember that first day way back in the first week of our first term here?"

"January 1944?" suggested Dike. As if we could not have figured it out by ourselves. I gave him the colonial smile.

"Thank you," I said condescendingly. "The principal was talking to a group of us freshers on the steps of—which dormitory was it now?—and I discovered you were the Anthony Achara about whom Headmaster Akweke spoke so often. I remember I looked at you then, and I wondered, could this be the fellow who'll make the rain that will drench me?

"Well, the old headmaster knew his stuff, didn't he? Here you are, finishing a year ahead of us, with a major scholarship to a wonderful place called the University College, Ibadan. So why am I not angry with you?"

And then he said something I have never forgotten and will probably never forget.

"It's because," he said demurely, looking at his hands on his lap, "you know it was only luck that did it for me. After all, we would have remained classmates if the principal had not *chosen* to promote us in the middle of the year."

Without consciously knowing what I was doing, I put an arm around his shoulders. And the words I spoke came from deep within me.

"You're too modest, my friend. I don't want to sound like our old headmaster, so I'll not predict anything about rainmaking. But I'll say this: if there'll be any students in Ibadan capable of beating you, I'll be honored to make their acquaintance next year. That's, of course, if I'm lucky to get there."

"Beat me?" asked Achara. "I've no intention of fighting—"

"Oh, shut up! You know what I mean—academically."

"Will you stop embarrassing me!" said Achara, looking distinctly uncomfortable. "What d'you think I am? A genius?"

I could not immediately come up with the apposite words to confirm that assessment. Neither could my other two friends. So we just looked at one another and then at our mutual friend Achara—in a silent tribute that was immeasurably more eloquent than any words would have been.

CHAPTER XXVI

SIXTH YEAR

I returned to Umuahia, after the summer vacation, aglow with the high encomiums the principal had showered on me. For the first time in several years, my end-of-year report had given entire satisfaction to my parents. This, notwithstanding that in the earlier part of my fifth year, I had suffered the mortification of sitting in the front row at the morning assemblies—with the littlest youngest boys in the school. And for what had seemed to me, at the time, like a long, endless week of shame.

Not only had Mr. Graves commented expansively on my academic performance during the year, he had been unusually positive in assessing my conduct and character. "He has been an asset to his house and the college," wrote the big man. "I am pleased with him."

I could not recall when I last felt like this at the beginning of any term or, as now, a new class. Class 6. My final year in Umuahia Government College. I had heard it said that one's years in high school are the best years of one's life. As I entered this sixth and final year, I actually began to have a sense that there might be some truth to that saying. For notwithstanding the somewhat checkered course of my life so far in the college, I knew I would not have exchanged it willingly for any other experience.

Adamma might also have had something to do with my feelings. She had certainly made the vacation one that I was not likely to forget for a long time. Now rising sixteen, she looked more woman than I thought she had any right to look. She had latterly developed this habit of coming to my place, two or so days into my vacation, without giving notice. I loved it and, I think, her. If I sound uncertain about this matter of love, it is for a good and solid reason—in my mind, at any rate. The fact was that, despite everything that had happened or not happened between us—notwithstanding that we had exchanged a not-inconsiderable volume of correspondence in the course of every term since she too became a high school student—I had never actually called her my *bloke,* our favorite Umuahia term for "girlfriend," which had little or nothing to do with the dictionary definition of that slang word. Not that this little lacuna mattered in the least to her.

In one of her letters to me, she had stated, rather artlessly, "You are my man, and I am your woman." I know I could never have written such words to her. This particular letter, unfortunately for me, had somehow fallen into the hands of Innocent Dike, who, as I later discovered, told Chidi Ebele about it. A chain reaction followed. So much so that by the time it got back to me, it was—as a master of inevitability—considerably embellished. The story was that the sister of my best primary school friend had not only declared undying love for me, but was ready to give up her education if I promised to marry her before going up to the new university in Ibadan.

I was, I suppose, flattered that I was considered a certainty for the University College. But that apart, I was thoroughly embarrassed by the currency given to the gossip. My classmates ragged me endlessly about it. Worse still, when I told Adamma about the story, she actually smiled contentedly and set at naught my embarrassment.

"They're jealous," she said quite seriously.

"No, they're not," I replied. "Some of them have their own girlfriends." I might have said "bloke," but she would not have understood.

"So if they have, why are they teasing you?"

Because their girlfriends had not made the type of declaration of love and marriage you were supposed to have made to me. That was the answer that jumped to my lips. But I decided not to give it utterance since Adamma clearly was not concerned about the details of the gossip.

Instead, I said, "Because I've not been lucky enough to see any of the letters from their girlfriends."

"Who are they? I may know some of them."

"That's exactly it," I said. "You might know them. So I'm not telling. They're careful to hide their letters, that's all."

"So it's your fault for letting them see your own," said Adamma sweetly. "I'm sure Kofi and Chidi—"

"I said I'm not telling you. There's no point guessing."

She looked hard at me and then gave up. And she never afterwards referred to the matter.

She came to my place, as she always did, without notice. She knew my room. Knew too that it was now exclusively mine. She did not knock on the door, it never having occurred to her that she might find me in an awkward situation.

Sometimes I found myself wondering if that was—well—complimentary to me. I could, for all she knew, have been dallying on the side with some other girl. But she obviously knew me better, perhaps, than I knew myself. There was another girl, to be sure. Evelyn was her name. I had seen her sister Catherine at Asaba, by the River Niger, with the debonair Prince Nwafor Orizu. That was a little over a year earlier. Our cricket team was returning to Umuahia after a match we played in Benin City against our sister Government College from Ibadan. I had been too timorous to cross the road from where we were standing to talk to her. I could have asked her about Evelyn. That was definitely a missed opportunity, though it probably did not matter since Evelyn was, at the time, more dream than reality to me.

Adamma went out of her way, even more than she had done one year earlier, to show me how much she enjoyed my company. Her father's mild anger, her brother Ben's occasional disapprobation, even her mother's tantrums—none seemed to make any impression on her. She was, she loved to tell me, now a big girl. Her mother, when roused, could still wield a mean whip. But Adamma said she was now grown past all that. I myself had once heard her mother say to Ben and his siblings, "When I married your father, they told me he was a very gentle person. I didn't understand then, but now I do. And I have no intention of standing by and doing nothing while you children develop into something that will bring shame on this family." I had no idea what terrible things her children had done to get her all worked up. But she was scary.

I do not mean that Adamma threw caution to the wind. Her inbred sense of right and wrong meant that she had to play a careful game with her mother so as not to needlessly offend her. She generally only came to see me on those occasions when her mother sent her to the Ekeoha market to buy things for the family or to deliver sundry messages. She always offered to go to the market for her mother, who suspected nothing. Ben perhaps should have, knowing the lie of the land, so to say. But whenever I asked Adamma about Ben and if he wasn't suspicious, she dismissed that worry with a wave of her hand. "Not to worry," she would say, which led me to think—indeed to believe—that the two of them had some kind of an understanding between them. Fortunately, my house was very close to the big market.

If my parents noticed anything, they said nothing much to me. My father only once cautioned me about girls in general. I refrained from asking him if he had any particular girl in mind because I was afraid of what his answer might be. I did not like the fixed stare he gave me as he pronounced his cautionary words. That stare told me that he knew, but that he chose, for his own reasons, to say nothing more, for the moment.

My mother was mostly in her shed in Ekeoha when Adamma came to the house. Almost the only time their paths crossed, when my mother unexpectedly returned to the house in midafternoon, I could have sworn she winked conspiratorially at me. But I do not want to misconstrue that wink—if indeed it was a wink. It could have been a mere twitching of her eye muscles or whatever tendon controlled their movement. Mothers did not generally conspire with their sons to ensnare unsuspecting young girls.

Only Nneka, my younger sister, would have had the mind to come into my room when Adamma was there. My elder sister, Grace, was too preoccupied with a middle-aged trader who was courting her without seeming to do so, to pay much mind to us. She saw Adamma sometimes. And always, she welcomed her—profusely. I could see they liked each other, which was to my advantage.

I knew Nneka's game. She was herself now a college girl, in a girls' high school in Uyo, about forty miles from Aba. She was getting wise to the ways of the world and of young girls and boys like Adamma and me. I had not as yet seen any boys hovering around her. Perhaps few dared to approach her, though she was quite comely. She had a sharp, cutting tongue when provoked, which might have discouraged unwanted familiarity. She would saunter into my room occasionally. She would not say so directly, but I had no doubt that her undeclared intention was to make sure Adamma and I kept strictly to the straight and narrow.

Against all odds, we did—but only just. Adamma permitted me more liberties than I knew what to do with. We lost control a few times. It was as if we were discovering the erogenous zones of our bodies for truly the first time. I do not know how or why these things happen. But whenever I felt a surge of passion drive through my body, somehow I thought of my friends. And oddly, when I did, I knew the right thing to do and found the strength of mind to do it—that is, to *not* do it. My dad was fond of saying "To each his own." I doubt he had Kofi Bentsil or Friday Stoneface in mind when he said that. But my friends did their thing, and I would do mine. If my friends chose to laugh at my virginity, let them.

When I boarded the train at Aba to return to Umuahia for the first term of my sixth and final year, I felt like someone who had been through fire and brimstone. And I came away with a surprise gift from Adamma: a rather fanciful handkerchief, on which she, or someone else, had embroidered the word "love." I did not know if she could do needlework. When I asked her if she did, she replied with her own question: why did I want to know? And because it was quite evident why I had asked the question, I took her riposte as a sign she did not want me to know. So I let the matter rest there. Her gift had sentimental value for me. But I knew better than to show the handkerchief to any of my friends, or I would have been made to regret the indiscretion. I decided therefore to bury it at the bottom of my clothes in my bedside locker and to only take it out if I was sure there were no prying eyes.

*   *   *

I struggled to settle down to the rhythm of life in the college because, for a week or two, I could not get Adamma out of my thoughts. I knew I had to do something about this quickly because the Cambridge School Certificate examination was fast approaching. I threw myself with more than my customary zeal into everything I did, whether it was housework or cricket or boxing. I won my cricket colors after the first two matches against local teams, in which I had batted very well.

The high point of the cricket season was the match against the Ibadan Government College, a repeat of the encounter two years earlier between the two schools. This time, the teams met, not in Benin City, but in Warri, some thirty miles south of the former and, like it, also on the west side of the River Niger and equidistant between Umuahia and Ibadan. Ughelli College, in Warri, played host to the two teams.

Our opponents, fortunately for us, had lost their cutting edge in the person of Andrew Ighodaro, the mulatto boy who had dominated the match at Benin City. We still had our two geniuses, Ebong and Obidike. The match ended in a respectable draw for both sides, though I made no contribution to our relative success. For as so often happens in all human endeavors, my first match, after I was awarded my cricket colors, was a personal disaster. I was trapped leg before wicket, offering no stroke to my first ball, which swung wickedly into my pads. It took me a moment or two to realize what had happened. The walk back to the pavilion, head hung in shame was, for me, the low point of my last cricket season in Umuahia.

I was glad to have the match against Ibadan behind me so I could devote my time to the next most important task: the Cambridge exam. I think I was well aware that it would take a major catastrophe for me not to do well. But I was not going to take any stupid chances with an examination, the importance of which was clear to all the boys. The Cambridge-Man was finally going to decide who was who in the class.

It was an open secret that most, if not all, class 6 boys infringed the lights-out regulation, which required all the boys, without distinction of class or status, to engage in one sole activity or rather, inactivity: sleep. Till the wake-up bell at six o'clock in the morning.

Those class 6 boys who were school or house prefects, and therefore enjoyed some privacy in their rooms, were able to study far into the night in relative security. All they did was cover the narrow entrances to their rooms (which had only half doors) with their red blankets or other pieces of cloth, such as wrappers. Nonprefects, who shared the open dormitory with all other boys in the house, had perforce to adopt other methods of studying beyond the lights-out bell.

I tried reading my texts with a torch or a flashlight under my red blanket. But the red glow always gave away such shenanigans. The alternative was to steal away from the dormitory, when everybody else was asleep, and find a shady nook in the nearby buildings. The classrooms and the library provided hardly any suitable niches. The long Administration Block was the best.

Gregory Okoroafor and I were simply doing what others, of our classmates, did fairly regularly. We found an obscure poorly lit alcove in the Admin Block where we often ensconced ourselves, safe from the prying eyes of the principal and the masters. We were so careful about what we were doing, we mastered the art of breathing without sound, even when an unwelcome insect or other nocturnal creature surprised and startled us. Bats, for example.

When, one day, the light of a torch breached the outer darkness surrounding our little alcove, we sprang up, fearing it was either Black Cat Pepple or, worse still, Mr. Graves himself. When the intruder revealed himself, we were considerably relieved.

"Oh, it's you, Agwuna," said Okoroafor, who was always quicker with words than I.

"What time is it now?" asked Agwuna, tight faced and flashing his torchlight at his own watch.

Neither of us answered his question. The way I saw it, since he could read the time on his watch, he did not need my help. I could not guess what went through the mind of my companion in misconduct. Surprise, and not a little shock, perhaps. At what seemed like Agwuna's excessive officiousness, if not downright meddlesomeness.

"One a.m.," Agwuna read from his watch. Then he peered closely at us.

"What d'you think you're doing here?"

Okoroafor was quickly ready with his answer, but I would not let him. Before he could get a word out, I clamped a hand over his mouth.

"When there is need to talk," I told him, "I will do the talking. After all, he is the prefect in charge of my house, not yours."

"That's where you're wrong," said Agwuna gleefully. "I am a school prefect, not just a house prefect."

"We know. And we are yeomen."

"It's not my fault," said Agwuna, "that you were not made prefects."

"That's why we're called yeomen. So?"

"So I want to know what you're doing here, at this time." For emphasis, or perhaps because we had stared him down, he looked down again at his watch.

"Unless you're blind or something," I said, struggling to maintain my composure, "it's quite obvious. I can't even believe you're asking such a question."

"I don't know what you mean."

"If you're so stupid you can't see what we're doing," said Okoroafor, unable to restrain himself any longer, "I'll tell you. We're doing exactly the same thing, for the same exam, that you do in your room, night after night."

"How would you know? You're not in my dormitory. Ask Okoye if he has ever caught me—"

"Oh please, stop that nonsense!" I shouted softly. "If you don't read after lights-out, why do you bother to cover the entrance to your room? But enough of this. If you've finished interrogating us, please leave us alone and go back to your room."

A thought suddenly struck me. "By the way, how did you know I left the dorm if you were not awake yourself? And how were you able to find us here?"

"What does it matter?" asked Agwuna. "I might have gotten up to go to the urinal."

"That's laughable. You're always boasting you never need to do that and that God gave you a bladder—"

He interrupted me. "You left the dorm when you know you shouldn't have. And you're here swotting after lights-out. That's all that matters."

He paused. We waited, but not necessarily with bated breath. What could he do to us in the circumstance? He seemed himself to be in considerable doubt on the matter because after seeming to take an eternity, he frowned and said, "I'll decide on your punishment by breakfast time."

So saying, he turned and walked away. He did not insist that we, too, return immediately to our dormitories. Perhaps he sensed he did not need to.

He had clearly achieved his objectives, which were to catch us, as it were, with our fingers in the proverbial soup pot and to destroy the tranquility of our night.

We stood stock-still for several moments, Okoroafor and I, trying to digest what had just transpired—angry beyond words, incredulous that our classmate and my almost-friend could behave so churlishly toward us. That we were also acutely aware that we were in breach of school regulations by stealing out of our dormitories, in the dead of night, did not in the least mitigate our outrage at Agwuna's threat of a punishment.

"Let's pack up and go," suggested Okoroafor.

"Right," I said. "My concentration is gone."

"D'you think he was serious?"

"Something," I said, "tells me we are in deep trouble with him."

Whatever it was that told me was deadly right. Agwuna pronounced our sentence after breakfast. Perhaps not wishing to make a public spectacle of our humiliation, he called us to the prefects' room.

"Because you're my classmates," he said, "I decided not to report the matter to the principal—"

"Oh, so you finally understood—," Okoroafor began.

"Wait a moment," said Agwuna. "I didn't say that was the end of the matter."

"So what are you going to do?" I asked as he paused.

"Well . . ."

"Well what, man?"

Then he said it. "I have decided that your punishment will be to go to bed thirty minutes early every night for five nights."

We had been standing and talking, all three of us. Out of the corner of my eye, I saw the school captain, Fidelis Nnochiri, seated at his customary spot in the prefects' room, deep into the room, by the window that looked out on to the pada tennis court. I could tell right away that he was watching and listening with interest, though he sought to camouflage it.

I groped for a chair and sat down as the wind went out of me. I think my mouth must have fallen open, in shock and stupefaction.

"Surely you're not serious?" I heard Okoroafor ask. At least I think it was his voice. But it could have been Nnochiri's. It would not have surprised me if he was also in shock.

"I am," answered Agwuna, sotto voce. Perhaps so Nnochiri would not hear him.

"Then you must be really out of your mind," asserted my friend. "I refuse to carry out this ridiculous punishment. You may report the matter to the principal if you like."

Wiser counsel prevailed, however, after Agwuna haughtily strode out of the room. The school captain called Okoroafor and me aside and spoke compellingly to us.

"What will you gain," asked Nnochiri, "if Agwuna goes to the big man? Nothing. The principal will, in all likelihood, uphold the punishment if only because he gave prefects authority to punish even their own classmates. And there's no question but that you broke college rules. Think about it."

I liked and respected Nnochiri. Besides being a good athlete, specializing in the sprint events, he was also one of the most brilliant boys in the class and was especially strong in mathematics and physics. When he had anything to say, he usually made a lot of sense. It always seemed to me that he chose his words more carefully than most. His voice, measured and deep, was modulated skillfully to suit the occasion. We called him affectionately FCN, after his initials.

In the upshot, Okoroafor and I carried out the punishment. But we had only done it for two days when Agwuna had an apparent change of heart. At the end of classes on the third day, he spoke to us.

"You may stop now," he said.

"Stop what?" I asked.

"The punishment, of course."

"Why?" asked Okoroafor, exactly echoing my thoughts at that moment. "Did you suddenly see the light?"

"I don't have to explain," said Agwuna. "Your punishment is over, that's all."

My friend and I looked at each other with a wild surmise. I knew what he was thinking, and he knew what I was thinking. We did not need words to articulate those thoughts. When finally I spoke, I could see right away that Agwuna had not been prepared for our reaction.

I stood up, slow and deliberate, so as to be eyeball-to-eyeball with him.

"Who begged you to change your mind?" I asked angrily. "We don't need your mercy. You punished us, and we intend to carry out your stupid punishment to the full."

"And if you think," added Okoroafor, "that making us go to bed thirty minutes early will affect our performance in the Cambridge exam, let me assure you it will make no difference. You will not gain any advantage over us, I promise you."

Agwuna visibly recoiled from our combined fury. "I didn't mean to gain any advantage—"

"Then what the hell did you mean?" Okoroafor spat at him. "Why did you punish us for doing exactly what you are doing in your room, behind your screen of blankets and bedsheets? If you think that I will stop this midnight swotting—and now I'm only speaking for myself—"

"Me too," I chimed in. But he went on as if I had not spoken.

"If you think this will make me stop, then you had better stop too."

"I'll be watching you," I said, to help my friend out. "If you stop, I'll stop. We'll stop. But if you continue, we'll continue. As to the punishment, we'll carry it out to the bitter end. Thank you!"

For once bereft of words, Agwuna stared at us for a long moment, taking two or three steps backward. Then he turned and walked out of the classroom.

From that day on, Agwuna was a changed man. Towards Okoroafor and me. Indeed, in the last few weeks of our preparations for Cambridge, he actually invited me into his room long after lights-out.

CHAPTER XXVII

My class went on a picnic the day before the Cambridge School Certificate examination was due to start in early December 1948. It was a bright, sunny day, with just a touch of the dry, dust-laden harmattan winds.

As with Achara's class the previous year, the picnic was scheduled to be a full day's affair, from eight o'clock in the morning till six in the evening. Most of us had largely reconciled ourselves to the inevitability of the outing. Some even looked forward to it. I might have been one of them had it not been that one of my boxing friends, Paul Ogbo, had put the fear of God, as they say, in me. He had warned me not to get into the water.

"Why?" I asked, amused.

"Simple. You've often said you fear water, not so?" he asked me. "Is this not the first time in your life you'll be going to a river to play in the water?"

"Yes," I said. "But the Yorubaman said it will be in shallow waters, very shallow waters. And he also said there's a sandy bank on which we can play games or just lie around if we want to."

"So just lie around on the sand. You've heard of *mammy water*, I'm sure."

"That's only in the River Niger, at Onitsha," I said.

"Yes," said Ogbo. "But how d' you know other rivers don't have their own *mammy waters*? If you enter the water and you're not careful enough, she might entice you to follow her. And you know what can happen if you do?"

It was all really too silly for words, but Ogbo was absolutely right on one point. I was scared of water, especially flowing water—in other words, a stream or river. I was touched by his concern for my safety, but he need not have worried on my account. I knew I would not likely be getting into the water since, at the time, I was nursing a jigger-infested toe on my right foot, which itched maddeningly.

Mr. Babatunde, the Yorubaman, had gone to a lot of trouble over the preparations for the picnic. To find the right spot for us, he had scoured the villages and countryside within a wide radius of the college. And he found what he sought at the confluence of the Imo River and a minor tributary, some twenty-five miles from the college.

We left the college promptly at eight o'clock and reached the picnic spot in under an hour. It was a scene of considerable beauty, with large mahogany and iroko trees providing some shade from the sun, if one needed a shade. The temperature, because of the harmattan, must have been very comfortably in the lower eighties.

From the banks of the tributary, we looked across the wide expanse of the Imo River to a sandy beach on the other side, some two hundred yards away. The river looked impressively large at this point in its course southward to the Niger Delta and the Atlantic Ocean.

"This is great!" shouted a boy, running toward the edge of the river. Several others followed him, most of them clearly raring for a swim. But Mr. Babatunde called them back.

"You like it?" he asked us.

A crescendo of voices answered in the affirmative.

"D'you think you'll have a good time here?"

"Of course, yes!" cried several of us.

"Good," said the Yorubaman. "But you must be patient. I've arranged for a canoe man from the village to come and ferry us across the river to the beautiful beach you can all see over there."

"Why?" asked several voices. "Why can't we just swim to the other side?"

Mr. Babatunde smiled. It was the smile of a seasoned adult who understood the impetuosity of youth and adolescence.

"Come," he said patiently, "and I'll show you why you shouldn't."

He led us a short distance along the bank and pointed to an area where the tributary joined the big river.

"You see those swirling eddies?" he asked. "They're caused by the confluence of the rivers. It is dangerous to swim there, and as far as I can see, there's no way you can cross over to the other side without coming perilously close to those eddies. That's one reason I arranged for the canoe man. And that's why you should not risk swimming on this side. Okay, boys?"

Some voices said yes. Other boys, eager for action, demurred.

"Where's the canoe man anyway?" we asked.

"I wonder what's keeping him," said the Yorubaman.

He looked around for several moments and then decided to go look for the man. "You all stay put here. No one should go into the river till I come back. I won't be long."

He might as well have been talking to deaf-mutes. I knew what would happen the moment the master turned his back. And it did. Several boys stripped themselves down to their underwear, ready and eager to plunge into the waters.

"Let's see who is the best swimmer in the class," said one voice.

"Where are the saltwater boys?" asked another voice. "This is your chance to show you can stay underwater as long as fishes do, without breathing."

"I'll race you to the other side," said a challenging voice.

Amid this furor, I sat disconsolately on the trunk of a tree by the tributary, dangling my feet gently, to and fro, in the water. I do not recall why I felt so gloomy and cheerless. The water, in which I dangled my feet, was actually rather soothing to my jigger-infested toe. I had indeed begun to wonder how I could concentrate on my examination paper, the next day, if the itching on that toe did not significantly reduce.

Someone tapped me lightly on the shoulder. I turned and looked into the smiling eyes of Kofi Bentsil and Friday Stoneface. Friday, especially, was in his element. I could see that the challenge of the river was more than he could resist.

"Afraid to jump in with the rest of us?" he asked me, a devilish twinkle in his eyes.

"But the Yorubaman said—"

"We know what he said," said Kofi.

"Wait for the canoe man if you want to," said Friday. "Kofi and me are going to swim to the other side."

"I hate to admit it," I said. "But I am afraid to cross the river even in canoe. What if it capsizes?"

Friday laughed. Kofi looked at me with pity in his eyes. Then they turned away and, in the next moment, plunged into the river. I watched Friday for a while as he swam with strong, coordinated strokes, his head bobbing up and down. And as he swam, he shouted continually to the boys closest to him, either to encourage their efforts or to challenge them, perhaps as the spirit moved him. Now and again, he would rear his body powerfully above the surface of the waters, only to plunge back in, in a sustained dive. If I needed proof that my old primary school mate was the best swimmer in the class, I was watching it now. None of the others could compete with him, either in the speed and certainty of his strokes or in his endurance under the water. By comparison, Kofi looked absolutely pedestrian.

The canoe man finally came, trudging behind the Yorubaman. But by this time, most of the boys—at least twenty of the twenty-six in the class—were already in the water. Some, notwithstanding our teacher's instructions to the contrary, were trying to swim across the river. I watched the Yorubaman closely and could see the alarm in his eyes.

"Come out of the water! Pronto!" he shouted. "The canoe man is here to take us across to the other side. And let's do it an orderly fashion."

The boys scrambled ashore, some with perceptible reluctance. I got off the trunk with little or no enthusiasm. The canoe, as it rocked gently in the rippling waters, looked old and weather-beaten. Momentarily, I wondered if it had holes in its bottom. I walked up to it and peered long and hard at its insides. It looked intact.

The master cleared his throat. "Okay now, boys, let's not rush for the canoe. If necessary, it will make two trips. We'll start with those boys who obeyed my instructions."

"Where's Stoneface?" Kofi suddenly asked, breathing heavily from his exertions. "I can't see him anywhere."

"But you two were swimming together," I reminded him.

"Don't be silly," he snarled at me. "Couldn't you see he was too fast for me?"

That was true. Our eyes scanned the surface of the waters, but Friday was nowhere to be found.

"Perhaps he has reached the other side," a boy suggested.

But the Yorubaman shook his head. "That's quite impossible," he said. "No matter how good he is. Let's take a count and make sure everybody else is here."

The senior boy, Nnochiri, took a count; and we were all accounted for. Except Friday Stoneface. As if drawn by a magnet, we all turned and looked at Mr. Babatunde. He looked back at us, but it was plain to all that he did not see us. His eyes looked pensive. Then after a moment or two, he broke away from us and walked quickly, all by himself, along the banks of the river for about a quarter mile. We stood where we were and waited. Some kind of paralysis, more mental, I think, than physical, had set in.

One look at the master's face, when he rejoined us, and we all knew that something had gone awfully wrong. He did not need to tell us he was himself beginning to worry. We sensed it. And with that realization came panic.

The panic increased noticeably when after another two or three minutes, there was still no sign of Stoneface. The Yorubaman, as was his wont, repeatedly brushed his very short hair with his left hand from front to back. He went and stood by the edge of the water and, from moment to moment, called out Stoneface's name. But only the echo of his own voice answered his shouts.

Kofi and I volunteered to walk downstream in search of our friend. The master agreed and sent two other boys with us. We walked in the only possible direction Friday could have taken if he had, as some had suggested, gotten out of the water and decided to take a lonely stroll along the banks of the river. Such a stroll seemed a trifle far-fetched to me, but Kofi and I thought any idea was worth following up.

When we got back, after walking downstream for about a mile, the master was engaged in an animated argument with the canoe man. Elijah, it turned out, was his name. He had, apparently, been asked by the master to do something.

"You wan' make I go in dere?" Elijah was asking, in some alarm, pointing toward the river. Did he think we could have been asking him to go into the adjoining forest?

"I no fit swim dere," he declared emphatically. "You wan' de water to swallow me?"

This time, he was pointing unmistakably at the eddies, where the two rivers met.

"I no even fit use my canoe dere."

I was beginning to think the man was a coward when he finally relented. With two assistants, he paddled toward the eddies because, as he told us, that was where something might have happened. His body language, as he rowed, told us he would have much rather been somewhere else than in the waters of the Imo River, tempting destiny. Suddenly, the paddlers seemed to lose control of the canoe, which lurched frighteningly for several moments. Fortunately, Elijah and his men regained control of their craft and eventually scrambled, cursing, to the safety of the bank.

Only then did we report to the master that not only had we not seen any trace of Stoneface, but that the nearest villagers had told us that no college boy had come anywhere near their village.

At this point, the entire class and the master knew that the worst had happened. I was numb with fear, overwhelmed by an indescribable mixture of emotions such as I had never before experienced. Not even when, about ten years earlier, two other kids and I had jumped from a three-foot embankment into a soccer field, and one of my friends had sustained what turned out to be a fatal compound fracture of his right leg. That experience had shaken me up. But this now was altogether a more profoundly devastating tragedy. There was an awful churning in the pit of my stomach that made me sick. I felt my knees give and quickly sat down by the river's edge, staring into the waters, wondering if, by some miracle, my missing classmate and friend would suddenly appear amid the rippling reflections.

In my mind's eye, I saw Friday one more time as he prepared to jump into the river. Like some of the other boys, he had seemed intoxicated with his own youthfulness—vibrant with life, supremely confident of his swimming skills, daring others, and being dared by them. Like the other boys, more than a dozen of them in fact, Stoneface had chosen not to listen to the injunctions of the Yorubaman and had plunged into the waters, as one might say, heedless of advice and careless of the consequences. And why not? Had not a dozen other boys done exactly the same thing? Why then did the Fates pick on the one boy who, oddly enough, was probably the best swimmer in the class?

There had seemed to be a strange look on my friend's face as he jumped into the river. The more I thought about that look, the more I found it eerily disturbing. Stoneface had smiled and laughed a thousand times before that fateful day. But the smile on his face, at the moment he entered the waters of the Imo River to meet his destiny, was unearthly. Why I had focused on my friend's face was, and remains to this day, a mystery to me. Was that macabre vision merely a figment of my own lurid imagination? I mentioned the matter to only one other boy, Gregory Okoroafor, who, like me, was no swimmer and had therefore remained on the banks of the river to await the canoe man and his canoe. Okoroafor told me he had seen nothing untoward and gently dismissed my vision as quite incomprehensible to him.

"It's just hindsight," he said. "I'm sure the smile was his regular smile."

What would he know? He did not see that ghastly smile. But I had seen it. I had not actually thought about death when I saw it. But it had been there; and my emotions, I was sure, had nothing whatsoever to do with hindsight.

There was nothing else to do but to pick up the pieces. Mr. Babatunde ordered us to pack up our things, including our untouched lunch. We moved like automatons as we clambered onto the school lorry and spoke hardly a word during the long drive back to the school.

The Yorubaman's face, drawn and haggard, was an unforgettable picture of agony. Intermittently, he brushed his left hand over his close-cropped hair. Other than that, he did not seem to know what to do with his hands or where to place them. He muttered endlessly to himself, staring vacantly into space. Once or twice—bless his good heart—he essayed a reassuring smile and told us there might yet be a slim hope that all would be well. His words might have carried some conviction if he had looked as if he believed what he was saying. Glumly, we stared at him. We felt our loss of a classmate and friend acutely. But we knew he felt worse. The tortured expression on his face told us that he felt as though his world had collapsed around him.

He asked the driver to drive straight to the acting principal's house. Mr. Alan Black, a middle-aged Englishman, was at home. As soon as he saw us, he knew something had gone terribly wrong.

"What happened?" he asked breathlessly and listened as Mr. Babatunde told the story. Stoically, he called for his steward and driver and, while we waited, searched for and found a long strong rope. He then dismissed us, invited the Yoruba man to go with him so as to show the way, and drove off in his minitruck. We knew he had no fondness for saloon cars.

Now would have been the perfect moment to sing the school's traditional chorus of lamentation. But we could not do it as we drove the last four or five hundred yards from the principal's house to the Administration Block. The words just stuck in our throats. But our faces said it all to a small group of boys who happened to be near the drop-off point in front of the wide steps of the big building. Soon enough, and I cannot recall how it came about, a sizeable crowd of boys gathered around us. They listened, in stunned and deafening silence, as we told our story and kept telling it, perhaps a hundred times, as more and more boys were drawn to the scene.

Later the same day, before supper, Mr. Black summoned the entire school to the assembly hall. The mood, as we awaited the arrival of the acting principal and the staff, was somber in the extreme. So profound was the silence that when a boy coughed, the sound was like a cannon blast.

Mr. Black entered the hall and stood in the middle of the dais, leaning heavily on a lectern. He was a barrel-chested man, about five feet four inches tall, and was, by repute, a classical musician. But I never heard him sing or saw him play a classical piece. We would have known if he did because he would have made a point of telling us who the composer was. However, he played the school piano with a marvelous virtuosity and brought back the quality of the singing in the school chapel and the assembly to the level it had attained in the days of Mr. Eagleton in my first year.

Standing by him, stiffly erect, was Mr. Babatunde, his anguished look clearly reflecting the torture in his heart. At a signal from Mr. Black, he stepped forward, cleared his throat, and began to speak.

"A tragedy has struck the college for which I take full responsibility. You know the saying, 'Man proposes, but God disposes.' Perhaps I chose the wrong spot for the picnic, but how was I to know that events would move inexorably faster than I could control?

"I want to thank Mr. Black for his understanding and his kindness to me. He has spoken to me like a father to his son. He has tried in many different ways to lift this terrible burden off my shoulders.

"He is also a man of infinite courage as he demonstrated when he and I went back to the scene of the tragedy. I was not surprised that he chose to disregard the dark warnings of the villagers about an evil spirit that supposedly lurks around the confluence of the two rivers and which preys on those humans foolhardily enough to swim in the forbidden waters. However, there is little doubt that the eddies there are extremely dangerous to swim in, but not, apparently, for our principal. He dove into the waters, hardly pausing to take off his shirt and swam to where we believe we lost young Stoneface. And he did not give up until it was clear the search was hopeless.

"There's little else to say. As you can well imagine, this is a burden I'll carry for the rest of my life."

So saying, Mr. Babatunde stepped back, yielding the floor to Mr. Black. The acting principal then spoke, still leaning on the lectern, in his soft, measured voice.

"Little did I think, when I was asked to replace Mr. Graves as your principal for three months, that I would be called upon to face something like this. I want to make it absolutely clear that what happened today was in no way the fault of Mr. Babatunde. He took the boys out on a similar picnic last year, and I had no hesitation giving my approval to this year's outing. It was an excellent idea that just went badly wrong. By the way, he omitted to mention that I had a long rope round my waist, which would have been used to pull me out of the river had the necessity arisen.

"We have to deal with this loss, individually and collectively. I appeal especially to the class 6 boys to try and put this tragedy as quickly as possible behind them. The Cambridge School Certificate exam commences tomorrow as scheduled. It may be hard for them to write their papers as if nothing happened. But they must realize that their lives must go on. They must face the examination.

"One more thing. It is quite possible that Stoneface's body will surface . . ."

A stab of pain went through my heart, even as another boy let out a long, hoarse groan of agony. A wave of anguished sobs rolled over the assembly as several boys were unable to control their emotions.

Pausing only briefly to let the moment pass, Mr. Black continued to speak, though now even his voice had lost a little of its steadiness.

"As I was saying, Stoneface's body will probably surface in another day or two. We have made arrangements with some villages downstream to bring word back to the college, should that happen. I have also arranged for the Stoneface family to be informed of this tragedy. I know that all our hearts go out to them.

"Thank you all."

* * *

The next day was probably the worst day in all my years in Umuahia. The loss of my friend Friday Stoneface was thrown into its sharpest relief when we assembled in the examination hall and the desk that should have been occupied by him remained vacant. I stared at that desk for several moments until somehow I understood the futility of my anguish and that my old schoolmate and friend was gone forever.

* * *

The body surfaced the following day, two days after the tragedy. And it surfaced, according to the report relayed to us, more or less in the area where fruitless searches had been made by Elijah, the canoe man, and by Mr. Black. What held the body so long in the water was a mystery to the acting principal, his staff, and all the students. But Elijah, the canoe man, knew what it was.

"The water spirit, no less," Mr. Babatunde told us. "I couldn't convince him to the contrary."

The college held a short emotion-charged funeral service the day after the body was found. Friday's parents and several other relatives were present at the service. The college chapel was packed to capacity. The service, though conducted by an Anglican priest from the Umuahia parish, was essentially nondenominational.

After the service, the funeral procession walked the short distance to an area, cleared for the burial, between the chemistry-biology laboratory and the cricket oval. In a brief funeral oration, Mr. Alan Black declared that the maintenance of Stoneface's grave would be the responsibility of my class in our two remaining terms in the college.

"This is your work," announced Mr. Black, "on every housework period, every day."

Bentsil, Ebele, and I tarried a while longer at the grave after everybody else had left. We held hands silently for several moments and then, at Chidi's suggestion, began to sing, "God be with you till we meet again . . ."

Which was the only way we knew to say our final good-bye to a friend who had been a classmate for more than a decade. The bond that had been forged in our primary school years had endured, though in our Umuahia years we had cultivated other friendships and had seemed to go our slightly separate ways.

More than a half century has passed as I write this. But there are still moments when this tragedy seems only like a bad dream from which I might awaken at any moment. And to my dying day, I will always remember Kofi's last words as we left the grave.

"Why did he have to go and die like that?"

To which there was no answer. Only puzzlement. Puzzlement that life could be so unfair. And so screwed up.

CHAPTER XXVIII

To this day, I cannot explain what came over me. I found, in January 1949, at the beginning of the second term of my last year in Umuahia that I was suffering from a very serious academic malady. A malady I can only describe as a sudden diminished mental capacity for the sciences and mathematics. It was as if an intellectual wall suddenly sprang up, from nowhere, cutting me off from those subjects. The more I reflected on this strange and totally irrational aversion for the sciences, the more I thanked my stars that I had not developed that phobia before the Cambridge examination.

What particularly bothered me was the looming entrance examination to the University College, Ibadan. This was an examination for which we had to enter seven subjects, each paper to be of three hours' duration, which meant that there was no way I could avoid the sciences and math. Or I would have had significantly fewer than seven subjects. And no chance whatsoever of success in what seemed to me, at the time, as the last most competitive examination of my life—what one might call a very crucial academic rite of passage.

Integral and differential calculus were anathema to me. These were new additions to the mathematics curriculum. If the truth must be told, I had never been totally comfortable with mathematics, and I needed to flog myself into acquiring a reasonably high level of competence in the subject. By working hard at it. And by receiving lots of encouragement from cousin Samuel, to whom the subject seemed to come more easily and naturally. Paradoxically, it was watching Samuel working at sets of advanced mathematical calculations, calculations that looked like mumbo jumbo to me, that set off alarm bells in my head. I knew then, two years before my turn came to make a decision on the subject, that I wanted no part of it.

It was fortunate for me that this "additional" mathematics (that was what we called it) was not a compulsory subject. And was not a required part of the mathematics paper in the university entrance exam. I was not so lucky with physics and chemistry, two subjects I absolutely could not dance around. I had held my own quite competently in these two subjects over the years and hoped and prayed that the competence would carry me forward through my remaining six months. Or at least until I had sat the entrance exam.

Organic chemistry, that branch of the subject dealing with the carbon compounds of living and dead matter, was the worst. The hexagonal representation and the structural formula of molecules and compounds confused me.

An extra effort, on my part, was therefore called for to, at least, salvage something from the general wreckage. Instead, I did everything I could, including absenting myself from classes on the flimsiest of excuses, to avoid the subjects. It was so bad, I was not above faking the occasional illness. And when I had to sit through a class session, I really only took notes when I thought the master was watching me. Otherwise, I read my novels surreptitiously or let my mind wander.

In the midst of all this academic lassitude, the results of our Cambridge School Certificate exam came out, in late March 1949. It was, predictably, a major triumph for the class as a whole. And for me personally. It did one other important thing, emphatically. There was that refrain "the Cambridge man will decide," which the boys had begun to chant several months before the examination. It had been half-serious and half-jocular and had been informed by the stifling academic rivalry in the class. Well, the Cambridge man finally decided. And except for the odd exception here and there, there was no overarching comfort in the results for those boys who sang the refrain the loudest, which, simply put, meant that the best in the course of the years came out best in the Cambridge exam.

Almost inevitably, a new chant arose: "Mellanby will decide." This time, however, there was no trace of an underlying seriousness about it. It seemed that those boys who had been quieted down, not to say discomfited, by the predictability of the Cambridge results simply felt the urge—strictly for the heck of it—to raise the new refrain for our next important academic hurdle. That hurdle was the entrance exam to the University College. Its principal was Dr. Kenneth Mellanby. We wrote that exam in the last week of the second term, in mid-April or thereabouts.

*   *   *

Mr. Walter Graves came back from his home leave in England. He seemed in extremely fine fettle for a man who had spent his three-month vacation wintering in Europe. We supposed that after the sweltering and unrelenting heat of Nigeria, a cold spell might have been exactly what his doctor ordered.

He promptly endorsed Mr. Black's decision that class 6 should tend Friday Stoneface's grave as our regular housework. For us, that meant loads of free time. Free time, which we used most profitably for serious study. I would be exaggerating if I said that the hesitant friendship between Agwuna and me blossomed. But it did grow somewhat; and we studied together for the university entrance exam, closeted in his room, as we had done in the last weeks of our preparations for the Cambridge examination.

Our academic rivalry had now all but dissolved into thin air. It is entirely possible that my sudden and rather inexplicable loss of interest in math and science had everything to do with this. I could no longer seriously challenge his preeminence in the class, overall.

The school, in general, and my class, in particular, received the results of the university entrance exam, when it came out in the second week of June, with mixed feelings. Not a single one of us achieved a merit scholarship, which was cause for acute disappointment for several of us. By the logic of my performances, year in and year out, I should have been among the two or three boys most devastated by the results, insofar as the merit scholarships were concerned. But I knew, between me and my god, that I had no reasons to have expected such an outstanding result. How could I, when math, physics, and chemistry had become nightmares to me; and I had had to write a three-hour paper in each of them? Agwuna felt crushed—as well he might. He had been, if truth be told, our one hope to win a university scholarship. Reports from the University College itself, sent to us by my old friend and mentor, Onyewuchi, indicated that a total of only three scholarships had been awarded in the entrance examination. This time, there were no *minor* scholarships.

I suppose I was sorry my name was never going to get inscribed on the scholarship board in the assembly hall, alongside Achara's and cousin Samuel's. Eight boys, including Agwuna and myself, secured ordinary passes, which was not at all bad, considering that only just over one hundred places were available nationwide. Once again, Umuahia had justified the status *we claimed* for it as the primus inter pares of the country's secondary schools.

"I wish they would remove that board from the assembly hall," Okoroafor said to me the day after the results were received.

I knew what he meant. The board was so prominently displayed, it was all we could do to avoid seeing it every time we went into the hall. It drew our eyes like a magnet, though I struggled to avert my eyes from it.

Of the eight of us offered admission to the University College, only two—John Agu and myself—were invited to Lagos for Nigerian government scholarship interviews. This was doubly disappointing for Agwuna, who had placed all his hopes on securing a scholarship, whether awarded on merit by the University College or through interviews by the government. He had set his mind on engineering. But because Ibadan had no such faculty, we all knew already that those who wanted to study engineering would have to go abroad, especially to England, after two years in Ibadan, where the most they could hope for was an intermediate bachelor of science degree.

"Where will I find the money to pay my fees in England?" Agwuna asked Mr. Graves during a class meeting with him.

The big man pondered the question for a moment or two. "Don't give up hope," he finally said. "You never know. The government, I'm sure, will find a way to help boys like you. The same goes for Nnochiri, who I understand, also wants to read engineering."

He stopped and beckoned to Agu and myself to get up. "You will leave tomorrow for Lagos by train. I have arranged for you to stay in King's College during your stay in Lagos. How's that?"

"Oooh!" said several voices.

"That's not fair!" shouted Okoroafor, but he was laughing as he spoke.

I was elated. Very few of us had ever been to Lagos. Except, of course, John Agu. And to be boarded in King's College was—as one might say—the icing on the cake. King's was the number one secondary school in the country in splendor (from all accounts), if not in academics. Agu, who never saw an opportunity to toot his horn, which he did not grab with both hands, boasted openly that he knew every corner of Lagos. "I'll show you," he said to me, preening himself.

The train journey from Umuahia to Lagos took three nights and nearly four days. We traveled some six hundred miles up north to Kaduna. Then about seven hundred miles in a southwesterly direction to Lagos. John Agu, who had never previously traveled by train between Lagos and Eastern Nigeria, seemed every bit as excited as I was on the long trip. We saw, with our own eyes, what we had learned in our geography classes. We saw the full range and the striking variety of the Nigerian vegetation, as the thick impenetrable tropical forests of the south gave way to the more open deciduous woods of the middle regions, which, in turn, faded away to the savannah grasslands of the north.

We marveled at the long magnificent bridge over the Benue River, at Makurdi, where we dined on *foofoo* and a scrumptious sauce of fresh fish, for which the Makurdi railway station was justly famous. And we feasted our eyes—if that is not too indelicate an expression—on the stark nakedness of pubescent girls as we approached Kafanchan Junction. I had of course seen naked nubile girls before, some ten years earlier, in my own village. But those had been the days of my own and their innocence.

There were scenes of unsurpassed natural beauty as the train reached the open savannahs: rolling rocky hills interspersed with piles of boulders that looked as if they had been arranged, not so much by natural or divine action as by human intervention.

We were totally unprepared for the utter commotion at the Kaduna railway station. We had been told we would have to change trains there. But no one had warned us that the change would be a riot. We fought a thousand other passengers for the privilege of finding two seats, not necessarily side by side, on the Lagos-bound train. This train, coming south from Kano, was already packed to near capacity with passengers and luggage, very few of whom disembarked at Kaduna. Apparently, this commotion was a daily feature of life at the station and was common knowledge among train travelers. Agu and I watched, with mounting horror, as other passengers threw their luggage and themselves into the train from Kano even before it had come to a halt. Incredibly, this riotous, rambunctious activity was accompanied by uproarious hilarity. Indeed, had I not known my fellow Nigerians as well as I did, I could have been misled into thinking that the rabble enjoyed self-inflicted pain and suffering. Eventually, Agu and I found two spots, separated by two or three rows of seats. And long before we reached Lagos, we were sitting next to each other.

We were received in the King's College compound by a kindly old man, who, on learning that I was a bit of a cricketer, immediately sent for two members of the school's cricket team: Roy Omotosho and Ernest Nnamdi. It turned out that these were class 5 boys.

I had my old primary school buddy, Titus Nwangwu, in mind and asked about him. I was not prepared for Roy's answer.

"You did not hear?" he asked me. "The entire class 6 went on strike and were expelled from the college a few weeks ago. You didn't hear about it?"

Of course, I had not heard. News about King's College was not a daily fare in my college. Besides, what were the odds that Titus, on his trip home to his parents in Aba, would have thought of breaking his journey at Umuahia for the sole purpose of telling me the story of their strike and of its aftermath? But, I remember thinking, perhaps King's College boys assumed that any hiccup in the life of their college was national news.

I had really looked forward to spending some time with Titus. I had especially looked forward to watching him and listening to him rave about his King's College as he took me around the compound. Now it seemed his school years in King's had come full circle, so to speak. In Titus's first year, the senior class had led the school in a strike that had convulsed the relative tranquility of the island colony. Three of the senior boys had been bundled off into the army. The year was 1944, and World War II was still raging in Europe and the Far East. None of the three King's College boys saw action in any of the theaters of that war, but one of them took seriously ill suddenly and died within a few weeks of their conscription.

But the times, as it is sometimes said, they had changed. There was now no war for which conscripts were needed. That, and the increasingly clamorous demands by our politicians for the respect and dignity even of colonial peoples, presumably stayed the punitive hands of the colonial office, through its Nigerian government extension, against the strikers.

My first surprise about King's College was that the entire school was in cramped quarters. But what it lacked in acreage it certainly made up for in perpendicularity. In Umuahia, not a single building—not even the imposing Administration Block—was a storeyed building. In King's, none was a bungalow.

King's College was an eye-opener in two other significant ways. In their general comportment and behavior, both toward one another and to their teachers, King's College boys were infinitely more relaxed than we were in Umuahia. Lagos being Lagos—the free-swinging capital city, at once more gay and sophisticated than any other Nigerian city—this was perhaps not surprising. The food served to the boys was an even bigger eye-opener. I knew next to nothing about European foods. But John Agu and I were in agreement that King's College boys enjoyed meals that must surely have been as close to European as made no difference. Bread, butter, and jam, with tea, coffee, or cocoa were routinely served to the boys. Chicken was served two or three times a week. In Umuahia, bread and its accompaniments were considered luxury items. We sometimes ate bread, but only when we spent our pocket allowance on it, on our Saturday outings, in Umuahia town. I do not believe we were ever served butter in our dining hall. If there was no bread, what would have been the use of giving us butter? And if there was no bread, there was no jam.

Chicken, generally, and certainly in my family in Aba, was reserved for feast days. Like Christmas and Easter. And very, very occasionally, for Sunday afternoon meals. For the three months of Mr. Alan Black's tenure as the acting principal, chicken was served to us once a week, regularly. Apropos of which, on his return to Umuahia after his home leave in England, Mr. Graves had publicly praised Mr. Black for his frugal management of the funds at his disposal. Then strangely, he had withdrawn chicken as a weekly item on our menu. On the grounds of it being wasteful of resources, he announced at a morning assembly. King's College used chinaware for their meals. In Umuahia, we used enamelware.

Sometimes, it seemed to me as I took in the situation, the informality in the interactions between staff and students in King's College bordered on cheekiness, if not insolence. I was concerned about this and mentioned the matter to Omotosho.

He laughed. "You know the old man who introduced us?" he asked. "We call him the Ancient of Days. Actually, his name is Mr. Ogunjobi. One day, in his class—"

"Oh, he teaches?" John Agu asked, echoing my feelings. "I thought he was only . . . well, you know . . ."

"I know what you mean," said Omotosho. "He's always giving the impression he's not educated and speaks Yoruba all the time, even to people he's meeting for the first time—that is, until he realizes they do not follow what he's saying. He knew you were coming from the East. Otherwise, he might have done the same to you. Anyway, as I was saying, there was this boy in his geography class who was carrying on until Mr. Ogunjobi angrily rebuked him. 'I taught your father, my boy—,' he started to say when the boy interrupted him and said, 'And you'll no doubt be here to teach my son.'"

"And what did the old man say?" I asked.

"What could he say? The Ancient has a very soft heart, which is why so many of the boys take advantage of him. In fact, it was the other boys who shouted the cheeky boy down."

I talked cricket endlessly with Omotosho. We compared notes on the relative strengths of our teams, matching the members of the teams by their specialties in batting or bowling or both. We agreed it would have been exciting had we played against each other, even once. He had heard that my Umuahia team had twice played against Government College Ibadan. I knew that Ibadan played annually against King's (twice a year, in fact, home and away). Why the same school authorities did not succeed in, and perhaps never even seriously considered, bringing Umuahia and King's together was a mystery to both of us.

I never had the opportunity of seeing the sights of much of Lagos, though Agu and I were there for about one week. We were allowed a tour of only the immediate vicinity of the college and the racecourse near it. I found the racecourse to be a beautiful open space, with impressive buildings all around it. But it was along the marina that I saw the tallest buildings of the metropolis. And if it were not for Omotosho, who helped us break a little out of our bounds, we would not have wandered that far from the college. Some of the buildings on the marina were five or six stories high—much taller than any buildings I had ever seen in Eastern Nigeria. I had seen pictures of even taller structures in Europe and America, but those two continents could as well have been on the moon or on another planet.

The government scholarship interviews turned out to be a mere formality. I do not recall how it happened or who leaked the news to us, but we knew unofficially that we were going to be awarded the scholarships. I do not believe we were really surprised about this, seeing we had, a month earlier, had preliminary interviews, along with Nnochiri and Agwuna, in Enugu, Eastern Nigeria. We, therefore, left Lagos, aglow with our success and talking excitedly about the future and what it might portend for us.

I had plenty of time to do just that on the slow three-night journey back to Umuahia. My father would be relieved and doubly so. First, cousin Samuel, the previous year had won a merit scholarship to Ibadan—a minor scholarship admittedly, but still a scholarship. And now, I was poised to win a full government scholarship, which would include the princely sum of twenty-five pounds as my annual pocket allowance. I am ashamed to admit that I worried that my dad might make me share this allowance with Samuel. Twenty-five pounds was a lot of money, to me. But share it with Samuel?

I counted myself extraordinarily lucky to be where I was at that point in my life. The founding of the University College could not have been more propitiously timed. If it did nothing else for me, it ensured that I would not have to seek employment with only a high school certificate in my hands—inevitably, of course, as a lowly clerk in some godforsaken government department or a commercial house.

Just before we left Lagos, John Agu made a sweet suggestion. "How about if we buy some tins of jam for our trip? It tastes so good. Better than butter."

So we bought two cans of the delicious substance and four loaves of bread and gorged ourselves over the four days of our journey until we had a surfeit of it. By then, we were very close to our destination. But, not wishing to return to the college compound trailing any evidence of our gastronomic dissipation, we threw away a half-full can of jam and scrupulously wiped off any telltale spots from our clothing.

CHAPTER XXIX

I lived out the remaining weeks of my life in Umuahia in the most leisurely manner imaginable. Convinced about the utter pointlessness of our final internal end-of-year examination, I became even more lackadaisical in my attitude toward the sciences and math. They could not hurt me any longer. I was not going to do my undergraduate studies in either discipline. The liberal arts were my future. Not calculus or organic chemistry.

There were nightmarish days as well. If this sounds a bit contradictory, let me briefly explain. Having turned my back on the subjects of my disinterest, I kept such spare notes in physics and chemistry that I was in very serious danger of scoring close to zero in each of them in the final class exams. That would have been terribly ignominious and shamefully anticlimactic. Not exactly the manner in which I had hoped to exit from the Umuahia Government College. I simply could not let myself sink to the bottom of the class in my final exams. That would have been too mortifying for words. I knew therefore that I had to do something extraordinary.

Several decades have come and gone since those last few days in Umuahia. But I have continued to debate with myself whether the solution I adopted was not a little bit of chicanery.

The tests for mathematics and physics fell on the same day. Chemistry was scheduled for the following day. That sequence was fortuitous for me, and I grasped it with both hands.

I approached Okoroafor in the classroom. Lowering my voice to barely above a whisper, I asked him, "Can I borrow your chemistry notebook?"

Okoroafor looked up from his desk. "My what?"

"Shhhhhh!" I whispered desperately. "You don't have to shout. I said, can you lend me—"

"I heard what you said. I have two of them. So it depends which one you want. What exactly are you looking for?"

"Well," I said, "actually the organic chemistry notes."

"You don't sound sure. And why are we whispering anyway?"

"Because I don't want others to hear us."

Okoroafor looked askance at me for a moment or two. "What d'you want it for? I'm not sure I like the sound of this. D'you want to copy a whole year's notes in just one day? The chemistry paper is the day after tomorrow."

"Listen, my friend, I only asked because—"

"I know. I've sat next to you these—what?—five or so years. I know for some time now you've hardly taken any notes, even when the master dictated it to us. So I'm asking you, what do you want to do with it between now and the chemistry paper? Tomorrow is physics and math. What—?"

"None of your business," I interrupted. "If you won't give it to me, I'll ask somebody else."

I turned to go away, and he reacted exactly as I had hoped he would. He put out a hand and stopped me.

"Hey! Wait! I didn't say I won't give it to you. Here!" He lifted the lid of his desk, rummaged through it, and produced the precious notebook. "Here it is. But I want it back tomorrow after the physics paper. Okay?"

"Okay," I said. I moved away quickly, hugging the volume to my chest, and carried it to the dorm.

The next day, while the other boys were performing their morning chores, I lay under my bedsheet and blanket, stiff as a ramrod, wearing a pained look. And as I expected he would, Agwuna soon came to inquire what the matter was.

I partially opened my eyes and shut them quickly as if the glare from the window was unbearable. "I feel bad," I said. "Really bad. My head is aching. It's as if someone is pounding on it."

"What's that stuff on your forehead?"

"Mentholatum, of course."

He thought about that for a moment. "How bad is it? What about the papers we're taking today?"

"Math and physics? I really don't know. I'll have to see how I feel in the next hour or two. The way I feel now, I doubt I'll be able to make it."

Agwuna seemed genuinely concerned to hear that. He leaned over, all of a sudden, and put his left hand to my head. Then he straightened himself. "Funny, you don't feel as warm as I expected."

"I didn't say I am feverish," I countered.

"Okay," he said finally. "Do you want me to have one of the boys bring you your breakfast later?"

"Yes, please."

As soon as I had the dorm to myself, I took out Okoroafor's chemistry notebook and did what I had planned to do. I read it assiduously. I was interrupted when a boy brought me my breakfast. I fell to immediately, making appropriate sounds from time to time to give the impression of continuing pain. Before I had done eating, Agwuna came back to inquire what message I had for the math and physics masters.

"I don't believe I can make it," I told him, "for the math paper, which should start in another hour or so. I don't think I'll be well enough even for the physics paper."

The physics paper was in the afternoon. I had never before missed even one paper in any of our examinations for whatever reason. The fact that I was doing so now, and not exactly for the noblest of reasons, made me feel awful. But not awful enough to change my plans.

Okoroafor was wrong in his surmise of those plans. I had not the least intention of copying out a whole year's notes. That would have been the stupidest thing to do. For starters, had I done so, I would not have had the time to study the notes before the next day. And I would not have had any use for them afterwards. Chemistry was not in my future.

What I did was study the notes meticulously. In fact, I did much more than study them. I memorized the entire notes, formula by formula, structure by structure. I had no illusions about what I was doing. Or about its aftermath. My head literally ached from the sheer volume of the stuff I forced into it. And I knew that after disgorging what I had crammed—on my chemistry paper the next day—I would, without the shadow of a doubt, promptly forget it all in a matter of weeks, if not days. I was prepared for that and had no regrets on that score.

In the upshot, I stunned everybody: my classmates, Mr. Kalaga, our chemistry master, and, most of all, myself. Two days after we wrote the chemistry paper, Mr. Kalaga called me aside after he had dismissed the rest of the class.

"I do not exaggerate," he told me in his inimitable, deliberate manner, "when I say that this is one of the greatest surprises of my life as a teacher. I knew you were making little or no effort whatsoever in my classes. But I also know you're no dunce. So as I watched you fiddle away the last term or two, I thought you'd probably eventually make out okay in the subject. But not quite this okay, I must confess."

"I was surprised myself," I said modestly.

"To achieve the highest score of the class in these circumstances should certainly surprise you. What I'd like to know is how in the world did you do it?"

He was certainly entitled to ask that question—a natural one in the circumstances. But of course, I was not about to confess that I had deliberately skipped the math and physics papers to cram for the chemistry paper.

"I hardly know, myself," I said. "I studied hard for it, of course, but I did not expect this result. I'm glad I did well."

"You should be, my boy. You should be. I'm proud of you. With your performance in the sciences in the Cambridge exam and now this, I wonder why you're going to Ibadan to read arts. You should study medicine, if you ask me."

I chose not to ask him and let the matter rest there. Some of my classmates were waiting for me outside the classroom in the veranda. They pounced on me as soon as they saw me. The same question was on every tongue. "How did you do it?"

Well, not quite on *every* tongue. Okoroafor and Agwuna had no interest in my answer to that question. Agwuna spoke for both of them. "We now know you were only pretending to be sick so you could swot for chemistry."

To both the question and the observation of Agwuna, I said nothing. Instead, I walked away, holding my head high, sensing that no one seemed to bear me any grudge for what I did. I think they knew, everyone of them, that I had, absolutely, to do something, however desperate, to avoid the ignominy of a woeful performance in my last exam in the college.

CHAPTER XXX

Three days to go! As I lounged on my bed in the waking hours, my thoughts centered on my six years in this, the most renowned high school in my part of Nigeria. We liked to boast to our friends from other schools that Umuahia was the best in the country, if not in the English-speaking world. Mr. Walter Graves, our imperious headmaster, certainly gave us the impression that a solid case could be made for those claims.

I was not involved in any housework. These last days were the freest I had known in Umuahia. I was a class 6 yeoman, but the prefects knew better than to apply the rules rigidly to us yeomen. No person in authority seemed, in fact, to pay us any mind. It would have been extremely churlish of them had they done so. Though we felt as free as the birds, we only abused those college rules that did no one else any harm. Like stealing a few minutes—well, perhaps an hour or so—of additional sleep. As I was doing now, lounging on my bed when the other boys were scurrying around doing this or that housework. Like turning up in the dining hall a little later than others. Or like chatting with our friends long after the lights-out bell, provided we did so discreetly and did not involve the very junior (classes 1 to 3) boys.

At the morning assembly, Mr. Graves announced that he would like to meet with my class the next day, the penultimate day of the school year. He did not elaborate. But it seemed obvious to us that it might be for the purpose of saying good-bye to us. Perhaps he had done the same thing the previous year, with Achara's class. If he did, I had not noticed. He had certainly not announced it at any morning assembly.

"If your final reports are ready," the big man added, "I will certainly give them to you to take to your parents."

I could not recall any end of term or year—and I had seen sixteen previous terms come and go—when our reports were ready for us to take away. I never knew if trust had anything to do with this. Trust, that is, that if the boys saw their reports before their parents or guardians did, some—that is, those whose reports were not laudatory—might not be tempted to try a little bit of skullduggery. Like deliberately misplacing the reports. Or destroying them.

During the afternoon rest period, I spent the entire hour—and more—in a brown study. Reflecting on what had been. Sometimes on what might have been. For some odd reason, my mind dwelt mostly on a master who was no longer there with us. Mr. Bisi Babatunde, the Yorubaman, had left the college in circumstances that might have been extremely sad for him—soon after the picnic tragedy that so cruelly snatched Friday Stoneface from us. But the man had been like a beacon for us. He was, relative to some of the masters, a young teacher, but one who could talk on equal terms with any white man. Our geography teacher, Mr. Mokelu, whom we called Jaw-Bones, once said to me that the Yoruba man had studied in the best universities in Britain and, with his two degrees, was arguably better educated than several of our white teachers. It did not escape our attention that Mr. Babatunde was the only Nigerian master who was allocated a house in what might otherwise have been an exclusively European zone. He was a very empathetic teacher. But beyond all that, we saw in him what we could ourselves achieve, given a little luck and the right circumstances. I hoped and dreamed that the University College—though it was no Cambridge University—would provide the threshold some of us absolutely needed to make something of ourselves.

I reflected on the big man himself, Mr. Walter Graves. Hard as nails and ironfisted. But very fair. And sometimes unpredictable. The regulations under which we lived were so many, we sometimes felt they were like a spider's web. A web that could ensnare us at anytime if we were not eternally vigilant. He seemed to take an impish delight watching us twist in the wind a little, when he caught us red-handed straying from the straight and narrow or in breach of one or the other of his cast-iron regulations.

The man knew every nook and corner of the compound. He had certainly surprised a few of us in the most unlikely hideaways as we swotted for our exams in the dead of the night. He would appear like an apparition, clad in a voluminous nightshirt and a matching cap, a sardonic smile distorting his features in the uncertain glow of the common kerosene lamp he always carried on such occasions.

He could look fearsome, especially when provoked. But he had a smile that lit up his face and did often soften his features. And as Mr. Kalaga once observed, his bark was mostly worse than his bite, which was not to say—Mr. Kalaga was quick to add—that one should, or could, take liberties with him. We had no clue as to the dynamics relating to his interactions with the masters, especially the Nigerian masters. But he seemed, at least to the superficial observer, to be a difficult man to come close to. Deliberately or unconsciously, Mr. Graves did not appear to encourage too much familiarity with any Nigerian, staff or student. Not even, or so it seemed to me, the Yorubaman. And with the sole exception of the latter, the Nigerian staff seemed to be in perpetual awe of him.

He had one mission in Umuahia, which he liked to proclaim, so to say, from the rooftops whenever an opportunity presented itself, which was too often, if I must speak the truth. He wanted, he said, to turn out the best bunch of boys possible. To that end, he did everything he could to stamp out ostentation in us. Or anything bordering on overindulgence. His overarching article of faith was *modesty*. "If I had my way," he once proclaimed, "I would impose a limit on the amount of pocket allowance your parents can give to you." Which was perhaps the first and only situation in which we ever knew him not to have his way.

Always solicitous for the welfare and the feelings of his poorer students, he was known on more than one occasion to take away a scholarship, won on academic merit in an entrance examination to the school, from a boy who *appeared* to him to be of comfortable circumstances. He would then transfer the scholarship to a more-needy boy. He did this, however, only if the poorer student performed meritoriously in that exam.

As I lay in my brown study, the rain pounded hard on the roof of the dormitory, with a sound that put me in mind of my childhood years. They were the years of my innocence, when I could indulge in such simple pleasures as gamboling in the rain, naked and uncaring. Those years had long slipped away, almost unnoticed, perhaps without regret—certainly never to be recaptured. At eighteen going on nineteen, I was close to being a young adult. Indeed, I *was* a young adult, ready to go out into the world, to fend for myself, which I would undoubtedly have had to do had I not been headed for Ibadan and to a higher level of studentship.

Years of innocence! Idly, I tossed the expression around in my mind. I was still innocent, come to think of it. Or was it not innocence to be still a virgin at an age when some of my classmates had, so to say, perhaps crossed the Rubicon? Adamma and I had come close, perilously so, several times as we had lain side by side, with our bodies in quite inflammable contact. But we had recoiled, at always the last searing moment, from that final step.

Kofi Bentsil and the others, our late lamented Friday Stoneface included, had laughed whenever I unwisely recounted one or two such close encounters to them. They had laughed so much that I had felt my very manhood slipping away from me. I had therefore resolved then that never again would I tell my friends the stories of my misadventures with girls. Perhaps until the day when I too would have crossed the line. And then I could be sure that there would be no more laughter.

Six years had passed since my three classmates and I from St. James School, Aba, embarked on our Umuahia journey, brimful of hope and optimism. But for me, it seemed like only yesterday. As I lay on my bed and thought about our foursome, I was forcibly struck by the disparateness of our fortunes. Through our many years of academic rivalry, we had remained essentially friends. At least, until the cold hands of death took Stoneface away from us.

From the day of that watery tragedy, I had struggled vainly to come to terms with the cruel finality of Stoneface's passing. He had been the most happy-go-lucky of the bunch. The one most likely to jump at the chance of making friends with a pretty girl. He seemed always to have a mischievous twinkle in his eyes. But withal, he had been as steadfast and true a friend as any boy could have wished for. I could imagine him from the great beyond watching us three as we struggled through our lives, with a kindly but impish delight.

Poor Chidi Ebele! Of us three remaining old schoolmates, Ebele had the most reason to feel hard done by. For not only had he lost his father in his first year in Umuahia, he had suffered the quite unjustifiable indignity of having to repeat one class. Ebele had taken this last misfortune, after a very brief period of despondency, like the stouthearted young man he was and had not allowed it to turn him sour. As it might well have done to me had I been in his shoes.

Kofi Bentsil was not going with me to Ibadan. Inexplicably, he had failed in the University College entrance examination, which was quite an astonishing outcome to both of us and to several others in the class. Bentsil had been consistently one of the best five or six in the class, almost from our first day in Umuahia till the last. What would he do now? A little stronger in math and the sciences than in the arts, Bentsil had the choice of a number of government technical departments. Such as the Public Works Department and the Posts and Telegraphs Services. Or he could take up teaching, at least temporarily, in one of any number of lesser high schools. Then hopefully, he would resit the entrance exam the following year.

I was mightily excited at the prospect of moving smoothly from high school to university. Six years earlier, I had done the same from primary to high school. But I was not so excited that I did not spare a thought for the friends I was soon to leave behind. Innocent Dike and Okon Ebong, in class 5, were due to sit both the Cambridge and the university entrance exams during the following school year. Dike, confident as ever, assured me we would meet up at Ibadan before I would have had time to settle down there. Ebong, less assured but hopeful, said he would pray for good luck in his exams.

Dike, at just over six feet, had grown into one of the two or three tallest boys in the school. He loved to stand close to me, at every opportunity, to show off his greater height. I suppose I did not mind letting him. As I repeatedly asked myself, what are friends for if not to accommodate one another's idiosyncrasies?

Ebong had reached a point in his cricket where all he needed was to demonstrate his superlativeness in the game on a wider, more national stage. That stage, I firmly believed, he would find as soon as he left the narrow confines of Umuahia, either for Ibadan or Lagos, the following year! He was also, next to Chidi Ebele, the best hockey player in the school.

I had friends in every class. But the two other boys whose friendship filled my mind now were Paul Ogbo and Alfred Onwudinjo. I would miss Ogbo's artful boxing. I just loved to watch him box. He would float around his opponent, arms moving like rapiers, hitting with blinding speed on all the lawful parts of the anatomy. And when you thought you had him in a corner and moved in for the kill, he invariably wriggled out, leaving you with an empty space. I know because I practiced often with him and can bear firsthand witness to the frustration his slipperiness can cause.

He was not a boy of many words. As a companion, he could sometimes be boring, answering questions in monosyllables, hardly ever asking any questions himself. But he would come to life if you channeled the conversation to boxing and to such renowned names as the fabulous Joe Louis, the Brown Bomber, or the incomparable Sugar Ray Robinson. Then a light would come into his eyes, transforming him. And he would glide effortlessly from taciturnity into a strange loquacity, prattling on and on. Not caring if you were listening or not. Seemingly in a world entirely of his own.

To Alfred Onwudinjo, in class 2, I was essentially a big brother—a relationship I found at once practical and uplifting. There was not anything, in my power, I would not do for him, so long as it was legal and fair to other boys. So though I would explain a subject matter to him, I scrupulously avoided helping him directly with his class assignments. For the two years we were both in Umuahia, I was guide and mentor to him, taking as my model the way Patrick Onyewuchi had counseled me in my first few years.

How I wished that my sibling and younger brother Ndubisi—the copycat—had joined me in Umuahia! But he had found his way to the Dennis Memorial Grammar School in Onitsha. And he seemed quite contented there and often took me to task whenever I dared to claim primacy for Umuahia over all other schools, including his own. Which was something I tended to do whenever the opportunity presented itself. But I always accorded second place to his DMGS, a missionary school for which I had the highest regard.

Had Ndubisi come to Umuahia, I dared to think he would have been friends with Onwudinjo. They were, I think, the same age. And they looked to be interested in similar subjects: math and science. Oddly too, and though too immature really to know what they wanted, each expressed a strong inclination for the medical sciences or engineering. However that be, he liked his school, though the feeling stuck in my mind that he would have given anything to have been with me in Umuahia. Only the feeling!

Suddenly, and I had no clue whence it came, an idea began to germinate in my mind. I fought it for a while, but it refused to go away. I fought it some more, and then it dawned on me that the harder I tried to resist it, the more alluring it became. That night, I tossed and turned on my bed, barely able to sleep. By the morning light, the idea had become an obsession.

Immediately after breakfast, I sought out Gregory Okoroafor and Kofi Bentsil. I invited them to a corner of the library where I thought we would neither be disturbed nor overheard by other boys.

"The principal is meeting with our class this morning at ten, right?" I asked them.

"Yes, why?" asked Bentsil, looking as if he had immediately smelled a rat.

"None of us knows for sure what he wants to say to us, but we can all guess."

"A farewell speech, no doubt," suggested Bentsil.

"And to wish us luck," said Okoroafor. He looked hard at me for a brief moment. "What's all this about? Why did you call—?"

"He'll probably tell us," I said, "how lucky we've been to be in the best secondary school in the country and so on and so forth. He is so proud of this college—"

"Aren't you?" asked Okoroafor.

"Isn't it the best?" chipped in Bentsil.

"Which one shall I take first? Anyway, both your questions are beside the point. It doesn't matter what I think. It's what he so strongly believes that matters. He seems so proud to be the principal of Umuahia that he is sure to get really upset if one of us were to say something uncomplimentary—"

"To him or to the school?" asked Bentsil.

"Either," I said. "Or both."

"So what is it you're going to say?"

"I'm not sure myself," I said. "I suppose it depends on what he says to us. I'll just have to listen and then see what happens."

I stopped because both my friends were staring at me dubiously. "It's really only going to be a practical joke," I said reassuringly.

"Sounds to me like one of your *stupid* jokes," said Okoroafor. "In any case, why are you telling us about all this? D'you want us to join you in pulling the big man's leg?"

"Not me," said Bentsil promptly and with some feeling. "Oh no! You're not going to involve me in this kind of thing now. It's easy for you, and you also, Okoroafor. You're both going to Ibadan and do not need any further references from the man. I might still need him to say good things about me, you know. Like if I want to change jobs if it turns out I don't like the PWD job the government's offered me. You know what he can write about you if you provoke him."

"You're telling me!" I said, laughing. But it had not been a laughing matter when the big man wrote some quite scathing remarks about me in a few of my reports. In the last year or so, however, he had changed his tune, though I had not been aware I had changed my ways.

"D'you recall what he once wrote in what's his name . . . Ufot O. Ufot's report? 'Ufot is capable of doing anything.' And the poor fellow came back from that vacation, bragging about it to anyone who cared to listen to him, thinking it was a compliment. Oh yes, I know what he can write about any of us, anytime."

Okoroafor was persistent. "I asked you why you're telling us about this. Though I'm also going to Ibadan, I don't think I want any part of your practical joke."

"Why am I telling you? To be honest, I hardly know myself. I suppose I couldn't keep the thought bottled up in my mind. I had to share it with somebody."

"I'll be watching you," said Bentsil.

"So will I," added Okoroafor. "I don't like the smell of it."

EPILOGUE

The boys stood up smartly when Mr. Walter Graves strode into our sixth form classroom. Every one of us would forever remember the sight of the stern-looking giant as he walked in, favoring his right leg. None would ever forget his piercing eyes or his luxuriant mustaches, which he had the habit of stroking when he was in a pensive mood. When he scowled, he inspired fear. But when he smiled, his personality was somehow transformed as the fierceness dissolved from his face. At a signal from him, we sat down.

Mr. Graves stood for several moments in silence, surveying the class row by row. Indeed face by face. It was as if he wanted to imprint on his memory, forever, the picture of every one of the young faces looking up at him. When he began to speak, his voice was strangely soft and emotive.

"It is never very easy to say good-bye," he said and then paused. He seemed to be more affected by the occasion than I had thought a man like him would be. He clearly struggled with himself as his mouth worked briefly, but no words came. Then he regained his composure.

"Always, always remember the words on your school badge: *in unum luceant,* which, as you all know, means "May they shine as one." Whatever tribe you come from—Ibo, Yoruba, Efik, Itsekiri. Whatever your nationality—Nigerian, Cameroonian, Gold Coaster—you must never forget. It is the whole purpose for which your teachers and I have striven these many years to try to educate you.

"It is our hope that, like the others before you, when you leave Umuahia, your light will shine so brightly that people will know you've been molded in a good school, the very best, if you ask me."

Kofi Bentsil, who sat in the front row, half turned to look at me. Gregory Okoroafor, who shared a desk with me, did the same. Our eyes met, and then they both looked quickly away. I was certain no one else observed us. Or if they did, they were of course totally innocent of what it might portend.

"From the days of the Reverend Fisher, our first principal, the name of Government College Umuahia has inspired deep respect, even reverence, from every corner of Nigeria. It is our duty, yours and mine, to ensure that that reverence never dies. It was to that end that we have spared no effort to try to inculcate in your minds an appreciation of what is good and noble.

"Academic excellence is one of the yardsticks for measuring schools. I do not think I need to tell you that in that particular respect, this college is truly second to none, and I do not confine this assessment to Nigeria or to West Africa or even to Africa. Any way you like to look at it, Umuahia is, and hopefully will always remain, a beacon for the times.

"This is not quite coming out the way I had intended. I did not want to sound preachy or sentimental. But what I am trying to say to you is that you must do all you can to let the light continue to shine through you, wherever you are and whatever you do. That, in a nutshell, is the purpose of this last farewell meeting. I am proud of every one of you. And speaking on behalf of the staff and all the other students, I wish you all God's blessings and the very best of luck."

There was a brief moment of silence, and then someone started to clap. Soon, we all joined in. The applause reverberated round the room. Fidelis Nnochiri, school captain and therefore senior boy, then got up and, still clapping, stepped out in front of the class. He waited for the applause to stop. Then he cleared his throat nervously.

"I think I speak on behalf of everyone here when I say we are all extremely proud to have been students of Government College Umuahia."

He stopped, and his look took us all in as his eyes ranged from side to side. Several heads nodded in affirmation of his statement.

"So how about three cheers to the principal. Hip—"

"Hold it there, my boy," Mr. Graves interrupted. "Not just the principal; the masters also and indeed every staff of the college, high and low."

Nnochiri smiled. "Yes, sir. Three cheers to the entire staff of the college, especially the principal. Hip! Hip! Hip!"

"Hurrah!"

The cheers were raised three times as was customary. Then Nnochiri resumed his seat.

"And how about three cheers to yourselves?" asked the big man. "You've been an important part, even the most important part, of the Umuahia story. Hip! Hip! Hip!"

"Hurrah!" We bellowed so loudly the very foundation of the building seemed to quake.

"Once is enough," said the principal, smiling. Then arms akimbo, he paced up and down once, twice, and asked, "You're all happy to have been students here, you say?"

"Yes, sir!"

"Would anyone like to say, briefly, in what way or ways you think you have benefitted from the college?"

"Let every boy speak for himself," suggested a voice from behind me. "In that way, you'll know exactly how each of us feels about the college."

"Oh my god!" someone in the front row said in a half whisper, hoarsely. It might have been Bentsil. In fact, I strongly believed it was him. He did not say it loud enough to distract the big man. But I heard him all right. And he did not need to look at me this time. Neither did Okoroafor. But I knew what both of them were thinking. I was thinking exactly the same thoughts.

The principal nodded. And I knew right away that the die was cast.

"Good idea, my boy," he said, "provided it doesn't get too repetitive. Why don't we start with you, Agu, and then work through the class in order? Stand up where you are and speak when it is your turn." So saying, he walked around the teacher's desk and sat on the teacher's chair, facing the class. He listened pensively as each boy got up and spoke his piece.

John Agu did not at all look nervous. I had thought he would be, seeing he was the first boy called upon to make such an important statement. But evidently, that streak of braggadocio, which he exhibited on the steps of house 1 on our first day in the college and which had never totally left him, now kicked in.

"The college has sharpened my brains," he declared.

"How?" someone asked.

"No interruptions!" said the big man in a voice that meant *no interruptions*. "Go on, young man."

John Agu looked witheringly at the boy who had interrupted him, cleared his throat, and went on.

"This will be very important in Ibadan, where I'm sure we will face fierce competition from boys and girls from all over the country and perhaps from the Gold Coast, Sierra Leone, and the Gambia. I've heard there's a student from DMGS, Onitsha, who not only got seven As in the Cambridge exam, but won one of the three scholarships in the Ibadan entrance exam. I hope he's not going to do medicine, which is the course I'm going to do."

Agwuna did not wait for the principal's signal. He sprang up from his seat even before Agu resumed his. "I'm not afraid of any boy or girl from anywhere. My course will be engineering, and the fellow from DMGS is welcome to take the same course. Other than that, what I really want to say is that the college taught us order and discipline above everything else."

Kofi Bentsil, when it was his turn to speak, first turned to look at me. There was apprehension in his eyes, which I could not quite erase, though I gave him my most reassuring smile. His voice, when he spoke, was soft—unusually soft.

"I think the greatest thing the college did for me is that it has given me a sense of humility. If you ask me what I mean by that, I'm not really sure I can explain it, even to my own satisfaction. The point is, don't you see? This is the greatest secondary school in the world—okay, in Nigeria. Laugh all you like, but it is the best, and we all know it. But when I meet boys from other colleges and they start bragging about their colleges, most times, I remain quiet and just let them talk."

He looked back at me one more time and then sat down. Naturally, we had been often together during our vacations in Aba. We had moved in the same circle of friends. So I was familiar with the situation he had described. I know I wasn't quite as taciturn as he had tended to be when it came to extolling the merits of our respective schools, whenever such comparisons came up in conversations. I was fiercely proud of Umuahia and seldom refrained from letting it all hang out if provoked.

I watched the principal closely, saw him stroke his mustaches as encomium followed encomium. He looked as proud as any father would be, listening to the heartfelt expressions of gratitude and appreciation from his sons. His smile widened especially when Fidelis Nnochiri declared that Umuahia had given him a sense of balance, which he said meant discipline; a proper appreciation of hard, practical work; and an understanding that, as the saying has it, "pride goes before a fall."

As I listened, I began to fight a mental battle with myself. Bentsil's agonized look tore at my heart. Okoroafor was due to speak just before me. But he had elected, as the boys spoke in their turns, to pretend I did not exist, though our bodies were within just a few inches of each other. He made no gesture towards me but sat stiffly, looking everywhere else but at me. But I had always been sensitive to his moods and mannerisms. And I understood the cause of his present unease. How could I not, seeing I had deliberately dragged him, and Bentsil too, into my half-formed scheme earlier in the day? I knew therefore that what was afflicting my two friends was a sustained attack of nervousness. On my account.

I became increasingly anxious myself as my turn approached. So much so that my mind began to lose its concentration on the unfolding situation. I was only vaguely aware of Okoroafor getting up to speak. And I was, unbelievably, still wrapped up in my thoughts, struggling with myself, when Okoroafor stopped talking and sat down. But of course, I came back to full consciousness when my name was spoken and my friend dug an elbow into my side.

"And now, Obinna Okoye!" boomed the principal's voice. Perhaps he had not actually called out my name any louder than he had the other names. But in my state of mind, it had sounded unnecessarily loud. It certainly woke me up. And he had also used my first name, when he had called the others—most of them at any rate—by their last names only. But he had developed that manner of address over the several years cousin Samuel and I had been in Umuahia together. So I supposed it was okay.

I gathered myself to my full height and, in a voice over which I seemed to have no control, spoke the momentous words.

"I DO NOT THINK I GAINED ANYTHING FROM THIS PLACE!"

I know I spoke those words as if they were composed in the innermost recesses of my mind and on my tongue, which spoke them, in capitals. It was a shattering moment. The big man went red in the face, staring at me as if he was looking at a ghost or something. Okoroafor unavailingly tugged hard at my shorts, trying to force me to sit down before another unconscionable word came out of my poisoned mouth. Poor Bentsil simply threw his head down on his desk.

*   *   *

Okoroafor and Bentsil were very angry with me. No surprise there. Nnochiri was too. Even—but to a lesser degree—Agwuna also! The latter, who knew nothing about my "practical joke," grudgingly acknowledged that it required tremendous guts to say what I said.

"Not that I agree with you," he was quick to add.

Okoroafor and Bentsil more or less dragged me to the principal's office an hour or so later.

"You must apologize to him for your stupidity," Bentsil said. "You must explain that you had meant what you said only as a joke to see how he would react."

"And suppose he doesn't believe me?"

"But it's the truth," said Bentsil.

"And you can call us as witnesses," added Okoroafor.

"Yes yes. But still, if he doesn't believe any of us—"

Bentsil gave me a hard shove, which propelled me to within a yard or so of the first window of the big man's office. "I'm afraid you have no other choice in the matter. You have to take that chance."

I do not believe I would have taken the last few reluctant steps into the principal's office if I did not realize that I badly needed to mend my fences with the big man. My friends, I noted as I walked through the door of the office, came as close as they dared to eavesdrop on my conversation with Mr. Graves.

It was quite a long conversation. Mr. Graves was in a very dark mood. Even after I had explained the genesis of my strange behavior, he remained very angry for several minutes. And then strangely, he—not I—began to recall the main events of my life in the college. He recalled, with startling clarity, the day of my interview, in October 1943, when I had sat on his lap in the same office in which we were now talking. He had sweet words for my cricket—and not because I was anywhere near being one of the more successful wielders of the bat, but principally because of what he described as the textbook straightness of my bat. He alluded to the times he had made me share the front row seats at the morning assemblies with the littlest boys in the college, though I was—on each occasion—a senior boy. Then he summed it all up with praise for my academic performance over the years.

"I think you should do well in the University College," he said.

I cannot truthfully say how mollified he was with me at the end of it all. Mr. Graves was a principal who loved always to keep a little in reserve, rather than to unwrap the whole package. But we shook hands as I prepared to leave him.

I wore my broadest smile when I finally emerged from the office. And straightaway, Okoroafor and Bentsil wanted to know how it went with me. But they could get nothing out of me.

"It is a long story," I said and walked away ahead of them.

THE END

CHIKE MOMAH (Nnabuenyi): A SHORT BIO

C hristian Chike Momah was born on October 20, 1930. He was educated at the St. Michael's (C.M.S.) School, Aba; the Government College, Umuahia; and the University College, Ibadan, where he earned a Bachelor's degree in History, English and Religious Studies in 1953. In 1959, he obtained the Associateship of the Library Association from the University College, London.

He was the first Nigerian graduate Land Officer (1954-1956) in the Public Service of the Eastern Nigerian government. Then he worked as a librarian in the University College, Ibadan (1956-1962); the University of Lagos (1962-1965); and the United Nations, first in Geneva, Switzerland (1966-1978), and then in New York (from 1978 till his retirement in1990).

He has four other published novels: (1). FRIENDS AND DREAMS (1997); (2). TITI: BIAFRAN MAID IN GENEVA (1999); (3). THE STREAM NEVER DRIES UP (2008); (4) A SNAKE UNDER A THATCH (2008). He has written several articles on Nigeria and on the USA.

Chike Momah has been married to Ethel, nee Obi, since 1959. The couple has two sons (Chukwudi and Azuka) and one daughter (Adaora), and has been blessed with seven grandchildren, and counting.

He is an involved member of the Nigerian community in the U.S.A., and has been honored with awards recognizing this involvement, including the first meritorious awards given by Songhai Charities, Inc., and by the Government College Umuahia Old Boys Association, Inc., both in 2003.

In 2003, he was honored with a chieftaincy title *(Nnabuenyi-Nnewi)* by HRH Kenneth Orizu, Igwe Nnewi.

Arlington, TX 76012   March 11, 2010

Edwards Brothers Malloy
Thorofare, NJ USA
July 25, 2016